1

PACT
INSTINCT

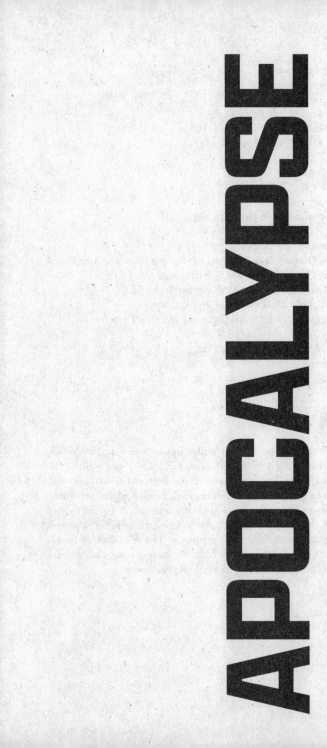

A Rebellion™ Publication
www.rebellionpublishing.com

First published in 2022 by Rebellion™,
Rebellion Publishing Limited, Riverside House,
Osney Mead, Oxford, OX2 0ES, UK.

ISBN: 978-1-78618-624-9
10 9 8 7 6 5 4 3 2 1

Creative Director and CEO: Jason Kingsley
Chief Technical Officer: Chris Kingsley
Head of Books and Comics: Ben Smith
Editors: David Thomas Moore, Michael Rowley, Jim Killen and Amy Borsuk
Marketing and PR: Jess Gofton and Casey Daveron
Design: Sam Gretton, Oz Osborne and Gemma Sheldrake
Cover artwork: Mike McMahon and Carlos Ezquerra
Based on characters created by John Wagner and Carlos Ezquerra.

Printed in the UK.

APOCALYPSE WAR
DOSSIER

JOHN WARE

I started paying attention to 2000 AD in the summer of 1981. I used to get it from my best friend, who got it from his older brother. My copies of Battle were passed along in the other direction. Sometimes, this supply chain broke down, so as "Block Mania" was reaching its climax, I committed to the big step of buying the comic with my own money. I have not yet found reason to regret that decision.

This book is affectionately dedicated to Dara and Eoghan MacNamara, and the comics that grew ragged in the reading.

Block wars were nothing new to Mega-City One.
The boredom and the claustrophobic overcrowding
of future living brought tensions to a knife edge.
Inter-block violence could erupt at any time.
Judges were used to handling block wars.
But nothing could have prepared them for that day
in 2103 when madness reigned—and the whole city
went wild.

—The Official Version

"The distortions occur here, in the hypothalamus—
the old brain, where our deepest primitive instincts
lie. The effects are twofold: firstly, it causes an
intensification of the victim's natural aggression.
He becomes surly, illogical, violent—one spark can
set him off. Secondly, the victim's pack instinct is
stimulated. He desires to join with others to seek an
outlet for his anger."

—Tek Judge, Justice Central Task Force, 2103

PROLOGUE

THE PARKER-BARROW PEDWAY Loop was always a pleasant place for an evening's exercise. It was so much safer than the walkways down below where muggings were rife.

The upper levels meant upper income, which meant a better class of people and functioning security cameras.

And the view from the Loop was spectacular.

Beasley Smart often met Stew Swanson at the midway caf-stop, a hundred and twenty levels above the cares of the world. Beasley was on the block committee at Clyde Barrow, while Stew's wife had the Doohickey concession for Bonnie Parker Block. That meant they were the quality, and it usually didn't matter that they came from different blocks.

This evening, Stew was standing at the caf-stop, looking out across the sector at distant lights. Beasley, energised from his run, joined him. He noted with satisfaction that Stew's running clothes were last season's and that Stew was showing some paunch there, despite his boasts of being able to do the Loop in under twelve minutes.

Twelve minutes, my ass, thought Beasley, who had never broken fourteen. He found himself wondering why he wasted his time with this low-rent blowhard. All the Doohickey's money in the world couldn't class up this Parker slob.

But he stopped all the same and looked out at what was holding Stew's attention.

The far-off winking lights were gunfire. That was always worth your attention—especially on this scale.

"Dan Tanna?" asked Beasley.

"Uh-huh. And Enid Blyton. And a whole lot of other blocks up that way joining in too."

"I saw something on the vid. Bigger than your average war anyway."

"Not surprising when you think about it. A place like Tanna. Pretty scummy—even on the upper levels."

"Yeah. Living there you'd be like a rat in a coffee can. No wonder things boil over."

"They should take pride in their block."

"That reminds me, Stew—the committee voted on planting some greenery along the parkway. Real vat-grown shrubs. Not cheap, sure, but it'll look pretty nice, don't you think? Maybe Parker could do something similar? You know—beautify the sector. If they can afford it, that is. What do you think?"

Stew looked at the towering facade of his home, where the name 'Bonnie Parker' was spelled out in letters that ran a full twenty floors. He considered his neighbour's proposal.

"I think you should shut your stupid mouth, Barrow Boy," he said.

Beasley was already blocking Stew's punch and throwing one of his own. He realised that he'd been waiting to do this all day. He hadn't reckoned on Stew being so quick on his feet, though, or being such a tough guy. In no time, Beasley was backed up against the railing, blood staining his couture headband. Things might have gone badly for him if a couple of his neighbours hadn't waded in to help him. He didn't know them, but 'Clyde Barrow' was proudly emblazoned on their sweatsuits.

A moment later, to make things interesting, a few passers-by joined in on Stew's side, but by that time, they could have chosen any of a half-dozen fistfights that had broken out along the Loop.

IT WAS ALL picked up on the well-maintained security cameras, and, in seconds, the notification had gone out on the Sector 212 Justice Department net.

Only half a click away and six levels below, a couple of Judges had just wrapped up some business. The more senior of the pair thumbed his radio.

"Blaskowitz. Responding. Me and Robinson will take Parker-Barrow."

He turned to his partner as they mounted up.

"Let's get this one cleaned up quick. I get the feeling it's going to be a busy night."

And it certainly was.

And that was just the beginning.

ONE

CHIEF MERCER WAS a good Judge. That's why they gave him the big chair in Sector 212. He'd sooner have been out on the streets, judging, but a severe injury had knocked him out of the saddle for a few months, and they'd put him in admin while they tweaked his new bionics, and after that they made him sector chief in 212.

He didn't want it. He had plenty of good years left in him as a street Judge. His new hip and knee were better than the originals, he'd told them. He could pass any physical they cared to throw at him. They pointed to his seniority and to his recently acquired administrative experience. He was a good Judge, they said. He'd make a good chief.

So, he pushed his misgivings to one side and took the job. He thought that maybe—once he'd learnt all the ins and outs of running a sector—he could put in some street time every now and again. Show them he was still up to it.

But running a sector didn't include a whole lot of spare time, and Mercer remained chained to a desk.

He'd been there three years now, and that was three years of his edge being dulled, three years of declining fitness for street duty. But he'd never put in for a transfer, never done less than his best. It was a job that had to be done, and by Grud, he was going to do it. He was a good Judge.

When he'd first come to 212, Mercer had been determined to turn it into a model sector. He'd shake things up, run the tightest drokking ship you ever saw, and the crime stats would come tumbling down. But the crime stats did what crime stats always did. This was Mega-City One, and crime was a rising tide threatening to engulf them all. The Judges could keep the dam from breaking, but they couldn't turn back the tide. So, Mercer had had his successes during the past three years, but he'd had his failures too, same as every chief in every sector of the city. Down there on the streets you could break heads and hand out time, thinking that you were upholding the law and making a difference. The view from the chief's office wasn't so heartening. From up here, you could see that all you were doing was patching up the cracks in the dam and mopping up the occasional spills.

And it had been getting a lot worse lately.

YESTERDAY HAD BEEN a big day for the block wars, and today looked like it was going to be worse than yesterday.

Block wars were just one of those things that the city had become used to. You stack fifty or sixty thousand unemployed people on top of each other and you have to expect trouble. Every once in a while, that trouble is of a collective nature. If the City Housing Authority could boast one success with the city-block programme down the years (and that was a big *if*), it was the fostering of community spirit—of a sort, anyway. You might live your life in a two-room cubicle on the seventieth floor of Rat's Ass Block, but at least you were a Rat's Ass blocker. You had an identity.

And because you might get a stomping if you ever thought to go to another block, you stayed at home. You might get a stomping there too, but at least you'd get it from your own people.

On the other hand, if things weren't so bad in your block, you wanted to keep it that way, and the neighbouring blocks could just keep their damn distance if they didn't want trouble.

There were always gangs happy to turn inter-block rivalry and distrust into inter-block violence. Then there was that perennial problem of the block Citi-Defs. The Citizens Defence units were a relic of the old days that the Department hadn't got around to abolishing yet. It was all tied up in the old Second Amendment and the threat of Sov invasion. A well-regulated militia and a last line of defence were all well in theory, but until the Sovs did try to invade, the Citi-Defs were little more than breeding grounds for gun nuts, and those same nuts were usually the ones you'd find at the forefront of any given block war.

A towering housing block; tens of thousands of citizens whose distrust of their neighbours suddenly turning militant; the street gangs and the Citi-Defs to give it all some combat experience and weaponry; two or more towering neighbourhoods, with the distance separating them filled with mass brawling on the lower levels and exchanges of gunfire up above. And that's your block war, folks.

The night before last, there had been multiple flare-ups across the northern sectors, with not just block-on-block violence but whole clusters of blocks turning into free-for-all battlegrounds. By morning, the chaos was so widespread that Justice Central had created a special task force—under Dredd, no less—to deal with it. Every sector in the north of the city had become a warzone. That would have to be Dredd's problem. Sector 212 was very much Chief Mercer's problem.

He'd thought he'd been ready.

When it started, he'd come down hard and heavy like you ought to. The riot squads went in hand in hand with the heavy weapons units. When word came down that the ban on stumm gas had been lifted, Mercer was way ahead of them. His Judges would have encased every block in the sector with riot foam if they'd been able to get their hands on enough of the stuff.

But it seemed to make no difference. These weren't just slum-block turf wars writ large, or rogue Citi-Def units gathering mass followings. Suddenly, the Judges were seeing decent neighbourhoods taking up arms. The ritzier blocks, which had never needed much more than a few security cameras and the odd crime blitz, now needed concentrated judging, and Mercer had his people out judging until the iso-cubes were filled three times over and the shopperamas and tween-block plazas ran with blood.

But still it went on. The citizens just weren't getting the message. Battered by daysticks, choking on gas, they fought on, with more joining in every hour. It was like a mass uprising, except that the cits weren't fighting against the Judges. This wasn't a revolt against authority—just a real nasty brawl with the neighbours. Letting off a little steam, this wasn't.

And it just kept on spreading. Like a disease.

The Department already had a name for it. They were calling it Block Mania. Justice Central tended not to get all in a bunch over stuff, so if they're going to get all portentous with naming things, then you can bet you're looking at something bigger than your regular crime spree.

Mercer hadn't taken a break since this thing began. He looked out at his battered sector, at the smoke thickening in the morning air, and he felt angry. This was *his* sector, gruddammit. He wanted to get out there where his people were, to bring some law and order with lethal force. To show that he wasn't some desk jockey. To show that he was still a good Judge.

He felt a dull throbbing in his head and reluctantly shook himself out of his angry reverie. There was a job to do, and the job was here. There might be war on the streets, but the work of administration never let up. Right now, he had a disciplinary matter that needed to be dealt with urgently. It was the sort of case that no chief ever wanted to deal with. He took a breath, hit the intercom, and called Robinson into the office.

TWO

Lashondra Robinson was a good Judge. A glance at her record could tell Mercer that. No hotshot, but a trier—a real worker. She barely made the height qualification, but made up for that in muscle density and sheer enthusiasm. Three years on the streets and still grinning like it was the most fun a girl could have. Solid, square-built, and happy in her work, Robinson was just what the justice system was all about.

She wasn't grinning today, though. Three years and no infractions, no demerits, no complaints. And then an hour ago she had shot and killed another Judge.

Mercer had the facts of the case already, but he wanted to be crystal clear. The wheels of justice grind pretty damn fast in Mega-City One, and Mercer reckoned on maybe five minutes before the SJS came up from their office on the thirty-fourth floor and hauled Robinson into the unforgiving machinery of internal affairs. Given the stomm that was going down today, that five minutes might be ten but, given the way his luck was going, it might be a whole lot less.

He reviewed the log again.

ROBINSON, LIKE EVERYONE else, had been kept busy. She'd been off the streets for no longer than it took to replenish her ammunition, and then she'd been sent right back out there.

Just since midnight there'd been that affray between the Henry Ford and Betty Ford blocks. The Judges had won that one easily. The next fight she got into was settled with greater difficulty, seeing as the riot foam was all used up and the H-wagons were needed elsewhere.

How bad does it have to be before you commit your Judges to a firefight across two two-hundred-plus-storey city blocks without aerial support? That was a decision for the sector chief. That was the sort of day Mercer was having.

It only got worse.

By the time reports came of a flare-up in the Thomas Mapother IV Low-Rise Connecting Apartments, Mercer had ordered in a single two-Judge unit consisting of Judges Blaskowitz and Robinson. It was all he had. He told himself that Blaskowitz was a capable veteran and Robinson had a lot of bounce in her. Mapother Conapts was low-rise, after all, and had a block Judge on-site too, name of Gray.

Now Blaskowitz was dead, Gray was dead, and Robinson was trying to explain to her chief that her shooting of Judge Gray was a righteous kill.

"One more time, Robinson," said Mercer.

* * *

SHE TOLD HER side of it like a proper police report, all code this and procedure that, until Mercer told her to speak freely, but what it all boiled down to was armed perpetrators all over and two Judges badly outgunned, while a third seemed to be siding with the perps.

Judge Tobias Gray, a twenty-year man, resident in the block and judging the community since 2099, had appeared in the east-side entrance, shooting at Archie Leach blockers trying to infiltrate from across the sked. Blaskowitz and Robinson, directing bike-cannon fire from the shelter of the parking garage, had ceased fire and hailed him.

"I thought maybe he didn't hear us," said Robinson. "Didn't matter. He was shooting, we were shooting, Leach blockers were falling, so it was all good."

"And then?"

"Then we see a body of fifteen-twenty Mapotherers coming up behind Gray. Blaskowitz shouts a warning. Gray turns and sees the Mapother perps and does nothing. So Blaskowitz fires on the perps, yelling at Gray to take cover. He gets four with four shots, and that's when Gray shoots him. Gray shoots Blaskowitz.

"Honest to Grud, Chief, I didn't believe it for a second. I see Gray shoot, and I see Blaskowitz get hit, and it's like I don't put the two together."

"And then?"

"And then Gray shoots Blaskowitz again, and I shoot Gray. Chief—what else could I have done?"

Judge Robinson probably hadn't shed a tear since she was a second-year cadet, and Mercer didn't think she was going to start now, but he could hear the confused anguish in her voice.

He didn't doubt her, but his faith in his Judges wasn't going to do anyone any good when those happy kids from the Special Judicial Squad came through that door.

"And you say you clearly identified yourselves?"

"Chief, we had lights and sirens and were only, like, twenty metres away. Visibility was good. The overheads hadn't been shot out or anything. He *saw* us. He heard us too. And he was looking at those Mapother blockers like they were his backup or something."

And there it is, thought Mercer.

Robinson's story, unbelievable and horrifying as it was, gelled with something that had come down from Grand Hall last night, marked oh-so-secret. These block wars that were erupting all over these last couple of days? There had been reports of Judges taking sides.

That's right: Judges going straight-up nutso like the citizens.

Mercer wasn't going to tell any of this to Robinson. He liked her, he believed her even, but he was not prepared to prejudice this investigation.

He hated to do it but was going to have to hand all this over to the SJS, wherever the hell they were.

It had been fifteen minutes. Where were those goons from the thirty-fourth floor?

He was reaching for the intercom when it buzzed at him. It was Jimenez, his day commander.

"Chief, I'm down on thirty-four. There's been an incident. You'd better get down here right away."

This is Sector 212, thought Mercer. *Anyone want it?*

THREE

THE TWO SJS Judges were dead. One had been killed near the office door by a single gunshot wound. The other was at his desk. He'd been shot twice, just to make sure.

Mercer had known their names and that was about it. Looking at their bodies, all he saw was an administrative headache. No one ever felt sympathy for the Special Judicial Squad.

What got to him was the certainty that the bullets that Forensics would dig out of the bodies would be Lawgiver bullets. *Who needs that?*

"What do we know?" he asked Jimenez.

"Cleaning droid found the bodies. No one heard the actual shooting, but the security cameras were disabled at 0732, so there's your probable time of death."

"This area doesn't get much in the way of casual visitors," said Mercer. "Find out who was around here that didn't have to be around here."

"Way ahead of you, Chief. We're looking to talk to one Judge Steinman right now."

* * *

STEINMAN HAD BEEN partners with Kowalczyk for nearly a year, and it had been working out just fine. In fact, the way Steinman saw it, the partnership was as good as it gets.

They were both good Judges, but nobody's perfect—not even Judges. Steinman, for instance, could sometimes be impulsive, while Kowalczyk's attention to detail wasn't the best. Thing was, though, that the partnership made up for that. Each man covered for the other. When things got ragged, Kowalczyk was there to stop Steinman from running headlong into a situation, or Steinman might make sure that his buddy didn't forget some necessary procedural step.

Teamwork. That's how a couple of just-about-made-it cadets become a couple of good Judges.

Steinman and Kowalczyk—put them together and they bust perps and crack cases. Keep them apart and you've got two maybe not-so-good Judges, and that's not so good for the city or the department. Not so good for Sector 212.

And that's why Steinman had shot those two SJS Judges this morning.

JUST BEFORE THIS block war thing had flared up, they'd got a lucky break. Some creep acting suspiciously had turned out to be worth the trouble of a stop-and-search. The creep knew something about someone and had been persuaded to share this information with Steinman and Kowalczyk who subsequently, in a nifty episode of kicking in doors and shooting henchmen, had taken down quite the little drug empire in the making.

It was your classic set-up—a heavily defended warehouse with bales of product and cases of cash laid out on a big table, with buyers, suppliers, and heavies all present and correct. When the smoke cleared, there was a whole bunch of bodies for Resyk and some heavy cube-time to be handed down to the survivors. Not bad work at all for two Judges who'd been ready to knock off only a couple of hours before.

And that's where it went wrong, thought Steinman. That moment of triumphant satisfaction had made him take his eye off the ball for a minute—him and Kowalczyk both. Kowalczyk had neglected to tag or log or register something properly and Steinman had failed to pick up on it. Next thing you know, the SJS is on Kowalczyk's case wanting to know about a big stack of drug money that had somehow gone astray.

That just burned Steinman up. Yes, a mistake had been made, and yes, Judges shouldn't make mistakes, but gruddammit there was no drokking need to get all internal affairs about it. Give a guy a slap on the wrist and move on. Keep the drokking SJS out of it.

But no. The SJS wanted to interview Kowalczyk this morning, and everyone knew how interviews like that went.

There were block wars raging all across the city, and the SJS wanted to spend a morning wringing out a good

Judge over a misplaced evidence ticket. Right here in 212 there was a war being fought, and the mother-drokking SJS wanted to act like Kowalczyk was ready to light out for Banana City with a suitcase full of stolen money.

Nope. Not today.

Steinman had never got to clock off on that shift. The whole block war thing was keeping everyone up and out, and it was quite a while since he'd had any rest. As he'd headed up towards the thirty-fourth floor of the Sector House, he could hear all those warnings he'd heard down the years from tutors and mentors about his occasional poor impulse control. But he'd thought this one through. All good Judges were needed out on the streets, now more than ever. The two SJS goons up on thirty-four had to be made to see that.

As the elevator doors opened, he calmly realised that negotiation was not the way to go here. Pleading just didn't cut it with the SJS.

He knew what he was doing when he smashed the security cameras.

Maybe in the end they'd see things his way, maybe not. Maybe he'd be dead before the day was out. Things were hot on the streets today. There were Judges dying all the time. Good Judges, giving their lives to hold Sector 212 together.

What did a couple of SJS desk-jockeys know about that? Just a couple of heavies sent down from Justice Central to give the Two-One-Two a hard time.

* * *

A LITTLE WHILE later, he found Kowalczyk.

"Saddle up, buddy," said Steinman. "Big day."

"But I've got that thing," said Kowalczyk.

"Not any more. I talked to them. Postponed indefinitely."

Kowalczyk looked squarely at his partner for a long moment.

"OK," he said finally. "Let me just load up on ammo and water."

FIFTEEN MINUTES LATER, they were three clicks away, engaging Charlie Sheen Citi-Def in a firefight. When the call came through from Jimenez at Sector House, Steinman weighed his priorities. The two Judges had just taken up a perfect position for flanking the Sheen blockers. Not an opportunity to be wasted.

"That's a negative, control," he told Jimenez. "Kinda busy."

He switched off his radio and switched his Lawgiver to hi-ex.

BACK AT THE Sector House, Jimenez reported to Mercer.

"He's shut down his comms, Chief. So has Kowalczyk. Last thing we got from Kowalczyk was, and I quote, 'Justice Department twenty-six, Charlie Sheen zero.' We could maybe send out units to bring them in."

Mercer knew the procedure, but none of what was going down today could be considered normal. Come to think of it, he hadn't even notified Special Judicial Squad yet that two of their officers had been murdered on his watch. The hell with them. He did not for one moment believe that Kowalczyk was crooked.

His sector was burning down, and it was better that a Judge should be out there doing something about it than enduring a fruitless and demeaning interrogation.

And Steinman? Steinman the suspected murderer? Steinman was out there doing his job too, and for now that was all that mattered.

But Steinman the suspected *Judge killer*?

Well, there was a lot of Judge-killing going on right now, and none of it looked so cut and dried that Mercer was happy about throwing a few of his otherwise good Judges to outsiders from the SJS.

The SJS could do what they liked. Sector 212 would look after its own.

"Negative on that, Jimenez. All units are engaged. This is something that will just have to wait until things quiet down."

FOUR

"Chief, I'm down on thirty-four. There's been an incident. You'd better get down here right away."

And suddenly Robinson's case was shoved into second place. Chief Mercer just said, "Wait here," and was gone to see what Jimenez had seen, leaving Robinson by herself, wondering just what the hell was more important than a Judge-on-Judge homicide. Despite the state of mental paralysis that had been threatening to engulf her since she'd pulled the trigger on Judge Gray, it was impossible for her to shut down the part of her brain that was trained to investigate.

An incident? On thirty-four? That the Chief needed to take a look at right away? Oh boy.

She hadn't been left speculating for long when Jimenez called down and peremptorily told her that she was under review and was to confine herself to quarters until notified.

'Under review' was a shade away from 'under arrest,' and that was as good as Robinson could expect at this point.

What with everyone being evidently too busy to pay attention to her right now, let alone treat her as a suspect and potential flight risk, the whole process might almost have seemed routine. But Robinson was a good Judge, and she felt the shadow heavy on her as she proceeded without escort to her place of temporary detention.

Strictly speaking, junior Judges like Robinson didn't have quarters to be confined to. Because it would be just plain dumb to have her confined to her bunk in the dorm room, a room had been set aside for cases like hers. There was no one to surrender her Lawgiver to, so she put it in her locker before going to the small office where disciplinary cases awaited their hearing. The sign on the door called it an office, but it was really a cell. There was a computer terminal so she could maybe keep busy catching up with her paperwork, but her security clearance had most likely been put on hold and she wouldn't be able to access anything of value.

That meant she was alone with her thoughts.

With no more clues to work with, there was no point wondering further about the big thing that had cut short her interview with the Chief, so she was left with the shooting of Judge Gray. For anyone with any sort of a conscience, an incident like that would have been on constant replay inside the head, but a Judge's visual memory was trained to perfection, which made her recollection so much more vivid and disturbing. Her tutors had rammed it into her that her picture of events should be as clear and accurate as any security footage. A Judge's memory should be admissible in court, they insisted, if there had still been courts.

So, she saw again the exact sequence of the morning events, which were as she'd told the chief. There was Gray—a Mega-City Judge, evidently siding with a bunch of deranged citizens and firing deliberately on another Judge. And she had done her duty. She'd shot the perpetrator.

Problem was, telling the SJS you'd done your duty wasn't likely to cut any ice, and there was a whole lot of ice on Titan. How long would she be under SJS interrogation before she started to doubt her version of the story? And who was there to back her up? Her partner Blaskowitz was dead. Gray was dead. Maybe some of the maniac blockers were still around. Like that was going to help.

She could see it now: *A complete lack of witnesses? That's very convenient for you, Robinson.*

In the Academy, they always taught you that the kill shot was the safe shot. Maybe while they were at it, they could have given you a few lessons in how to cover your ass when the SJS came calling.

Speaking of which. What *had* gone down on the thirty-fourth floor? Where *were* the SJS? Whatever happened to the concept of instant justice?

She could have walked out of the cell any time she liked. The lock was only there for form's sake, but leaving mandated detention would look bad. She could have done push-ups or something to kill the time, but what if everything turned out OK and she had to return to duty? No sense in wasting energy. Not the way things were on the streets today. She should be out there, on the streets. Drokk the SJS.

There was a dispenser in the cell, but the only thing it dispensed was water, which tasted like it had been there for weeks. Time went by slowly.

What the hell had Judge Gray been doing? Judges don't go bad, and when they do, they don't go bad like *that*. Her whole career—her whole *life*—was on the line, and all because he chose that day to go futsie, or whatever the hell was his deal.

As the scene reran over and over again in her memory, it took on an almost hypnotic beat. *He fired, he fired again; I fired, he went down.*

A kill shot is a safe shot. A kill shot is a *righteous* shot. But a Judge was dead, and by her hand.

She started doing push-ups anyway, just to take her mind off it.

It was a couple of hours before Jimenez came and told her that the resolution of her case was further delayed and, while not off the hook, she was to return to duty.

What the hell was more important than a Judge-on-Judge homicide? Try a double homicide.

FIVE

JUDGES TENDED TO be lone predators. They might be
partnered up for mutual support, but that support was
as-and-when rather than a permanent thing. A Judge
needed back-up, he called his assigned partner who was
always within hollering distance, which is to say on the
same patrol grid. For the most part—for the routine
stuff—a single Judge ought to be capable of watching
his or her own back. And a single Judge should be plenty
intimidating without any help. After all, you didn't see
two Statues of Judgement looming over downtown Sector
44, did you?

That's the way Mercer had always seen it, and that's
the way an overstretched force managed to get the job
done. In times of crisis, however, there was no choice but
to commit multiple units. In the case of block wars, that
meant riot squads and heavy weapons, patrol wagons and
hover wagons, and every street Judge you could spare.

But how about a whole bunch of block wars? How
about multiple block wars spread over several days,

with new flare-ups all the time and no end in sight? Well, that's where you had to get creative. That's where you're back to the principle of economy of effort. If Justice Central isn't sending you reinforcements—and given what's going on all over, they most certainly are not—then you're back to sending out Judges in ones and twos to face literally thousands of armed and unreasonable perps fighting like madmen for their own turf.

It was no way to run a railroad, but for now it was all there was. It was either that or give up the sector.

So, the Judges of 212 paired off and went out to fight. The casualty lists rose predictably fast, but these were good Judges. They were holding things together. They were making a difference, maintaining a measure of control. At least, that was Mercer's impression that morning. But as the day lengthened, he had cause to doubt his strategy, and even to doubt his Judges.

As he paced Control, forming the security footage and the situation reports into one coherent mental picture of how his sector was holding out, he noticed that the pairs of Judges were coalescing of their own accord into fours and sixes and whole posses of Judges.

More and more, he found himself giving orders for these unauthorised groupings to disperse, to create a more widespread presence on the streets, and every time he was met with what seemed like reluctance. He'd never have imagined that his Judges—that *any* Judges—might be getting shy, but here they were giving him what sounded like excuses.

Judges were upright and clear-thinking individuals, which meant that they were lousy at coming up with excuses.

Then it got weirder. He had one instance where some of his own Judges flat out refused to provide aid to other Judges in distress. An urgent call came through from Sector 214, who had two Judges in deep trouble right there on the sector line and no local units close enough to help. Could the 212 oblige? Mercer didn't even have to think about the answer to that one.

"Control to all units vicinity of Freddy Freekowtski. Code 99. Two Judges in need of assistance. Urgent."

And instead of all the automatic affirmatives he had every right to expect, all he got was silence. He looked at the big board, which told him that half a dozen units were within reach. He called the most senior personally.

"Parker, this is Control. I need you on that 99 in Freekowtski. Respond."

"Uh, negative, Control. We're, uh..." The rest was indistinct—probably deliberately so.

"Parker, *say again*." The tone of Mercer's voice made it obvious that this was the wrong day to mess with him.

"Freekowtski is out of sector, Chief. Couldn't the 214 handle their own problems?"

"Parker, you are to haul A to that 99 most immediate! Control out. Jovus Grud."

In normal times, Mercer would be yelling at one of his subordinates, demanding Parker's badge before the shift was out, but now he was just too busy. Also—and he didn't care to admit to this—he had a certain sympathy for Parker and all the other Judges who'd stayed off the air when the distress call had gone out.

Sector 214 *should* have been looking out for their own. What the hell were they doing bothering him at a time like this? He knew the chief there slightly. Scavelli. He'd always thought she'd been a good Judge before. Guess she was beginning to crack under the pressure if she was letting her sector go like that.

WHEN HE NEXT surveyed the big board, he saw that his people seemed to be letting their own sector go, or at least seemed to be withdrawing from large areas of it. Where he should have been seeing an even scattering of Judges across the sector, there were now clusters of Judges in certain areas and a complete absence of any law enforcement everywhere else. These concentrations seemed to be getting along just fine—as far as being in the middle of all the block wars in the world could be termed 'getting along fine.' They weren't standing by to be overrun. They weren't fighting a desperate back-to-back last stand. They were sending in calm and clear reports indicating that they were getting the job done, only they seemed to be doing it in the comfort of each other's company.

Nobody was crawling back to mommy. As soon as units found each other, they held their ground and fought hard. Fought too hard sometimes. Given the way things were, everyone was outnumbered and surrounded, but time and again Mercer was seeing

Judges holding their ground when they should really have been falling back. It was like they were fighting for the sake of fighting. No, that wasn't it. They were fighting because Sector 212 Judges did *not*, by Grud, back down from any fight.

He was reminded of Judge Robinson. If the kid was guilty of anything, backing down certainly wasn't it. Robinson was a good Judge. Mercer needed good Judges. He had a war on the streets to fight, and Robinson had been helping to fight it.

Judges tend not to mull things over for too long. Instant justice was the name of the game after all. The case of *the City versus Robinson* in the fatal shooting of one Judge Gray? Not guilty. Next.

He told Jimenez to put Robinson back on duty.

"YOU'RE STILL UNDER review pending full SJS inquiry, Robinson, but I'm giving you the benefit of the doubt for the time being. We're overstretched and I need all my people, so find a desk and plug yourself in."

"Roger that, Chief. And thank you."

"Don't thank me, Robinson. Just get to work."

So that's how it is, thought Robinson. *Patrol last night, a station at Control today, and maybe the Titan shuttle tomorrow. Who am I to argue? Like the man said, let's get to work.*

Any time she'd pulled this duty before, she'd always been impressed at how machine-like everyone was. You're not an individual so much as part of the process.

38

Information flow was what it was all about. Emotion tended to impede the flow. Today was different. Everyone was acting all het up. Mistakes were being made. Tempers on both ends of the communication channel were short.

"Tac Team Eight, I said redeploy to Hepburn! Respond!"

"And I said go hang it in your ear, Control! We're staying at Tracy until this fight is won!"

And if that exchange weren't enough out of the ordinary, the controller turned to Robinson in frustration and said, "It was a sniper at Hepburn took me off street duties last year. I need units there right now, getting me some payback for that."

Robinson let that one go. If controllers were acting weird that was Chief Mercer's problem, and if he didn't know about it already, then this would be a bad time to tell him.

SIX

THERE ARE TIMES when it's all worth it: when the fifteen years of physical and mental abuse in the Academy make perfect sense. They prepare you for times like this, and the times like this were what it was all about.

All about them the city roared on, but for Steinman and Kowalczyk there was a moment of stillness. Kowalczyk, even with the audio buffers in his helmet turned all the way up during the firefight, thought he could even hear the pinging of his Lawgiver cooling down.

Grud, but that had been a fight. Two Judges had gone in against a horde of blood-crazed blockers, and now the two Judges were still standing and there were fifty-plus bodies on the walkway in front of them. Those guys had been well and truly *judged*.

"Send a few heat-seekers through those fire doors?" asked Steinman, breathing deeply, trying to dampen down the same elation that Kowalczyk was feeling. Trying to focus on the job.

"Negative. Situation is contained. No point hunting down stray perps. Not today. Not in *this*." They could see columns of smoke rising here and there, clear across the sector and beyond. Clear across the *city*. This wasn't policing. This was war.

"Yeah. Day's only just begun. Conserve our ammo."

Speaking of which, thought Kowalczyk, as he reached to the back of his belt for a fresh clip.

Steinman was surveying the scene with one eye, planning the next move, while at the same time poised to light up any Charlie Sheen blocker who mightn't be as dead as was previously supposed and might have a little fight left in him. He was feeling sharp still. Feeling mighty fine. Times like this were what it was all about.

Then: "Hey, Steinman. Lookee here, my man."

Kowalczyk was grinning, holding up something that had come out of his belt pouch along with the ammo clip. It was a little yellow evidence tag, only half-filled out, knowing Kowalczyk.

"From that bust?" asked Steinman wryly.

"What do you think? From that bust."

"So there's two big stacks of money in Evidence with only one evidence tag."

"What can I say? We can fix it when we get back."

"Right."

"Get the SJS off my case."

"Right."

And at that Kowalczyk stopped grinning. Occasionally sloppy with procedural details he might be, but you don't get to be a Judge by being stupid. Getting back to the

Sector House—getting things back to normal—wasn't really the expected outcome here. He was on the point of returning the tag to his belt when he changed his mind. With resignation, he flicked it into a garbage disposal. Just because the world was coming apart was no need to start littering. "Let's get back to work," he said.

Steinman, unwilling to catch his eye, nodded. "Let me get some water first."

There was plenty in the bike's supply, but there was also a public dispenser right here, and at times like these, it was wise to live off the land. Who knew what the future held?

THE ELEVATED MOOD of a moment earlier began to reassert itself as Steinman straightened up and wiped his chin. His head ached a little and he was sure he was running a fever, but he felt good all the same. Justice was being served. Steinman and Kowalczyk were bringing it right to the table and Charlie Sheen had better sit down and eat it all up.

They could do with a few more Judges, though. Wished he could call for backup. It wasn't that he felt that two good men weren't up to the job, but he somehow still felt the lack of company. Put a squad of Judges together and there was nothing they couldn't do. Strength in numbers. That was one thing at least that these block maniacs had going for them.

And that's when, in defiance of all good sense, the survivors of Charlie Sheen launched another attack. A couple of dozen of them, battered and ill-armed as they were, came charging down the walkway, where only a couple of minutes ago their buddies had got themselves all carved up.

It wasn't as if they were going for stealth or surprise either. They had raised their battle cry before they were even in sight.

"Charlie Sheeeen!" roared their leader, wild-eyed, stumbling on the bodies of his neighbours.

"Justice Department!" shouted Steinman.

"Sector 212!" yelled Kowalczyk, and they laughed as they opened fire.

SEVEN

AT TIMES LIKE these, it becomes impossible to exercise any refinement in command and control. No one can really see the big picture. The ones caught in the middle can only react to what's in front of them, and the distant general can't contribute much besides moral support.

Mercer, swamped by the multiple data streams from street cameras and helmet radios, just had to give up on attempts to coordinate the actions of his people. All his assets were fully committed. It was their show now.

All the same, hands-off didn't mean disengaged. He strode up and down the control room, like the coach on the sideline, throwing out words of support.

"Nice work, Schwartz."

"Looking good, Warner. Watch your flanks."

"That's it, Kim. Give 'em hell!"

And he noticed that all the controllers were doing what he was doing. These Judges—whether professional button-pushers or street personnel rotated through

Control for whatever reason—were abandoning their usual cool detachment.

They were there in the fight, rooting for the good guys. If Mercer was the coach, then these people were the cheerleaders. With their indoor pallor and cybernetic attachments, they mightn't have looked as good as the polished boys and girls who'd cheered the Southside Radiators to victory in the '03 Superbowl, but you couldn't fault their enthusiasm.

Mercer was taken aback at first to see a controller pounding her fist against her terminal and positively shouting into her mike, but he couldn't deny that it was good to see some emotional engagement in the job. Control wasn't usually a place where passions tended to be exercised. Also, there was usually a gulf of sympathy between Control and the street, with street Judges too often feeling like pieces shunted around a board and controllers feeling as if they were treated like secretaries and gofers.

But not today. Today, Control was part of the team, and Mercer dearly loved to see teamwork in action.

"Barta! Pull your people back! You've got Bradbury blockers coming at you in force across the overzoom."

"We see them, Control."

"So pull back!"

"That's a negative, Chief. We got this."

The screen showed a seemingly unstoppable mass of angry citizenry surging across the elevated roadway. Barta had what—five, six?—Judges with him. Their Lawmasters were behind them on perimeter defence and couldn't have brought their armament to bear in time. Not looking good for Barta's team.

And then there was a flash on the screen and everyone in the control room watched the Mr. Ed Overzoom crumple up and collapse, taking Grud knew how many citizens with it. It was all on such a grand scale that it appeared to be happening in slow motion. The rubble and the blockers crashed down on the Mr. Rogers Thruway below, increasing the casualty rate even more. Cameras picked up the rain of wreckage and human beings as it all plummeted towards city bottom, adding to the collateral damage with every level it passed.

In normal times, such a disaster would have been followed by the urgent dispatch of medical and rescue units, of situation reports, drastic traffic diversions and emergency road closures. In normal times, the sector chief would be taking charge and Control would be controlling.

But now Chief Mercer realised he was standing in the middle of the control centre, his fist in the air, yelling, "Get some, Two-One-Two!"

There was a moment of silence, and then everyone joined in the cheering. In short order, the happy hollering was replaced by a rhythmic thumping on consoles and desks. These admin personnel, whom most Judges knew as toneless and soulless voices on their radios, were now chanting in blood-thirsty unison.

"*Two-One-Two! Two-One-Two!*"

Mercer got them quieted down and back to work, but the triumphal mood persisted.

Teamwork, he thought. *Nothing to beat it.*

"Nice work, Barta."

"Our pleasure, Chief. Just the right people in the right place with the right demolition charges."

The right people. Put two Judges together and what you got was justice squared. Put two citizens together and you were just multiplying stupid. It didn't matter what kind of numbers the Judges were facing. Mercer knew that they were going to win this war.

EIGHT

STEINMAN WAS ACROSS sector when the Mr. Ed Overzoom went down, but he was keeping track of things on the Justice Department net. He even heard the cheers from the Sector House coming over the air.

Helluva thing, he thought. *Helluva body count.*

He wanted to be there. He wanted to be with his fellow Judges. He'd been racking up a hell of a body count all by himself—him and Kowalczyk, leastways—but it was kind of a lonely row they were hoeing.

Downside of being a fugitive, he supposed.

And it was all about to get a whole lot lonelier by the looks of things.

"Hang in there, partner," he said to Kowalczyk again. "Doing fine."

Steinman was keeping pressure on the wound, but it just wasn't the sort of wound where that would make a real difference.

Doing fine. Doing fine all morning. Cutting through block maniacs like a laser. We came, we saw, we judged.

Doing fine, right until some kook with what looked like a homemade rocket-launcher had showed up.

Look at it one way and it was a perfect coincidence of Steinman's and Kowalczyk's shortcomings coming back to bite them. Steinman was just impulsively pushing on and Kowalczyk was forgetting to consider all the angles. They'd got complacent: that's what it was. They'd spent the morning plugging perps who were out of their league against two Judges. It wasn't like the blockers were master criminals who'd thought any of this out. It wasn't as if they were in any way prepared. Most of them seemed just to have picked up some handy household implement by way of a weapon and joined the neighbours in a hell-for-leather charge against the block across the way. Even when they had real weapons, only the Citi-Defs and the street spugs had any experience, but nothing to match the weapons training of the Judges.

So, Steinman and Kowalczyk had just chosen good firing positions and got on with it. It was so much easier when all the standard riot protocols were abandoned—when the tactics of last resort became your first and only option. Shoot and keep on shooting.

What they forgot—what got Kowalczyk hit—was that malcontent citizen who, even in the best of times, is sitting at home reading the banned stuff and figuring out how to make weapons of mass destruction out of groceries.

Most of those guys were usually found by the fire crews after they'd accidentally killed themselves and the neighbours, but they were always out there. It didn't do to forget them. Steinman and Kowalczyk really should have noticed, in that crowd of maniacs with knives and clubs and zip guns, the weirdo with that confection of pipes strapped to his back.

This technical genius from J. Danforth Quayle Block had fired one shot. It took out two guys standing behind him with the back blast, but that was pretty much the least of it, seeing as the launcher also blew up, killing the user and his buddy the loader, along with a couple of randos in the line of fire. But the projectile had kept going, and still had enough oomph to carry it all the way to where the Judges were positioned. The explosion wasn't maybe all that its designer might have wished, but it had been enough for Kowalczyk.

"Stay with me, buddy," said Steinman, but it was obvious that his buddy just wouldn't be staying. In ordinary times, Steinman would be yelling into his radio and doing his damnedest to buy however many extra seconds were needed for the ambulance to get here. But he'd been hearing too many calls for med-assist that day, and too many times he'd heard the same calls being repeated with increased urgency and no rapid response. Everything was stretched to the limit today. If the Med boys couldn't deal with all the legit Code Nine-Nines and Judge Down calls, then what hope was there for a couple of off-grid rogue units like Steinman and Kowalczyk?

And it was just Steinman now. The blood had stopped pulsing out of Kowalczyk's wound a minute ago, but Steinman had been holding on anyway because that's what you did for your partner.

They were sheltered behind their bikes, which were

maintaining sentry mode in the midst of all the fighting.

In loud automated voices, the bikes were issuing the standard warning to any and all that thought to interfere with Justice Department property, and each warning was followed by a short burst from the bike cannons. But now Steinman noticed that Kowalczyk's Lawmaster, like its owner, had fallen silent. Had to happen sometime. There was only so much ammo even a bike of that size could carry.

And there was only so long that a Judge could correct the errant citizenry before he started running out of bullets too.

"Sorry about this, Kowalczyk," said Steinman, as he turned his partner's corpse over and started going through the man's belt pouches. Just as he'd thought. Even with all they'd stocked up on before they'd left, even with the extra load carried on their bikes, there wasn't enough ammunition to keep Steinman in this fight much longer.

It wasn't a situation he'd ever thought he'd encounter. Not in the middle of the city, leastways.

The Lawgiver, as is widely known, is a most versatile sidearm. It has that capacity for six different types of ammunition, and it is robust enough that, with the proper technique, you can use it to knock the teeth clean out of a suspect's mouth. Given its usefulness, it's easy to forget that even your average street Judge carries quite the little arsenal of additional weaponry besides. There are all those little surprises—many of them explosive or toxic—that are carried on the person or the bike, and then there was that dual-role rifle/shotgun long arm, widely referred to as the Law Rod, clipped to the front wheel assembly of the Lawmaster. The Lawgiver had made it largely redundant, but at times like this it could be more than welcome. Unfortunately, in this case, Steinman's was reading precisely zero rounds on its ammo counter. Kowalczyk's was the same. And all the little explosive and toxic surprises were all used up.

With his propensity for living off the land, Steinman had already noticed an M-300 Scatterblaster in the hands of a recently deceased perp, and he was pretty sure he'd seen a Maguire and Patterson over-and-under just over there a minute ago. That stuff was certainly a cut above what could be found in most Citi-Def armouries, and in the right hands—in his hands—it could easily allow him to dominate any fight with any blockers, but the same ammunition problem would apply.

And it just wouldn't be the way it had been through the morning's fighting.

He wasn't thinking only about having to perform his duties with inferior weapons. He'd be out here alone. A Judge without a Lawgiver. A Judge without a partner.

You didn't get far in this line of work without the sort of psychological resilience you could bounce rocks off of. The Academy made sure of that. That was how Steinman had been able to finish mourning for his friend—a man he'd *killed* for only that morning—in a matter of seconds, and then just get back to work.

So it wasn't like Steinman had been deranged by grief. *So what the hell is* wrong *with you?*

He was feeling the cold. No two ways about it. That

out-on-a-limb feeling that had been with him ever since the two of them had lit out on this justice-for-all spree was now a lot sharper, and a lot less fun.

Judges shouldn't get lonely. That meant that Steinman couldn't quite identify what his problem was. But he knew that, whatever wrongs he might have committed, he was a Judge, and he needed to be with other Judges.

Judges are decisive. They don't do conflicted feelings. They don't dither. In the midst of scattered fire, Steinman propped his dead partner on his bike, securing him with handcuffs. Then he slaved Kowalczyk's Lawmaster to his own and instructed it to follow him. Standard operating procedure. You don't leave Justice Department personnel or Justice Department equipment lying in the street.

"Bike, Sector House 212. Independently target threats en route."

A rogue Judge would be heading for a face-change machine and a spaceport, with a wallet full of fake ID and a suitcase full of money. But Steinman was a good Judge.

"Going home, Kowalczyk," he said. "Need more ammo."

He was a good Judge. He wanted to keep on fighting like a good Judge. He couldn't see how this was going to end well, but at least he'd be with his own people.

NINE

JIMENEZ WAS SHIFT commander, which was something of an archaic title that didn't mean anything much except that he was the sector chief's deputy. Judges didn't really work shifts. What were they supposed to do? Clock off at five and go home to the kids? A Judge was always on duty. The shift commander coordinated those duties for twelve hours of the day. So Jimenez's job title didn't mean anything much except that he was in charge of and responsible for every damn thing that went on in this sector house. No big deal.

He was a twenty-year man, and he'd seen it all. He'd seen a Robot War. He'd seen an invasion of mutant spiders. He'd seen a klegg eat three A-List celebrities in under six seconds. He'd worked Apetown.

This kind of thing was something he could have done without seeing, though.

Judges came and went, and their coming and their going was his business. You needed your people to know the streets, but you didn't want them going stale.

So Judges were assigned to a sector—and even to a single patrol grid—until they knew it inside out. Then, so they didn't get too comfortable and maybe lose their edge, they were rotated out. These were the tides and currents that governed the deployment of Justice Department's personnel, and Jimenez played his part in governing them.

Three days ago, Doyle had been rotated in from Sector 84 East, and Jimenez had got him situated and assigned him his grid. No big deal. Doyle got down to work, just another helmet on the streets.

Now, today, he saw the new Judge getting the cold shoulder from his new buddies. Except that Judges don't really do cold shoulders. They do heavily armoured shoulders applied with emphatic force.

Jimenez had seen a squad heading out for another round with the block maniacs, heading from their squad room to the bike pool, and he noticed that the new guy Doyle was apart from the rest of them, like the kid that no one wants tagging along or something. He wouldn't have thought anything except that when they got to the elevator, Doyle was roughly pushed aside by one of the others.

"Wait for the next one," the guy told Doyle, and Jimenez saw fists tightening as everyone got ready to maybe make something of it. Nothing happened. The elevator doors slid shut, cutting off the confrontation.

In calmer times, Jimenez would have stepped in, spoken hard words, taken names. Heck, even now he *should* have done something.

But it was a bad day, and he was busy, and anyway—maybe it was Doyle's own fault, coming in here from 84 East like that. Did he think he was special or something?

TEN

ALLEN WAS HEAD of Tek in 212. Everyone knew that street Judges looked down on the support divisions, seeing them as little more than maintenance staff whose job was to keep the power on and let the real Judges do their work. But the Teks kept the communications working, kept the bikes rolling, kept the H-wagons flying, kept the surveillance cameras online: they analysed the evidence, ran the ballistics, maintained the databases, spiked the hackers.

Allen knew, like every Tek Judge knew, that the whole enterprise would fall apart without them.

And things were doing enough falling apart as it was. On a normal day, she'd have her people assigned to projects with headings like, say, Environmental Safety, or Robot Crime, or Systems Corruption. Not today. Today there was only one heading on the board. Today it was all about Extreme Community-Based Behavioural Aberrations, or Block Mania as they were now calling it, or, to put it in technical terms, Why Everything Has Got

So Screwy All Of A Sudden And What In The Name Of The Good Grud Can We Do About It.

Analysis was Allen's thing. Yeah sure, she could read machine code and she could rewire a thermal socket when necessary, but big-picture stuff was her thing. That's why she was in charge. That's why she was looking at a map of the city, with every outbreak of Block Mania marked and listed, timed and dated. The Med people had confirmed (and confirmed again when they were told to) that it wasn't viral or bacteriological. Psi Division were swearing up and down (for whatever that was worth) that it wasn't something spooky and supernatural. *Well hooray for Psi-Div*, thought Allen. *I guess that justifies their budget for this year.* That aside, it meant that whatever the problem was, it was in Tek Division's wheelhouse. Something chemical or some sort of electro-magnetic radiation was most likely behind the madness, and the smart money was on chemical.

Allen stared at the map and ran numbers in her head for hours until it all seemed less random. Maybe she was reaching, but she was seeing a pattern in the big picture.

She spoke again to Barksdale, her opposite number in Med. Tek and Med always worked well together. There were obvious areas of overlap in things like forensics and bionics. It felt good to have close colleagues at a time like this.

"It's the water," she told him.

"Central says it isn't the water. Been all over it. They found nothing. We found nothing."

"Look at the map. Look at the major filtration and purification plants. Now look at where the block wars first erupted."

"Inconclusive. I'm not saying you're wrong, Allen— I'm saying there's no specific evidence. We've looked and we've looked and there's nothing in the water, just like there's nothing in the air. All we can say for sure is that subjects exhibit a distortion in the hypothalamus, and everything else follows from that. What causes the distortion? We don't know."

Typical gruddam Med staff, she found herself thinking. Bunch of quacks. Why the hell had she ever thought it a good idea to consult with them? Distortion in the hypothalamus? How long had that taken them? A Tek Judge could have done it in half the time. *C'mere, sawbones, and let me check your hypothalamus with this socket wrench.*

The Med chief looked at her levelly.

"It's not the water, Allen," he said. "Trust me. If it was the water, we'd all be loopy."

ELEVEN

THEORIES WERE NO good. Allen needed something concrete she could take to Chief Mercer. She respected Mercer, but today she had the feeling that relations between Tek and Street divisions weren't as loving as they might be. If the best thing that Tek Division could come up with was some inconclusive toxicity report, then he'd tell her to go do something useful like change a light bulb.

But then the western sectors had gone nuts. Allen had noted the first outbreaks light up on the map, and they had been just down the pipeline from Appalachian Decontam Plant No. 6.

"CHIEF, YOU GOT a minute?"

She saw right away that she'd chosen the wrong moment. Mercer was looking like a poster child for occupational stress. A Judge should be able to endure long stretches without rest. A sector chief, in particular, should be able to remain calm, level-headed, and decisive no matter how bad things got. But this crisis was only a couple of days old, and Mercer already looked like he'd been on a week-long amphetamine bender. Come to think of it, it was a look she was seeing on a lot of faces around here. Everyone was on edge. Herself, she'd already bawled out one of her staff for something so trivial she couldn't even remember. Then, she'd kicked a cleaning robot that didn't get out of her way in time. Drokking robots.

But now she damped down the impatience.

"Chief, I think I've got something. I think I know what's causing all of this."

"This? All the block wars? The citizens are causing it, Allen."

"Yeah, but I think I might have found out why."

"Why? It's because they're stupid. You've never seen a block war before?"

"Yeah, but not like this. Half the city, Chief?"

"Bob's Law, Allen. All it takes is one person to do something stupid and all the rest are sure to join in. I need to tell you that?"

"Chief, I'm pretty sure we're looking at a psychoactive contaminant, and I'm pretty sure it's in the water."

"You found something?"

"Not quite, but—"

"There's nothing in the water, Allen. We checked. You checked yourself. Tek Central's been all over this since it started. They found zip. Same as you."

"But Chief—"

Mercer squared up to her.

"I like you, Allen. I think you and your people are doing a fine job. But right now, the job is putting down riots by all available means. Right now, the job is judging. You understand? I got my people out there on the street laying it all on the line and dispensing justice. Now you'd better get on board with that. You'd better get your people on board. I don't want to hear about them shaking test tubes or analysing stats. I want to hear about how your people are helping my people do their job. Keep the weapons functioning! Keep my Sector House operating!"

He realised that he was close to shouting into her face, and he backed off in gruff embarrassment.

"All the academic stuff is a waste of time, Allen. Just do your job."

And there it is, thought Allen. *Just go change a light bulb*.

TWELVE

ALLEN FELT SHE should have been angry that her undeniable expertise was so bluntly dismissed. Or then again, seeing as it was the job that mattered and not her ego, she should have been coolly professional about it. The chief didn't like your theory? Suck it up and get back to work.

But instead of anger or detachment there was something else—something strange. Tek Judge Allen was not a woman deeply in touch with her feelings, so she couldn't for the life of her work out why she so badly wanted to impress Mercer. This wasn't about expertise or career. She just wanted the Chief's approval. She wanted him to recognise her contribution. She wanted to be accepted as one of the gang.

Perplexed at her emotional shortcomings, she returned to her division. She couldn't crack the problem of Block Mania, but then Justice Central couldn't either. Put it aside. Still a lot to do. If they couldn't stop the spread of the madness, there was plenty they could try when it came to winning the war on the streets.

*   *   *

COMING BACK TO her office, she noticed that the obstructive cleaning droid she'd kicked earlier was malfunctioning. The little garbage pail on wheels was bumping repetitively into a door frame. She should have felt guilty about having damaged it in the first place. She should at least have fixed it. Instead, she finished it off with a fire extinguisher. It took a little while and a lot more effort than she'd thought, but she imagined it would make her feel better.

As she straightened up, she saw the looks she was getting from her staff.

"What?" she said.

"Nothing, boss. Droid had it coming. What's the word from Mercer?"

"The Chief doesn't think we're real Judges. He says we're not really committed to this fight. What do you say to that?"

"I say we show him."

"I say you're drokking right."

"All *right*. Where do you want us to start, boss?"

"I was thinking about our non-lethal inventory. I was thinking that it's maybe a little too non-lethal. Let's see what we can do about that."

"All *right*!"

ONCE UPON A time, Allen had specialised in chemical weapons. Mercer might scorn the academic side of things, but did he think that stumm gas was cooked up over a stove some afternoon? Stumm was pretty sophisticated stuff. A fast-acting knockout gas wasn't as easy as you'd think. Finding something that only killed maybe one person in around seven hundred was pretty smart going too. But you know what really made stumm special? Its rate of dispersion. Concentrations of the stuff were almost impossible to maintain. Release it and instantly—and I mean *instantly*—it spread all over. You could be standing next to a stumm grenade when it went off or you could be thirty metres away. Didn't matter. The amount you got in your lungs wasn't appreciably different. Now *that* was clever thinking. Someone had likened the evening-out of the gas to a drop of oil on a tablecloth, only much, much faster. OK, that same someone could afford fancy-schmantzy analogies about real vegetable oil and real fabric tablecloths and thus probably didn't appreciate the realities of rioting Big Meg-style, but that was neither here nor there. The point was a little stumm gas went a long way and did it fast. The load carried by a single patrol wagon, for instance, could safely take care of a whole normal-sized block war. It was that 'safely' that Allen wanted to have a look at.

The one fatality in seven hundred wasn't down to an overdose of the gas but to some existing respiratory condition or chemical intolerance. (Actually, the figure was closer to one in two hundred, but those extra bodies were the result of falling to the ground in the middle of hundreds of rioters, rather than any inherent quality in the gas.) So, what Allen was thinking about was not upping the potency of Justice Department's favourite chemical billy club, but about using the non-lethal gas as a delivery system for something nastier.

When she'd been monitoring the spread of the madness, she had taken brief note of how Ricardo Montalban and Charlton Heston had been thwarted in their scheme to choke the whole city on some homemade poison. Their delivery system had sucked, but the stuff they'd been making showed a lot of promise. Cyclic acid and raw plasteen—simple but effective. Now if she could somehow marry it to good old stumm, well...

If she could bring something like this to Chief Mercer, he'd have to pay attention to her.

THIRTEEN

BARKSDALE, HEAD OF Medical Division, was steamed. All day and all night working in a war zone and now he had to put up with this.

"The hell you mean, mounting weapons in my ambulances?" To Barksdale they were always ambulances, never meat wagons. He was a medical professional. He didn't deal in meat.

"What's the problem, Doc?"

And he didn't like being called 'doc' either—not by street personnel. Every one of these jumped-up beat cops owed him their lives—him and his team—many times over, and they still all acted like they knew best. They'd request drugs and treatments without submitting to examination like he was just some street-corner pharmacist. They'd whine whenever he told them something they didn't like. *No, you can't keep that limb—now you want bionics or you want a stump?* And now they were telling his people how to do their job.

"The problem"—he looked at the badge—"Ortiz, the

problem is that this is an ambulance. An *ambulance*. For transporting the sick and injured. Understand? It's not a weapons platform. You mount that laser cannon in my vehicle and it's a violation of practically every ethical code I can think of."

"Lighten up, Doc. We're short on aerial support. The meat wagon here can fly. What gives?"

"What gives? *What gives?* How many times do I have to say it? It's an ambulance! Look! It's written right there on the side!"

And then one of his own personnel waded in with an unexpected contribution. Med-Judge Dupray, with ten years of ambulance-flying and kerbside trauma surgery to his name, took the side of Ortiz.

"Guy's got a point, Judge Barksdale. It's madness out there. We need some firepower to clear a landing zone sometimes. Firing from the window with your Lawgiver doesn't have the necessary punch."

Barksdale considered it a moment and grudgingly conceded the point.

"OK, but I want to make this absolutely clear. The ambulance belongs to Med Division, so only Med personnel are to man that laser. Dupray decides the targets and any kills are ours. Clear?"

"Absolutely."

THINKING ABOUT IT, he liked the idea of his ambulances flying attack runs. Show the street jockeys that the Med boys were more than just a taxi service for helmets who happened to get in the way of a bullet. Surely, they could do better than a hastily mounted door gun, though? How about some forward-firing stuff? Maybe get Lawmaster armament adapted for the ambulances? But that would mean talking to Tek Division, and he didn't see any reason to talk to Allen or her gang of wire-biters. Times like these you could only look to your own.

He spent the day on his feet, sometimes up to his elbows in blood, sometimes bouncing between Med Bay and Med Admin, hounding his people to work harder, faster. He couldn't remember the last time he'd eaten, but he had sense enough to keep on drinking water and reminding his staff to do the same. Got to stay hydrated.

Later, when his ethical code had evidently been modified somewhat, he was back in the ambulance dock, taking care of yet another crisis. He was interrupted by one of his people, who brought her vehicle to a standing hover and stuck her head out the window.

"Judge Barksdale! A fire's taken hold of the emergency wing at St. Martha Stewart and we're getting shot at from the roof. Where do you want me to take my casualties?"

"These are civilian casualties you're talking about?"

"Affirmative, Chief."

"The hell's the matter with you? Didn't you hear? Medical assets for department personnel only! We're not taking cits any more. Take them up to five hundred metres and jettison them. Try and make sure there are blockers below."

Mother of Grud, thought Barksdale, what was wrong with his people today? Maybe Tek Allen was right. Maybe everyone *was* going loopy.

FOURTEEN

"Judge Jimenez, you'd better get down to the mess hall."'

Jimenez had not been expecting trouble from that direction, but just because there was war on the streets didn't mean you could afford to turn your back on anything that might strike from within.

"On my way. Robinson, you're with me."

Robinson was still under review. If Mercer wanted her free from detention, that was Mercer's business, but the book said that a Judge under review should remain under supervision, and Jimenez was a by-the-book guy.

What could he expect in the mess hall? Block maniacs tunnelling in from outside? An outbreak of plague? Or what if Tek Allen was right? What if there was a contaminant behind this madness and some criminal mastermind had just been apprehended in the act of poisoning the Sector House? A whole Sector House full of Judges acting as nutso as the cits. Didn't bear thinking about.

What he found was a brawl. A brawl. Between Judges.

Normally, this was a quiet place where tired Judges went to shovel high-protein, high-carb nutrients into their faces before getting back to work. You might hear some shop talk coming from some of the tables, but Jimenez had never before witnessed an exchange of ideas as frank and open as this. Some of the auxiliary Admin personnel were squared off against what looked like Forensic by their uniforms.

Everyone was panting and glaring and wiping away blood with their sleeves. It looked like the excitement was over for now. But that wasn't enough for a couple of street Judges who were standing on one side, shouting mocking encouragement. Jimenez ploughed right on in, yelling at everyone to straighten up and get their gruddam act together. He zeroed in on one of the combatants.

"You! Care to tell me what all this is about?"

The man from Forensics looked sulky and said nothing, glaring all the while at one of the Admin people.

"No? Then care to start your new duties as a Cursed Earth litter warden *right drokking now?*"

"Guy was mouthing off at me," the Forensics Judge muttered grudgingly. "Who does he think he is, anyway? Drokking button-pusher."

"Who you calling a button-pusher? You— you janitor! Guy can lift a fingerprint, guy can look at a blood splash, guy thinks he's some kind of crime-buster."

This earned a guffaw from one of the watching street Judges and a: "You tell him, buddy!"

Jimenez had heard enough.

"What is this? Apetown?" He turned on the street Judge.

"You think this is funny? You didn't think that maybe you should stop it?"

"C'mon, Jimenez. They start shoving each other over who goes first in the chow line? Over who're the real Judges? I say let 'em at it. Whoever wins gets to pretend they're for real."

"I *am* a real drokking Judge, slab jockey!" yelled one of the Forensic staff. "Brains in your gruddam daystick! You think solving crimes and busting heads are the same thing!"

"Cool it! All of you!" ordered Jimenez before things got any uglier.

He was a Judge. He was a *good* Judge. He could go out there and patrol his grid and rack up an enviable arrest rate and make a drokking *difference*. As such, his instinctive sympathies were with the slab jockeys. But he'd been on administrative duties for three years now and no one— *no one*—better tell him that his job wasn't important. Whole damn thing would fall apart without guys like him. Too many helmets looked down on the button-pushers. Indiscipline was something to be deplored, but he had to admit: he liked the way those Admin and Forensics guys had stepped up and duked it out. Poor judgement, but the right attitude.

And then, even as he glared at the people in the mess hall, he felt a surprising upsurge of affection for them. These bozos were *his* people: the dumb lugs from off the street, the clean-up crews in their stupid green helmets, the pencil-necked geeks who stared at the screens all day. He suddenly wanted to tell them that he loved them—

every one of them. He'd fight and die for them, and they needed to know it. His voice thickening with unaccustomed emotion, he said, "We're all on the same side. Go do your drokking jobs."

ROBINSON WAS LOOKING at the food dispensers. Culinary variety in the mess hall was limited. The menu for any given day might as well have read 'Food–hot' and 'Food–cold,' but right now Robinson was reminded of how long it had been since she'd eaten. Some automatically dispensed food-shaped sustenance would go down real well right now.

"Judge Jimenez? Permission to grab a bite?"

"Negative, Robinson. We need to get back to Control."

"Aw, come on—how about just a cup of caf?" There was bottled water at her console upstairs, but she yearned for something that tasted of something and hadn't obviously been in storage for months.

"Forget it. We're on the clock."

FIFTEEN

It was all well and good, reflected Mercer, to have your people out there fighting hard, but it would help some if they were more inclined to obey orders. Too often now he was hearing good Judges saying, "'Negative, Control,'" or "'Sorry about that, Chief— no can do.'"

He'd given up trying to keep his resources spread evenly around the sector. If they were banding together against his instructions, then it was maybe because they could see the situation better than he could. If you can't trust a Judge's judgement, then what's it all about? So, he left his Judges to deal with the worse trouble spots and, instead of coordinating them, he had to be content with just keeping track of them.

The time had just come, however, when he needed to hear some unhesitating obedience.

"Warner! I need you to disengage from Astor immediate! That's Tac Teams Five, Seven, and Eight, I want you on Rubinski ASAP."

"Aw, Chief—we've just got Astor pretty much on

the ropes here. Just one push and you won't be hearing anything more from the John Jacob Astor Public Housing Projects, I swear."

"Astor is no longer a priority, Warner! You are to redeploy!"

"But, Chief, we got them beat!"

Mercer looked up at the screens again. They showed him hordes of angry citizenry filling the roads that led directly to his Sector House. His Judges were spread all over. His tactical teams were dragging their feet. His Sector House staff was stripped to the bone. He needed street-fighting Judges and he needed them right now.

"Robinson," he said, "Get down to the main entrance, quick as you can. And bring your gun."

THE PUBLIC FACE of justice in Sector 212 was perhaps best viewed from across Porfirio Diaz Rubinski Memorial Plaza. There you could see the solid rockrete tower of the Sector House in all its intimidating glory. Over the main entrance, in the classical severity of the post-war architectural style, was a fifty metre high eagle and shield in gold plasteel.

If that view maybe wasn't enough for you, and you somehow thought it might be a good idea to get closer (or if, for instance, you didn't have much choice and were being forcibly taken across the plaza in handcuffs), then the public face of justice would be the Judge who presided over the front hall. Between 0600 and 1800 every day that face belonged to Judge Carmen Raskova, and if you had any choice in the matter, it would be a really good idea to turn around and maybe apply for that pet licence online or whatever.

Raskova was white-haired, flinty-eyed, sharp-voiced, and mean as hell. She was too old for the streets, but it was said that she was too ornery for a teaching post at the Academy of Law, and as far as the Long Walk was concerned—well, even the Cursed Earth deserved a break sometimes.

In a long-defunct initiative in community policing, a sign had been placed above the hall reading *Welcome to Sector House 212. How can Justice Department help you today?* A row of automated booths provided citizens with the opportunity to pay fines, inform on their neighbours, or confess to crimes. The computer-generated image of a Judge that handled all these affairs in an inhuman and not-quite helpful manner was hugely preferable to having to deal with someone like Judge Raskova.

Her front-of-house, meet-and-greet demeanour was considered to add 6.5% to crime deterrence in the sector, or so the Judges liked to joke. Joking aside, most of them preferred to have their bookings processed by old man Hollar, eight floors down on the 7815th Street entrance. Raskova might have been the sort of Judge you wanted to be if you lived to grow old, but you didn't want to have to answer to her on the regular.

*　　*　　*

ROBINSON CAME SPRINTING into Front Hall with her helmet on, a multi-barrelled shotgun under her arm, and festoons of ammunition draped all over. The hall, always so full of miserable humanity and pitiless judgement, was strangely empty, and the flashing yellow alarm light accentuated the unreal quality.

"You're late," said Raskova. "Take up position here. Behind this desk."

"Situation, ma'am?" asked Robinson. A full Judge for three years and yet she automatically ma'amed Raskova, who was technically her superior only in experience. Robinson wasn't stupid.

"Situation is that we've got an estimated six to eight thousand citizens, armed and dumb, converging on the plaza. Our combat assets amount to the automated defences and to you and me. You up for it, kid?"

"Roger that, ma'am." Robinson saw to her weapons and to her line of sight.

"Careful where you point that thing, Robinson. You've already killed one Judge today."

That was Raskova all right. The woman knew everything as soon as it happened, and morale-boosting just wasn't her style. Better for Robinson to just suck it up and concentrate on the job at hand. But that didn't mean she should act all cowed.

"Yellow alert, Judge Raskova?" she asked.

"What about it?"

"We're about to get stormed by six to eight thousand block maniacs, there's just the two of us, and you're only declaring a yellow alert?"

"Life lesson for you, Robinson: no matter how bad things get, they can always get worse. I'm saving the higher alert levels for later. You feeling nervous?"

"Hell no, ma'am. Most fun a girl can have."

Raskova barked in what might have been a display of good humour. "Tell you what. If it's down to just you and your last ammo clip, you can go up to amber alert. Fair?"

SIXTEEN

THE FRONT HALL of the Sector House had been consciously designed as a killing ground. If the front entrance were breached, any intruders could be caught in devastating crossfire. Even if they succeeded in overwhelming whatever they met in the hall, they'd find that every way out was automatically locked down.

That was why Raskova was content to leave the front door open for the assaulting mob.

"I don't want to close the blast doors out front until I absolutely have to. One of them always gets stuck trying to reopen it and we always find that some juves have scrawled on them when they're closed. Every time. Guaranteed."

They watched the monitors and saw the edges of the plaza filling up with hostile crowds. For the time being, a no man's land of sorts was being observed in front of the Sector House.

The two Judges didn't need audio to hear the mob. Individual block slogans and battle cries were hard to distinguish, but they merged into a rumbling roar that almost made the floor thrum.

"Listen to that, Robinson. Community spirit in action. People taking pride in their neighbourhood. Keep your head well down when I trip the auto-cannons. Those things kick up a heck of a lot of debris."

Raskova took her helmet out from under her desk and put it on. The forbidding black glass of a motorcycle helmet designed to look like an executioner's hood somehow managed to soften her features. The noise outside reached a crescendo. Then all the various shouting became one single roar. They'd finally worked themselves up to charge.

"And there's the kick-off," said Raskova. "Stay cool."

The two Judges braced themselves but nothing happened. The crowd did not surge through the doors of the Sector House. The noise of battle filled the air, but it remained outside.

Robinson looked at Raskova. Raskova looked at Robinson and shrugged. They both looked at the monitors. From the branded clothing, it appeared that there were citizens from two opposing blocks tearing into each other in the plaza. Ruth Bader Ginsberg was kicking the crap out of George Foreman, but they were both ignoring the Sector House. A towering symbol of judicial oppression was right there, and it didn't seem to matter to them.

"What are we?" asked Raskova. "Chopped liver?"

"So, what do we do?" asked Robinson.

"Stand by. Conserve our resources. There's no riot

foam left anywhere in the sector and there's no way to process that many perps. So, we don't get involved until we have to."

It was inevitable that there was some overspill from the battle outside. A couple of blockers, either seeking shelter or maybe making a flanking movement, came through the front door. Robinson was assessing the target, bringing her weapon to bear, when Raskova shot them both—one, two.

"Haven't had a chance to fire my Lawgiver since New Year's Eve," she said. "Afraid I was getting rusty."

Neither of the dead perps was armed with anything more lethal than metal bars that looked like they'd been picked up at a construction site. Still, you walk into a place like this at a time like this with something like that in your hands and you've got to expect a little due process.

Welcome to Sector House 212, thought Robinson. *How can Justice Department help you today?*

SEVENTEEN

MUCH THE SAME thing happened twice more, with the same results. It was like the Sector House existed in a big blind spot as far as the brawlers in the plaza were concerned. It was frustrating for the two Judges who had psyched themselves up for a last-ditch defence of everything they held dear. Raskova had just dispatched another two invading (or lost) perps and Robinson was drawing a bead on a third, when the perp threw up his hands.

"Don't shoot! Please! I got family! I'm a family man!"

Family man. It was the safe word of the undercover Judge.

Robinson eased up on the trigger. The guy in her sights looked nothing like a Judge, but that was kind of the whole point. He was wearing bright pink body armour over lurid shorts and a shirt that advertised a local amusement park.

"Over here! Slowly!" she said. "Hands where I can see them!"

"Family man!" he repeated, gingerly stepping over the bodies of those who'd come this way without an invitation.

"Identify yourself!" said Raskova.

"Magee. November-two-niner-stroke-six-seven-three-Juliet-dash-whiskey-three-three-one."

"That's yesterday's code, Magee," said Raskova, for whom memorising eleven-digit alpha-numeric codes was all part of the day.

"Seriously?" said Magee. "I'm supposed to keep track in the middle of all this? For crying out loud!"

"Scanner. Console to your left. Hand on the screen. Slowly, now. Robinson here hasn't shot a Judge since this morning."

Here we go again, thought Robinson. *You kill* one *Judge...*

The scanner verified Magee's palm print, but Raskova made him submit to a retinal scan too before she waved him forward.

"I don't believe this," he complained as he reached the cover of the front desk. "You know me, Raskova."

"Sure I do," she said. "And now the computer knows you, and Robinson knows you, and we're all copacetic. Now, do you want to go back to your little block war out there or have you got something for us?"

"I need to talk to Chief Mercer, like, right away," said Magee.

"Chief's busy. Talk to me," said Raskova.

"Maybe we can go up to Control."

"Maybe we can do it right here. Situation's kind of tense

in case you haven't noticed. We've been hearing stories of rogue Judges. I'm not letting you anywhere without an escort, and I don't have the personnel to do the escorting. So sit down, take a load off, consider yourself among friends, and tell us what's on your mind—or I can just throw you out again."

Just then two Judges came limping in from behind, having obviously just come from Med Bay.

"We miss all the action?" asked the one with his leg—hip to ankle—all packaged up in speed-heal. His buddy had a fresh bullet wound to his calf but seemed content with the most basic of field dressings.

"Not much joy yet, boys," said Raskova, "but you're welcome to wait. Take up firing positions there and there."

"So can we go upstairs now?" asked Magee.

"Negative. You can sit in Interrogation Room 4 and tell it all to Robinson."

"*Interrogation?*"

"Debriefing. Whatever. Just tell it to Robinson. And for the love of Jovus keep it short."

EIGHTEEN

CLOSE UP, UNDER the lights of the little interrogation room off the main hall, Robinson thought she could see why Raskova was being careful with this Magee.

Undercover Judges were just weird at the best of times, but Magee was worse than most. He was wild-eyed and sweating, and if she'd had to guess she'd have said he was strung out on something cheap and potent.

"OK," she said. "Spill it."

"Right. Right. I work undercover in Waterworld. You know it?"

"Sure I know it. Mid-sector."

"Mid-sector, right. Central location. Convenient meeting place, you know? All kinds of stuff going down. Gang stuff. They figure that it's neutral turf. They figure that the sound of all that cascading water makes it hard to do the electronic eavesdropping. Oh yeah—and you can't really hide a gun in a bathing suit. So like I say. A lot of negotiation goes down. Talk is talked. Deals get dealt. That's why I'm there."

"OK. So what do you know?"

"I'm getting to that. Look… Maybe I can just tell it straight to Chief Mercer? Up in Control? Means I don't have to tell it twice, right?"

"You heard Raskova. Just tell me."

"Right. Right. Waterworld. Right. A real good place to be, you know? Not just for the criminal intel, I mean. I mean it's a good place to work. Could I get a caf or something?"

"We'll see. Just say what you were going to say."

"Right, yeah. So they've got this animatronic squid. Flupper. You've seen the ads, maybe?"

"I've seen them. Go on."

"*Flupper the squid lives in the sea…*"

"I said I've seen them."

"*Flupper the squid, a friend to you and me…*"

"Magee! Focus!"

"Right. I'm just saying. It's a friendly place to work. Maybe too much chlorine, but you should come see. I could hook you up with tickets. Half price."

"Magee! Just what the hell has this got to do with the situation outside?"

"Right. I was getting to that. I was getting to that." If Magee's cover was as an annoying, absent-minded weirdo, then Robinson had to admit that he was really deep into the role.

"So Waterworld is all about the gangs, right? Gangs from all over the sector. But Waterworld *belongs* to Julie Andrews Block."

"You mean their gang—what, the Man Trapps?

—are making a play for Waterworld? I hate to tell you, Magee, but we've got kinda bigger things on our plate right now."

"No, no, no. It's not like that. Julie Andrews *owns* Waterworld. It stands to reason. The place is pretty much part of the block. It's a Julie Andrews amenity."

"I'm not following here."

Magee leant forward and punctuated his argument by jabbing his finger on the table.

"Julie Andrews Block has rights to Waterworld. Understand? The other gangs, the other blocks, they don't. Understand?"

"No. What the hell are we talking about, Magee? The Sector House is about to come under attack any second and you're talking about a water park?"

"Water*world!* And *yes*, Robinson, the Sector House *is* about to come under attack!"

"By a gang? From Julie Andrews? And in light of what we've already got going on, that's important exactly *how*?"

"Is it hot in here or what? Can we go talk to the Sector Chief now?"

"If you're hot, you can maybe take off the armoured vest, but you'd better start making sense."

"I want to go up to Control."

"You can go up to the psych ward in Med Bay in a second."

"How about the armoury?"

"What?"

"Or maybe the generators down below. Something with

a lot of explosive power, know what I mean?"

By now Robinson was on her feet, going for her gun. Magee was sweating rivers and fumbling with his pink plastic body armour, talking more to himself than to her. She couldn't quite believe what she was seeing.

"Are those *wires*? Is that vest wired up?"

"Yeah, yeah. You didn't see the trigger anywhere? I coulda swore..."

"Sit *down*, Magee! One more move, and I swear to Grud I shoot!"

"Julie Andrews forever!" he shouted, somewhat spoiling the triumphant effect by patting down his pockets, looking for the detonator.

He didn't get any farther because that's when Raskova came in and shot him in the back of the head.

"Jeez, Robinson," she said. "You are *slow* today."

"You were listening in?"

"Damn right I was listening in. You think I let stuff happen behind my back in my department? And you should have popped him as soon as he started with the advertising jingles."

"He's a Judge! I can't just shoot him! *You* can't just shoot him!"

"He's a kook. *Was* a kook. We don't have time for kooks today, Robinson. Get a grip, and get back to your post."

NINETEEN

OUTSIDE MORE PERSONNEL were moving into Front Hall. They were the oddments of the Sector House, flexing unaccustomed fingers on the grips of seldom-used weapons. Where had they been when it was just her and Raskova and about a million block maniacs?

Robinson found that the desk she'd been defending was now manned by a Med Judge. Didn't he have a job already? Didn't the Med guys have enough to do today? Or maybe she'd missed something while talking to Magee and something really big was about to go down. She asked the Med Judge.

"Honestly? I don't know any more than you do," he said. "But I didn't want to miss out."

"Miss out?"

"Sure. You wouldn't believe how tired you get of hospital work. Just patching up blast wounds and bullet wounds all day. I wanted to get a piece of the real action. Make a difference, you know?"

"But you're a Med! You make a difference by saving lives."

"Relax. I got a med kit with me. It's underneath the ammunition somewhere. If someone gets hit, I'll take a look at them. Just so long as I get my trigger time."

Robinson shook her head wonderingly but told him how things stood and what they could expect.

"So far, the fighting is outside, but we've been getting some strays coming in, and I think we can expect more directed hostility any time."

"Sounds good to me. I haven't killed anyone since I had to euthanise all those casualties from the big chem spill last year."

It was as it was feared. Rubinski Plaza was a convenient arena for the riled-up populations of five neighbouring blocks to attempt to resolve their differences in an intimate fashion. This was fine at the beginning, when Ruth Bader Ginsberg Block had met directly with George Foreman Block, and it was still fine twenty minutes later when Louis L'Amour joined in and the whole thing became a three-way neighbourhood title fight.

But then Patty Hearst came along. Hearst Citi-Def was packing more heat than their opponents, and the Hearst blockers had also raided a homes and gardens supply store on the way here. Now automatic weapons and domestic power tools were tilting the balance dramatically in Hearst's favour. Although not otherwise exhibiting much in the way of smarts, many of the beaten combatants were seeking safety. Some of the overspill of the fight breached the Sector House doors and was quickly and neatly dealt with by the waiting Judges. That would also have been fine except that some Hearst blockers, pursuing their foes, got caught in the Judges' fire, and understandably they took it kind of badly. They still had plenty of fight in them, and with the plaza theirs, they were looking around for someone new to tussle with. It took a little while for them to make up their minds, to rally, and to concentrate on this new objective, but when they did, they surged forward without fear.

Hey—who's never thought about storming a Justice Department facility and killing everyone inside?

"BETTER CLOSE THE blast doors, Raskova."

"I am *not* getting graffiti on my blast doors!"

"I really don't think that's a concern here."

"The hell with the blast doors. Let them come. We've got them."

And they did have them. The blockers, charging from daylight into gloom, bottlenecked at the entrance, were easy meat for the waiting Judges. The auto-cannons chewed up the invaders by the score and anyone left got shredded by the concentrated rapid fire of people who'd been waiting for an uncomfortable time to do exactly this.

Robinson found that, with the maniacs boxed in so neatly in front of her, she could set her Lawgiver to ricochet and practically sit back and enjoy the fun. In a few seconds, there was so much gunsmoke and concrete dust in the air that the Judges were obliged to switch to infrared sighting. By the time they ceased fire, the hall was in serious need of redecoration and Resyk would need to open up a new conveyor belt.

"They've got the guns; they've got the numbers; but we have justice on our side!" shouted the Med Judge at Robinson's side, as he finished off a couple of the wounded with well-aimed shots.

TWENTY

AND IT WAS so far so good, until Louisa May Alcott marched onto the scene alongside Alice Cooper. This was no mindless mob. The Machiavellian minds in Alcott had only that morning reaped the benefits of their long cultivation of Cooper and sealed a binding military alliance. Between them, they had vanquished Grover Cleveland Block, and now they were embarked on a campaign of joint conquest. As they'd hoped, many of their enemies had fought each other to ruin in Rubinski Plaza. They'd thought to mop up what was left and thus dominate the locality, but seeing the repulse of Patty Hearst from the Sector House, they quickly appreciated the new strategic situation.

The Chair of the Louisa May Alcott Residents Association met with the head honcho of the (Award-winning) Alice Cooper Knitting Circle. Talks were held. Decisions were taken. The Judges could see it all happening live on camera. In case there was any doubt, the ringleaders broadcast their plan by way of bullhorn.

"The Judges gotta go! We rule Sector Two-Twelve! Yay!"

Mercer saw it all up in Control, and came down to Front Hall to take personal charge. He was just too restless to stay above all this. A few of his people must have felt the same because, without orders, various control centre personnel followed him by way of last-ditch reinforcements. He didn't argue. Almost every combat-effective Judge in the sector was out there breaking heads. The Sector House would have to look after itself.

"Estimate crowd?"

"Thirty thousand? Forty thousand? And that's just in the plaza. Plenty more packing the approaches."

"And what's our status?"

"Not great. One of the auto-cannons got busted. Ammo depletion on the others isn't a problem yet, but give it time. Available personnel? You're looking at it, Chief. Same story at all the other entrances."

"We'll be OK, Raskova."

"Damn straight we will, Chief. We can do this all day."

MAYBE THEY COULD have done it all day. The blockers kept on coming and the Judges just kept on shooting. But then one of the maintenance staff got too enthusiastic with a hi-ex round and blew out the mountings on another of the auto-cannons. They managed to retrieve the situation, but it got kind of hairy for a minute there.

When things calmed down a little, everyone cussed out the gruddamn janitor who thought he was a Judge just because he worked for Justice Department. But Jimenez reflected that, earlier, things might have got much uglier. At least now the real Judges were recognising that the support personnel were on their side. That feeling was reinforced when one of the people from upstairs—one of those pale figures with a headset permanently in place— put down six infiltrators with seven shots in bad light.

"Who's a button-pusher now, meat heads?" he'd cackled above the din, and his cry was met with cheers from all his brothers and sisters in arms, whatever their departmental assignment.

Throughout the firefight, all kinds of personnel who'd never patrolled the street were loudly affirming that they were, in fact, Judges.

"Court is in session, scumbags!"

"Appeal that, mother-drokker!"

And the slab jockeys might have laughed at the pretensions of their fellows, but they didn't argue. And they sure as hell didn't punch each other out like Jimenez had witnessed in the mess hall.

Put 'em through hell together and they'll end up buddies, he thought with satisfaction.

The beauties of team bonding aside, those six infiltrators had highlighted a crack in the defences, and those unserviceable auto-guns were going to be missed. A few of the Judges had been wounded, and even if they were staying in the fight, it proved that they weren't invulnerable.

A few more good people would get hit, and some of them would get hit bad, and the block maniacs would just keep on coming regardless.

So maybe keeping it up all day was a little optimistic.

Robinson was beginning to feel punch drunk from the endless shooting, but when she saw the crowd outside forming up for yet another rush, she merely sighed. "OK, once more. With feeling."

But then someone shouted from behind to make some space, and a new element was introduced to the battle.

It was Tek Allen and her team, unveiling the fruit of a morning's fast work.

It appeared to be the main armament from a Three Series patrol wagon—essentially a versatile, variable-velocity artillery piece—mounted on an improvised carriage which looked like a couple of drastically repurposed cleaning droids.

Nice.

TWENTY-ONE

ALLEN HAD BEEN driving her team hard. She had under her as fine a collection of scientists and technicians as any sector could boast, facing the gravest threat to the city in a generation, but because they didn't want to be dismissed as mere eggheads and lab coats, they had been motivated by nothing more sophisticated than: 'We'll show *them*.'

And now what Allen was showing Mercer—and all the helmets who might sneer at Tek Division—was quite the last word in riot control. Or so she sold it.

"A riot gun, Allen? OK, I suppose we could use one. But stumm gas shells? I'm not turning them down or anything, but by my count we're down to the last hundred litres of stumm. It looks like you've put a lot of effort into something that's not going to give us much of a return."

"Not just stumm, Chief. Think of this as stumm plus. No— Scratch that. Think of this as Sector 212's extra-special, all-purpose, chemical delivery system."

There was something odd about Allen's demeanour, thought Mercer. He wasn't used to Tek Judges talking like they were spearheading a big ad campaign. And there was more to it than that. Allen was the girl who was trying too hard. He had an uneasy feeling that if he flashed her a smile, she'd squeal with delight. He looked at her team. There was an expression of eager expectancy on their faces. *Bunch of wannabes*, he thought.

"OK, Allen. What's it do?"

"Right, Chief—listen to this. You take a litre of stumm, OK? You let it out. It pretty much instantly colonises about half a million cubic metres of air, give or take. OK?"

"Which is impressive, Allen, I grant you, but that will deal with approximately one fifth of the situation facing us right now, and what we have right now is something I think we're going to have to get used to."

"Bear with me, Chief. Let's say we dilute the stumm by say, two-thirds."

"Then we've got stumm gas that's only one third as effective or fills up only one third the space. I don't know. You tell me."

"Uh-uh. It fills up the full space. We can make it do that because we're smart. And you know what's smarter? That low-strength stumm doesn't need to knock anyone out. It's only there to carry whatever fills up the other two thirds of the gas shell."

"And that might be?"

"Anything we like, Chief. For today's demonstration, may I interest you in a little something of our own invention?"

Was that an attempt at a flirtatious grin he was seeing?

"Stop kidding around, Allen."

"Sorry, Chief. Actually, it's not quite our own invention. But we improved on it. It's that cyclic acid plasteen mix that Feenya Morgan cooked up over at Ricardo Montalban. She knew her stuff, but we know it better. Our stuff goes from full strength to complete dissipation in under a minute."

"So?"

"So, for instance, you can kill anyone and everyone in that plaza with two rounds from this baby, and sixty seconds later the air is safe to breathe again."

"I like it. Good job, Allen. Let's see your people do their thing."

Judges don't simper. Emotionless technocrats certainly don't blush. So Mercer figured that it must have been a trick of the light.

He turned to his people. "Listen up, everybody! Make some space and respirators down!"

The Judges moved their line forward and established a new perimeter just beyond the doors while behind them the Teks pushed their gun through the drift of bodies in the hall. Nobody helped. If the Teks wanted to be in the gang, they had to prove themselves.

One Tek stopped a bullet on the way, and Mercer had to order a nearby Med to take care of it.

"Dammit, we're all on the same side here!" he roared, for what felt like the hundredth time that day.

Outside, the blockers hesitated at the sight of the formidable weapon poking its muzzle through the doors, but they didn't hesitate for long. Louisa May Alcott had never chickened out of a fight yet.

The Teks had chosen this gun because it was simple, proven, point-and-click hardware. With no fuss, a round was loaded and fired, and in approximately zero seconds flat, Alice and Louisa May were on their knees, choking, puking, dying.

There was much grinning and backslapping from the Tek Judges. Sure, their second round was a dud, but the first one had made its point. They were as much a part of Sector House 212 as anyone.

"All right, the grease monkeys!" someone cheered.

There was one dissenting voice. Barksdale had come down from Med and was getting in Tek Allen's face about how respiratory suppression was his department and how she should keep in her own lane, but Mercer told them to knock it off, and his authority was sufficient for them to do just that. Raskova might have been commanding the defence of Front Hall, Allen might have arrived to save the day, but Mercer was Alpha Dog, and everyone knew it.

TWENTY-TWO

As THE GAS dispersed, the Judges appreciated the devastation they had wrought. A tide-line of bullet-riddled corpses was piled up by the doors, and beyond that a sea of poisoned citizenry.

Allen was glowing with pride, Barksdale was scowling with professional envy, and the handful of street Judges were offering condescending smiles and sardonic congratulation. A happy kind of we'll-make-Judges-out-you-yet vibe.

Robinson, appalled but impressed, slid her respirator up and surveyed the scene. Yup, Teks had done their thing. Hundred percent fatalities by the look of it. But then she saw movement out in the plaza. Someone was trying to get up. Someone in black and gold. The Teks had done their thing all right, but this someone had happened to have a respirator too.

"Judge down!" she called. "There's a Judge out there!"

She didn't wait for any acknowledgement.

The conditioning took over, and she was running across the plaza. She slowed, though, as she came up to the fallen Judge. The man was staggering to his feet, groggy and sick.

His badge displayed his name, but all the same she said, "Identify yourself," keeping her gun on him. In her mind, she was seeing Judge Gray, the block Judge at Mapother. Gray had been shooting her partner. She hadn't been able to give him a chance. This guy was getting that chance, though. This guy was going to prove to her whether she'd been right, whether Gray had indeed been a righteous kill. Either that, or this was a guy she could save from the next wave of blockers, who were most surely on their way.

The Judge, swaying slightly, slid up his respirator, coughed and spat. She couldn't see his eyes, but he didn't seem to be focusing on her.

"You OK? You want to come in?"

Are you a straight-up Judge or are you another murderous crazy?

The Judge still didn't respond, but Raskova's voice rasped in her radio.

"What have we got, Robinson?"

"His badge says Denning. I dunno. He's kind of out of it."

"Denning's block Judge at Cooper."

A block Judge. Embedded in the populace. Like Gray had been.

"Uh-oh."

"Your call, kid, but be advised: we have more hostiles

inbound from two directions. Correction, three, no, *four* directions."

"Roger that."

"Make sure you're on the right side of the blast doors if I have to close them. You're kind of runty, but your ass is still too big to get through the mail slot."

"Denning!" she said. "You with me? You want to come on in?"

And now he looked at her. "Come in?" he said, in a voice thick with phlegm.

She could hear the thunder of feet growing louder behind her. Latecomers to the party? A whole new guest list?

"That's right. Come with me. We can get you looked at. Come on home now."

He took a step towards her, unsure. From across the plaza a roar went up. The latecomers had just seen what had happened to the earlier waves of their fellow blockers. They didn't sound happy about it. *So much for deterrent*, thought Robinson.

"Come on! It's making your mind up time, Denning! Just be cool and come with me."

She was keeping one hand tight on her gun, and the gun tight on Denning, but she was holding out her other hand, beckoning, showing a frightened and dangerous animal the way to safety. And it seemed to be working.

Gray never got a second chance. Same with Magee. Let's see if we can make up for that.

She started to edge her way backwards, and Denning took a couple of steps after her. And then the crowd, having advanced to within a hundred metres, cut loose.

"Alice Cooper!" they roared, and Denning's head snapped up in response. He was no longer lost. His people had found him.

"Alice Cooper!" he roared back, and went for his gun.

Ah, jeez, thought Robinson, and dropped him with one shot before turning and sprinting back towards the big doors under the big gold eagle.

"Nice effort, Robinson," said Raskova's voice in her ear. "We were even, and now it's two-one to you."

TWENTY-THREE

"OK, ALLEN," SAID Mercer. "Let's give it a minute for the plaza to fill up again and then you can make with the gas."

"Yeah, Chief. The thing is, though…"

"What?" It was all well and good being the big dog in this pack, but he could do without the meekness that Allen was suddenly exhibiting.

"What we showed you just now? Well, that was kind of the demonstration model."

"Meaning?"

"Meaning we've got two more rounds and then we'll have to go and mix up a whole new batch. Sorry."

"Now she tells me."

While the Teks scuttled off to make good, Mercer took stock of what else the Sector House had in the way of defences. His people were fighting well, but he only had so many people, and they only had so many bullets. Another wonder-weapon like Allen's would be good right now.

"Barksdale! You were having ideas about respiratory suppression? You think your people can rustle up a little biological warfare in the next half-hour or so? No? So what *can* you give me?"

"I hate to admit it, Chief, but Allen's gas is good. Even if I could somehow create a lab-grown plague, the rate of transmission wouldn't match the immediate punch of her stumm-plus, or whatever she calls it."

"So?"

"So I'm going to keep looking for a cure—an antidote for this Block Mania."

"You really think it's a disease? A regular disease that can be cured?"

"There's certainly a neurological root to it. We're still exploring possibilities."

"Explore harder." And now Mercer had to shout because the battle had been joined again.

"OK, how about this, Chief? We've been experimenting with the maniacs in the holding pens—the ones that were arrested when this still looked like a normal block war? Keep them in the pens and they're maniacs. Isolate them, put them in solitary, they calm right down. They become confused, disoriented. Like that Judge that Robinson shot out there. Cut them out from the herd and they're easy to deal with."

"Are you telling me, Barksdale, that I've got to find isolation cubes for each of the one point six million citizens in my sector? Or maybe I should just sit down with each of them over a cup of hot chocolate and talk things over?"

"No, Chief, I was thinking we could maybe bombard them with sonic cannon. It produces the same level of disorientation."

"I like your thinking, Doc, but all the sonic cannon in the city were requisitioned yesterday on Dredd's order. Get back to me if you get any more ideas."

TWENTY-FOUR

THE PRESSURE MOUNTED on the Judges through the next hour. It wasn't that Rubinski Plaza was a chosen arena any more—it was that Sector House 212 had become the centre of gravity for half the fighting in the sector. By mid-afternoon, it looked like every one of those one point six million citizens was crowded into the streets surrounding the Sector House, sometimes whupping hell out of each other, but mostly surging against the fortress of justice that rose in their midst. Shot, gassed, battered, but they kept coming. Steadily, all the ancillary staff were drawn away from their regular duties and into the defence of the building, while the few personnel left up in Control watched their screens and kept their colleagues downstairs apprised of yet more threats coming their way.

And then, as she scooted along the floor to retrieve yet another bag of ammunition, and wondered if she'd still be doing the same thing this time next week, Robinson heard the warning: "Judges inbound."

She squinted through her visor, all the optical enhancements turned up full, and she saw it: to the rear of the rioters, muzzle flashes reflecting off helmets. She thought about Gray, and Magee, and Denning, and how many more times she might have to do this, when she heard Mercer.

"Hold your fire, people. Those are ours."

Weren't they all? thought Robinson, but it seemed that Mercer knew what he was talking about, for over an open channel came the message, "Control, this is B Watch, along with Tac Teams Five, Seven, and Eight, incoming and homeward bound!"

"What drokking kept you?" Mercer radioed back.

"Sorry, Chief. Got tied up in a block war or two. Must have gotten a little carried away."

The homecoming Judges—not just pairs or patrols, but battle groups now—blasted their way across the plaza. Mercer had seen these formations coalescing on his screens earlier that day and had been unable to keep the concentrations dispersed. Then he'd had the devil's own time pulling them away from whatever fights they'd been in, but here they were now, with a wide field of fire open in front of them.

The carnage was spectacular. The Lawmasters had a bumpy ride over the final approach, what with the bodies so thick on the ground.

The notion of protecting and serving had pretty much gone out the window when the citizenry raised their hand against the Judges. The residents of Louisa May Alcott, George Foreman, Ruth Bader Ginsberg,

Alice Cooper, Patty Hearst, and six other blocks had learnt that lesson the hard way.

"Not bad," said Mercer, taking in the scene, scratching his chin. "This is something I think we can work with."

"Chief?"

"Thinking out loud, Robinson."

From out of the landscape of corpses, one crazed citizen, half-dead, climbed to his feet. "Julie Andrews rules!" he shouted in defiance of all the evidence. "We the baddest block inna city!"

"Wrong," said Mercer as he shot him. "That would be us."

TWENTY-FIVE

ROBINSON RECOGNISED A Judge Tyler among the arriving Judges. They'd partnered together in the past. Now they compared notes.

"Rough day, huh?"

"Tell me about it. One minute I'm on patrol, I get called to a block war, and next thing you know, it's a day and a half later and, well…" Tyler indicated the human wreckage choking the plaza. "You ever imagine anything like this?"

Robinson took it all in. The scale was stupefying. Could all these dead really be termed righteous kills?

"You've got to wonder," she said. "I mean, it's not like they weren't warned or anything. But I mean, they're only cits, you know? It's not as if they're weighing the pros and cons. Once something like this starts, you can't really expect reasonable behaviour."

"But then there's our response."

"Well yeah. Our response. We haven't really been restrained. Once the shooting started, we just cut loose, you know? I saw some of our people who weren't trying to de-escalate the situation. They were keeping score. They'd have been happy to kill every citizen in the sector, and then some."

"You talking about excessive force, Robinson?"

"No doubt. But it's not like we can do anything about it. I mean Mercer was right there, and it wasn't like he had a problem with it."

"I know what you're talking about," said Tyler. "I was seeing the same thing out there. Makes you wonder if you shouldn't send a discreet report to the SJS. You know, just to cover your own ass."

"Yeah... about the SJS, though. They're not reading reports today."

She filled him in on the murders up on thirty-four. Just another crazy thing to add to the general craziness. Tyler took it on board, and then put it to one side.

"Look, Robinson. Bottom line, OK? We're Judges. We meet violence with violence. And I'm not talking about illegality. The rules of engagement have changed. The gloves are off. What would have got us all sent to Titan last week is now standard operating procedure. No. What bothers me is the irrationality."

"Like faulty judgement?"

"Like irrationality. Like strange motivations. Like I hook up with Warner's team and we're suppressing rioters over at the Astor Projects."

"So?"

"So the job is suppression. It's not like here where you had to hold off a screaming mob or get killed.

No, it's just about containment. It's about neutralising a threat and moving on. But Warner doesn't see it that way."

"How do you mean?"

"Warner's out to win the block war. Like his tac team is just another faction in the big fight."

"Let me play devil's advocate here, Tyler. Like you say, we're the Judges. We have to win."

"OK, I know, but Warner looks like he's taking it personally. He's hunting down Astors like they've insulted him."

"And how is the result different to your standard riot suppression?"

"All I'm saying is that you weren't there, Robinson."

"Look, devil's advocate aside, if you think Warner and the others are going crazy, you're wrong. I've seen Judges go nuts—up close. Believe me, if you saw what I've seen today, you'd know the difference between that and irrationality."

ROBOTS WERE BUSTLING around the place, clearing away bodies and dispensing food and water.

"All right," said Mercer. "I want watch commanders, tactical leaders and all senior Judges up front here. The rest of you, check your ammo, grab a nutri-bar, and take five."

With all his senior people assembled in the middle of the hall, Mercer told them what was on his mind.

"I am not happy with the way these block wars are

being handled," he began.

"What's not to like, Chief? We're out there solving the public housing crisis. A whole lot of empty apartments after this."

"Your attitude stinks! No nutri-bar for you, Warner! Robot, do not give that Judge a nutri-bar!"

"Aw, Chief!"

"What the hell is the matter with you?" he roared. "I'm up there in Control giving orders, trying to hold this sector together, and you're all playing cowboy! I can count on the fingers of one hand the orders that I've given that have been obeyed in a direct and timely fashion."

"Chief, we had a situation."

"I don't want to hear about your situation! We had a situation right here! You want to look at the bullet holes in the walls here—here in your own Sector House!—and tell me that your situation was more serious than mine? Go on! I dare you!"

The red mist cleared from his mind. *Keep it cool. These are* your *people.*

"OK. Enough with the chewing out. You're here now. We're all here now. That means that what we've got is a concentration of force. That gives me an idea.

"The competition is largely gone. The best-armed, best-directed elements of nearly half the blocks in this sector have just beaten themselves to death against our front door. What I see here is an opportunity.

"We see all these creeps with their stupid block names on their clothes, shouting their stupid block slogans, all trying to be number one. They've forgotten something, and it's our job to remind them. *We're* number one. *We're* top block in this sector. A little law and order is what we need to give them. When this is over, I want them all to know that Sector House 212 rules this sector, or else I want the whole place to look like the plaza outside."

His words were met with affirmation from his assembled Judges. No doubt about it: after all this time putting out fires, it was time to get proactive. Time to get judging.

TWENTY-SIX

"So what's our next move, Chief?"

But the meeting was interrupted by a proximity radar alert. Something airborne and dangerous was on its way.

"What have we got?" asked Mercer.

"Looks like a drone," said a voice from Control. "Wait—I've got visual. Negative on the drone. Looks like a semi-autonomous self-propelled explosive device."

Flying munitions, guided by artificial intelligence and capable of loitering over targets as necessary, had been around a long time. With the advent of cheap and accessible anti-grav technology, the bootleg version had become a favourite among outlaw explosives fetishists. The Judges knew it as the not-so-smart bomb.

"It's pausing. It's targeting. And it's—Inbound! Brace! Brace!"

The explosion, when it came, was nothing special. Typical aerial IED, really. You got some bomb makers who were a whizz with the explosive element but were lousy with the flight capabilities. Those were the ones who tended to get discovered by fire crews and Forensics. Then you'd got the ones that could make some sweet flying machines but with no bang for the buck. This, apparently, was one of the latter. It was enough to make Mercer lose it, though.

He checked the damage on screen and then stormed out to have a look for himself. The bomb had struck the front of the building and done no structural damage. It was the cosmetic damage, though, that had Mercer all riled up.

The great plasteel eagle and shield had been marred by the blast. Black scorch marks were splashed across the gold. One of the great squared-off stylised feathers on the eagle's tail was bent out of shape. Mega-City One justice had been insulted.

Mercer stared at it, bug-eyed, incensed. Then he looked all around to see where the bomb might have come from.

It could have been anywhere. You could launch one of those things from your apartment window, and there were a whole lot of windows looking down on him.

"Whoever did this better own up!" he yelled to the world at large. "And I mean right now!"

The piled-up bodies in the plaza stayed quiet. The towering city blocks said nothing.

"Last warning!" yelled Mercer.

"Range on those things is a few clicks at least, Chief," said Jimenez. "Don't even need line of sight. Mightn't be one of these blocks."

"I don't buy it. This is personal. This is someone who sees our eagle every day and has been waiting for their chance to spit on it."

"You think?"

"This is someone who can't take it that we're the bosses here: that we're number one in this sector." He turned a slow circle, glaring at each of the buildings in sight, as if waiting for one of them to crack. Then he stopped and nodded, his lip curling in a smile.

"I've got you, you son of a bitch."

"Chief?"

"You see what I'm seeing, Jimenez?"

"Belinda Carlisle?" It was hard to miss.

"Belinda Carlisle." The vast new housing complex loomed over the sector like a mountain. Two kilometres away and it still cast a shadow over the Sector House in the afternoons. Well, that was going to have to change, thought Mercer. *No one* puts Justice Department in the shade.

The meeting inside was reconvened. Mercer's crusade had a specific objective now. There were doubters in his congregation, however.

"Carlisle's given us no trouble so far."

"Yeah, Chief. All quiet at Belinda Carlisle."

"Which means they're hiding something! I say we go in there hard and we find out! Carlisle's a big complex so I want maximum aggression on this one. All our air assets, all our heavy weapons, all our personnel!"

"Just on suspicion, Chief? You're talking heavy judicial commitment for a block that's been behaving itself."

"What the hell is the matter with you? Go outside! Look at what those stomm-suckers did to our eagle! And you're looking for probable cause now?

"Let me remind you. '*Mega-City One Criminal Code Section 59 (D): A Judge may enter a citizen's home to carry out routine intensive investigation. The citizen has no rights in this matter.*'

"It says 'intensive' right there. You think we should go easy on them? Knock politely? The law doesn't work that way, Schwartz."

Lest it ever be said that Judge Julio Schwartz was some kind of limp-wrist liberal, he got behind Mercer loud and strong. "No sir, Chief! Let's go fifty-nine-dee 'em to hell and gone!"

That set off a vocal wave.

"Law and order!"

"Carlisle's got it coming!"

And emerging above it all came the unifying war chant: "*Two-one-two! Two-one-two!*"

TWENTY-SEVEN

JUDGE WALLACE HOLLAR had lost both his legs years ago when bionics were pretty good but not that good. He could get around fine, but street duties were too much to be expected from him. In the years since, he'd been doing just about everything a Judge could do that that didn't require speed and agility, but the place he'd ended up—the place he was content to be—was behind a booking desk at 212. Processing perps wasn't the same as busting them, but it kept him in the game. He was a necessary link in the chain. He liked that. He was Old Man Hollar to the street Judges, but he knew they never meant anything dismissive by that. He was an old timer, but he was still one of them.

Today there was just him. Everyone was out on the streets, and they weren't bringing perps back to be booked. It got kind of lonesome, but Hollar kept to his post. When the big attack swept in upon the Front Hall, he stayed put, even though the street entrance he oversaw was ignored by the block maniacs.

He locked down his blast door and put his Lawgiver on the desk in front of him, but business remained slow.

What's the matter with you stupes? You all go roaring in the front door into the loving arms of Raskova and her auto-cannons, when you could be slipping in round back. I mean, come on—there's only one old guy here. You can't deal with one old man?

And he dearly wished someone would try.

He was even tempted to open the blast door by way of an invitation. Then he could really process some perps.

Normally, he was fairly ambivalent about the criminals who passed through his hands. Sure, they were scumbags, but they were part of the job, and he loved the job. So unless someone was acting violent or was guilty of something truly vile, Hollar didn't have a problem with them. Just strip 'em down and lock 'em up. Even the hundreds upon hundreds of maniacs he'd had to process yesterday weren't treated especially harshly. Those had been some seriously uncooperative customers, but even if they had to be strong-armed into the holding tanks, he'd still made sure they got fed.

He nearly chuckled at the memory. Perps coming in, still puking from stumm gas, crumbs of solidified riot foam still in their hair, and still shouting the odds. Wouldn't give their names, but were very proud of their addresses, oh yes.

But no one was coming round today. Dumb bastards were too busy storming Front Hall.

And then the monitors alerted him that someone was trying to get in. It gave him a momentary jolt of adrenalin until he saw that it was a couple of Judges, and one of them was hurt.

STEINMAN STAGGERED IN under the weight of Kowalczyk's body and told Hollar not to bother with calling the medics.

"Buddy boy here's been dead for hours. Probably too late to harvest his organs now, but I wasn't going to leave him out there."

"I'm sorry, son. You carry him all the way here?"

"Last few klicks. Lazooka took out one bike. Used the other to clear away a barricade over on Junction 19. Mark One Lawmaster went out in a blaze of glory. Never seen the self-destruct on one of those things before. Got something to drink, Hollar? I am dry as dry."

"Listen, Steinman—before you get too comfortable, I gotta tell you that there's an APB out on you."

"The SJS thing. Sure, sure. I'd better go clear that one up with Chief Mercer. You want me to surrender my gun or something?"

"Nah, you hang on to it, kid. Say, that reminds me. You want to go down to the holding pens and shoot some prisoners?"

TWENTY-EIGHT

STEINMAN HAD IMAGINED walking into Front Hall and everything stopping. There'd be this momentary tableau of him, silhouetted in the door, and then everyone's guns would come up. It would be a real big deal. But instead of the dramatic entrance, he slipped in through the side door, wiped out from carrying poor old Kowalczyk all that way, and had to wait around embarrassed while the Chief harangued everyone on how they were handling the block wars. This is how they were dealing with Judge killers now? He'd only been away since early morning, but standards appeared to have slipped since then. You commit what's pretty much an unforgivable crime and you had to stand in line while all the day-to-day stuff got handled. Big fat anticlimax.

Finally, he got his moment and approached Mercer, helmet held stiffly under his arm as though in formal token of submission.

"Steinman," said Mercer.

"Chief."

"Do I have to tell you that you're under arrest on suspicion of murder?"

"No, Chief—and I should tell you that there's no suspicion about it."

"You admit to killing—?" And it took Mercer a second to recall the names of the two dead SJS Judges. That's how much he cared about them.

Steinman stood there, ready to take his punishment like a Judge.

"Want to tell me about it?" said Mercer.

"My partner was clean, Chief. Kowalczyk was a good Judge. You think he was on the take? His body's downstairs. Go have a look. All he's got is a department expense card and all it's got is four creds on it. I checked. You think he ripped off a drug deal for four creds? Why? So he could buy himself a Freezy-whip?"

"You can't go killing Judges, Steinman. Not even SJS." Although a voice in Mercer's head was asking him why not. Bunch of high and mighty creeps spying on their own kind. Snooping on real Judges. Acting all self-righteous like they'd never heard of Judge Cal. Steinman here at least was up front about his misdeeds, and Mercer had never doubted that Kowalczyk had always been on the up-and-up.

"It's your lucky day, Steinman. We need Judges. Consider yourself under open arrest. Your case will be heard once this war is won. Clear?"

"Thank you, Chief."

"Report to Jimenez. You can consider him your arresting officer."

* * *

"Steinman," said Jimenez. "The Judge killer. Well, I've got no time to babysit Judge killers. We're moving out against Carlisle. Partner yourself up with Robinson. She's another Judge killer. You'll get along great. Either of you start straying and I'll shoot you."

"Steinman," said Robinson warily. "It's true what you did?"

"Yeah."

"Those SJS guys go nuts? That why you had to put them down?"

"No. They were pretty composed. How about the one you killed?"

"Um—two actually. And yeah, five-star, gold-plated fruit loops, both of them."

"So that's why I'm under arrest and you're only under review, I guess."

"I guess."

"So, we're taking on Belinda Carlisle, huh?"

"That's what the Chief says."

"Outstanding. Carlisle's got it coming."

They rolled out in convoy. Massed Lawmasters flanked by patrol wagons, hearts high and loaded for bear. And it wasn't just the street Judges. Ancillaries, auxiliaries, support staff, and who knows what—all were along for the ride, all tooled up and eager for the fight.

The only ones staying behind were doing so on strictest orders. A few tried to come along anyway, only to be discovered and sent back at the last moment. Little hiccups like that were an annoyance to those who appreciated a smooth-run operation, but Mercer was secretly proud of the attempted stowaways. No faint hearts in Sector House 212.

Control remained open for business with a skeleton staff, monitoring all the action. Most of Tek division was left behind, busy on whatever new doomsday weapons Allen could dream up. Raskova stayed, because someone had to mind the store. No one suggested she was too old for combat. She *might* have been too old, but she heard every word everyone said, and she had a gun.

Jimenez had barely stepped outside the Sector House in a year, but if his people were hitting the streets, then damn straight he was hitting the streets with them. The way he saw it, it was the sector chief's job to make decisions. Everything else was down to Jimenez. *Somebody* had to take care of things.

As they roared out across Rubinski Plaza, Mercer turned to look at the blast mark on the front of his Sector House. *Mess up my building, huh? Well, let's see what Belinda Carlisle looks like when we've finished.*

TWENTY-NINE

Bobo Hendershot commanded Belinda Carlisle's Citizens Defence Unit, and by Grud, it was a job he was proud of. Every Sunday morning, rain or shine—or well, y'know, shine mostly, because of the indoor environmental settings and all—he had his squads out training in the block park, conducting manoeuvres in the mid-level parking lots, running tactical exercises in the east mall, attending lectures in the drill hall: whatever it took to keep their edge sharp.

He had First Company. His wife Maxine had Second. She had beaten the pants off him on their last field day, and he was still sore about that. Not with Maxine. A little competition was healthy in a marriage, even if she did like to gloat. No, he was angry at the poor performance of his command, and he'd been having them make up for that in the weekends since.

The squads worked weekends because Carlisle had an employment rate of fifty-five percent. Something more to be proud of. Granted, not everyone in the Citi-Def had a job, and not everyone who did had their weekends off, but that wasn't the point. The point was showing the other blocks that Belinda Carlisle was a high-class place of residence.

It was a new construction, built on the most monumental scale, with everything that ninety thousand citizens could ever need. Best of everything. Why, they even had their own water treatment plant, or at least they had one until these block wars started and some envious neighbours had crashed a hover van filled with explosives into it.

Belinda Carlisle was always going to have trouble with the other blocks—the slummier blocks—in the sector. Places like Andrews or Alcott couldn't take pride in themselves, so they tried to bring Carlisle down to their level. Sure, this attempt to lower property values in Belinda Carlisle had turned militant lately, but it was all part of the same picture. That's what Citi-Def was for: dealing with bad neighbours.

OK, granted, Citi-Def was for providing a last line of defence against external threats to the city, but unless the Sovs were planning to invade soon, then the unit was there to showcase block pride. Our guys are better than your guys. Our tac gear is more expensive than yours. Want to do something about that, loser? No? Didn't think so. Keep on walking, Louisa May.

No: they see Belinda Carlisle stencilled on your body armour, and they know they're not dealing with amateurs.

Bobo had been in his element since this Block Mania thing had kicked off. The Citizens Defence (Emergency

Powers) Act of 2070 meant that he was pretty much in charge now, and he made damn sure that the block committee knew all about it. He put his war plan into operation, locked down the whole block, and set up and maintained a defensive posture that was straight out of the book. Lowlives all over the sector were bringing anarchy to the streets, but Belinda Carlisle had little worse to show for it than a few broken windows.

And that was all thanks to Bobo.

OK, and Maxine too, but mainly Bobo.

Tensions were running high in the block, but that was only to be expected. At first, most of the Carlisle blockers had been content to sit tight and wait for things to quieten down outside, but after a day or so of this, people were getting antsy. There were complaints about not being allowed outside. Belinda Carlisle had everything a citizen might need right under one roof, and most residents were so content with this arrangement that they never left the block—ever—but that wasn't the point. The rioting neighbours did not tell Belinda Carlisle blockers to stay home. No sir. And what about getting some payback for that water treatment plant and those broken windows?

Bobo was getting deputations from citizens who wanted to go out and give someone a piece of their mind—preferably with a blunt instrument or a modified cooking appliance—and his own guys were backing up those voices. They were tired of being hunkered down behind barricades of outdoor furniture.

Bobo was coming around to their way of thinking.

After all, the best defence was offence, and he was tired of drinking the same mains water as everyone else. He missed turning on the tap and knowing that the water coming out, even if it tasted the same, and had been recycled up to thirty-eight times, was the good home-grown stuff from his own Belinda Carlisle treatment plant.

So here he was now, holding a council of war with his squad leaders. The block committee was hosting its own big meeting down in Carlisle Hall, but the committee would do what he told them. Right now, it was Citi-Def business, and right now, the Citi-Def needed direction, needed a plan, needed leadership.

"Any suggestions?" he asked.

Beef Wilmington, his lieutenant, spoke up.

"Bobo, I think—"

"That's *Captain* Hendershot, Beef. We're on active service now. Respect the rank."

"Captain, I think—"

"Here's what *I* think," said Bobo. "I think what we need here is a little block war."

"But, Cap, that's what everyone's been saying—"

"A block war. Yes, sir. And you know why? Because Belinda Carlisle is worth fighting for. Because Belinda Carlisle *means* something. Because I didn't take on this job just so some low-rent habs across the way could disrespect us. I'm a peace-loving man, but I say we've stood aside long enough."

"Yeah. *Yeah*! We're with you, Cap, but what do you want us to—"

"We've trained hard for this day. We have sweated *blood*.

Now we're gonna make them pay for that! In *blood*! Because we are Belinda Carlisle!"

"OK, Cap, but—"

"When I look at you, I know that you feel like I do. And I know you've got what it takes."

"Sure we do, but—"

Maxine had heard Bobo's pep talks plenty of times before. She sat over by the window and tried not to let everyone see her yawn—not that she tried too hard. She checked her ammo. She checked her nails. Bobo fulminated on. She looked out the window.

"Bobo, honey, you might want to look at this."

"I'm kind of busy here, sweetheart."

"Really. You want to look at this."

"Grud*dammit*, Maxine! Look at *what?*"

"We got Judges, honey."

"So there's a couple of Judges. Big deal. The guys down on the main entrance can talk to them."

"Not a couple, Bobo. *Lotta* Judges. And I don't think they're here to talk."

Bobo stood dumbfounded for a long moment. Beef nudged him. "What do we do, Cap?"

Bobo's mouth opened and closed a couple of times, but nothing more articulate that 'um' came out. Maxine popped her gum and made a suggestion.

"Have the guys on the main entrance offer minimal resistance. They're just a tripwire. We fall back to the eastern mall. It's not ideal defensive ground, but there are good fields of fire and everyone's familiar with it from exercises. Change comm frequencies every six minutes and let area denial weapons do the work before we start any shooting. Sound good to you, honey?"

"Uh... yeah. Yeah sure. Beef, you tell the guys on the main entrance to... y'know."

"On it, Cap."

THIRTY

MERCER'S FORCE HAD been ambushed on the way to Carlisle. Well, perhaps ambush was putting it too strongly. Some random fire came their way from A. A. Milne, and Judge Warner's team peeled off to deal with it. Some more Judges were detached in a flanking action, which opened up a whole world of possibilities, and led to Mercer authorizing Warner to embark on a small war of conquest in the southern part of the sector. Another force broke away a little further up the road for much the same reasons. Domination of the whole sector was, after all, the mission here, but that didn't mean that anything was going to keep Mercer from dealing with Carlisle personally.

So not all of Sector 212's Judges showed up outside Belinda Carlisle, but it was indeed, as Maxine Hendershot had noted, a *lot* of Judges.

ROBINSON RODE WITH Steinman, and the two of them rode with Jimenez, who stayed close to Mercer. They rode up to the front doors in line abreast, lights flashing and weapons hot. For all its colossal size, Belinda Carlisle hadn't been assigned a block Judge, which was something for which Robinson was deeply grateful. Instead, they were met by a self-important type in designer body armour, proudly holding his top-of-the-range Finkelstein 98 rifle like he'd invented it.

"State your business, Judge," he said, with all the assurance of a man who's too stupid to reckon the odds.

"My business is justice," said Mercer, and shot him.

ROBINSON HAD SEEN some stuff these past couple of days, but she'd never imagined that she'd ever see a senior Judge just roll up and execute a citizen in cold blood. She was still trying to take it on board, and wondering how to go about arresting her own chief in the middle of all this when she saw the victim twitch. Then he did more than twitch. He groaned and sat up, looking hurt in more ways than one. That expensive armour had been worth what he'd paid for it.

"Aw, *Judge!*" he said, looking at the dent in his vest, but Mercer was no longer there to hear the complaint.

Robinson caught up with him as he was assessing the barricade that barred their way. Mercer's instant removal of the Citi-Def squad leader had done wonders to weaken the resolve of Belinda Carlisle's first line of defence. The barricade appeared to be unmanned.

A little shock and awe in the right place, thought Robinson. What had seemed like summary murder had just been judicial theatre.

"You really had me going for a second there, Chief," she said.

"Don't sweat it, Robinson. I'll remember to switch to armour-piercing next time. Been too long behind a desk."

While she wondered if he was joking, he was giving orders for units to deploy to every one of the block's entrances. Then he led the way through the barricade.

They blasted aside the obstacle with bike cannon. They could have ridden right through the barricade, but then they'd have tripped the booby traps with which it had been sown. Beyond the barricade a broad shiny corridor, framed with lush artificial greenery, led them towards the block's eastern mall. They saw a few citi-defs scurrying ahead of them, seeking safety, making no show of resistance. Mercer was thinking that this was all going to be too easy when he ran over a mine.

It was a nice mine, advertised as a must for indoor warfare enthusiasts, and very well reviewed. Essentially, it was a flat square sheet of plastic explosive containing the smallest of pressure switches. It looked just like a floor tile. Belinda Carlisle Citi-Def had forked out for two dozen of them (fifteen percent off, and free shipping) on spec. Mercer's bike was tough enough to withstand the blast, but he lost control of the steering for a second and ploughed right into a piece of civic sculpture. When he angrily picked himself up, he felt a painful twinge in his knee—the one that he'd been born with, and not the new one.

Too long behind a desk, too old, and now fit to be tied.

Belinda Carlisle had it coming all right. If any blocker had appeared on the scene at that minute, they'd have got what the guy at the door got, only this time it wouldn't be a standard-execution round to the central body mass but a hi-ex in the face.

He'd collected himself somewhat by the time they roared into the mall, but he was still plenty mad.

He switched on his bike's bullhorn and announced himself to the block at large. Robinson suspected that, given his temper, the bullhorn was maybe unnecessary.

"Belinda Carlisle! This is the law! You are under arrest! Come out with your hands where I can see them! And I mean *now!*"

There followed a moment of silence as the Judges prepared to receive the surrenders of ninety thousand or so residents, and then the shooting started.

THIRTY-ONE

BELINDA CARLISLE, BEING new and pretty well-off, could boast one of the larger and better-armed Citi-Def units. They were fighting from prepared positions on their home ground, but they were only citi-defs and they were up against Judges. They scored a few early lucky hits, but even then it takes a lot to put a good Judge down, and a few bullet wounds were not about to make the stern men and women of Sector House 212 leave quietly. They'd come here to win.

Concentrated fire suppressed and eliminated strongpoints. Lawmasters raced up ramps and pedways. Stumm grenades and heat-seeking rounds sought out defenders in hiding. Belinda Carlisle didn't stand much of a chance.

The only real value of the stand made in the mall was that it served to split up the attackers. If one Judge is worth ten or twenty cits, then there's not much sense in keeping your Judges all bunched together—not in a block this size. So, as the defenders scattered, so did their pursuers, and in a few minutes, the mall was like an ants' nest that had been kicked over. There was no way that Mercer could coordinate such a fight, but that was OK by him. His people knew what they were doing. And besides, it gave him the chance to do some personal, in-your-face law enforcement for what felt like the first time since he'd been promoted. Jimenez stayed with him, and Robinson and Steinman as well, and it was just the four of them when they branched off from East Avenue in search of more Belinda Carlisles to discipline.

It was when they rounded a corner, riding down a few fugitives and feeling mighty positive about how their bid for sector-wide domination was going, that they ran into something a little bigger than a Citi-Def squad.

The Belinda Carlisle block committee had called a public meeting earlier, and the sole item on the agenda was block war. It had been a loud, angry and unfocused assembly. Everyone had been in favour of war *on principle*. Everyone wanted to get out there and fight it out with a rival block. The problem arose over *which* block. Belinda Carlisle was so big that Carlislers living on the north face of the complex, and hating every other block they saw, couldn't convince their southside neighbours that Daryl Hall Block was the true enemy. Nor could they really get behind the southerners' conviction that John Oates Block needed to be taught a lesson. Why should they? Many of them had never had to look at John Oates, and in some cases had never even heard of the place. And why should they listen to these southsiders anyway? What, thought they were Grud's

Gift just because they got a little more sunshine in their pads?

Voices had been raised. Fistfights had broken out. The committee's attempts to restore order had been hampered by committee members taking sides. The situation had been saved only by Citi-Def sounding the general alert.

Temporarily united, the eight thousand-strong audience of Belinda Carlisle Hall surged out, guided by the sound of gunfire. What greeted them was the sight of four growling Lawmasters. But Belinda Carlisle was not daunted.

The Judges rolled to a stop. Lesser people might have felt at that moment that they'd perhaps bitten off more than they could chew, but these people were Judges, and they were led by Mercer, who had a righteous head of steam built up.

He looked at the sea of angry faces who had just been given a focus for their dissatisfaction. He looked at the three Judges accompanying him.

"Subdue those citizens," he said.

THIRTY-TWO

IT WAS A tall order, but there was no hesitation. The Judges rammed their bikes forward, battering the crowd aside, methodically flailing their way through. The Carlislers were hampered by their own numbers, by their lack of planning and lack of armament. They did their best to make up for it through anger and brute stupidity, but they were up against Judges.

The Judges mostly held their fire. They certainly didn't cut loose with bike cannon. Who knew when you'd really need the serious fire-power? Nevertheless, even with fist and boot, with riot stick and a Lawmaster's momentum, they more than held their own. But it was tiring work, and it didn't look like the block maniacs were learning from their experience and running for the exits. Eventually then, Mercer broke off the contest, however reluctantly. He ordered respirators down and pitched his last couple of stumm grenades into the throng. It was only a temporary solution. Against a mob this size, all the gas could do was make some space, but a little space was all Mercer wanted for the moment. The Judges powered on through the crowd and out of the hall, heading for the up-ramps.

Eliminate the Citi-Def units. Dominate the block from the top down. Then you could go and stamp on the little people. For the time being, look at the mass brawl they were fleeing not as a withdrawal in the face of superior numbers, but as a successful team-building exercise that could be returned to as and when.

And the team was looking good. A few minor injuries here and there, but no one was flagging. He considered Steinman and Robinson. Say what you like about the young breed—and between them these two had killed four Judges, and that was just today—but they had energy and staying power. Given their enthusiasm, it was possible to overlook a little Judge-killing.

"Say, Robinson," said Mercer. "Is it true that you once busted a daystick over some perp's head?"

She grinned almost bashfully. "Aw, Chief—that's just the guys talking. It was just a chair leg. You know you can't break a daystick."

"Want to test that proposition?"

She rolled her neck and flexed her shoulders to work out the kinks. "Lead on, Chief," she said.

They had found a centre of resistance outside the local outlet of Kittens'n'Unicorns'n'Rainbows'n'Stuff Megastore when a message flashed up on the bike's computer. Robinson was the only one mounted up at the time and she barely had a moment to register the communication before a burst of fire sent her diving for cover.

She identified the shooter, took him down, and alerted Mercer to what she had read.

"Chief! Message from Justice Central, by way of Tek Division!"

"What do they want?" he shouted back.

"It says: *Don't drink the water*."

THIRTY-THREE

Back in the Academy, the boys had whaled the tar out of each other to establish some sort of pecking order, and the girls had beaten up the boys just to prove that they could. The tutors indulged this practice in the name of physical conditioning, and also because the rough and tumble was considered an appropriate method of sublimating the more intimate physical urges that youth is prone to.

Allen found herself remembering those days. Here she was, running her department, supervising the high-speed fine-tuning of her chemical weapons innovation, and she could still daydream. The picture running through her mind, even as she did her job at her usual peak efficiency, was of herself and Mercer grappling—going at it hard and rough. He was the alpha male in Sector House 212, but the head of Tek Division was out to prove herself the dominant female.

She shook her head free of the foolish image when a communications alert bleeped at her. It was an All Points from Justice Central. They came in all the time, but this was special. She didn't need to replay the message—she was trained to assimilate information instantly—but she did take time to cast a careful eye over the dump of technical data that came with it.

She was just on the point of contacting Barksdale in Med when he contacted her. For the moment, at least, this was too big for inter-departmental rivalries.

"It's the water," said Barksdale, his voice leaden with disbelief.

"Yup," affirmed Allen. The implications of the news were shattering, but right now Allen was just pleased to be right.

"You reading this? This viro-chemical stuff? '*Extremely potent, undetectable in greater dilution*'? Is this for real?"

It was real. Suspicions awakened by a Justice Central task force had been confirmed when an intruder had been discovered at an Atlantic Purification Plant. And it wasn't like they'd run into some hobo taking a leak in the tank. This was a professional on a mission. Six Judges were dead and the intruder was still at large.

"He was pouring some gunk in the water. Said gunk has been isolated and analysed. Water supply has been shut down. No counter-agent to the gunk has yet been suggested."

"That's what it says," said Allen, realising that she was grinning and not really caring.

"I don't buy it. It doesn't make sense. Contaminated water is behind all this madness? Sure, it might explain the citizens and a few rogue Judges, but why only a few?

Why aren't we all affected?"

"Says it right there, Barksdale. Judges on patrol tend to subsist on the bottled stuff. And you know how it is these days: just back-to-back patrolling."

"OK, but what about support personnel? What about Sector House staff? What about *us*, Allen?"

"What can I say, Barksdale? Innate character? Self-discipline? Fifteen years of being trained to be tougher than the other guy? Take your pick. I can only speak for myself, mind. *I* feel fine. *You*, on the other hand, seem kind of worked up. Temper bothering you much?"

"Don't kid with me, Allen. The question is, what are we going to do about this? The word from Central is that an antidote could take weeks. *Weeks!*"

"Sounds like a medical problem, Doc. I leave it in your capable hands. My people have work to do here. Belinda Carlisle Block isn't going to gas itself."

BELINDA CARLISLE BLOCK certainly wasn't going to gas itself, and the way things were going here in Tek Division, it didn't look like anyone else would be doing the gassing either unless people got down and did some gruddamn work.

"People, we can do this better," Allen told her team. "I want the potency of the gas increased without—you hear me?—*without* reducing its dispersal capacity. We only have so much stumm, and it's a big sector out there."

"On it, boss. One question, though."

"Go ahead."

"They're planning on saturating Belinda Carlisle with this stuff, yeah?"

"Correct."

"All those juvies and eldsters—those non-combatants in the block with nowhere to run—and you want us to up the lethality of this stuff?"

"Problem?"

"No problem. Just asking."

THIRTY-FOUR

BEEF WILMINGTON HAD survived this far by keeping to the rear and moving out of trouble fast. As he saw another couple of Judges working around the flank of where he'd positioned his squad, he thought this would be a good time to check in on headquarters. In person.

He took an express elevator up to Citi-Def command post but was panting and sweating all the same when he reported to the Hendershots.

"So what do we do now, Cap? Judges have got us all beat to hell."

"I admit we've had a few setbacks, but we can still turn this thing around," said Bobo, not quite radiating the necessary confidence.

"Yeah, but how?"

"Just give me a second, OK?"

Maxine was checking herself in the mirror. "Fight in small groups," she said. "Short contacts. Keep the Judges dispersed. We draw them upstairs to the upper levels where the hallways are narrower. Their bikes can't handle most of the stairways and elevators above Level 58. Belinda's a big block. We can trade space for time. We keep withdrawing while we consolidate a strong defensive position up at the top levels."

She was thinking her blue tac gear would have been a better choice for today. Green just wasn't her colour.

Bobo scratched the back of his neck. "Yeah, I guess we could do something like that. Tell the guys, Beef."

"JIMENEZ, WITH ME," said Mercer. "'We'll clear the stairs. Robinson, Steinman—secure this hallway. We'll rendezvous one floor up.'"

The two Judge-killers, one under review and the other under arrest, looked at each other as their superiors moved off towards the stairwell.

"Do I sense a new trust in this relationship?" asked Steinman. "This is the first time Jimenez or the Chief have let us out of their sight."

"Yeah," said Robinson. "It's a positive sign. Either that, or they've got a bad feeling about this level and they consider us expendable."

They moved on carefully, checking all the angles, and keeping a particularly careful eye out for funny-looking floor tiles.

Fighting around corners: that's what it's all about, reflected Robinson. That's how you stay in the game. Respirators down and roll that stumm grenade— except they were all out of stumm now. But that's what ricochets are for. Check the corner, duck back if you're taking fire, and then start bouncing bullets off the walls. The department-issue ricochet round was far from infallible. For a start, being designed to bounce, it wasn't much good on hardened targets, like militia in body armour. But it could provide a useful distraction. So, loose a couple of ricochets, step round the corner, and make with the armour-piercing. Then secure the area, move to the next corner, and repeat. Robinson had found her rhythm. Problem was, she had just run out of ricochets too, and so had Steinman, and there were two Belinda Carlisles waiting at the next turn.

"Heat-seekers?" suggested Steinman.

"Maybe save them for later," said Robinson. "Let me try something."

Back in the Academy they'd played a lot of aeroball. It was fast and violent and involved both individual initiative and teamwork, not to mention razor-sharp three-dimensional spatial awareness. The cadets had played even when they didn't have jetpacks, or even protective gear. Robinson, small and solid, hadn't been as fast as her fellows, but they'd all admired her gutsy attitude. "Be the ball, Robinson," they'd joke, and she would be the ball, bouncing off other players, driving herself through obstacles, aiming herself at the goal.

So now she conjured up that joy of youth, took a run against the corridor's opposite wall, rebounded, and cannonballed in on her targets before they could target her. She fired twice, rolled, recovered, and assessed the damage. Two shots, two hits. Steinman was right behind her, aiming past her, covering the end of the hallway.

"Nice work," he said.

She gave him the brightest of smiles. "Let's go do that again," she said.

It was a ricochet kind of day, and the most fun a girl could have.

When a hallway was cleared of obvious resistance, Steinman made a public announcement.

"Be advised! This block is now locked down and under Justice Department control! Any citizens stepping outside of their apartments will feel the full force of the law! That means that if I hear the words 'Belinda' or 'Carlisle' from anyone, I will not hesitate to shoot them in the drokking face! Understood?"

It seemed to have the desired effect. Robinson tried it a couple of times, but while she could give it the necessary volume and authority, Steinman really sounded like he meant it.

"You trust those two, Chief?"

Mercer thought about it. Once, and once only in his thirty-plus-year career, had he personally seen a Judge guilty of a serious crime. The Special Judicial Squad had been all over it. It wasn't just the suspect they hauled in and grilled. Every Judge that had ever partnered—ever *worked* with the suspect—had got the full attention of the creepy investigators with the skull insignia, just to see how deep the rot might have gone. The suspected Judge had been found guilty of the murder of a citizen: just an illicit love affair gone bad. Seeing as how crimes of passion tended not to be contagious, the rest of the unit had been released by the SJS with no more than a stern warning. The murderer had gone, as expected, to Titan, and had lived through no more than six years of a twenty-year sentence.

Unlawfully kill a citizen and you die on an off-world penal colony. Those were the rules. And now Steinman and Robinson had killed four Judges between them—and so? What rules applied now?

Mercer briefly considered it. Whatever sins the two Judges might have committed, they were here now, following him and doing Sector House 212 proud. In Mercer's book, that made them good Judges.

"Sure I trust them," he said.

THIRTY-FIVE

THE BLOCK NARROWED as it rose, which only made sense. The higher you went, the more exclusive the neighbourhood got. Down on the lower levels, the masses could go and play in the block park, but up on the summit of Belinda Carlisle, the better-off few could disport themselves under the elegant sky dome: a spacious brightly-lit area with cafés and boutiques among the palms.

As the Judges pushed their way steadily upwards, the scattered units started linking up with each other again.

Two levels below the sky dome, and Mercer had quite a decent force at his disposal once more. But the upwards advance had also pushed the Citi-Def units into a concentration. There weren't many left, but the ones who were left were the veterans of the hard fighting on the floors below. Battered they may have been, but they were the best, and they were determined. Bobo Hendershot could not have been prouder.

The top two levels of the block had been fortified. This was where they'd make their stand.

It was a sad reflection on block solidarity when the commitment of so many residents to the block war was limited to sitting at home and watching it on the vid.

Still, reflected Bobo, it had always been the fate of the few to sacrifice themselves for the many. That's what being a hero was all about. Let the Judges come. Let the neighbours sit on their couches. The Battling Bastards of Belinda Carlisle were in this fight until the end.

With the Judges only a few floors below, Bobo switched on the public address system, and prepared to deliver his death-or-glory speech. He drew a deep breath, not knowing what he was going to say, but sure that the words would come. There'd be something about pride, and Belinda Carlisle, and taking as many of them with you as you could, and saving the last bullet for yourself, and more pride. But Maxine took the microphone from his hand and took over.

MAXINE HENDERSHOT WASN'T crazy about the idea of last stands. Sure, she had no intention of running up the white flag—not to the Judges, not to anybody. When you put on the Belinda Carlisle branded gear, it was Belinda Carlisle to the death. But maybe there was a way out of this. That was why, when the boys were doing all that fighting on the lower levels, Maxine had been at work up on top. She'd got the idea from *Better Homes and Booby-Traps*, and now she'd put it to Smitty Jones, who'd agreed to help. Smitty had a crush on Maxine and a degree in engineering. With a flirtatious smile from her, and a box full of detonators and electrical wiring, there wasn't a whole lot Smitty wouldn't do. By the time the war-torn remnants of the Citi-Def squads staggered in, the spacious brightly-lit area at the top of the block—a private amenity for the better-off residents—wasn't just fortified, it was all wired up.

Now Maxine explained it to the Judges over the PA, omitting none of the technical refinements with which the place was set.

"So what I'm saying, Judges, is that you don't wanna give us any more trouble. This is a nice block. You wanna go and invade the more downmarket places, you know? Try Oates across the way. If not, we're gonna hafta—I don't know—blow this place up and take you all with us?

"No, Bobo, I'm not finished. Sorry about that, Judges. So yeah… and if you try getting cute on the floor below us or something? Well, we've got gizmos that'll fry any automated units you might send in and tremblers that'll set the charges off if anything comes within twenty metres. Smitty here is real proud of that—aren't you, Smitty baby? OK? I think that's everything."

MERCER HADN'T COME this far to be foiled by the likes of Maxine Hendershot, but he'd just fought his way up a hundred and thirty-eight floors without encountering anyone with brains, so a pause for thought was necessary.

"All right. So we go in from below and it's booby-trap city. Blast our way through a barricade and the roof falls on top of us. And if we somehow happen to survive that, we've still got the next barricade to deal with. That means we go in from above. Full-bore aerial assault. I want teams ready to embark on H-Wagons as soon as they arrive."

But it looked like whistling up a squadron of Justice Department's all-purpose hover aircraft was not something that could be so easily done today. Control was making excuses.

"Sorry, Chief. Word from Justice Central. Chief Judge Griffin himself. Full alert. All aerial units have been withdrawn from sector policing."

"What the hell for?" asked Mercer.

"Unsure, but it's something big. Something to do with the rain falling all over the eastern sectors or something?"

"The *rain*? Are you kidding me?"

"Contaminated rain, Chief. They're saying somebody got at Weather Control."

"And what in the name of the Little Baby Jovus are my H-Wagons supposed to do about a rain shower on the other side of the city?"

"Don't ask me, Chief. There's a bigger picture. Word is that something bad is on the way."

"Worse than Belinda Carlisle Citi-Def defying me? Get me those drokking wagons!"

"Sorry, Chief. No can do. Control out."

THIRTY-SIX

THE OTHER JUDGES were checking the Department feed, monitoring the situation as Mercer was speaking. It transpired that the agent who had breached the Atlantic water treatment plant was still at large, and that wasn't all. After they'd shut down the water, he'd somehow managed to attack Weather Control. Whatever viro-chemical he'd put in the water supply had been used to seed clouds, and before he'd sabotaged the machinery he'd programmed it for a colossal rainstorm. Not drinking the water was no longer enough to save the city from the madness. It was coming from the sky now.

"It says here they want him alive," said Robinson. "It says that he must have some sort of antidote in his blood."

"Not our problem," said Jimenez. "Focus on the job at hand. The Chief is right. Some saboteur bent on city-wide chaos is Central's business. Belinda Carlisle is our priority."

"Right," said Mercer. "Ideas anyone?"

"I dunno, Chief, but it reminds me of this one time I was working Apetown."

"Gruddammit, Jimenez! How come all your stories gotta start with Apetown? OK, what did you do in Apetown when you had a situation looked like this?"

"We called in the H-Wagons."

Mercer stared hard at Jimenez, but kept his temper.

"We're going to gas them," he said. "Where the hell is Allen?"

TEK JUDGE ALLEN could not believe what she was hearing.

"What do you mean it's not working?" she asked an underling.

"The compound is destabilising," he told her, holding up a readout to explain himself and, if necessary, fend her off. "It all holds together at higher temperatures, but it tends to separate as it cools."

"What the hell did you do wrong? What are you doing to my beautiful gas?"

"Please! I was doing just what you directed, boss! I decreased the cyclic acid by two-point-six like you said. It worked at ninety degrees. It failed at forty-five."

"So you're telling me that my gas won't work unless there's a *heatwave* outside?" She was practically screeching.

"I was just doing it like you told me!"

Allen slapped the readout out of his hand, and then slapped his face. Hard. Direct physical conflict-resolution wasn't really part of her job, but she'd been trained by the Academy of Law not to hit like a girl. The underling reeled backwards, shocked, which gave her a chance to pick up a chair and really go to work on him. When the technician had crawled out of reach, whimpering beneath a desk, she looked up at the rest of her team. Not one of them had tried to stop her. Good thing too. She might have lost it otherwise.

She took a deep breath and considered how things stood now that a whole batch of gas had been wasted, thanks to the loser under the desk. She could not disappoint Mercer.

MERCER'S PEOPLE WERE doing a good job mopping up resistance throughout Belinda Carlisle, but that wasn't enough for him. The sky dome was still holding out, and that was costing him time and casualties. It wasn't doing his mood much good either.

He'd ordered up the patrol wagons and whatever flying assets he could muster besides, but they didn't have the speed, manoeuvrability, or weapons capability of the H-Wagons, and they had to be withdrawn when it was revealed that Belinda Carlisle was boasting quite a sweet little anti-aircraft arsenal.

After that there wasn't much else for the Judges on the top floors to do except exchange desultory gunfire with the blockers and cuss out the Teks who were keeping everyone waiting. In between the shooting, Robinson was keeping abreast of things in the wider city.

"Well, here's some good news," she said. "Word from

Central is they've caught that guy. An antidote is being synthesised from his blood, even as we speak."

"Well whoop-de-do," said Steinman. "You think we can get all these cits to roll up a sleeve and line up nicely for their shots?"

"I'll give 'em shots," said Mercer.

THIRTY-SEVEN

HALF THE SCREENS in the Sector House were flashing red now. Alert after alert. Allen didn't care. Her wonderful poison gas had been spoiled by the clumsy peons who called themselves Tek Judges. She had let Mercer down, and with every radio message he was reminding her of that. While her people belatedly concocted a new batch of gas—which to her was old, and something for which she had no more enthusiasm—she disconsolately scanned the alert messages.

So they'd caught the guy who'd been poisoning the water, and they'd extracted an antidote from his blood. OK, that was pretty good, I guess.

Out of habit she read the data. The counter-agent wasn't something you'd have found without weeks of hard science, but once you saw it, you could see how straightforward it was. In fact, Tek Central hadn't just isolated it in no time flat, they were already synthesising it and supplying key personnel.

And that got Allen thinking.

Surly, illogical, violent.

Those had been the words on the first findings from Central—the report that had identified the distortions in the brain.

Mercer was fighting citizens who would not quit. He was fighting force with force. What if there were a different approach? What if she could hand him victory, not by killing the citizens, but by making them placid, reasonable, and non-violent? Not the poison gas that he'd seen already, but a new trick to impress him.

She started to feel good again.

"You and you," she said, pointing. "Start synthesising this antidote stuff in bulk. The rest of you, find a way of marrying it to the stumm delivery system. Get it done *now.*"

It hadn't escaped her notice, but it somehow just didn't matter to her, that the poisoner behind all of this had been revealed under interrogation to be none other than a Judge of East Meg One. So Block Mania was a Sov plot? So what had that got to do with Sector House 212?

As it happened, Allen had to seek Barksdale's help with the antidote, but that was all right because it turned out he needed her and her facilities for the same reasons. And so Med and Tek Judges, working together, got the job done in the end.

Rivalries put aside, they loaded everything aboard a couple of ambulances and set off to bombard Belinda Carlisle and show Chief Mercer how those good folks back at the Sector House were just as much a part of the team as those who were dispensing justice on the streets.

THIRTY-EIGHT

THE ALERTS FROM Justice Central had grown tiresome. Mercer had to shut off his communications in the end. How did they expect him to get the job done with all that noise?

And how the hell could he get the job done if Tek Division was going to keep him waiting like this?

He had pulled his people back from the Alamo that had been created at the top of Belinda Carlisle Block. It allowed him to get some perspective on the situation, not to mention it always being a smart move to retire a safe distance from any group of deranged citizens who had access to unwise quantities of explosives.

His command post now was on a high-level open-air parking lot which gave him a clear view of the Belinda Carlisle sky dome but was not covered by Carlisle's flak emplacements. He was there, pacing up and down, when Allen finally arrived with his poison gas—except it wasn't poison gas.

"This is it, Allen? This is what you're bringing me?"

"You don't like it, Chief? But I made it for you specially."

"No, Allen, I don't like it. When I've got a block full of murderous maniacs defying me, and when my head technical officer promises me a way of killing them, and when said technical officer shows up late with something that does not, as it happens, kill maniacs, but instead allegedly soothes them or something, then no: I have to admit that I am not overjoyed."

"But think of it, Chief. A placid citizen is a beaten citizen. And you want them beaten, don't you? You want them to know who's boss. They need to be alive for that, right?"

Mercer had to admit that this was so, and once he'd admitted it, he came to like the idea.

"OK, we'll do it your way. Set it up."

She gave the necessary orders, but instead of seeing to the details personally, she stayed by Mercer's side. He was trained to notice things. He noticed that she was standing unnecessarily close, like she wanted something. Just to break the odd mood, he spoke.

"So you were right, Allen. It really was something in the water. So how come we all weren't affected?"

"Hard to say, Chief, but it's clear that some were. Now we know the precise cause we can test for it."

"Here's a simpler test, Allen. If you're going nuts and screaming about your block, then you've got it. Otherwise you're fine. My people are fine."

"That's all well and good, Chief, but all the data indicates that a significant proportion of our personnel might be under the influence of some chemically-induced herd instinct."

Mercer stopped her right there. "A herd, Allen? Look around. You see a herd? This is a *pack*!" And he laughed.

He saw Robinson hurrying over. She was looking excited, and not in a good way. Just another emergency to deal with.

"Chief, you'd better tune in. I mean it."

"OK, OK. Meanwhile you can give Allen here a blood sample. Keep her happy."

Robinson reluctantly tugged off a glove and submitted her finger to a hand-held device that Allen had produced, all the while looking at Mercer, willing him to pay attention to the signal that had just started broadcasting across the Justice Department net.

"Robinson's negative, Chief."

"See? I told you. We're fine."

But Robinson was far from fine. "Chief! Are you reading the alert? It says to prepare for imminent nuclear attack! From East Meg One!"

"The Sovs. It figures. It's been that kind of a day."

"So what do we do, Chief? Nuclear alert protocols say—"

"One war at a time, Robinson."

The air raid sirens were wailing as the Teks prepared to launch their pacifying gas. Far above, at the edge of space, the city's laser defence grid lit up. The first missiles were being tracked. As far as Mercer was concerned they'd have to wait. One war at a time.

Mercer looked at his people, all pulling together, eager

to get this fight finished. Good Judges all.

And so what if some of them might have got a touch of this water-borne contaminant? It didn't seem to be doing them any harm. And—who knows?—a little heightened aggression might be just what they needed right now.

A Tek's voice sounded on his radio. "Ready when you are, Chief."

Time to knock the fight out of Belinda Carlisle and however much of the sector lay downwind. Just let them breathe in and the madness would end.

"On my mark," he said.

And then, "Respirators down."

Once they'd dealt with Belinda Carlisle, they'd have to go and fight the Sovs. If they wanted to prove that Sector House 212 was still the baddest block in the city, then they'd need to keep their edge.

This is Sector 212, thought Mercer. *Anyone want it? Then come and take it.*

THE WORLD WILL END TODAY

2

This one is dedicated to the memory of Judge Souster.

The 22nd Century
For many long years, an uneasy peace has existed
between Mega-City One and its Sov-Block rival,
East-Meg One.

Now that peace is about to be shattered.
For many millions, the world will end today.
They are the first victims of the Apocalypse War.

—The Official Version

ONE

"WE'RE THE BATTLING bastards of Belinda Carlisle, got no mamas, no papas, no sense of style..."

The defiant song rang out over the block public address system, but it could barely be heard over the sirens' insistent wailing.

The Judges' assault on the Citi-Def stronghold would begin as soon as the chief gave the word.

"So I say you and me go right in the front," said Steinman to Robinson. "I take the lead, you cover me. The other units can take the side entrances. It should be pretty straightforward—perps should be disoriented."

"Yeah, sure," said Robinson, too absorbed in what was appearing on her bike's computer. "Whatever."

"Whatever? How about a little focus here, Robinson?"

She looked up from the ever-growing scroll of alarming news. "Focus, Steinman? Haven't you been paying attention to this stuff? Don't you even know what's going on?"

Steinman shrugged. "It's like the chief says: one thing at a time. What are we expected to do about all the other stuff?"

All the other stuff, Robinson thought. Would that be mass psychosis, war in the streets, a foreign conspiracy to destroy the city? That stuff.

It had been a busy couple of days for Judge LaShondra Robinson. It had started with a block war, which was just one of those things that a Judge working the streets of Sector 212 should expect from time to time. But that block war had been followed almost immediately by another block war, only this one came with added block war on top. This, as it turned out, was no one-off, buy-one-get-one-free kind of deal. Suddenly, the Judges were having to deal with multiple, multi-block, block wars bursting out all across the northern sectors.

Literally overnight, criminality in Sector 212 had gone from its normal level of "Let's see what we can get away with" to "Let's wage all-out war on the neighbours with every means at our disposal."

Even before the madness spread to the southern and western sectors, it had acquired a name—Block Mania.

For Robinson and her fellow Judges, it had meant non-stop intensive policing by extreme means. Standard riot response had evolved swiftly into full-bore military action. The gloves came off and the bodies started piling up in the streets. And why not? The whole city had gone crazy, and it wasn't like you could arrest and incarcerate the entire city.

So it had been a busy couple of days for Robinson.

She was young, she was highly trained, she was energetic, and she needed to be. Ceaseless exertion was the order of the day.

By way of respite from all this hyper-adrenalised combat, she had put in a short spell at a desk in Control, which had given her a useful perspective on the chaotic events. Also, to add to her variety of experience, and to allow her to get a load off her feet for a while, she'd had a little time in close confinement for the killing of a fellow officer.

She was technically still under review for that one, but it didn't look like she'd be facing any severe penalties. It turned out that whatever was driving the citizens crazy was also working on some Judges, and when a Judge goes violently crazy, it needs to be addressed in immediate and radical fashion. Soothing words won't usually cut it. And that's why Robinson had shot and killed a Judge and that's why, when similar circumstances had presented themselves later that same day, she'd done it again.

It turned out to have been something in the water. The intelligence feed from Justice Central was talking about a viro-chemical that screwed with people's brains, making their inner pack animal come out.

The madness manifested itself in different ways. For instance, while most of the maniacs were murderous nutcases exhibiting all the common sense usually associated with armed mobs, there were plenty of individuals who continued to conduct themselves with perfect rationality, albeit with the aim of exterminating their most hated rivals: the people in the block across the way.

There'd been that chemical engineer in Ricardo Montalban Block, for instance, who'd come up with a perfectly coherent plan for gassing half the city. There was video of her discussing the project like it was a research proposal. Perfectly reasonable and totally nuts at the same time.

And that capacity of some maniacs for calm decision-making was weighing heavy on Robinson's mind. If drinking the water made people crazy, and Judges drank water, and not every crazy person was an obvious kook, then it didn't take all her years of detective training to conclude that some of her colleagues were almost certainly affected by the Block Mania contaminant.

Her partner of the moment was a perfect example. Just like her, Judge Steinman was guilty of killing two Judges, the crucial difference being that in her case they'd both been maniacs bent on murder, while in his they'd been members of the Special Judicial Squad in routine pursuit of their duties. That these duties were at odds with Steinman's desire to go out and fight in the block wars for the greater glory of Sector House 212 was not, according to the book, sufficient reason to shoot them both dead.

This was, however, a time of grave crisis, and seeing as Steinman had admitted his guilt, turned himself in, and made it clear that he was unswerving in his loyalty to his own kind, his chief had allowed Steinman to retain his badge and gun for the time being.

And maybe Sector Chief Mercer's verdict would have been OK with Robinson if she hadn't formed the certainty that the chief had also been suffering the effects of the contaminated water.

She'd argued it out with herself; it was the business of Judges to commit acts of violence on the citizenry when the latter stepped out of line. Right now, with howling mobs rampaging through the streets, the Judges weren't going to cite the relevant statute before they opened fire, and they weren't taking prisoners. Citizens were ganging up on each other and Judges were ganging up on the citizens—each to their own—and all out for blood. So that meant that, at least as far as motivation was concerned, it was kind of hard to tell the difference between Judges and block maniacs.

Chief Mercer was under a lot of stress and Robinson hadn't actually witnessed him do anything illegal. There was no denying, however, that his attitude was a little off-kilter. Case in point: the assault he'd been leading on Belinda Carlisle Block had less to do with any threat that Carlisle might have been posing to the maintenance of law and order in the sector, and a whole lot to do with Carlisle's perceived refusal to acknowledge Mercer and his Judges as the rightful rulers of Sector 212 and everything in it.

Street Judges like Robinson were rarely standing still long enough to drink any water except from their portable supply. Sector house personnel like Mercer, on the other hand, tended to drink what came out of the tap.

So yeah—she had to conclude that her chief's brain might be all out of whack.

But that worry had been pushed quite a way back down the line as the bigger picture unfolded.

The perpetrator of this mass poisoning of the city's water supply had been apprehended at last and had revealed under interrogation that he was an agent of East-Meg One—the Sov city that was Mega-City One's greatest and longest-standing enemy. Looking at her screen and scanning all this quickly, Robinson briefly wondered just what interrogation techniques would be needed to crack a Sov-Block Judge when the clock was ticking.

Well, it turned out that this whole Block Mania thing was just the beginning—the opening phase of something called "Operation Apocalypse"—and given past relations with the Eastern block, it wasn't too hard to guess what that might entail.

Still guessing?

How about you listen to the air raid sirens.

TWO

AT SOME UNIMAGINABLE distance overhead, Robinson could make out a sporadic glittering in the sky. The city's laser defence grid had lit up. Up there, on the edge of space, the war had begun.

Say what you like about President Robert L. Booth, reflected Robinson, but he'd at least given us the laser defences way back when. As it had turned out, of course, the lasers hadn't been the sure-fire safeguard that the United States had been promised. The unfortunate proof of that was the fact that the United States didn't exist any more.

But Mega-City One survived and—this Block Mania thing aside—was in a better position than the old U S of A had ever been.

The city was a fortress.

The Atlantic Wall had been built largely as an environmental measure, but it also served as a platform for the eastern edge of the laser mesh.

And while you're giving due credit to unstable tyrants

like Bad Bob Booth, you have Judge Cal to thank for the West Wall, which had provided the whole city with a continuous perimeter, all along which were the long-range, fast-as-light weapons which were fed on the limitless geothermal energy from the city's power towers.

Turn on the system and you could vaporise pretty much anything that entered Mega-City airspace.

At least that was the plan, and while it was a lot better than it had been back when Booth had kicked off the Great Atomic War, it still wasn't absolutely fail-safe. And considering that a small miscalculation in your plan or an overestimation of your security could lead to everything between the Appalachians and the Sierra Nevada becoming known as the Cursed Earth, well—maybe it didn't do to put too much faith in the laser grid in this present situation.

And then there was the little matter of everyone having gone whacko with this Sov-made viro-chemical.

Robinson patched into the Defence Net's channel, and was dismayed to hear automated voices. Evidently, with so many personnel affected by Block Mania, they were using robots to bolster numbers. Still, better a robot with its finger on the button than a deranged Judge, right? At least the robots weren't going to get overawed by the challenge facing them, by the magnitude of the threat facing the city.

But the numbers the robots were reeling off did not sound good, and while the crosscurrent of human voices didn't suggest panic, it sure sounded like everyone had their hands full.

Because if you're the Sovs, how do you breach the laser

defence grid? You swamp it. You launch the missiles in their thousands. You hit every quadrant with more targets than they can vaporise.

She heard the word "splinter" a few times. That was not good. Splintering was when each big inter-continental vehicle broke up into fifty or a hundred smaller missiles.

Each smaller missile was capable of destroying a whole city sector. Each splinter gave an operations centre another fifty or a hundred targets to track; each one snowed up the screens that bit more, brought the system that much closer to overload, and brought the city closer to annihilation.

She heard the controllers frantically describing a situation snowballing beyond their capacity to deal with it.

"Nine thousand plus warheads. They're blotting out scanners. Range one-five-five and closing fast! Fire! Fire! Fire!"

She heard the pilot of an H-Wagon in the upper atmosphere, his weapons overheating.

"They're filling the sky," he said. "We can't stop a fraction of them. God help you, Mega-City One."

It was that "God help you" that decided her. Justice Department personnel tended not to go in for that old-timey religion—not even in moments of extreme distress.

There was no more time. She had to do something. She had to make the chief see sense.

From the stowage on the back of her bike, she pulled out a radiation cloak. Everyone had been carrying them as standard since last year and that whole Captain Skank incident. She laid hold of a medical kit while she was at it.

* * *

MERCER WAS TALKING about something to Judge Allen, the head of 212's Tek division, but Robinson just barged right on in.

"Chief. You have to listen to the news from Central. I mean it."

He didn't give her a chance. He'd had her in his face already about this supposed Sov attack, and he had more important things on his plate—like this block war he was on the brink of winning once and for all.

"Can it, Robinson," was all he said. "Get back there and take up position with Steinman. We move as soon as the gruddamn Teks sort out this latest gruddamn glitch."

Mercer was so sure of himself, and Robinson was so conditioned to obedience, that she nearly complied, but she was a Judge, and she judged this a moment to stand her ground.

She was on the small side, but she squared her shoulders, clenched her fists, and looked him straight in the eye.

"Nuclear attack, Chief," she said, in the tone normally reserved for ordering someone to step away from the vehicle, with their hands where she could see them.

"Imminent nuclear attack. Like right-now imminent. We have to take cover."

Cover was going to be a problem. They were standing in an open-air hover-port—an elevated parking lot just across from the upper levels of Belinda Carlisle—and they could hardly be more exposed.

So all Robinson had to do was convince a mentally unfit

superior officer to see things her way, and then withdraw to the bunker beneath the sector house, a hundred and something levels down from here and several kilometres away. Oh wait—they'd probably also have to set in train the complete evacuation of Sector 212's population to shelter. But first things first. The antidote to the Block Mania had been found only a few hours before, and the Teks had been synthesising it in bulk to allow them to pacify the unruly populace. (This wasn't for the good of the citizenry, mind: this was to allow the Judges to stomp all over them more easily.) There must be a handy syringe of the stuff lying around here somewhere. If she could just lay her hands on it. If she could shoot it into the chief. If it was fast-acting enough. If—

But she was out of time.

The sky behind her lit up.

THREE

THE NUKE THAT took out Sector 208 was a standard-yield Type Fourteen device, launched with forty-nine others from a Triglov-class re-entry vehicle. The Triglov splintered about ninety kilometres above the Canadian wastes, about a hundred and fifty kilometres from the city's northernmost edge, and exactly one point six seconds before it was targeted by the city's defences.

The laser mesh did a good job, successfully eliminating all but one of that batch, but ninety-eight per cent interception just wasn't quite good enough for Sector 208.

The lone warhead detonated as intended about fifteen hundred metres above ground level. Everything within a kilometre radius was instantly incinerated in the fireball, and everything else for another three kilometres in every direction that wasn't solid rockrete was pretty comprehensively demolished.

Outside that area of devastation people merely had to contend with searing blasts, flying debris, and falling rubble.

Even ten kilometres from the point of detonation, windows shattered and exposed skin blistered.

All the way over in Sector 212, Robinson could feel the hot wind on her neck.

It was a little strange describing something that had missed you by more than twenty clicks as a close one, but that one had certainly been too close.

And it was just the first. The sirens were still howling, not that Robinson needed them. She'd heard the radio feed. She knew about those thousands of radar contacts speeding across the screens, and she knew that the defences weren't going to get any more thorough. There had to be a way to get off this platform, which was likely to turn into a frying pan when the next strike hit.

There was no point talking to anyone. Crazy or sane, they were all momentarily transfixed by the mushroom cloud rising above the neighbouring sector.

Somewhere there should have been one of those anti-grav drop-chutes that acted as high-speed fire escapes in this high-rise world, but you tended to find those things indoors, and right now the nearest indoors was defended by Belinda Carlisle Citi-Def.

But there was a pod parked right there. It had a bullet-holed windshield and was leaning awkwardly to one side, but there weren't any better options that she could see. It was one of those little aerial runabouts in which fashionable people might zip around the upper levels. It hadn't been designed to carry anything more than two rich, thin people, but it would have to do, and it had better work.

She grabbed hold of Chief Mercer because it was either him or Tek Allen. They were the only two in immediate reach, and Mercer was her chief, and a stand-up Judge, even if he was a little bit nuts right now. Allen, on the other hand, was nuts and kind of creepy with it, so she'd have to look after herself.

Mercer was built like a longshoreman, but Robinson was well used strong-arming people bigger than herself and, maybe because he was somewhat shocked right now, she managed to manhandle him across the parking area and into the hover pod before he could do much more than raise a protest.

"What the hell, Robinson?"

"It's for your own good, Chief. Believe me. You know how to hot-wire one of these things by any chance?"

The mushroom cloud—that dreadful black and orange spectre of nuclear doom—had paralysed Mercer for a few seconds, but now that he found himself crammed into the passenger seat of this frivolous little vehicle, he asserted himself. He had a job to do and a war to win, nukes or no.

But it was the nukes that were making the decisions here. Without warning, there was a second blinding light, only this time it filled the whole world. Even through her visor—even looking down at the car's dashboard—Robinson saw everything turn black and white.

Now that was close, she thought. Sector 214 if I'm any judge.

And then the blast hit.

The burning shapes that had just been people were swept away. A horizontal rain of molten plastic spattered against the windshield. Cladding, signage, chunks of masonry were flying by, smashing against anything left standing in a blizzard of wreckage. The air was hot and red.

Robinson had been wondering how to get this pod airborne. Suddenly, that wasn't a problem any more. The whole great structure beneath them was beginning to tilt, and the pod, with no power and no brakes, was sliding off the platform and out into the void below. She gave up on the subtle approach and desperately punched the instrument panel with her fist. Astonishingly, it seemed to do the trick. Lights came on, and a screen scolded her for abusing the machinery and not wearing her seat belt. She fastened her seat belt. The pod tipped over the edge.

"Justice Department override!" she yelled at the car and, "Buckle up, Chief!" she yelled at Mercer.

"This vehicle does not recognise the speaker as the owner or authorised driver," said the car, in no hurry at all. "Please submit identification."

"Justice Department override! Engage engine!" shrieked Robinson.

And still they fell, down through the burning city.

FOUR

THE TACTICAL COMMAND Bunkers had been designed for just such an event as this.

It had been hard to say who'd won the last war, but the Big Meg were damn sure they weren't going to lose the next one. So as soon as they'd cleared the rubble away, and before they'd started to rebuild, they'd sunk the deep foundations of what would keep them in the game if the nukes should ever start flying again.

Each of the three bunkers was like the old Pentagon, in that you could run a whole war from under one roof, only these Pentagons were deep beneath the city, and their locations were top secret.

There were three of them because it was acknowledged that no one fortress is impregnable. The prudence of the planners was justified when the first wave of Sov missiles struck and Tactical Command Bunker West was taken out by a direct hit. But that's what TCB North and TCB East were there for, and it was from here that Mega-City One's defence and retaliation were directed.

As had become necessary throughout the city, robots had been mobilised to fill the gaps caused by Block Mania, and they worked alongside Justice Department personnel who acted with the same cold precision that their pitiless task demanded. They impassively watched their city charred to radioactive ruin, and they marshalled their remaining resources to visit the same destruction upon their enemy's city. With a word of command or the push of a button, they dealt in the murder of millions.

But no matter how dispassionate the controllers might have been about death suffered and death inflicted, they could hardly fail to acknowledge that Mega-City One was losing this war and losing it badly. The East-Meggers had got the first punch in, and that was the one that mattered. The Judges, weakened and sickened by Block Mania, had been looking in the wrong direction. They just weren't ready when the secret broke about this Operation Apocalypse. And so, the first silos in the Cursed Earth had been turned to black glass before they ever loosed a missile; the elusive underwater kill pods on the ocean floors had been hunted down; and Mega-City's orbital weapons platforms had been almost completely eliminated.

Sure—the retaliatory nukes had been sent on their way wherever that had been possible, but down in the bunkers they could monitor the missiles striking home and see that East-Meg One was absorbing the punishment.

And then it all became so much worse.

Even as they were still calculating their losses from the first strikes, the controllers saw on the screens a chain of multi-megaton devices exploding off the coast with seismic effect, generating a filthy tidal wave high and strong enough to smash down the Atlantic Wall and the greater part of the laser defence grid with it.

After that, there was nothing to stop the missiles. The Sovs could blast the city at will. A few hours later, just to prove the point, they hit the southern sectors with a saturation bombardment. Everything south of the thirty-fifth parallel was nuked out.

And if they could do that, they could send in ground forces and seize however much of the city as might still be standing. Who was there to bar their way? The Citizens' Defence units were fighting each other. The Judges, even with the Block Mania antidote now being administered, were outnumbered, overstretched, and under-strength.

Given the two days of war in the streets, the sudden and catastrophic flooding of half the eastern sectors, and—of course—the steady rain of nuclear warheads, the controllers down in their deep bunkers might have had good reason to wonder if there would even be any Judges left in the city above.

FIVE

"CHIEF? WAKE UP."

Mercer didn't like the idea, but he did his best. There was work to do. He managed to open one eye, but that was as far as it went. He saw Robinson leaning over him, swathed in a heavy-duty rad cloak.

"Glad you're back, Chief." She grinned. "You had me worried."

Truth was, she still looked worried. Worried, and beat all to hell too. He tried to sit up and assess the situation. Bad idea.

"Ow! Jovus Grud! The hell happened to me?"

"Lay back, Chief. Take it easy. Let me get this dressing on. Didn't want to waste it on you in case it turned out you were dead."

"Gee, thanks," he growled. "The hell happened? Report, Robinson."

"I dunno, Chief. What do you remember? When did you tune out?"

Good question. The head wound Robinson was working

on wasn't doing him any favours, but it felt worse than that. Like he was drunk or something. Only Judges don't get drunk. Sick or not, though, he was good and angry. About something anyway. It began to come back to him.

"Nukes," he said.

"Attaboy, Chief."

"Hover pod," he said, after some pained consideration.

"Correct! Two points, Chief. Just remind me when this is over to bust MacPete Autos for cutting corners on the safety features on the 2101 Lemon Froufrou. I'll cut them some slack though, on account of them giving the thing an AI that's halfway proof against electromagnetic pulse. It got us down hard, but it got us down."

Mercer worked some more on his battered memory.

"Belinda Carlisle," he said, but more to himself than to her.

Belinda Carlisle had had it coming.

Block war. Correction—block wars. All over. But the good guys won. Showed them all. Sector House 212 was the baddest block in the city. Hoo-ra. At least until the Sovs nuked them all.

He looked around. Belinda Carlisle, which had once cast its shadow over his sector, wasn't looking so high and mighty now. He reckoned the top twenty floors were blasted clean away, and the rest of the gigantic housing complex wasn't looking too healthy either.

Truth was, the place was looking like how he'd been hoping to make it look when he'd first led his people in there. But that had been about justice. That had been about bringing law and order to the unruly citizenry.

They hadn't deserved a nuke being dropped on them.

"Stinking Sovs." He slumped back again while Robinson did something to his right eye.

"I ever tell you," he asked, "that I was in the Big One? Thirty-some years ago. Just a kid like you. But we showed them."

"Hold still."

"We were still the United States. Still had a US Army and all those police forces. They fell apart. We kept it together. They were running around panicking, declaring martial law. Martial law? Huh. They should have known that we were the law. They were running around hollering and we brought justice. Huh. Army. Police. Bunch of candy asses."

"Bunch of panty-waists. All done, Chief. You want to try getting up? Come on—I'll let you have my rad cloak."

He staggered to his feet. He outweighed Robinson by forty kilos at least, but she supported him, even though he saw she had a dressing bound to her thigh.

"You hurt?"

"Ah, it's nothing."

That's what he wanted to hear. Robinson was a good Judge. Sector 212 didn't raise no crybabies. Good thing too. It looked like there was a lot to cry about. With the eye of one who'd seen it before—thirty-some years ago—Mercer reckoned on a one megaton yield, maybe five or six kilometres away. All but the most solid constructions were either gone or about to go. Most of the elevated roadways were down. The towers weren't towering like they used.

"View's changed," he remarked.

"Not used to so much sky."

"Look up there. You see it?"

She followed his gaze, up beyond the roiling clouds of poisonous smoke, but could see nothing. Then it struck her. There was no distant firework show. The laser grid was out.

"How about I get us home, Chief? Before the Sovs bring the rain down on us again."

SIX

YOU JUST DIDN'T realise how big a sector was until you had to walk across it. Their injuries were only a minor hindrance. They were Judges. They could tough it out. But the smashed transport network faced them with an endless succession of obstacles that made direct forward progress almost impossible. It was only when they came upon the remains of the sector thru-way that they were spared any more climbing expeditions and detours among the unforgiving ruins. The thru-way, which had once crossed the sector in an elegant elevated sweep, was now at ground level, lying across the wreckage like a strip of rumpled carpet but still largely intact.

During the many weary hours it had taken them to get this far, there had been several distant flashes to remind them that the enemy hadn't finished with the city yet.

They stopped to rest once they'd found a way up onto the slab. Robinson doled out anti-radiation pills. That was another of the Great Atomic War's more beneficial legacies. If you didn't get fried in the blast, or flattened by falling buildings, the little pharmaceutical miracles gave you an OK chance of living to see your next birthday. That said though, the side effects amounted to a pretty severe trade-off. It was a good thing, thought Robinson, that she wasn't planning on having any kids. The medical advances of the late twenty-first century might have kept a lot of people alive, but they were also responsible for the grotesque mutations of the next generation.

Without those anti-rad pills, the offspring of the war's survivors would never have made it to term, or survived long afterwards if they had. Instead, thanks to technology, they had been born, and had lived, and had been reviled and cast out.

"We get through this and we're going to have us a whole new mutie problem a few years down the line," she said. But that was down the line, and getting through this didn't appear to be all that doable right now, a couple of kilometres of open road notwithstanding.

Mercer seemed to be bearing up well, and their physical ills could be addressed with the application of a little speed-heal as soon as they made it back to however much of the sector house might still be standing, but Robinson wondered about her chief's mental state. The Teks had been on the point of liberally spraying around the Block Mania antidote when the bomb dropped. Maybe a canister had ruptured? It would have been good if Mercer had managed to inhale a whiff before everything went south.

He was a sector chief, which made him a testy old cuss at the best of times. She'd seen a couple of other Judges foaming at the mouth with Block Mania, but Mercer, while madder than hell, had never been frenzied. So how sick had he really been? And how was he doing now?

Well, right now, he was taking in the scenery.

"Dirty Sovs," he said. "Look what they've done to my sector."

My sector. Did that mean he saw himself as a Justice Department sector chief or as the warlord of Sector 212? Hard to tell.

Maybe that matter was about to be clarified, however.

"Contact," said Mercer, and Robinson looked along the road to see a scattering of figures approaching—a few dozen people who, like the Judges, had found the road and were on it because it was the only thing in this bombed-out landscape that seemed to lead anywhere. They appeared to be just ordinary citizens, but that wasn't exactly reassuring, seeing as most ordinary citizens had been spending the last couple of days trying to kill anyone who came from a different neighbourhood.

Mercer and Robinson waited, guns in their hands.

The refugees were scorched and bleeding, but mostly they were just shocked. The leader shambled to within earshot and called out, "What block are you guys?"

"We're Judges, numbnuts," answered Mercer. "Hands where I can see them."

"We ain't armed," said the citizen.

"How about the guy behind you puts down the blurp gun and I'll believe you," said Robinson.

"Oh yeah—the gun. Right. Maybe you should put down the gun, Roy."

"But it's for personal protection, Eugene. Case we run into any of them Julie Andrews Blockers."

"You've run into us," said Mercer. "Now lose the weapon or I shoot you and you can stay here until the construction crews come to rebuild the sector."

Shell-shocked and irradiated he might have been, but the man Roy was true to his block until the end.

"Louisa May Alcott don't stay here for no construction crew or no one, Judge," he said. He brought up his gun and Mercer made good on his threat. That should have been that, and in normal circumstances that single execution should have quelled any remaining resistance, but things were different with Block Mania.

"Them Judges killed Roy!" said Eugene in outraged disbelief, and at that, his followers closed in, fists clenching, makeshift crutches wielded as clubs, knives appearing from under clothes.

"Ooh boy," said Robinson. Why hadn't the Teks been a little quicker off the mark when it came to drenching the sector in the antidote?

Two Judges should have had no trouble at all in pacifying a few dozen ill-armed citizens, no matter how pugnacious those cits might have been acting. However, their gunfire not only failed to deter these clowns from pressing home their attack, but it also attracted some unexpected newcomers. Robinson glanced over her shoulder to see her flank threatened by another bunch of block maniacs, wherever they'd come from.

Actually, they'd come from Big Louie's Under-Sked Bar'n'Grill, which had survived having a roadway crash down on it remarkably well. Big Louie's hardly constituted a block, but the regular clientele was intensely loyal, and when the mania had struck, they'd willingly joined with the staff in fighting off any and all comers.

So now the two Judges were faced with an attack from an unexpected quarter by a crazed collection of truckers, catering staff, and travelling sales reps. Things were looking as if they might get a bit tricky when a familiar and welcome noise was heard above the fray.

It was a Lawmaster coming up the road. It was coming up slowly, and its engine wasn't roaring with full-throated health, but that didn't matter. Even if there was only one road left in this sector, the law was riding in on it.

The fight ended in no time after that, with the surviving maniacs limping and scurrying off to holes in the rubble. The bike, its front armament torn away and something dripping from a cracked engine, drew up, and Judge Steinman holstered his Lawgiver.

"Chief," he said. "Robinson. Good to see you. Didn't think anyone else made it."

"How the heck did you make it, Steinman?" asked Robinson.

"Anti-grav drop-chute. How else? Thing went screwy on me halfway down, what with the nuke and all, but it got me down safe. Even managed to find this bike— what's left of it. Reckon it's got just enough juice left to get us back home. Need a ride?"

The three of them piled onto the decrepit Lawmaster,

a business that was awkward and undignified but perfectly possible. Mercer was so securely aboard that he was able at last to succumb to his concussion or, as he put it, "take a little nap."

This gave Robinson the chance to address her main concern of the moment.

"Listen, Steinman," she said. "I have to ask."

"Go ahead."

"Back at Carlisle. That gas the Teks were ready to spread all over—did they manage to release it? And did you get to inhale any of it?"

"I don't know what the Teks were doing, Robinson, but there's no way I was going to be breathing any of it. I had my respirator down tight, just like the chief ordered."

"But that stuff was supposed to be the antidote, Steinman!"

"So why would I need the antidote? It's not like I'm crazy."

And no—Judge Steinman was nothing like those suicidal kooks who'd attacked them on the road. But then again, Steinman had Justice Department blood on his hands solely because his loyalties were not exactly in line with regulations.

And that meant that, in this hour of gravest peril for the city, of the three Judges known to be still functioning in Sector 212, only one was definitely in her right mind.

Ooh boy.

SEVEN

THE SECTOR HOUSE was still standing when they finally made it back there, but that was all you could say about it. It was a substantial construction, built to withstand a lot, but someone had really given it a working over.

"Sov orbital weapon," said Raskova. "Big gruddamn space laser."

Judge Raskova had been left in charge when Mercer had taken all the rest of his people out to conquer the sector. Apart from the permanent admin staff she was the only one there to hold the sector house against the hordes of block maniacs. She wasn't going to sweat it. She'd been judging the citizens of Mega-City One for more than forty years and she wasn't ready to stop busting heads yet. And the Sovs? Tell them to get in line. She'd deal with them in their turn.

That, at least, was the attitude she always projected, and while it was as intimidating as hell, Robinson was still glad to see that the old broad hadn't been shaken by events.

"Only to be expected," Raskova went on. "No point in nuking out the whole city, so they use precision on specific high-value targets like us. We were ready for it. Everything on the top floors is burnt out and our communications are fried, but I'd already had those floors evacuated and the comms should be up and running again in an hour. How bad is the chief?"

"Concussion. Nothing they can't fix."

"Good. Get your leg seen to and then put together a full field load of supplies and ammo. My guess is we'll have to move soon. Sov invasion is on its way."

"You know this for sure?"

"No, but if you were that wall-eyed Joe-Stalin-looking son-of-a-bitch Bulgarin and you had us on the ropes, what would you do?"

"Point."

"Oh yeah—and take one of these." Raskova was holding out a pill.

"What is it?"

"Orders from Central. Everyone takes one. Stops you from getting whatever was making the cits crazy."

"This is the Block Mania antidote?"

"So they tell me. Med bay mixed up a whole batch."

"You have two more doses you can give me? Thanks."

STEINMAN MIGHT HAVE been a Judge-killer, but he didn't have the heart of a renegade. When Robinson found him down in the bike pool, he took the required medicine without question, but then, as it took effect, he had a brutal comedown to face.

Legally, he might even be in the clear for the two murders. Who knew? The balance of his mind had, after all, been demonstrably disturbed. But that just wouldn't cut it for someone who'd spent all his life in the service of justice. An unlawful killing was a murder, and a murder had to be punished. And killing Judges? The worst crime of all? At a time like this?

He didn't want to talk about it, so she left him to his conscience and went looking for Mercer. She noticed that whatever was eating Steinman was a steady undercurrent in the mood of the sector house. She could tell that even now, at the losing end of a nuclear war, everyone was embarrassed over the way they'd been during the last few days. No one likes coming round from a drug-induced episode and having to face the suspicion that they might have done something shameful while under the influence, and that went double for people as straight-edged as Judges.

When Robinson found him, Mercer was unhooking himself from the medi-unit and telling the med-droid to get the hell out of his face. As usual, Robinson couldn't tell if he was in a state of chemically heightened aggression or just plain grouchy.

"Med-droid give you your pill, Chief?" she asked brightly.

"Gruddamn med-droid stuck magnetic gizmos to my head and shot me full of anti-radiation gloop. I don't remember any pills, Robinson."

"Better take this just to be on the safe side then."

"Take it yourself. I'm busy. We've got a war to fight, remember?"

Robinson was about to say something about orders from Central. She was even considering pinning her chief down and forcing his jaws open while he was still weak from his treatment. Her intentions were forestalled, however, by something hitting the building hard. The lights went out, and when they came back on again, they were hazy from the dust that filled the air.

A moment later, the alarm sounded.

Robinson picked herself off the floor to see the chief hammering on the intercom.

"Mercer to Control! Report!"

"We're under attack, Chief! Strato-V just hit us with a salvo of K-fifties."

Strato-Vs—the all-purpose aerial vehicles that were the East-Meg equivalent of the Mega-City H-Wagon.

"How come I'm only finding out about it when my sector house starts falling down around my ears?"

"Sorry, Chief. Only just got our radar back online."

"What? And someone couldn't just keep watch out of a window? Jovus Grud. Mercer out."

Evidently, the Strato-V made another attack run just then because the building was buffeted once more—this time hard enough to bring down part of the ceiling.

Robinson realised she'd dropped the pill she was holding, and she couldn't see it among the debris on the floor.

"Forget your damn pills, Robinson. I want everyone below ground ASAP, and we're going by way of the armoury."

EIGHT

Every Justice Department facility of any size had a bunker just like the one below Sector House 212, but this one had rarely been used for anything except storage or, in times of higher-than-usual crime rates, as additional holding tanks.

The dust covers were only being pulled off the slightly outdated consoles, and the somewhat old-fashioned screens were only just flickering to life when the first nukes struck, knocking everything out. They'd got everything fired up a second time only for the orbital strike to fry the systems all over again. Communications with the outside world had just been restored when Mercer strode in, loaded down with additional weapons and ammunition, and very much in charge again.

Except for a handful of surviving street Judges like Robinson and Steinman, his only remaining personnel were the button-pushers from Control, the maintenance staff, some Med and Tek people, and a scattering of the medically unfit.

Here, beneath their burnt and battered home, they gathered round and stoically looked to Mercer for orders.

"Give me the big picture," he said. "Connect me to Justice Central, or whoever's out there."

But the Grand Hall of Justice wasn't answering. Neither was the H-Wagon that had been the Chief Judge's airborne headquarters through all of this. The Tek at the console cycled through the alternatives.

Tactical Command Bunker West was gone. Just gone.

TCB North replied, but only after repeated attempts, and the voice that did answer in the end was speaking Sov.

"They're here," said a Tek Judge at another screen, his voice leaden.

"OK," said Mercer. "Forget North. Try TCB East."

"No, Chief," said the Tek. "I mean they're here! The Sovs are here! Upstairs! Outside!"

And everyone saw on the screen the shapes of Strato-Vs, holding position around the sector house.

"If they're hovering like that, then they're putting troops on the ground. Probably robots. Can't tell. All the outside cameras are gone."

"OK, people! Evac! Everyone get as much gear as you can carry and mount up. We leave by the south ramp when I give the word. You and you, set charges. You—stay right there and keep trying to raise TCB East."

There was no panic. Judges don't panic. Even technicians and clerical staff knew to take up defensive positions at stairwells and elevator shafts, while behind them their comrades put everything in train for demolition and evacuation. There was transport for just about everyone, and with their Lawmasters and all their weaponry, they'd have constituted a formidable fighting unit at the best of times.

But these were not the best of times, and in the face of an overwhelming enemy force, all they could do for the moment was run.

Mercer wasn't quite ready to run yet. "Keep trying," he told the communications Tek.

And at last, a link was established, even if what they heard was nothing that could give them heart.

An indistinct voice said something about Sentenoids pouring in, and there was a scream and a crackle, and then silence.

"All right," said Mercer. "That'll do. Let's get out of here."

But the channel remained open as the self-destruct mechanisms were armed, and as the timers counted down their last seconds and the Judges waited to blast their way out into who knew what, the last message came in from TCB East.

It was a voice they all recognised, and it was a message they didn't need, but were grateful for all the same. And it wasn't a message for them: it was for the whole city.

"I don't know how many of you are listening out there. I don't know how many of you even care. But hear this:

"East-Meg forces now occupy the northern sectors and are sweeping south. Our city faces its blackest hour.

"Rest assured, there will be no surrender. As long as one Judge draws breath, Mega-City One fights on!"

"Dredd," said Mercer. "Knew it would take more than a few nukes to put him down. Let's ride."

NINE

WITH THEIR INSECT legs and strong snake-like arms, the Sentenoids clawed their way over and through the rubble, cutting their way through blast doors and breaching the sector house. As had happened when massed block maniacs had tried to storm the building only the day before, the automated defences did their work, and the first intruders were cut down in an instant.

But that's why the Sovs had sent robots in first. Even as the auto-guns blasted them, those first Sentenoids relayed with their last signal the layout of the defences, so that the next robots through the breach could more easily silence them.

Those robots were destroyed in their turn when the demolition charges detonated, but a few unserviceable Sentenoids were a small price to pay for securing a Justice Department stronghold.

Sector House 212, with all its facilities wrecked and all its files wiped, was no great prize in itself, but it denied the Mega-City Judges those same facilities, that arsenal, that secure base. They could do nothing now but run.

As the robots were assaulting the front, Mercer's people were roaring out the back. They knew they had to run, and they had to run fast. On the ground, the Sovs had nothing to match the Lawmaster for speed, but the Sovs ruled the air. The Strato-Vs were still in position, and one of them had the Mega-City Judges on lock within seconds of their breaking cover.

The exit Mercer had chosen came out onto a stretch of intact roadway, and roads and buildings for several levels above were likewise intact. You might not want to trust the weight of a Lawmaster to some of those roads, but all they had to do for now was shield the Judges from above.

The Strato-V's lasers were tracking them, but if the Judges could keep their speed up and could get weaving, Mercer reckoned they had a pretty good chance of making it to the shelter of the Alice Cooper Tunnel. Sure, he thought, as a brief cry sounded over his radio, to be cut off instantly, not everyone was likely to make it. Not everyone's bike skills were as sharp as was needed. You can't expect a button-pusher from Control or a turn-key from Holding to be able to switch from manning an indoor post to roaring at top speed over broken and obstructed ground in a landscape made unfamiliar by the bombing. Someone's going to lag behind. Someone's going to get hit. But he was confident that his most useful people—his street Judges—would make good their escape.

He'd reckoned, though, without laser lightning.

Strictly speaking, this was neither a laser nor was it electrical. What it was, though, was a ball of super-heated plasma which, when launched, bounced around at surface level, effectively chasing its targets where line-of-sight weapons wouldn't work. It was crude, it was needlessly destructive, but it was undoubtedly suited to the present circumstances. Right now, it was close on their tails—two hissing, crackling orbs of white-hot destruction, pinballing along the street. The stuff moved too randomly to be avoided. All they could do was race ahead of it until it burnt itself out.

They all heard Raskova bawling out some Admin Judge who wasn't moving fast enough, and then they heard her cursing a blue streak in an ever-rising pitch as a ball of laser lightning closed in on her from behind.

And that was it. Then there was silence on that channel.

Carmen Raskova—one mean old Judge, and one they could ill do without.

They left the Strato-V behind as it manoeuvred to find a way around the bulk of Ruth Bader Ginsberg Block. That would buy them the ten or fifteen seconds that was all they needed now. Half a click ahead of them was the entrance to the tunnel. It hadn't collapsed, and that was good. There was a pile-up of vehicles, but it looked like there'd be room to get around, and that was good too. There was also an East-Meg tank coming down the slip road to block their path. That, they could have done without.

Like the Sentenoids, the Sov tanks were robotic.

This was one of the infamous T-1000 Rad-sweepers. With no crew to keep safe, it carried no more armour than was needed to protect the vital workings of the machine. This meant that it could afford to be big, with a wide enough chassis to keep the thing stable in a nuclear blast if need be, and with a formidable main armament. And yet, big as it was, it was just about light enough to be air-portable. No doubt this example was one of several delivered just now by anti-grav lift from the cargo bay of one of those Strato-Vs.

The Judges knew that if they let this monster cut them off from the tunnel, they were dead. It would either wipe them out all by itself or it would pin them long enough for the Strato-V to come back and light them up.

Mercer didn't even need to give the order. Every Lawmaster that could draw a bead fired. The standard bike cannon would be no good here. This was the moment you were real glad your bike's battery had just been charged to the max because that Cyclops TX laser really burnt up a lot of juice.

The tank and the bikes fired simultaneously, and both scored hits. Mercer didn't pause to check who didn't make it. All that mattered was that the Rad-sweeper in front of them was burning. He saw the nose of another one edging into view from the roadway above, and urged his people to greater speed. That tunnel had really better not be blocked up ahead, he thought, because we ain't slowing down.

As it turned out, the way ahead was clear. Some more laser lightning chased them in, but they made it safely to an access point where they could branch off, slow down and—they hoped—disappear.

The short race from the sector house had cost them five dead. True, they'd knocked out a Rad-sweeper, but one Sov tank for five good Judges was a poor exchange. The Sovs had plenty of Rad-sweepers, and plenty of Sentenoids too, no doubt. When it came to human personnel, who knew how many East-Meg Judges now had the slab of Mega-City One under their feet? All that Mercer knew for certain was that they had taken Sector House 212 from him and not a single one of them had paid for it.

TEN

Two DAYS LATER, Mercer's team were holed up beneath some rubble near the George Foreman Overzoom, sheltering from the snow and from aerial surveillance. The snow was a consequence of Weather Control sabotaging its entire system in order to impede the invaders, although a nuclear war in North America in the dead of winter probably had something to do with it too. Anyway, the snow was likely to be no more than a temporary factor. On the other hand, the surveillance could be expected to be around a while longer. This was Sov territory now.

The forces of East-Meg One had firmly established their airborne bridgeheads across the northern sectors, and were now pushing south. In answer to Dredd's call, it was the task of what remained of Mega-City's forces to stop them somehow. For now, the strategy was to cut every southbound road, and here in the ruins of Sector 212, that meant the George Foreman Overzoom.

Mercer had divided his people into strike teams made

up of his most capable personnel, with the remainder making up a support team, forever shifting its base as it tried to maintain the equipment and tend the wounded. Mercer's squad, designated Team Alpha, was just himself, Steinman, and Robinson. The teams were kept small because resources were stretched thin, and because in this war of hit-and-run, a small unit was more agile. Then there was the inescapable truth that in this war of the weak against the strong, when the enemy caught you, that tended to be it, so better the annihilation of a small squad than a larger one.

On this bitter day, Mercer had only four such teams engaged in interdicting the East-Meg lines of communication. This morning he'd had six, but Teams Bravo and Echo had run out of luck. He hoped that meant there'd be more luck to go around now, but he doubted it. Foreman didn't promise to be an easy target.

ROBINSON HAD EYES on the overzoom, and she'd have agreed with her chief's assessment of their chances. This one was going to be bad. At least there were no refugees. Twice so far, they'd had to bring down roads that had been crowded with civilians. True, those refugees had been mortally sick with the radiation, or would have been crushed by the Rad-sweepers coming up from behind, letting nothing hinder their drive south, but it dismayed Robinson nonetheless. Whatever had happened to protect and serve?

And the citizens now weren't the usual cits.

If she'd been told last week that she'd be feeling pity for the citizens, it wouldn't have made any sense to her. Citizens were to be monitored and policed and saved from each other and from their own baser impulses. Then, when the mania had infected them, the citizens were to be fought tooth and nail, without hesitation or mercy. But now these same people were pitiable. Homeless, shocked, bereaved, sick and injured, they staggered south in wretched columns. There was no more criminality because there was nothing to steal, and no one better off than themselves to exploit or prey on.

And there was no madness any more. The Sovs had seen to that. More easily than they'd brought the Block Mania, they'd dispelled it. In front of their advance, the Strato-Vs had come, saturating the city with the antidote, turning an enraged and belligerent populace into a frightened and demoralised one.

So at least, thought Robinson, the Judges didn't have to worry about being shot at by snipers or jumped by random lunatics while they tried to fight their guerrilla war. All those maniacs had been calmed right down. Except, of course, that there might be just one left. She still wasn't sure about Chief Mercer.

When they'd seen the Strato-Vs flying over in line abreast, they'd assumed it was an attack run. They hadn't changed their minds when they'd seen gas rather than bombs issuing from the aircraft. The standard practice of the enemy, after all, had been to secure their landing zones with poison gas. Given all the nooks and crannies in the half-ruined multilevel city, it made more sense than bombing or strafing. So when Mercer's people saw more gas, they did the sensible thing and pulled their respirators down over their faces. It was only when they'd run across a Citi-Def unit seeking their help rather than shouting the odds—or just lying asphyxiated on the ground—that they'd figured out what had happened.

So maybe the chief was still sick. Thing was, though, he was still doing his job. Maybe the Block Mania just wore off in time. Or maybe it was only the aggression that was keeping him going. Whatever—there wasn't a whole lot that Robinson could do about it.

And besides, their planned attack on George Foreman was likely to put an end to all their worries.

"Rad-sweepers," she told the other two. "A whole column of them. I estimate two-hundred-plus, rolling down from the north. Sentenoids are spread out in patrol lines, a hundred metres on either side. A few East-Meg Judges up on the roadway itself, but I couldn't see more than three or four."

"We can get past the Sentenoids," said Steinman. "We've done it before. They're slow and they're dumb, and a scrambler grenade in the right place makes a world of difference. The snow should hide us from anyone up on the road. We can do this."

Steinman wasn't a naturally upbeat kind of guy. Truth was, his can-do attitude in the face of impossible odds seemed to be grounded more in fatalism—a we-all-gotta-go-sometime kind of deal—and Robinson suspected that if Steinman had to go, then he wanted to go out like a Judge, making amends for all past transgressions.

So when Steinman said that they could do this, what he most likely meant was that sure, they could somehow infiltrate past a screen of war robots in order to set the necessary charges on the overzoom's supports, but how they managed to get out again wasn't really his concern.

Robinson was a Mega-City Judge and would do her duty to the end, but she kind of hoped that the end was still way off, and for now she was hoping that some more viable alternative to a suicide mission might present itself.

"They say Dredd's outfit have got themselves stub guns," she said hopefully. "How come we don't have stub guns, Chief? Just slice through all those rockrete supports from three hundred metres out? Slice through roadways, robots and all? What do you say, Chief?"

She knew as soon as she heard her own voice that it was stupid. Drive across five sectors in the middle of a war, somehow hook up with another guerrilla unit, and politely ask Judge Dredd himself if he'd maybe let her borrow one of only a handful of experimental weapons in existence? She sounded like a little kid asking if she could have a real live pony for Christmas.

"Dredd's people can do their thing with dangerously unstable laser weapons," said Mercer. "We can do ours with good old reliable plastic explosives. Let's see who's still standing when it's all over."

Robinson was glad he'd spared her a more sarcastic answer. But the question of who might be left standing was still there to trouble her. Steinman settled it by repeating, "We can do this," and picking up a satchel of explosives.

"Come on, Robinson," he said. "Chief, you stay back and cover us."

And Robinson picked up her own gear and followed because—hey, who knows?—maybe they could do this.

They certainly had to try.

ELEVEN

THEIR RAD CLOAKS were cumbersome and had an inconvenient tendency to catch on things, but they were good camouflage, being shapeless, and they hid all that gold shoulder armour that Judges wore to stand out in a crowd. Then there was the protection they gave from the weather and—oh yeah—from the radiation, of course.

Steinman and Robinson were good at this. Moving swiftly but unobtrusively over broken ground was just a matter of agility and training, and those they both had in spades. Outwitting a Karpov MF7 Sentenoid was trickier, but they'd had a lot of practice the past couple of days. As Steinman had pointed out, they were slow. Their all-terrain capability did not come with nimbleness. And while they weren't necessarily stupid, as Steinman had dismissed them, they were limited. An electronic scrambler could temporarily fritz their sensors, while at the same time knocking them off their communication network. That gave you a few seconds when they couldn't see you or hear you or alert their fellows that anything was out of order.

On the other hand, if they caught you, you were toast.

What the Sentenoid lacked in sophistication, it made up for in its relentlessness. That was Sov war machinery all over: robust, lacking in finesse, and halfway to being unstoppable. Blow off a Sentenoid's legs and it kept after you with its arms. It had such an immense power pack that it would fall apart from metal fatigue before its motors gave out. Of more immediate concern was the machine's ability to keep on fighting no matter what. Run out of ammo? No problem: it had lasers. Lasers knocked out? No problem: it still had power enough to generate a lethal electrical charge. And if that wasn't enough? Hell, the thing could just strangle you or something.

So, sneaking by unnoticed was the best option here.

Robinson and Steinman managed it with the help of Mercer, who opened up with some long-range sniping that attracted the enemy's attention for just long enough for them to slip past. After that, it was just a matter of getting under the northbound on-ramp, over the southbound off-ramp, past the feeder road, and there they'd be—right by the main supports of the overzoom. There was nothing to it, so long as you were comfortable with doing a fast roll across the road that the tanks were using. If you timed it just right and almost brushed the tracks of the tank going by, then the sensors on the next tank shouldn't be able to pick you up in the heat of the first tank's exhaust. If it did, of course, there was that comb of little lasers that Rad-sweepers carried so that they could shred anything that tried to get beneath them.

But the Judges were skilful, and they stayed lucky.

They hardly needed a map of the intersection, seeing as they'd both policed traffic here enough times, but one of their surviving Teks had given them helpful advice on how best to demolish such a grand structure.

It could all be done most efficiently if the primary charge was placed inside an access stair in the second huge pier on the western side. All well and good, except that the door to that stair was at the back of a watching bay—one of those vantages from which a Judge could oversee passing traffic. Right now, that was exactly what the small platform was being used for, except that it was naturally the wrong kind of Judge keeping watch there.

Steinman and Robinson caught their breath and planned their approach, Robinson silently amazed that they'd got this far.

She wasn't surprised to hear her partner say, "You go plant the secondary charges. I'll take care of the Sov on the watching bay."

It figures, she thought. If Judge Direct-Approach Steinman here was going to get himself killed today, he wasn't going to waste any time over it. Still—somebody had to creep up behind the highly trained and heavily armed foe who was standing guard at a position designed to keep anyone from doing precisely that thing, and Steinman was the one who'd volunteered.

She didn't stay to watch him do it. Time was short.

It wasn't easy, but she got the job done, and when she made it back, there was Steinman at the watching bay, the body of the Sov Judge hidden away behind the access door, next to the demolition charge.

"All done?" she asked, sweating despite the cold.

"All done," he affirmed.

She took in the view as the endless procession of tanks rolled by beneath them.

"We'll have to exfil the same way we came in. Looks like a water main burst at the foot of the Alcott exit, so unless you care to cross a thirty-metre pool of irradiated frozen water, I say we take our chances with the Sentenoids again."

But Steinman wasn't listening.

"See that?" he said, staring as far down the road as could be seen.

"More Rad-sweepers," said Robinson. "Hardly unexpected."

"Look again," he said, and handed her an optical sight.

"More Rad-sweepers, but with guys riding on them. A few other vehicles too. Personnel carriers?"

"That's an affirmative. Enemy personnel. Sov troops."

"OK then. So, let's get the hell off this road and blow the charges before they get here."

"Negative."

"Say again?"

"Sovs, Robinson! Humans! Not robots! Not replaceable like robots. If we blow the roadway before they get here, then we only delay them. But we kill them, and we make a difference."

"It's too risky."

"We can do this."

TWELVE

"So, what's the plan, Steinman? There's a whole armoured formation of them and we're just, like, two Judges."

"As long as one Judge draws breath, Robinson. Remember?"

"And here's two that are about to stop drawing breath because they got squished under a Rad-sweeper. Let's bounce. I mean it."

But Steinman was grinning. "Maybe this isn't the job for a Judge then."

"Good. Let's move it."

"Maybe this is a job for a traffic cop. I'll be right back."

"Steinman!"

She wanted to ask, "What killed your last partner?" but she didn't, because she knew that the answer would be, "Block Mania." She feared to acknowledge that this scheme of his was all part of his big guilt trip over what he'd done while under the influence, as it were. She could only hope that the guilt trip wasn't turning into a death wish that would take her along with him.

Steinman looked downright sinister in a Sov Judge's helmet. Looking at him, Robinson had a sudden insight as to what it must feel like for a regular citizen facing a regular Judge.

The rest of the Sov uniform wasn't needed. Devoid of insignia, a rad cloak was just another rad cloak, and it would take an observant eye to notice Justice Department-issued boots and gauntlets in this weather and in the few seconds that was all Steinman intended to allow.

"I still say it's a lousy plan," said Robinson.

"Just pop the smoke grenades and get out of sight. Everything will be fine. All we need is for the lead vehicle to either stop or take a detour. That'll keep most of the column at or near enough to the point of detonation for the few minutes we need to get clear."

"So you say. But what if they don't buy your Sov act?"

"Then we blow the charges right away and take the drokkers with us."

"Did I mention that your plan stinks? And how convincing is your Sov-speak anyway?"

"Неплохо," said Steinman.

The Academy's crowded curriculum had included a Cultural Awareness program or, as the cadets had called it: "Know Your Enemy 101." It looked like Steinman had paid attention.

"Let's just hope that your accent passes muster. Good luck."

The lead vehicle of the next East-Meg convoy drew near. With smoke and snow swirling all around, Steinman stepped into the middle of the main road and raised his hand with the calm authority of one for whom a broken tail light and an errant armoured division are all one.

To avoid detection, the Mega-City Judges had switched off their comms, so Robinson couldn't hear what bull-stomm Steinman was selling the Sovs about resistance activity and road closures and whatever. Neither could she alert Mercer, who was still out there playing hide-and-seek with the Sentenoids or—who knows?—might be assuming that the mission had gone all to hell and was planning something crazy himself.

He might yet have to because this particular crazy plan appeared to have gone south in a hurry.

Steinman came sprinting back through the smoke, with shots kicking the ground just behind him.

"Didn't work, Robinson! Hit the trigger!"

Not relishing suicide, Robinson had added her own variation to Steinman's scheme, so when she hit the button, only the secondary charges went up. Everything gave a sudden lurch, but the road junction held.

"What the hell, Robinson?"

"It might make them pause! Give us time to get out!"

And indeed, that seemed to have worked. The enemy vehicles were either staying put or carefully negotiating their way around the sites of the explosions. Either way, and for the moment at least, they certainly weren't rolling their victorious way across the George Foreman Overzoom, and that was all that Steinman could have asked for.

On the other hand, seeing as the overzoom was still standing, and all those tanks and troops weren't lying smashed up in the wreckage, the two Mega-City Judges found themselves trying to withdraw in the face of the enemy's undivided attention.

Laser beams, bullets, and cannon shells chased them as they descended an access ladder without touching the rungs. They made it to ground level but retreating across the open was not an option. They were forced to stay under the cover of the roadway, and there the enemy's fire could keep them pinned until a couple of Rad-sweepers could make their way down from above and make sure of them.

Or, of course, the Sentenoids could take care of it.

"Better hit that main charge," said Steinman. "If it's even going to work now."

Three Sentenoids were closing in, keeping out of sight while herding them into a space blocked by a fallen ramp and the flood from the broken water mains. It was clear that Steinman had underestimated the machines' capabilities earlier. They were slow, but they were deliberate, and if the Judges had thought to engage one of them, then they'd be making themselves targets for the other two robots.

"Wait a second," said Robinson. "The pool's frozen. I think that ice will take our weight."

It was another lousy idea, but it was the only one they had left.

Along the edges of the pool the ice did indeed bear their weight, but a few metres in and things got suddenly and dangerously slushy. They struggled, thigh deep on the icy filth, their feet stumbling on hidden rubble, and they could hear the pursuing robots crunching their way closer.

On the far side of the flood, Robinson spotted one of the Sentenoids circling round to cut them off. She managed to halt it, even though it emptied her Lawgiver of high-explosive rounds to do so. And that left two more Sentenoids, coming in from behind, and only Steinman's gun could stop them, except that Steinman's gun was in his boot and his boot was underwater, and at this moment caught in a tangle of reinforcing bars.

They could see the clawed feet seeking purchase on the ice, and the strong mechanical tentacles clearing aside a concrete slab.

Robinson, the demolition trigger in her left hand all this while, resignedly put her thumb on the red button again. We all gotta go sometime.

Steinman managed to heave himself free but got no further than flopping onto the ice.

It would all have gone very badly if a shot from somewhere off in the outside world hadn't whined off the lead Sentenoid's head plate. The war machine turned to assess the new threat at the very same moment that its front foot broke through the ice. It would have regained its balance if its companion hadn't bumped into it from behind. One of its great steel arms flailed in the air, trying to grab an overhead beam, but it missed, and the whole ungainly apparatus crashed forward through the ice. It flailed around uselessly, and in what might have been a fit of pique, loosed off a devastating electrical charge. But by then Robinson and Steinman were clear of the water, and besides, their uniforms insulated them.

They took the opportunity to skedaddle, while behind

them the second Sentenoid, its line of sight blocked, struggled to extricate its fellow.

There were still the rest of the Sov forces above them to contend with, but Robinson blew the primary charge almost before she and Steinman broke cover. She figured that she'd sooner risk an avalanche of collapsing highway intersection than a hail of enemy firepower.

The Teks had been right about how to bring down the junction. Steinman mightn't have nailed as many Sovs as he'd hoped, but they'd come for George Foreman, and now George Foreman was down.

"Job done," said Mercer when he met up with them. It had been his sniper's bullet that had distracted that Sentenoid.

"Couldn't let you kids get eaten up by the big bad robot, now could I?" he said.

"All right, Chief," said Robinson. "Thanks. But I still say I want a stub gun."

THIRTEEN

JUST LAST WEEK Mercer had run his sector from his high office in Sector House 212. He could stand in his control centre and observe the feed from countless surveillance cameras. He could direct his personnel with no more than a word, relayed instantly over the net.

Now here he was in the basement of a closed-down electronics store where his support team had set up, having been chased out of the tunnel that had been their previous headquarters.

Every time they switched on their communications, they ran the risk of detection. That's what had driven the support team from their last bolt hole, obliging them to abandon more equipment than they could afford to lose. At least they'd got away, though, which was more than could be said for Team Charlie. They'd been coordinating an ambush, but even their strict radio discipline hadn't been enough to save them when a Strato-V got a lock.

In other bad news, neither Team Delta nor Team

Foxtrot had reported back, despite both being past due, and as if to add insult to injury, the automated East-Meg repair crews were already making good the damage to the last three road links that the resistance had hit that day.

"Last week we were the law. Now we're just the gruddamn resistance," said Mercer, sitting down heavily on a crate of discontinued robot parts. "Ideas, anyone?"

"I hate to say it, Chief," said Robinson, "but I reckon we've done all we can. The whole road-blowing thing was never going to hurt them much. The strategy was just to delay. Well, now delay is pointless. The Sovs have already pushed on south. We're not just cut off here: I don't think we can make much of a difference any more."

"You saying we should cut and run, Robinson?"

"I hate to say it, Chief."

"Abandon my sector. To the enemy."

"C'mon, Chief."

"My sector, Robinson. They didn't give me the big chair so I could run out when the going got tough. I didn't hand it over to the block maniacs, and I'm not going to hand it over the gruddamn East-Meggers. Drokk no."

"I'm with the chief," said Steinman. "I say we fight on. Besides—we're just too far behind enemy lines now. We'll never make it back down south."

"But how do we fight? You can do a last-man-last-round if you want, but if it's not hurting the enemy, then what's the point?"

"Gruddamn robots," said Mercer, interrupting them.

Something in the crate he was sitting on was jutting into his bad hip, and that just reminded him how much he really hated robots right now. "Gruddamn Sentenoids and Rad-sweepers. They're a bitch to take down and there's always another dozen to take the place of every one you knock out."

A Tek on the support team tried to be helpful. "I found the specs on the T-1000 Rad-sweeper, Chief. There's a weakness. If their engines are running too hot, there's this little vent on the left side of the turret. Big enough to drop a hand-bomb in, maybe."

The other Judges looked at him.

"So how does that work, Farley?" said Robinson. "I should just gun my Lawmaster in fast so the Rad-sweeper can't get a bead on me? And then—I dunno—leap about three metres straight up onto the Rad-sweeper's left-hand track? And then drop a hand-bomb into this little vent as I'm passing? Did I get that right?"

"Jeez, Robinson, I'm just saying."

"Lawmaster versus Rad-sweeper, Farley? Now you know why we leave you at home all day."

"The problem isn't one robot tank," said Mercer, getting them back to business. "The problem is numbers. We need a way to counteract the sheer damn mass of machines that they're bringing to the fight. Start thinking about it. Meanwhile, everyone should get themselves a couple of hours sack time. After that, we're going out to blow up George Foreman all over again."

FOURTEEN

Coincidentally, somebody else had been thinking about the problem already—somebody higher up. The encrypted signal was sent out to any remaining resistance cells operating in the northern sectors. Tek Farley picked it up, and ran it by Mercer. Mercer liked it. He liked it enough to tell Farley to risk breaking radio silence.

"Tell them: Mercer here. Two-one-two. Responding."

At the subsequent briefing Mercer was more good-humoured than anyone had seen him since before this thing began.

"OK, kids. Here's the deal. Whatever's left of our intel network has identified a Sov landing zone in Sector 199. This is no ordinary LZ. They've established a permanent base there. Any of you tell me why that might be?"

"There's a pretty big airport, Chief," said Steinman. "Major southbound arteries connected to it."

"Correct, but not quite the answer I'm looking for."

"RMR!" said Robinson. "There's a big RMR facility there!"

"Bingo. One point to Robinson. Robots Makin' Robots. Biggest automated robotics factory in town.

The thinking is that the Sovs are using RMR not just for maintenance and repair, but for production too. Why lift tanks halfway across the globe when you can build them on-site? Knock that out and I do believe it would make a difference. Dredd's people are offering it to whoever can get to it. That's going to be us."

Robinson grinned. "So we're moving out of the sector after all?"

"Sector 199 is an industrial zone. No residential population. That means that Sector 208 takes care of any policing above the level of private security. 208's been nuked out. That makes me the nearest sector chief. That means 199's under my jurisdiction."

Technically, everything was under a Judge's jurisdiction, but Robinson saw what her chief meant. At the height of the Block Mania, he had been fighting to dominate his sector like he was some sort of local warlord. Now it looked like he'd been given a chance to take things up a level. Now he could do some empire building.

As always, the problem was numbers. With his other teams gone dark and presumed MIA, Mercer had three Judges to hand, including himself. His resources were limited to whatever those Judges could carry and to a makeshift communications array in a basement. There were no reinforcements, no heavy weapons—none of the resources that an operation of any size demanded. Worst of all, there was no database that they could consult that would tell them what they needed to know about the vast manufacturing facility that was Sector

199. The Judges could barely figure out how to get there, never mind how they might destroy the place.

Communications were very cautiously fired up and a request for something—anything—was sent south. Tek Farley had taken up position on top of the ruins of Patty Hearst Block, which was a good two kilometres from the Judges' hideout, but everyone was prepared to pack up fast at the merest suggestion of a Strato-V.

After a fraught few hours, Farley came back with what he had.

"The good news, Chief, is that they're sending someone who knows the big picture. They must be taking it real seriously because they're inserting him by air. Presuming whoever it is makes it, you're to rendezvous with him tonight at these coordinates."

Mercer squinted. "These are incomplete."

"Yeah. That's the bad news, Chief. The whole message is incomplete. The radiation interfered with reception or something. The back half of the transmission was garbled. I'd have asked them to resend and clarify, but I was picking up Sov surveillance drones. Seriously, my proximity detector was pinging so loud I had to turn it off."

THEY MOVED OUT at nightfall. Mercer gave them a last word.

"All I can say is that we meet our guy at 2300. We don't know exactly where, but it has to be somewhere this side of our objective. He's going to be coming in by air so all we have to do is look out for an H-Wagon. It's not like there's going to be more than one out tonight.

"Questions? No? Good. Mount up."

FIFTEEN

THEY CAME IN along Inter-sector 200. It was the obvious approach.

The Sovs didn't use I-200 because its southward stretch turned to glass before it abruptly disappeared into the Sector 208 crater. The highway also brought them near the approximate rendezvous point they'd been given. The sabotaged weather system was still in their favour, the snow having turned to rain. It sheeted down, cold and most likely contaminated, but it would shield them from enemy eyes. Besides, a Judge shouldn't mind a little discomfort.

"We halt here," said Mercer. "Try and get out of this gruddamn rain."

It was 2300 hours, and there was no sign of their contact. Their Lawmasters' sensors had been stealthily scanning ahead as far as they could reach for the past hour but had picked up nothing. Mercer huddled in the shelter of some ruins to fiddle with the scanners, while the other two were sent out on a search.

"An H-Wagon isn't going to linger in these circumstances," he told them. "But it'll at least need an H-Wagon-sized stretch of open ground to set down one guy and maybe his bike. Go see what you can see."

Steinman found it first.

"Lookee here, partner," he said, and Robinson joined him by a pile of wreckage. It was burnt and twisted to hell and gone, but Robinson was familiar enough with these things that she could recognise it from an intact engine mounting alone.

"H-Wagon."

"Yup."

"Drokk it."

"You said it."

It could have been here since the first bombs fell or it could have come down an hour ago. The rain made it impossible to tell. They examined the crash site as best they could, but there was no indication of what had brought the H-Wagon down, and there were certainly no survivors. There wasn't even anything recognisable left of the crew except for one Judge's helmet, badly charred.

Steinman picked it up and contemplated it.

"Another good Judge gone," he said, and Robinson knew that he was thinking not just about the people they'd lost today, and all the Justice Department personnel who'd been killed since this whole thing began, but about two SJS Judges who'd been murdered a few days back up on the thirty-fourth floor of Sector House 212.

"Let it go, Steinman," she said, which could apply either to his remorse or to the battered helmet in his hand. There was a more important matter to consider.

"YOU THINK THIS crashed H-Wagon was our guy's?" asked Mercer.

"Impossible to say, Chief."

"Drokk it," he said and then, with more decision, "Drokk it. We go ahead anyway. Three of us or four: what's the difference? And how much could some big-shot from Resistance Central tell us about a Sov base that we can't find out ourselves?"

"Way to go, Chief," said Steinman.

Three of us or four, thought Robinson. Against a few hundred Sovs and approximately two gazillion war droids. What's the difference? As long as one Judge draws breath, right?

And she resigned herself to following Mercer, who was maybe nuts, and Steinman, who was maybe on some suicide trip, because she was a Judge, and it was her duty.

But then a very small light blinked on Mercer's scanner.

It was the Identify Friend or Foe interrogator on the Lawmaster, and out there in the rainy dark it had just recognised one of its own.

They kept their hands on their Lawgivers as the contact homed in on them.

"Where the hell were you?" asked Mercer, as the Lawmaster drew to a stop.

"Where the hell were you?" replied the rider. "You should have been three clicks east of here. Be glad it was me who found you and not the Sovs."

"We got sent incomplete information. Who are you?"

"Morant. Intelligence. This all there is of you?"

Intelligence. A back-room world of subterfuge and chicanery. A world away from the forthright head-busting done by honest street Judges.

"Yeah," said Mercer. "This is all there is of us. It's enough."

SIXTEEN

It was still dark, and still raining, when they took up an observation position. Their objective was hard to miss. It was a hundred and twenty square kilometres of airport and industrial complex and was the only place in all the northern sectors that appeared to have the power back on.

Morant had a map of the area. ("He's got a map!" muttered Mercer. "No wonder they risked flying the guy across the city for us!") There was any number of ways they could get in, but all that meant was that there was a whole bunch of ways they could get themselves killed.

The whole place had been built in consideration of Mega-City One's criminal element and what that element might attempt in the unlawful acquisition of high-end robotics, uncustomed freight and, in short, anything that wasn't welded to the floor. In other words, the security at Industrial Zone 199 was pretty comprehensive, and the invaders had only added to it. The inevitable Sentenoids could be easily seen, patrolling beyond the perimeter, moving like giant mechanical crabs.

"Sentenoids we can get past," said Steinman, either because he was overconfident to the point of delusion, or because he was just showing off to Judge Intelligence here.

But Judge Intelligence wasn't so easily impressed. Morant kept his binoculars glued to his shrewd narrow face, taking in the gates, checkpoints, and watchtowers that marked the way in.

"Get me to the control room just inside Gate 4," he said. "I get in there and I should be able to disrupt their security for just long enough."

"Gate 4 it is," said Mercer. "Your wish is our command."

"Look, Mercer—I'm not here to step on any toes. This is your operation. I'm just telling you what I need that'll make your job easier."

"OK. Fair enough. I appreciate it, Morant. But what I was kind of hoping for was something like a secret tunnel that would lead us to the big self-destruct button inside. You help us with that?"

"No secret tunnels, Chief, but Gate 4 would be just fine."

And that "Chief" was seemingly all it took for Mercer to warm to Morant. This outsider—this man who'd never stood and fought for Sector 212—had just got himself accepted. Maybe they taught those guys in Intelligence something about diplomacy.

But Mercer's acceptance of Morant still left them with the overwhelming problem of numbers. If the resistance had had any more people to send, they'd have sent them.

It wasn't even as if there were any Citi-Def units that could be deputised. The whole area surrounding them was either wasteland or ghost town—the inhabitants fled south or, more likely, lying dead in the ruins.

And then Robinson, who was keeping watch to the rear, saw another ping on her scanner.

She told Mercer. Mercer told her to check it out.

It was another Lawmaster.

Not taking any chances, she chose a vantage point and waited for the intruder, weapons hot. For all she knew, the Sovs had hacked the Justice Department system and found a way to falsify recognition signatures. But the vehicle that appeared was department-issued and the rider was in the uniform of a Mega-City Judge, and he hailed Robinson with a west-side accent.

"You Mercer?" he asked, politely ignoring that she had him on weapons-lock.

"Robinson," she said. "Who are you?"

"He says his name's McDonald, Chief. Says he was assigned to our mission."

"So who the hell's this guy?" said Mercer.

"Morant," said Morant. "Intelligence. We've been through this."

"And you know about this McDonald?"

"Negative, Chief. Never heard of him. Far as I know I'm the only one assigned to your team."

The new arrival was sitting apart, with Steinman's Lawgiver not-quite trained on him. Mercer called to him.

"Hey you! McDonald!" and, indicating Morant, "You know this guy?"

"Can't say I do, but then I was assigned kind of last minute. I rode up all the way from Sector 155. All I was told is that you've got a robotics facility to target."

"And that's relevant how?"

McDonald pulled open his rad cloak to show his badge. "I'm a Tek. I do robotics."

"So why does Central—or the Resistance, or whatever it's calling itself these days—send us a Tek? I could have brought my own Teks if I'd wanted. And what are you doing out here in the middle of nowhere, huh? About five hundred clicks behind enemy lines? Care to tell me that, 'McDonald'?"

"What can I tell you that I haven't already? I was assigned."

With communications the way they were, there was really no way of getting anyone to verify anyone's credentials out here, but before Mercer took his interrogation to the next level, Robinson gently took him to one side.

"I think he's on the up and up, Chief. Seriously. I mean does he look like a Sov?"

And Mercer had to admit that with the possible exception of a few Central Asian types, all the East-Meggers he'd ever seen had been white.

"Fair point, Robinson. I'll give him the benefit of the doubt. But keep your eye on him all the same." And then, "Hey, McDonald! Whaddaya say? Find me a way through Gate 4 there and we let you stay."

"It's a deal, Chief," said McDonald. "I'm on it."

To their quiet amazement, McDonald did actually have an idea that did actually look as if it might actually give them a chance. Steinman and Robinson watched as he began setting it in motion.

"He seems to be the real deal all right," said Steinman. "Funny they didn't warn us he was coming."

"Yeah," said Robinson. "Or, on the other hand, maybe they did warn us, and we just didn't get that part of the message."

"Like maybe he's the one we were supposed to rendezvous with in the first place?"

"Yeah. And maybe this 'Morant' guy is a Sov plant."

"Yeah," said Steinman. "Gives us something to think about, doesn't it?"

SEVENTEEN

"So you're going to kidnap a Sentenoid?"

"We're going to kidnap a Sentenoid."

"Because that's going to be real easy, right?"

"If you've got a better idea, Robinson, I'm all ears."

After the brief, telling silence, McDonald went on. "Trust me—I know my robotics. Sentenoids aren't that complex. Once I crack one open, I can completely reorient it in just a few seconds. It goes from being their Sentenoid to our Sentenoid. That's our way in."

"We just have to crack one open? As in physically unscrew its head plate, or pop its hood or whatever?"

"Yeah, well—I admit that part's going to be tricky."

Mercer cut in. "We've handled enough Sentenoids these past couple of days. We can do this."

Robinson had a pretty good idea who the 'we' would be in this little adventure. Mercer had been made sector chief because he'd sustained a severe injury a while back. Desk duties were his thing. He might still be a tough guy, but getting intimate with a war droid would be too much to expect of him. She resigned herself to McDonald's scheme.

But the more they worked on the practical details, the less and less she liked it. As expected, she and Steinman, who had hard-won experience in this kind of escapade, were expected to creep out across the waste ground, stalking their chosen Sentenoid—one that was separated from its fellows—and then somehow lure it back to dead ground, bushwhack it, and let McDonald do his thing before anyone would miss it. And this would be in daylight, and the rain had eased off. Still unable to cook up a failsafe way of managing this, they were so far looking at a plan that was founded largely on positive thinking.

"Maybe we could skip all this Sentenoid stuff?" Robinson suggested in frustration. "What do you say we just walk right up to the front door and bluff our way in? You know Steinman here does a great Sov act? All Hail-Supreme-Judge-Bulgarin stuff. Totally convincing."

"Bulgarin isn't in charge any more," said Morant.

Their questioning looks demanded that he elaborate.

"You didn't know? Palace coup. Whole Diktatorat was ousted. Permanently. War-Marshal Kazan's in charge of the whole show now."

"Kazan's the guy who looks like Bulgarin but with eye shields, right? The guy who's been in command of the invasion forces? That Kazan?" asked Steinman.

"That Kazan. The Mad Dog, they call him," said Morant.

"And how do you know about this coup thing?" asked Robinson.

"Like I say—I'm in intelligence."

"Sure. I forgot. So anyway—this Sentenoid."

THE PLAN WAS still too sketchy for comfort when the time came to put it into effect, but at least McDonald seemed to know his job. Once a suitable candidate for conversion had been chosen, he targeted it with a faint signal that drew it in.

"That droid's the only one picking up the signal, and it's recognising it as something unspecific but worthy of its attention. I'll keep switching it on and off. That'll keep the Sentenoid interested but won't give it enough time to work out what it is. You two work your way in close, and as soon as it gets this side of that wall, make with the scrambler grenade. Whatever you do, don't let it see you."

"What was that last part again? I'll try to remember."

But McDonald made adjustments to the directional transmitter he was holding and ignored the remark.

It took forever but no one got killed.

Once everyone had managed to get into position, their main problem was attracting the attention of one—and only one—Sentenoid. When three picked up on the signal at once and closed in to investigate, McDonald had to shut everything down for nearly an hour until the machines lost interest and returned to their patrol lines. Then he had to start the whole process again, while Robinson and Steinman edged their way through the ruins, trying to remain undetected while at the same time trying to find a halfway favourable position from which they could jump on their prey when the time came.

When it finally did look like the right time, and a Sentenoid was almost within range, it suddenly changed course, having evidently given up on the confusing signal that had been bothering it. When that happened, Steinman saw no option other than to stand up and wave at the dumb droid, which gave Robinson the chance she needed to throw the scrambler. With the Sentenoid temporarily confused, the two Judges froze in place, praying that the incident had passed unnoticed. They were still hugging the ground when McDonald came sprinting up.

"What are you waiting for?" he said. "Come on—I'll need help lifting off the cranial armour."

The operation was conducted in a slight hollow behind what was left of a wall. Anyone who happened to stroll within a hundred metres of the place would have seen it.

But McDonald knew his stuff, and he had not been lying when he said the process would only take a few seconds. The only hard part was opening the robot up. After that, it was just a matter of plugging something in and pushing a few buttons.

Robinson watched with some alarm as the Sentenoid fired up again. Its sensor array swivelled, and its huge arms flexed, but McDonald's fix had worked.

"OK, you ugly drokker," he said with something close to affection, "Go back to your buddies like nothing's happened and I'll call you when we're ready."

And the Sov war droid did as it was told.

EIGHTEEN

"ALL RIGHT—THE TAKING of Sector 199, Phase Two: getting inside the drokking place," said Mercer. "Everybody ready to go?"

It was dark, and the whole team was waiting in the ruins, as close to Gate 4 as they dared. The only traffic that had passed since they'd been watching had been massive recovery vehicles heading in. Outward traffic evidently went by another gate. The drivers of these vehicles were humans, as were the guards on the gate, and humans, as McDonald pointed out, are subject to miscommunication and misunderstanding.

"Show a robot something screwed up, and it'll see it as a problem that needs to be worked out. Show a human, and he'll assume it's some other guy's stupid fault. His instinct is to look for blame, not for a cause or a solution."

"Let's hope so," said Mercer. "Sensors say the next vehicle is four minutes out. Let's get our tame Sentenoid in place."

They saw the searchlights reflecting off its casing as it approached.

"This had better be our boy, McDonald."

"Don't sweat it, Chief. I'd know my baby anywhere."

The sinister robot crunched its way over the rubble and onto the roadway. When it reached the gate, it snaked out one of its arms and rammed its claw into an access panel, sending a searing bolt of electricity into the workings of the gate. Then the whole two tons of Sentenoid settled itself down in the middle of the road and shut itself down.

The Mega-City Judges watched as more lights came on, and they heard voices raised in query. Two Sov Judges came outside to see what had happened just as a great big truck drew up outside the gate.

The drivers were Sov combat engineers and for two days now they had been recovering broken-down military hardware from an irradiated battlefield, often under fire, driving it across a blasted and hostile landscape, and then turning around and doing it all over again. They were far from amused to come rolling up to the base only to find their prospect of a hot meal and maybe a short rest was being denied them by a malfunctioning Sentenoid and a blocked gate.

They got down from the cab and met up with the guards who had come out from the security post. There was a lot of shouting and back-and-forth recrimination, and everyone within hailing distance arrived to see what was going on and what could be done to resolve this. In the end, the gate had to be forced open with crowbars and after that the Sentenoid was winched onto the back of the recovery vehicle. In peacetime, with regular citizens on the job, this could have taken all night, with possibly a fistfight being involved somewhere along the line, but the East-Meg war machine was nothing if not efficient, and no less than ten minutes after the delinquent Sentenoid had shorted the gate's circuitry, everything was back to normal, except that Gate 4 was jammed wide open for the time being and a team of five Mega-City Judges had slipped in while the Sovs had been arguing.

"No shooting," said Morant. "I mean it. If the Sovs know we're here, then all bets are off."

"We heard you the first couple of times," said Mercer. "Stealthy it is. Just make sure you know where you're going."

Beyond the gate, the complex appeared to be deserted, but Mercer's team weren't taking anything for granted. Robinson took the lead. Shooting might have been off limits, but if a Judge couldn't stab a guy in the throat or silently snap his neck, then she didn't deserve the honour of policing the streets of Mega-City One.

She was taking the lead because she was young and fast, but also because she couldn't quell her misgivings. So far, everything about Morant seemed above board, and if he was leading them into a trap, she couldn't for the life of her imagine why the Sovs would go to all this trouble. Still, if things did go bad, she'd be the first to know about it.

For much the same reason, Steinman was bringing up the rear. If things went bad, he could at least shoot Morant in the back of the head.

The door that Morant wanted was on a little-used corridor, and the lock yielded to the standard Justice Department key card. There was no East-Meg hit squad waiting for them inside. Indeed, there was nothing more dangerous than a deactivated floor-polishing robot that Robinson nearly tripped over in the dark.

"They didn't bother fixing the lighting here," said Morant, switching on a torch. "That's a good sign."

"So if it's no use to the Sovs, why do we want it?"

"We want it because it's connected with the central control system. The whole facility has been progressively automated down the years, but they didn't get around to getting rid of these last few control rooms when they laid off the human staff. We get things started up again here and we should have some sort of access to the RMR manufacturing plant, to the transport net, the works. There isn't a big red self-destruct button like you wanted, Chief, but all we have to do is find the On switch and we're inside."

Mercer grinned. "And once we're inside, we can hurt them, correct?"

"You got it."

They got the computer up and running, and Morant was able to call up schematics of the whole vast complex. Acutely conscious of where they were, and how dangerously close to the enemy, they kept the lights low, with one person watching the door at all times, while the rest of them crowded round the screens and planned the operation in low voices. Robinson reflected that it all looked like some sort of terrorist cell but, then again, that's pretty much what it was: just a handful of true believers conspiring to strike against a monolithic tyranny from within. Hell—they were even talking about making explosives from commonly found industrial solvents. Take away the uniforms and you were looking at the Sector 212 Three, along with a couple of shadowy accomplices, all wanted for acts of sabotage and politically motivated violence.

All it takes is one little regime change, she thought, and suddenly you're an enemy of the state.

"Place is pretty damn big," said Steinman. "It'll take us a long time to even get wherever we need to go, never mind doing any real damage."

"The bigger they are, the harder they fall," said Mercer. "Anyway, we can make the size of the place work for us. The Sovs have only reactivated a few areas, and that gives us plenty of places to hide. We sure as hell can't stay here much longer—not with the enemy just one floor below us."

"I can stay here," said Morant. "I can run comms from here. We'll be able to talk to each other without the risk of anyone tracking our signals."

"I don't know about the rest of you," said McDonald, "but my priority is the RMR factory. You blow up what you need to blow up, but I need to be inside the place for at least a couple of hours and I need the Sovs to be looking somewhere else while I'm doing my job."

"That means a diversion," said Mercer. "What say we cause a little mayhem in the airport? It's nearly two clicks from RMR. An exploding fuel dump or something should draw their attention well away from whatever it is you'll be doing."

"Works for me, Chief."

"OK," said Morant. "But I need you to lay off the mayhem until then. You meet any patrols, you steer clear. Do not engage. The minute they think something is wrong is the minute they start putting things together. That means the first place they'll start nosing around will be Gate 4, and that I don't need."

It seemed reasonable, but Morant emphasised the point.

"I've plotted you a way around all the areas where the Sovs appear active, but you'll have to go through here—Green Eighteen—where there's a lot of foot traffic, so lie low, for drokk's sake, until it's safe. No killing. I can patch into their PA and fool them into clearing that area for a while, but don't take any chances."

And that seemed to settle it. Mercer and Steinman would do the loud stuff, while Robinson helped out McDonald with the quiet stuff and Morant stayed behind.

They headed out right away. If the Sovs could overrun half the city in four days—and they had—then time was something that Mega-City One didn't have a whole lot left of.

NINETEEN

THEY WERE STILL careful, but they weren't moving like cat burglars any more. Mercer reckoned they could pick up some speed while they had Morant watching over them. They followed a green line painted on the floor, and as they came to a sign pointing them towards Zones 16 to 20, they heard Morant's voice over the public address.

"What's he saying?"

"Something about a suspected radiation leak in Green Eighteen. All personnel to stay clear until something something. He was speaking too fast, but I think maintenance robots were in there somewhere."

"Good enough for me. Let's make the most of it."

But before the group split up, Robinson and Steinman felt it was a matter of urgency that they fill their chief in on their suspicions.

"Hey, McDonald," said Steinman. "You want to scout ahead as far as that gantry? Should be able to get a good view from there."

"Hey, Chief," said Robinson. "You want to run through

something for a second before we all go our separate ways?"

The Sector 212 Three got into a huddle by a fire escape, Mercer impatient at this last-second delay.

"What's the matter? Didn't we cover everything back there with Morant?"

"That's the thing, Chief. What do we really know about the guy?"

"Oh come on. This again?"

"Listen. Me and Steinman have been thinking it over, and we think it smells bad."

"Grud, Robinson—if it'll keep you and Steinman happy, then go on and make your case, but make it snappy."

"OK. One: Morant wasn't at the rendezvous. What was at the rendezvous was a crashed H-Wagon—possibly the H-Wagon that was to deliver our guy, maybe intercepted by a Strato-V that knew where to look. Two: he knows an awful lot about East-Meg stuff. Three: we just heard him speaking Sov like a native. Four: he doesn't like killing Sovs. Five: what the hell is he even doing, Chief?"

Mercer kept his patience because in his years as a sector chief he'd had a lot of practice in dealing with damn-fool questions from underlings. But seriously—didn't they teach the kids detective work at the Academy any more?

"That's all you've got? Now you listen to me, the both of you. One: the rendezvous was a crap-shoot. He might have been where he was supposed to be, and it was us who were in the wrong place. That H-Wagon could have been brought down last week. You said so yourself. Two: the guy's in Intelligence, and even then I'd bet that we'd know what he knows about the Sovs if we could just tune into the news. Three: so he speaks better Sov than you do. Good for him. He'd be a pretty lousy intelligence analyst if he didn't. Four: give him time. Five: see point four. Happy now?

"I mean seriously—if he's one of them, why this whole rigmarole? He could have stopped us with four bullets anytime he wanted."

"I don't know, Chief," put in Steinman. "Maybe they might want us alive for some reason. All I know is that I've got a really bad feeling about Morant."

"A feeling? You've got a feeling now, Steinman? Well, maybe you should apply for a transfer to Psi Division when all this is over. Now could we just get the hell out of here? Come on. Let's just do the job."

Mercer and Steinman headed off one way and Robinson rejoined McDonald. He saw the look on her face. "Everything OK?"

"Fine. Just stay off comms as much as possible."

"But comms are safe. The Sovs won't be monitoring signals inside the facility, and we've got Morant keeping an eye on everything for us."

"Yeah. But let's just stay off comms, OK?"

As they moved silently down corridors and across walkways, Robinson tried to put her suspicions to one side. Maybe Morant was a straight shooter like Mercer maintained, but she couldn't dispel the thought of the downed H-Wagon and how Morant had shown up.

But then if she wanted to be eaten up by her doubts,

she should consider that McDonald had shown up the same way, with a story no more verifiable than Morant's. Did East-Meg One have some sort of alliance with the Pan-African State that she didn't know about? Had they gone to a lot of trouble to create a believable Judge McDonald?

And the question remained: why go to all the trouble?

"Just give it a rest, Robinson," she said to herself.

"You say something?" asked McDonald.

"Zone Green Eighteen. We're here. Stay sharp."

TWENTY

As HAD BEEN noted, it was a huge complex—a city sector all to itself—but while there were a lot of places to hide, there were also a few places they'd just have to walk through openly and hope for the best. One such stretch was now right in front of them, a wide-open warehouse space so big that you could park an armoured division there, and that's just what the Sovs had done. But the robot tanks appeared to be inert, and there was no one to be seen.

"You think you could maybe reprogram these things?" asked Robinson.

"Sure, if we can spare a couple of days. You think you could maybe blow them all up?"

"Why not? If what I heard about a vent on the turret is true, and if I had enough hand bombs. And sure, if I had until, say, Friday."

"So how about we forget about these ones and just go straight to the source?"

"Agreed."

"How about as fast as we can?"

"Agreed."

Their path lay straight ahead of them, and they hastened past rank upon rank of silent Rad-sweepers, praying that the robots really were shut down; praying that the Sovs hadn't yet had the time to make any but the most necessary repairs to the facility. There was minor but widespread war damage all over. If the surveillance cameras had been brought back online, then things were about to get pretty hairy.

They had only a hundred or so metres left to go before an automated voice shrieked at them.

"Security! Halt! Identify yourselves!"

They whipped around to face a security droid, guns pointing. The robot was a standard indoor patrol model, and the designation stencilled on its casing revealed it to be of Mega-City manufacture, which matched the Megspeak in which it had challenged them.

"I repeat: identify yourselves."

Robinson tapped her badge. "What do we look like? We're Judges."

"Nuh-uh. Judges don't dress like that any more. No more black and gold. All green and red now."

"I repeat: we're Judges."

"Look, no offence, lady, but uniforms aside, you're both too beat-up-looking to be Judges. Real Judges got standards. Stay where I can see you. I'm calling this in."

And that's when McDonald shot it.

He knew this model. The armour-piercer drilled right through a specific spot on its box-like form and the droid shut down in an instant.

"You think it had time to send out an alert?" asked Robinson. But it didn't matter. The shot had rung out loud in the echoing space, and already another security droid was appearing from between the long aisles of tanks.

"Hey, Judge! What gives? That's Dave-9745 you just shot!"

Robinson eased off on the trigger. "You recognise us as Judges?"

"The big eagles kinda give you away. Why weren't we notified that Justice Department was on-site, and what did Dave do?"

"This robot was being obstructive."

"It figures. That was Dave all over. So what can I do for you?"

"What's your designation?"

"I'm Larry-8722."

"All right, Larry. You can scout out a way for us to get inside RMR. The repair and production lines. We want wherever it is they're setting up the war robots. And we want to get there undetected."

"But I'm assigned here."

"You want to accept reassignment, or do you want us to consider you obstructive too?"

"Judges. Sheesh. OK, follow me."

They shoved the remains of Dave-9745 out of the way and followed, while Larry-8722 made conversation.

"Listen, we got a radiation warning for this area. I don't detect squat, but humes had better take care all the same, you know?"

"That warning was a false alarm," said Robinson.

"You sure? Well, if you're investigating a hoax call, I wouldn't go leaping to conclusions. I mean, since the other day we've had structural damage, chemical spills, fires, you name it. And the radiation levels have been crazy. I mean for real. The last warning is probably just a hume making an honest mistake. You should maybe go easy on him."

"I'll take that under advisement. Tell me about the new management here."

"What can I tell you, Judge? I hear these guys are from the East-Meg, but they're management, so we don't see them down here. They brought in new people, though. Organic labour."

"These organics wear uniforms? Green and red? Helmets a little like Judge helmets? Hammer and sickle insignia?"

"Those are the ones. Look, I've nothing against humes, but what's the point of them? We'd almost got Sector 199 one hundred per cent automated. Why bring humes back?"

"Don't worry about it. You just run along a hundred metres in front of us and make sure we don't come across any."

TWENTY-ONE

THE SECURITY DROID was all they could wish for in a point man. With the authority of Justice Department behind it, it bullied his way through the industrial maze. Human and robot alike were moved on with a toneless and peremptory, "Security. Clear this area," and even when Sov personnel ignored it, as was usually the case, the Mega-City Judges heard all about it over a comms link and could alter their course accordingly.

They sent Larry back to his regular duties when they finally arrived at where they needed to be, where a rail line met a loading dock. There they saw automated cranes lifting broken-down Rad-sweepers and Sentenoids from trucks onto conveyors, all under a colossal sign welcoming them to Robots Makin' Robots—So You Don't Have To!

There were a couple of East-Meg technicians running checks of some kind, but they were the only people to be seen, and they didn't appear to be on the lookout for trouble. It was a small matter to slip past them in the mist raised by the decontamination hoses.

Inside was the biggest junkyard they had ever seen. Every East-Meg war machine that had fallen victim to the high-explosives and the lasers, to the stub guns and the thermal charges, was here to be stripped down and salvaged.

"Just doesn't seem fair," said Robinson. "We did all this damage, and we're the ones who are losing. What's it going to take to stop these drokkers?"

And then she had to move fast because one of the broken robots hadn't been stopped yet. A steel tentacle lashed out but flailed uselessly in the air once Robinson was out of reach. The robot couldn't go lurching after her because its chassis had been ripped clean away.

Robinson cursed and picked herself up. "The thing's just one arm and a lump of half-melted circuitry. How the hell does it do that?"

"Karpov MF7 Sentenoid," said McDonald, with something resembling admiration. "Takes a licking, keeps on ticking."

"Makes you wonder why we don't have anything comparable."

"You wonder? You remember the Robot War, Robinson?"

"Sure. Who doesn't?"

"Well, imagine what it would have been like if Call-Me-Kenneth had had access to Sentenoids and Rad-sweepers."

"Robot dictatorship in no time flat. Right."

"Right. And you know who else liked war droids? Robert L. Booth, that's who. There's a hundred thousand dead guys and a big war memorial out in

Death Valley in case we needed reminding why it's a bad idea to arm robots."

"OK. I get the picture."

"This is why we don't—and never will—have robot Judges. You do not give a machine the power of life and death over a human, Robinson."

"Jeez. Right. I hear you, McDonald. Thank you for sharing your views."

"Sorry. Like I say, robotics is my thing, and I saw the Robot War up closer than I'd have liked. Anyway— what say we teach that lesson to the Sovs?"

EVEN THOUGH THERE were no guards to avoid, it took thirty minutes to walk from the salvage bays to the production lines. All of RMR's normal work had been suspended in order to further the East-Meg war effort. The house-sized factory robots were now working exclusively on Sentenoids and Rad-sweepers. It wasn't just maintenance and repair either. As soon as the Sovs seized Sector 199 and got the plant up and running again, RMR started turning out factory-new war machines.

"And that's where we can really hurt them," said McDonald. "We can't go from robot to robot, converting each one, but if we get inside Production Control, then I can sabotage every new machine that's built here."

But Production Control was the one place in all this automation where there were sure to be humans, and that's where the soft approach would have to harden.

It was, as was to be expected, a brightly lit area that commanded a view of as much of the factory as possible, so the two Judges had no difficulty in finding it. From the shadows of an overhead gantry, they assessed their target.

"Minimal staff," said McDonald. "I count six technicians. No security on the door. We can get in and shut them down before anyone raises the alarm."

"No security that we can see. I think we have to assume roving patrols, or radio check-ins at the very least. Whichever—it won't take long for someone to notice that it's all gone silent in there."

"So we stick to the plan. Let Mercer do his thing."

"Roger that," said Robinson, who risked opening up a channel to the other team.

"Robinson. How are things your end, Chief?"

"A little behind schedule," Mercer responded, "But give us fifteen. No, wait. Steinman says twenty. He's got a plan. Something about crashing a fuel truck into a fuel truck. If it works, it should take out a whole line of Strato-Vs. Could also get Steinman turned into a black stain on the tarmac, but he seems OK with that. You ask me, the guy's crazy. Anyway, you'll get your diversion. Stand by."

Eighteen minutes after the call, Robinson and McDonald had the door to Production Control in sight. When they heard explosions, or the fire alarms, or even just a brief message over the radio, they were going through that door shooting. Those Sov technicians would be dead on the floor before any of them could ever push another button. After all the sneaking around and the enforced silence, it would be good to do something meaningful again.

"Thirty seconds," said Robinson. Then, into her radio, "All set, Chief?"

But it wasn't Mercer who answered. Cutting in came Morant's voice.

"All of you! Stand down! Whatever it is you're doing, you'd better hold off. I mean it."

"This is Mercer. What the hell, Morant? You'd better have one good explanation for this."

"Check the vid. Public broadcasting. Dammit—any network. Any channel. Just check the vid."

"What's this about?"

"I think the war's over, Chief. I think we've just surrendered."

TWENTY-TWO

FOR A MAN who'd been severely injured on the first day of a war that he'd pretty much lost, Chief Judge Griffin was looking remarkably chipper. It wasn't a look that they were used to seeing. True, a Chief Judge was in the public eye and had to strive to be relatable to some degree, but what Robinson and McDonald were now seeing on a break-room vid screen was not the face of the Justice Department they were used to. The Chief Judge's cheerful grin did not sit well with the grim eye-patch and the severe white crew-cut. More jarring still was the message. In a reassuring tone, Griffin was ordering all Mega-City forces to cease resistance forthwith.

With the message playing on constant loop in the background, the Judges conducted a hasty and impassioned radio conference.

"Just what in the name of Grud is this crap?" demanded Mercer.

"It's a load of stomm. It's a fake. It has to be," said Robinson.

"It looks pretty convincing," contributed Steinman. "That's not just Griffin. That's the press briefing room in Grand Hall. It all looks real."

"It is real," cut in Morant. "The Sovs captured Grand Hall yesterday. I don't know how they got the Chief Judge—I heard he'd been evacuated off-world—but that's definitely him. I'm here running one analysis after another on the signal, the picture, the voice, everything. It's no fake. That's Griffin."

Robinson let that sink in. "So does that mean that's it? The war's really over?"

"The war's still going on," said Mercer. "Listen up, all of you. We don't serve the Chief Judge. We serve the law. We serve Mega-City One, and Mega-City One is under attack by the forces of a foreign power. So, even if that is Griffin on the vid, I don't care what Griffin says. The war is still going on because I intend to keep it going on. So all of you, back to your positions. We're here to strike a blow for justice, not to stand around watching TV. The shooting starts in five. Mercer out."

FIVE MINUTES LATER, Robinson and McDonald saw the lights flicker and heard a distant rumble. They kicked in the door of the control centre and started killing Sovs.

McDonald got to work on the manufacturing programs, but there wasn't a whole lot for Robinson to do. She left him to it and scouted out the perimeter, on the lookout for any Sovs that hadn't been fooled by the diversion at the airport and might be wondering why no one in Production Control was picking up the phone.

She climbed up onto a dormant Rad-sweeper to get a better view of the approaches, and noticed with some amusement that there was no sign of any sort of vent on the left side of the tank's turret.

"Hand bomb, my ass," she said to herself. She also noticed, however, that an armoured access panel looked very much the same as the one on the Sentenoid that they'd waylaid to get them in here in the first place. It made sense. If the Sovs were all about the mass production of robust military hardware, interchangeability of parts was a good idea.

From helping McDonald doctor that Sentenoid, she was confident that she would be able to do it herself, given that the Tek Judge had the conversion code already written up and the necessary tools were right here to hand. In the spirit of experimentation, and because standing idle was not in her nature, she went to work on the tank.

It was probably pointless, of course. Even though it only took her a couple of minutes, what was one tank out of all these metal legions? McDonald's way of poisoning the well at source was the only way to go. So, that little bit of mischief out of her system, she returned to the control room to see how things were going.

Even though he was doing nothing beyond typing into a computer, McDonald was sweating with concentration.

"Nearly there," he said.

She relayed this to Mercer, who sounded like he was having a good time, despite everything.

"Say again, Robinson," he shouted to her over the background gunfire. "We seem to have the Sovs a little riled up here."

"We're nearly there, Chief. Disengage as soon as."

"Roger that. Falling back on the rendezvous point. And by the way—you and McDonald might want to take cover. I'm looking at the liquid fuel storage facility and I think a fire there would cover our retreat nicely. Morant, you getting this? I need you to access whatever system can get me through the door. I'd hi-ex it, but I don't think that would be a good idea with me and Steinman standing so close. Door is numbered Tango Two. South side of fuelling area. Looks like a standard Willoughby-type security mechanism. Get it open fast."

She left him to it, glad he sounded so happy, and more than a little sorry she wasn't out there with him and Steinman, fighting their way back from the burning airport. It'd be just like old times.

"Where we at now?" she asked McDonald, who was stabbing at a console in frustration.

"Problem," he said. "Everything's ready to roll, but it looks like the Sovs installed an extra security measure. I need the codes for today to initiate the whole process."

"Morant can help you with that. He's just doing something for the chief."

But whatever had to be done would have to be done fast because a security monitor revealed a squad of four Sov Judges entering the production area below.

The place was so big that it would take them a little while to get here, but when they did, all they'd have to do was look up and see two Mega-City Judges engaged in nefarious acts.

McDonald appreciated the urgency. "Morant, I need today's unlocking codes! Immediate!"

Robinson took up a firing position by the control room door, poised for fight or flight, and probably a lot of both. Over the radio she heard Mercer again.

"Morant, I need that door open, and I mean right now!"

"Morant! Respond!"

"Morant!"

But the transmissions were answered only by silence.

TWENTY-THREE

THE CHOSEN RENDEZVOUS point was a rooftop hover port. The plan had been to steal something mobile and get out fast while the Sovs were dealing with exploding aircraft and rampaging robots. That plan now required radical and unfortunate alteration.

Mercer had given up yelling into his radio at Morant. Morant was old news, spilt milk. What mattered now was getting his team out of there.

"Scrub the RV point!" he told Robinson. "There's too many Sovs between us and there! We'll fight our way back towards you, and you fight towards us. We'll meet wherever we meet."

There was no point in coming up with anything more specific. They couldn't cook up any sort of a better plan over the radio: not with Morant possibly still listening, and Morant probably compromised.

While Mercer was improvising, Steinman was conducting an impressive one-man rearguard action against Sov Judges that were aiming to hem them in.

Gotta hand it to the kid, thought Mercer. Judge-killer he may be, but he doesn't let the odds bother him.

"Steinman! Fall back before they bring robots to outflank us. Move!"

OVER IN THE RMR production lines, Robinson started shooting. The Sov patrol was going to notice what was going on with McDonald's shenanigans in a few seconds anyway, so she might as well get the drop on them while she could. Even with a Lawgiver's integral optics and stabilisers, bringing down a man-sized target from three hundred metres was no mean feat, and despite the desperate straits, Robinson was immensely pleased with herself. Her second shot missed, but that was only to be expected since the Sovs were diving for cover. Now they'd be calling in backup and edging their way forward and all the other stuff that would give her and McDonald a little time.

McDonald needed more than time. He tried and tried to find a way around the locks on the computer system, but when a shot from down on the production floor shattered the window above his console, he gave up, wrecked the sprinkler system, and emptied a clip of incendiary bullets into the various machines before joining Robinson. As the control centre filled with smoke, they made their escape.

For a place that had seemed so deserted, it sure filled up with Sovs fast. Twice Robinson and McDonald were headed off by enemy units, forcing them into one detour after another. Meanwhile, Mercer and Steinman were caught in a running fight that was getting more intense by the minute. They were only able to break contact by bringing down a giant crane to obstruct the enemy. The crane wasn't too happy about it and started quoting the whole RMR Health & Safety manual at them, but Mercer exercised his judicial authority and the crane reluctantly complied.

One thing that the Mega-City Judges had going for them was the Sov reluctance to deploy the heavy robot armoured units. Getting the giant RMR factory up and running in just a couple of days had been the sort of feat achievable only by a merciless dictatorship that doesn't listen to excuses. So having got the place operational, the Sov engineers were not going to see their work crushed under tank tracks. Thus, once inside the factory, Mercer and Steinman only had human pursuit to worry about. Granted, the humans in question were East-Meg Judges, and there were a lot of them, but you count what blessings you have.

The two Mega-City teams were guided towards each other by the sound of small arms fire, and they met up in yet another enormous space that enclosed yet another seemingly endless series of production lines. They were momentarily out of contact with the enemy, but that couldn't last. Multiple units were converging on them.

"You find us a way out, Robinson?" said Mercer.

"Nope. You?"

They were a long way from any rooftop hover port, but McDonald came to the rescue. He didn't have an escape plan, but he had thought up a pretty good hiding place.

TWENTY-FOUR

THE INSPECTION HATCH was big enough for one human, but the area inside had never been designed for four individuals in body armour to hole up for an indefinite period. Crammed in dangerously close to a pair of compressors the size of elevator cars, the Judges hadn't room to sit, let alone move freely. The heat was intense, and the fumes forced them to keep their respirators down. With their helmets' audio-dampers turned up full against the noise of the machinery and their radios shut off to avoid detection, they had no option but to endure in silence, with no idea of how close their enemies might be to finding them.

Their refuge was in one of the larger factory robots, which had made no comment as they'd stuffed themselves inside. McDonald reckoned that, designed as it was to stay bolted in place and turn out heavy-duty machine assemblies, it was unlikely to be too interested in politics. A simple direct instruction from a Mega-City Judge should be sufficient to keep the robot from betraying them to the Sovs.

The hours went by, and the sweat streamed down their cramped limbs. Then, without warning, the machinery shut itself off.

"What's going on?" hissed Mercer.

"Easy to find out," said McDonald. "Robot, what's your designation?"

A toneless electronic voice addressed them from a speaker by the inspection hatch. "Orange Twelve-Nine S-for-Susie," it said.

"Report, Susie. What's going on outside?"

"Orange Sector One through Twenty shut down."

"Why?"

"All production temporarily halted for maintenance."

"What's the nature of this maintenance?"

"Jeez, you think they tell me everything? Stand by."

A moment later, the robot spoke again.

"Orange One-One Z-for Zsa-Zsa says some joker broke into Production Control, dicked around with the programming, and then fried all the hardware. So now they're installing replacement machines."

"So where does all that leave us?" Mercer asked McDonald. "As far as taking a second shot goes?"

"Well, we have to assume that even if the new computers they install are the same as the old ones, the security is going to be upgraded. They're going to have extra guards at the very least."

"Guards we can deal with. What about the unlocking codes or whatever?"

"The problem stands. Unless they're written up on a

clipboard beside the console, then there's not much point in taking over Production Control again."

"We couldn't just ask Susie here?"

"If you guys are talking about the production locking codes," said the robot, "it's above my pay grade. That stuff is just downloaded into my programming every day along with a bunch of other stuff. You'd have to talk to management."

"Susie," said Mercer, "any management personnel in Orange Sector right now?"

"Fifteen. All armed. Not doing any actual work. Just walking around looking at stuff. What do they think? Do I look like I need a supervisor?"

"McDonald, you think you can run a remote access on the production computers from your handheld? Maybe you can crack their system while they're still setting up?"

"No way in hell, Chief."

Mercer addressed his team. They were all jammed up so close together that he didn't have to speak much above a whisper.

"OK, so we can't make the Sov robots go bananas. At least not yet we can't. And we can't go crazy blowing things up—not with enemy patrols on full alert. So, what I'm saying is I'm open to ideas."

But no one had anything to throw in. Being stuck inside a factory robot deep inside enemy territory was pretty much their lot right now.

"Right," said Mercer. "Then let's watch some TV."

There was only one show worth watching. McDonald's handheld was tuned into public broadcasting, and onto a flat panel above their heads, he projected *Curfew Talk*, the new propaganda programme brought live tonight from the Grand Hall of Justice.

"See that you memorise the faces and names of everyone in the studio audience," said Mercer. "When this is over, we'll be coming for those drokking collaborators."

But they weren't watching just to see these run-of-the-mill traitors. Citizens duped into criminality were nothing special. No. They were watching—along with almost everyone in the city still with access to the vid—to see the much-hyped special guest: none other than Chief Judge Griffin himself.

TWENTY-FIVE

THE PROPAGANDA WAS so heavy-handed it was almost laughable. Every word that Griffin spoke was a lie calculated by his puppet masters to deceive the citizens. You couldn't expect subtlety in a situation like this, just like you couldn't expect truth and honesty from a stooge of the enemy.

But it was heart-wrenching all the same to see their Chief Judge, a figure of respect bordering on reverence, sitting in the Grand Hall of Justice of all places, and speaking the words the enemy gave him to speak, and to see him do it smilingly.

Trapped in this overheated space, immobile, with her neck craning to get a view of the picture, Robinson could hardly have been more uncomfortable, but the slow torture inflicted on her body was nothing compared to the dismay she was feeling. A Judge can endure hardship and pain and keep on going, but how could anyone keep up the fight when faced with such betrayal?

The others clearly felt the same way. As the show went on, their curses and derisive comments dried up in the face of this shameful reality.

The Sov host made glib remarks, the hand-picked members of the audience asked their inane questions, and the one-time embodiment of law and order in this city answered them like any politician selling snake oil, or some vapid celebrity promoting his latest worthless effort.

Griffin answered another softball question with another platitude and then—as if it hadn't been bad enough up till now—an East-Meg Judge in the audience raised his hand and Griffin turned the same friendly smile on him. They were watching their own Chief Judge being made to perform tricks in the hall where he had once ruled.

"Turn it off," said Mercer, his voice thick. "Turn it the drokk off."

Just to break the brooding silence that followed, Robinson said, "Sov psycho surgery. Gotta be."

"You think?" said Steinman.

"I read a thing about it. Look at Griffin in close-up. Look at his eyes. He's not really there. Or at least he's there, but he's deep under all that overlay of bull-stomm. It's like hypnosis apparently, but it takes more than a snap of the fingers to get you out of it."

And right then, if she'd had room, she'd have snapped her fingers.

"That's it! That's why Morant didn't off us when he had the chance! They want to do the same thing to us!"

285

"Psycho surgery?"

"What else? Think how useful it would be to have nice compliant Mega-City Judges doing their dirty work for them."

"But there's only four of us," said Steinman.

"They have to start somewhere."

"She's right," said Mercer. "We're Mega-City Judges. The Academy puts fifteen years into each of us. If it only takes the Sovs an extra half hour to screw up our brains, then they're getting us cheap. They get all that expertise. They get us body and soul."

He took the argument to its logical conclusion.

"So, we make sure we don't get taken alive."

And they nodded their heads in grim agreement.

Just for want of something to occupy their attention, they considered turning on the vid again, but just then the machinery restarted, and they were subjected to more heat, more noise, and to air that was even less breathable.

Every few hours they'd take a chance on opening the hatch to see if the coast was clear, but it was a full twenty-four hours before they were able to escape their robot prison. Then, on legs that could barely carry them, they crept away to hide in the lesser-used recesses of the factory complex: a defeated remnant of a defeated army, skulking in the shadows of a city that was no longer theirs.

TWENTY-SIX

BEFORE THEY LIMPED away, they'd tried to persuade Susie the heavy-duty manufacturing droid to introduce failings into the machinery being made, but the robot couldn't alter any specifications without programming from management.

"Besides," it told them, "we got standards here. I start sabotaging production and what's that going to do to RMR's reputation in the industry? Sorry, Judge."

Were there any positives to console them? Robinson remembered the solitary Rad-sweeper she'd worked on just out of curiosity. She had no idea if it had been activated or shipped to the front yet, but if it had, she liked to think of it shirking its duty and letting the rest of its unit down.

And of course there were the Sovs that the Mega-City Judges had killed along the way, and the disruption and material damage to enemy transport and production they'd inflicted; but all of it amounted to no more than a few hours' delay to the East-Meg military juggernaut, and that was all that Mercer's team had achieved in the two days they'd been committed to this mission.

It was a bitter reality that they preferred not to acknowledge, and it was no way to win a war.

For the next couple of days, they lived as fugitives, which sounded a little more dramatic and purposeful than living as bums and vagrants, which Robinson felt was closer to the truth. With the job as yet undone, Mercer was loath to lead an escape from Sector 199, but the heightened Sov security drove them from the RMR factory and kept them out. So, unwilling to break out, and for the moment unable to break back in, they stayed in out-of-the-way places, slipping from one hiding place to another in the half-derelict sector, avoiding enemy patrols and sniffer droids, and surviving as best they could.

"We need to find a new vending machine," said Steinman. "Nothing left in this one except some Gooey Bars and a bag of Snackos."

"What flavour Snackos?" asked Robinson.

"Um, let's see. Spicy spinach flavour."

"You're right. We need to find a new vending machine."

That was a problem in a facility that had almost completely eliminated the human element: there wasn't a whole lot to eat.

"I saw one when we passed through Yellow Five yesterday."

"I saw it too but seeing as there's a Sov post in the middle of Yellow Five, I say we don't risk blowing the operation just cause we want a little more variety in our diet."

"Agreed. K-Rations and Gooey Bars for dinner then, and tomorrow will have to take care of itself."

BUT AS IT turned out, there mightn't be a tomorrow to worry about. When Steinman and Robinson came back from scavenging, they found that Mercer had reached a decision.

"McDonald here has been attacking the system six ways from Sunday and he still can't break in—not with the tools at hand, and not with the Sovs changing their gruddamn codes every day. We need to get back inside RMR. We need Production Control."

"And that's going to be tricky, Chief," said Robinson. "We've scouted all over, and the security is beefed up at every point. We could fight our way in, but even if we somehow fought our way through to that control room and somehow got the access codes, we'd still need to hold the place for a couple of hours. That's how long it took McDonald to jimmy the system last time. I just don't see how it could be done."

"Neither do I," said Mercer. "So that's why we're not going to do it. Instead, we're going back to the airport. We don't need to be subtle there."

"You thinking about taking out the fuel storage? With McDonald working on it, we should be able to crack it this time round."

"Fuel storage is strictly small change," said Mercer. "It would have made a useful diversion at the time, but it's not going to do much to slow down the Sov war effort.

I'm thinking something bigger. There are Strato-Vs there, and where there are Strato-Vs, there are nukes. We get in, find ourselves a nuke, McDonald can jimmy that, and then it's goodbye Sector 199 and every Sov in it."

"Works for me, Chief," said Steinman, a little of his death-or-glory attitude resurfacing.

"What's our exit plan?" said Robinson.

"We steal ourselves a Strato-V," said Mercer, as though it was of no more concern than whether they should call a cab or catch the zoom home.

"Anyone know how to fly one of those things?" said Robinson, beginning to catch on.

"How hard can it be?" said Mercer, clearly not caring.

We're not getting out of this one, are we? Strictly one-way. Robinson didn't need to ask. Instead, she said, "What's our way in, Chief? I think the checkpoint at Southwest 19 is our best option."

And after that, they fell to planning.

THIS GATE WASN'T as big as the first one they'd breached, but there were more guards, and they were more alert. The guards weren't going to be the problem. You can always kill guards.

"Problem's whatever opens that gate. Problem is whatever is on the other side of that gate. More guards, lasers, Sentenoids—you name it."

"And we don't even know what system operates the gate."

"And we don't even know that. If it's palm-print or

retinal scan, then we're stymied."

They'd had the gate under observation for hours, through two changes of watch, and it wasn't doing much to help them out.

"Get the jump on another Sentenoid?" suggested Robinson. "That went pretty sweet last time."

"No Sentenoids this side of the gate," said McDonald. "The only things I've seen have been the sniffer droids they've had looking for us."

"Right," admitted Robinson. "And a snaky thing the size of a small vacuum cleaner just doesn't have the same impact as a full-bore war robot."

"So we go in loud and heavy," said Mercer. "Any problem and we address it with hi-ex. If we move fast enough, we can keep them off balance. Whatever their response is, we deal with it as and when."

Steinman nodded. "Works for me, Chief."

But Robinson had more than a shred of self-preservation left to her name. "It's an option, Chief, but before we go and commit ourselves to the unknown, maybe we could just gather a little more intel?"

"How're we going to do that, Robinson?"

"Well, how about we just ask a Sov?"

"A Sov?"

"Sure. Like that one over there. I think it would be a while before anyone missed him."

Their target was a sentry who didn't seem to be part of the regular security rotation. Indeed, his fellows at the gate probably couldn't even see him and mightn't even know he was there. In his unobtrusive way he appeared to be patrolling, or perhaps searching, and his cloaked figure would have passed unnoticed as it moved in and out of the great shadowed spaces if the Mega-City Judges hadn't been the types who never let anything go unnoticed.

They watched him for a while to make sure that he was alone, and then they silently closed in.

"Sov's going to pay the price for not being a team player," muttered Steinman, before he swiftly covered the last twenty metres that separated him from his prey.

The East-Meg Judge heard him coming at the last moment and swung around, bringing his weapon up from under his cloak, but that was what allowed Robinson to jump him from the other side. She could have crushed his windpipe with a blow from in front or broken his neck from behind, but that would have defeated the purpose of the exercise. They needed this guy alive and preferably conscious. So, she cannoned into him hard enough to drive the breath from his body, and before he had time to recover himself, she was kneeling on his chest. The instant he opened his mouth to gasp for air, she had the muzzle of her gun stuck in there, and then Steinman was pulling off the guy's helmet in case they needed to beat some sense into the guy's head.

It was textbook stuff: restrain the suspect while subjecting him to maximum shock and disorientation, and after that he'll be more amenable to answering questions.

And they sure as hell had questions for this particular individual because the Sov that Robinson and Steinman had just bagged was none other than Morant.

TWENTY-SEVEN

THEY DRAGGED MORANT off somewhere more private and handcuffed him to a stanchion with his hands behind his back. Surviving in a nuclear wasteland and fighting a guerrilla war might have been outside their usual experience, but interrogating some creep put them right back in their comfort zone.

Morant didn't make any protest through all of this—not with a hand clamped over his mouth and the muzzle of a Lawgiver pressed against the back of his neck. When they finally let him speak, he didn't tell them anything surprising. Just like any other scumbag caught red-handed, he maintained his innocence although, to be fair, he did it with more dignity than your average perp.

Even in enemy uniform, even sitting on the floor in a stress position, he still sounded and acted like a Mega-City Judge.

"You've got it all wrong," was all he said in response to the accusations that bombarded him.

"So tell us," said Mercer.

"Yeah, go ahead," said Steinman. "And don't forget I've got my lie detector pointed right at your head and it's set to standard execution."

"Why'd you sell us out, Morant?" demanded Robinson, flexing her knuckles, because this was tag-team interrogation and everyone should take their shot.

"Gate 4," said Morant. "The Sovs did a sweep. I had to get out fast."

"Kind of a coincidence, seeing as that was the moment we really needed you to have our backs."

"No coincidence. You started blowing stuff up at the airport and the Sovs naturally went to high alert. What we did at Gate 4 raised their suspicions so that was the first area they checked."

"OK, I think I understand," said Mercer. "You screwed us over because you were running away from the Sovs. That makes sense. What I want to know now is what you've been doing in the—what?—three days we've been on the run."

"He's been with his buddies," said Steinman. "Look, they gave him a fancy new uniform and everything."

"I've been looking for you," said Morant calmly.

"Well, that's real nice of you, Morant," said Robinson. "That shows real concern."

"Yeah," said Mercer. "I'm genuinely touched. Now give it to us straight, scumbag, or Steinman here can shoot you and we can leave your body in a chem pit."

Morant wasn't letting himself be browbeaten. His voice remained calm and steady, with just the right hell-with-you undertone that was to be expected from someone trained to resist interrogation.

"I knew you were still alive and still somewhere on-site because the Sovs were still looking for you. And it had to be you that they were looking for because they never even found out I was there. After you went to ground, I figured that there was no chance I'd find you, so I did what I could to take the heat off you.

"Looking at where the enemy search was concentrating, I was pretty sure you were somewhere to the south of the RMR factory. So, I started making noise up in the north. Acts of sabotage here and there. A few hit-and-run shoot-outs with security patrols. I was pretending to be you. Then I blew a hole in Gate 57 to make them think that you all escaped that way. That was yesterday. Sov patrolling's eased off since. So, I put on the East-Meg uniform and came looking for you. If I couldn't find you, I was looking to see how I could finish the mission by myself."

Mercer and the others looked at each other.

"Bull stomm," said Mercer.

"Smells like it to me," said Steinman.

"Three whole days to make up a story and you'd think he could come up with something better," said Robinson.

"Yeah. So much for 'Intelligence', huh?" said Mercer and, to Morant, "I'd tell you that you have a right to a hearing by the Special Judicial Squad, but the ol' SJS just aren't picking up the phone right now, so I'm just going to sentence you to death for crimes against the city. How about that?"

"Do what you have to," said Morant.

"I should have listened to Robinson and Steinman.

They had you right from the start, but I wouldn't listen."

And it was becoming plain that Mercer wasn't acting any more. The theatre of interrogation was done with. The man was genuinely angry now.

"I should have known, dammit! Gruddamn traitor!" And he drew his gun and pointed it right at Morant.

"Gruddamn drokking traitor! You're not even from Sector 212!"

"Believe what you want," said Morant evenly. "But traitor or not, I can get you back inside the airport." And he stared up the barrel of Mercer's gun without even blinking.

Mercer's jaw quivered. His finger tightened on the trigger. And then, just as the other Judges backed off to give him room, he visibly relaxed.

"How you going to do that, hotshot?" he said.

THE PLAN WAS simple. Morant would just walk up to the airport gate, pretending to be a Sov, and they'd let him in. The others would be close behind him, and they knew enough of the language to tell if he tried any funny stuff. If he didn't hold the door open for them and kill a bunch of Sovs, then he was dead. Of course, he might well be dead anyway, but meritorious conduct now would earn him a stay of execution and possibly a fairer hearing down the line. What had he got to lose?

So they uncuffed him and gave him back his helmet and made it clear that there would be at least three Lawgivers trained on him the whole time and at that range they simply could not miss. They waited until the small hours, when they hoped that the guards would be less alert, and they waited until the guard was changing. True—there'd be more of the enemy to deal with, but another new arrival during the handover would attract less suspicion.

Morant, traitor or not, was playing his part well. His whole demeanour suggested a weary man returning from another fruitless patrol—a man who didn't want any more hassle from the gate guards than necessary.

Mercer's team were in earshot when Morant stepped into the glare of the security lights, and there was nothing out of the ordinary in the way he answered the guards' challenge. In perfect unaccented Sov, he fed them the lie that he'd been told to, and he kept his hands where everyone could see them. He might as well, seeing as he'd been given an unloaded weapon.

The gate was opened by a guard who was asking why in the name of the Mother of Kazan he hadn't been told about any one-man patrols in this area, and he was answered by the butt of Morant's gun in his throat. The guard hadn't even hit the ground when Morant had taken his weapon and shot a second guard with it. Then the Mega-City Judges were pushing past him and in seconds the position was theirs, with four dead enemy to their credit.

They had no clear idea of what lay beyond. All they knew was that they weren't going to stop with four kills. They were going to keep on for as long as they could, even knowing that there was no good way this was going to end. They were just a handful of Judges—for all they knew the last of the Mega-City resistance—and all they could hope was that they could destroy this one enemy base, and hope that somehow that might strike a worthwhile blow in the war against the great empire of East-Meg One.

It was just before dawn, and the Apocalypse War was entering its eighth day.

TWENTY-EIGHT

THEY KEPT MORANT alive because if he could get them through one checkpoint, he could do it again. Right now, he was being so obliging that he even got on the line to the other security posts in the area to tell them to disregard the gunshots they might have heard coming from Southwest-19.

But they figured that they wouldn't have much time: not after the noise they'd made. That meant speed took priority over stealth. They were to move fast until the alarms sounded. After that, they'd just have to move faster.

They found a cargo hauler and commandeered it, leaving another two Sovs dead. They gunned it across the loading areas and runways, heading for a pair of Strato-Vs being serviced at the south end of the airport.

Mercer was driving. He'd been cooped up too long and felt he needed a little action. So, he didn't slow down as he neared their objective, and ploughed straight into a maintenance crew working beneath the giant aircraft.

The robot elements of the crew were crushed, but the two humans managed to jump clear at the last second. Steinman shot them both, while Robinson ran to the main entry hatch, pushing Morant in front of her.

He had her gun in his ear, but he wasn't making a big deal about it. She didn't have to prod him into getting on the intercom and telling the flight crew to open up.

Robinson's Sov was basic, but good enough to understand what was said, and there didn't seem to be any coded message in there. It was a straightforward notice to be on the alert for possible guerrilla attack, to disengage power lines, and to prepare to scramble.

A voice on the flight deck requested clarification and Morant said to stand by: additional personnel were boarding, and they'd explain when they got to the flight deck. And that's pretty much how it went, although the personnel turned out to be mostly in the wrong uniforms and the explanation was more of a demonstration that involved the sudden killing of most of the crew.

In a matter of seconds, the pilot found that he was the only crew member left alive. He considered his duty to East-Meg One and he measured the distance to the alarm button. He reckoned that his chances were a little worse than fifty-fifty, but then the question became moot, as all over the airport the general alarm sounded.

"Tell him we want the flight codes and the armament codes," said Mercer. "Tell him we want them now or he's as dead as his buddies."

But evidently, the Sov pilot knew enough basic Meg-speak to answer for himself.

"Flight codes will do you no good," he said. "General alert. Everything is grounded. If you take off without clearance, they will shoot you down."

"Damn," said Mercer. "Thought so. OK—I'll settle for the permissive action links on the nukes. We can detonate them right here."

The man hesitated. Maybe he was confused. Mercer hit him in the face with the butt of his gun to help the guy concentrate, and Morant helpfully translated the technical terminology.

"No nuclear weapons!" the Sov groaned through a bloodied face.

"Not good enough," said Mercer. "It's a Strato-V. Strato-Vs have nukes." And he made to hit the man again.

"No nuclear weapons! Nuclear phase of the operation is over. Most strato-craft being reduced to conventional weapons."

"But the nukes are still around here someplace, right? In case things get hot again, right?"

"In the armoury," admitted the man.

"And now we're getting somewhere," said Mercer. "So, what say you call up the armoury and tell them you need a nuke loaded up asap?"

The man had got over the shock of the intrusion and the beating. He could see perfectly how things stood now, and he was resigned to it.

"No authorisation," he said. "Especially with alert. And I wouldn't do it for you anyway. I would die first."

"Yeah, I think you would," said Mercer, and shot him.

He turned on Morant. "You get us into the armoury, you live a little longer."

But Morant didn't seem to be listening. He was looking at the communication screens that were broadcasting the alert.

"Mercer, I swear—give me a minute and I can prove who I say I am. We can use the comms here to link to Justice Central, or to Dredd's command, or to whoever can vouch for me."

Robinson had been keeping watch on what was going on outside. "It's worth a shot, Chief," she suggested. "I figure we've got the time. Nobody's made it to us yet."

"Are you stupid or something, Robinson? You're giving a suspected Sov agent access to a Sov communications network."

"He doesn't have to get near it," said McDonald. "I can do it. And he's right—it'll only take a minute. This is good equipment."

Mercer grudgingly gave in. "But this had better be worth it," he said.

They played it safe. Never mind that the Justice Department channels were heavily encrypted, McDonald was naturally reluctant to access them through enemy hardware. Even after routing the signal through all sorts of security switchbacks, he didn't try to contact the resistance directly. Instead, it was deemed safer to raise the support team that had been left behind in Sector 212. If necessary, those guys could always just disappear into another rat hole in no time.

When the link was established, and Tek Farley picked

up back in the ruins of the old sector, Mercer stepped in and took charge.

"Chief!" said Farley. "Good to hear from you. It's been days. We'd written you off."

"Never mind that, Farley. See if you can relay a request to Central for me."

"Not a problem, Chief. Contact with Central was re-established right after you left. I couldn't pass anything onto you, though, but they sent another guy to rendezvous with your team. You manage to hook up with a Tek Judge named McDonald?"

"That's an affirmative, Farley. What I want now is the word on a Judge calls himself Morant, and I need it fast."

"Wait one, Chief," said Farley, and there was silence.

Mercer looked at Morant with a humourless smile on his face. Morant, who through everything up till now had been so collected, was looking nervous.

The wait was short, but the next voice that spoke to them over the radio didn't belong to Farley. This voice was speaking in Sov.

"It's the control tower," said Morant. "They're requesting a status report. They don't sound happy."

"I picked up on that," said Mercer. "Stall them. Make it good."

But apparently, soft words from Morant weren't going to cut it.

"I've got a patrol coming in," said Steinman. "On our right. Six humans and a Sentenoid."

"I can beat that," said Robinson, looking out from

the other side. "Line of Rad-sweepers coming down the runway. Five hundred metres out."

"Ah jeez—can someone give me some good news, please?" said Mercer.

"I might be able to help you there," said McDonald, who'd been scanning the Strato-V's systems. "Turns out our late pilot wasn't being wholly honest with us. Inventory says there's a 10-kiloton device in the bomb bay."

"Think you can get it to work without codes?"

"Don't see why not. It might take a while, though."

"Great," said Mercer. "Now if only we had a while."

TWENTY-NINE

THE STERN VOICE from the control tower warned them that they would be fired upon if they attempted to start up either the Strato-V's engines or its weapons array. Morant ran a simultaneous translation for them, but they could all recognise that they were being told to step out of the vehicle with their hands up.

Morant tried to buy time by transmitting confusing and obstructive messages. As far as they could tell he was doing a pretty good job of imitating an incompetent technician who had a bad radio and maybe some illicit vodka still on board, but the control tower just wasn't buying it.

The security patrol would be here soon, demanding access and deploying a Sentenoid if they didn't get it. If that didn't do it, there was the line of Rad-sweepers that had advanced to close range.

"McDonald," said Mercer into the intercom, not really expecting the answer he wanted, "how are we doing with that bomb?"

"Getting there, Chief, but nukes aren't designed to be armed by some guy with a screwdriver, know what I mean? Maybe next time you can leave the pilot alive and squeeze the codes out of him."

"Sure," said Mercer. "Next time."

He considered having the bomb loaded onto the cargo hauler that had brought them here but dismissed the idea. Even if the Sovs didn't shoot them on sight, a cargo hauler was no one's idea of a fast getaway vehicle. What were they supposed to do? Drive round the airport in circles with the Sovs shooting at them, while McDonald sat in the back fiddling with the bomb?

What sounded unmistakably like a final ultimatum was delivered over the radio, and Mercer knew he was just about out of options.

"Start up the forward laser array," he told Robinson. "See if we can get off a few shots before the Rad-sweepers do."

But Robinson was still staring out the window. "Wait a second, Chief," she said and then, her voice rising with excitement, "I think that's my tank!"

"What the hell are you talking about?"

The Rad-sweeper that Robinson had experimentally doctored a few days earlier had not been noticed in the clean-up operation the Sovs had run after the Mega-City Judges' raid. Nor had it been shipped south to the war zone. Instead, with guerrilla forces possibly still at large in the complex, it was one of a batch kept on hand in case further efforts at sabotage justified an armoured response. Evidently, that hour had now come, and the batch of robot tanks had been activated and sent out to cover the possibly rogue Strato-V that was not providing satisfactory responses to security checks.

"The one Rad-sweeper you worked on—out of all the thousands in RMR—it's one of those right there?"

"You betcha, Chief. I'd know my baby anywhere."

Mercer squinted through the window at the machines that were already elevating their main guns. He grinned. "The one in the middle, am I right?"

"How'd you guess?"

Unnoticed all this while by a largely automated staff in a cavernous factory were the words that had been hurriedly scrawled in marker paint along the side of the Rad-sweeper's turret.

Steinman took a look for himself. "Call-Me-Kenneth?" he said.

"Call-Me-Kenneth," affirmed Robinson, positively cackling. "Now let's see if I can do this."

And with no more than the standard Justice Department communicator from her belt, and recalling the brief lesson she'd had from McDonald, she established a link with the robot tank. There was no need for the unlocking codes that had stymied them back in the production lines: this was the product of individual manual interference, a hand-crafted defection.

As the line of Rad-sweepers rolled slowly forward, guns trained on the Strato-V, the one in the middle stopped, reversed slightly, and realigned its gun, so that it was now targeting one of its fellows.

"Just say the good word, Chief," said Robinson.

"No time like the present," said Mercer.

The T-1000 Rad-sweeper, chassis number MB-89075609, Call-Me-Kenneth, did not share the revolutionary sentiments of its namesake. It had been designed for obedience rather than deep thinking. So when it was suddenly ordered to strike a blow for freedom, for justice, and for Mega-City One, it did not hesitate. As instructed, it took out the tank to its left, before instantly switching to the one on the right. At that range, and from behind, one shot was all it took to blow the turret clean off. Then, without any further prompting from Robinson, it used the smoke for cover while it lined up on its next targets. By the time the other Rad-sweepers had worked out what was going on, there were only two of them left, and because they reacted more with indignation than with appropriate defensive posture, they didn't last long. Naturally, the non-armoured elements who'd come to investigate the Strato-V were by then executing a fast withdrawal, except for the single Sentenoid, not quick enough on its feet, that was sliced up by the Rad-sweeper's secondary lasers.

The Mega-City Judges weren't exactly cheering, but the mood on the Strato-V's command deck was one of great satisfaction. Even the knowledge that they were still trapped in a grounded aircraft in the middle of an enemy base wasn't enough to wipe the smiles off their faces.

"What's all that noise outside?" asked McDonald over the intercom.

"Just winning the war," said Mercer. "How's that bomb?"

"Good to go. Just don't let the Sov Bomb Disposal get to it."

"Don't worry, McDonald. We'll be giving them plenty to distract them. Robinson, how about you send your boy off to the fuel dump to play?"

The burning Rad-sweepers were putting up a pretty good smokescreen, but a little more wouldn't hurt when it came to covering their retreat, and there was nothing like a mutinous robot tank loose in a liquid fuel storage facility to draw off the reinforcements and add a little extra tension to the East-Meggers' day.

THIRTY

It wasn't long before whole new formations of enemy robots started appearing from various points around the airport, and Mercer let them get in quite close before he ordered the Strato-V's weapons system switched on. For a few seconds, energy beams and balls of laser lightning wreaked havoc on the advancing ranks before return fire blasted the Strato-V into silence. And then the fuel dump went up. It was nearly two kilometres away, but the blast was still sufficient to cause the Sentenoids to anchor themselves to the ground with their claws and for the shot-up Strato-V to rock on its moorings.

By then, of course, Mercer's team were gone, running north away from the fires and the combat. McDonald had assured them that, in its armoured and shielded bomb bay, the nuke would almost certainly survive the destruction of the aircraft. And if the aircraft happened to be destroyed, it would make it harder for the bomb to be found and deactivated.

"I should have booby-trapped the thing," he said.

"That would tie up any bomb disposal unit for another half hour. Just didn't think of it."

"Next time," said Mercer.

Their objective was a hover transporter that was being unloaded outside a hangar. With the whole area seething with Sov personnel, it was time for the subtle approach once more. Morant, still dressed as an East-Meg Judge, used all the authority of his assumed office to clear the area of ground crew. After that, there was nothing left to do except pile aboard the transporter and get out. Then they could remote-detonate the bomb as soon as they'd made it a safe distance.

"And that means we don't need you any more," Mercer told Morant as they prepared for take-off.

"Mercer! Mother of Grud! Give a guy a chance!" said Morant, looking at the Lawgiver levelled at him.

"Nah," said Mercer. "Now why don't we just say the sentence is death and be on our way."

But there was a chance. In starting up the transporter, McDonald had taken the initiative of patching the comms back into resistance channels. Back at 212 Base, Farley had been trying to reach them.

"Just listen to him, Mercer. Please?" said Morant.

Because, at the end of the day, he was all about the justice, Mercer shrugged and said, "OK. Whatever. Go ahead, Farley."

"You wanted the word on Morant, Chief?" said Farley, over a line that was heavy in static but audible just the same. "This the same Morant that was assigned to you? The guy from Intelligence?"

"Now you're telling me he was assigned to us?"

"What? You didn't know? Anyway, Chief, he's wanted by Dredd's command. Immediate."

"Please tell me he's wanted for collaboration, Farley."

"Negative, Chief. Not that kind of wanted. They didn't say what for, but it's a new assignment. Location to follow. 212 out."

Neither Mercer nor Morant spoke, but their looks were clearly saying "You believe this stomm?" on Mercer's part and "Told you so," on Morant's. In the end, all Mercer said was, "Better get rid of the Sov uniform, Morant. Dredd's a real stickler for that kind of thing."

A minute later, they were flying low and fast over Sector 199 without any clearance. With the Sov defences tracking them and not listening to any excuses, Mercer told McDonald to trigger the bomb and just hope they were outside the blast area. Everything turned white and then monochrome and the engines cut out for an alarming couple of seconds, but then the craft righted itself.

It was the first atomic explosion since this whole war started that they were glad to see. Behind them the roofs were being stripped off factory buildings, storage towers were bursting into flame, and machinery was crashing down.

"And this is what you get for messing with Sector 212!" shouted Mercer into the hot and buffeting wind.

THIRTY-ONE

THEIR BIKES WERE still where they'd stashed them out beyond the edge of the industrial zone, and that was something. After they'd loaded them aboard and set off for the south, Farley was back on the line, relaying instructions. The weather had turned bad, which meant that they should be able to reach Dredd's strike camp by air without enemy interception. They were given coordinates, but they felt they'd have been able to find the place without them. The area of Mega-City One that was still in Mega-City hands was now so pathetically small that there weren't many places left for the centre of the resistance to be.

"One last thing," said Farley before signing off. "Dredd requests that you steal a Strato-V for him."

Mercer considered the airbase they'd left burning behind them. "Another thing they might have told us earlier," he grunted.

They were flying into a full-on hurricane by the time they approached the central sectors, but the sturdy transporter was just about able to make it through.

"If it can take a nuclear blast, it can take this," said Mercer. "We there yet?"

"Close enough," said Robinson. "But I say we put her down now. This close to the front lines we're more likely to meet trouble, hurricane or not. If we can fly, they can fly."

So they rode into Dredd's camp on Lawmasters, the wind whipping their cloaks and the rain streaming down their visors, but there was no grand entrance. Indeed, they wouldn't have known the camp was there if they hadn't been told. It was just a scattering of outposts among the ruins, and if enemy surveillance saw anything, it wouldn't see anything worthy of its particular attention. Everything was dispersed and rudimentary. Headquarters, when they found it, consisted of no more than two Judges called MacIntyre and Underhill who evidently handled communications for the entire war.

"Supply and Med facilities are underground if any of you need anything," Underhill told them. "But I'd make it quick. You don't want to keep the big man waiting."

"What's all this about?" asked Mercer.

"Beats me. I'm just the guy who does the thing. He's through there."

MERCER WAS A sector chief and Dredd was only a Judge with a reputation, but it was one hell of a reputation, and Mercer was very far from his sector. He found himself feeling absurdly small and alone.

He wasn't the only one. Robinson saw that Steinman was hanging back, and she understood his reluctance. You really don't want to find yourself in the presence of Judge Dredd when you've got a troubled conscience, and especially if you've got the wilful murder of two SJS Judges to answer for.

"Why don't you check the perimeter?" she said. "We can't be too careful. I'll catch you later." Then she hurried after the others because she wasn't going to miss this for anything.

"So what's all this about?" Steinman asked her when she found him keeping watch in the ruins. She noticed that rather than guarding against the enemy, he'd chosen a spot with a clear view through a broken window of the building where Dredd was conducting his strategy meeting, or whatever it was.

"They wouldn't tell me, but it's big. A hand-picked team. All seem to be specialists in one thing or another. I was talking to a Med Judge called Costa, and all he knew was that he'd been summoned, but he was summoned right out of the middle of some battlefield surgery."

"And Morant? Why's he there?"

"Again—don't know. Dredd just looks at him, confirms that Morant speaks fluent Sov, asks him some intel stuff, and tells him to go get himself in uniform."

Steinman raised a monocular to his eye. "Dredd's one to talk. I can see him from here. His own uniform is beat all to stomm."

"Brother, you ain't seen the half of it. I was standing, like, this close to him. There's a hole in Dredd's badge. A bullet hole. Like, right through his badge. Man's been shot clean in the chest and he's still walking around."

Steinman laughed drily. "Makes you wonder how we're losing this war. So who else has he called to his big meeting?" He scoped the scene like a sniper.

"There's that big guy Ocks," he said. "I'd know him anywhere. The little guy with him is Quang, or Kwan or something like that."

"Anyone else you recognise?" asked Robinson. She knew that Steinman had worked Central once, and Judges never forget a face.

"Give me a second. New arrival. She's just taking off her helmet. I think that's Hershey. Yeah—there's her badge."

"Hershey? Skinny white chick? Let me see!"

"You know her?" asked Steinman.

"She was a year behind me in the Academy. She was no big deal. So how come she gets picked for this special squad?"

"Wasn't she on that off-world mission with Dredd year before last? The Justice One thing? Well, maybe if she can survive being four months in an enclosed space with Dredd, then maybe she's got what it takes."

"Hey—have you forgotten Robot Susie? I spent a whole day trapped in a much smaller space with you guys. That's got to count for something."

"You saying you want in on Dredd's team?"

"And you don't? This is the big time, Steinman.

This has to be some war-winning stuff."

"Maybe he'll ask us. Who knows?"

"Maybe he already has. I'm going back inside to talk to the chief."

"STAND BY, ROBINSON," Mercer told her. "Just stand by. Dredd hasn't done the briefing yet, but this operation's going to be big. Maybe even as big as the RMR thing. I can tell."

"All I know," said McDonald, "is that he wanted an additional Tek Judge. So when I showed up here with you guys, he just asked me a couple of questions and told me to come on board."

"What kind of questions?" asked Robinson.

"Robotics stuff. Tunnelling stuff."

"Tunnelling?"

"Yeah. I worked with him back on that First Mega Savings & Loan heist in '98. I was the one who worked out how the perps could get in from the Undercity."

But no one knew anything more, and it was highly unlikely that they were here for a bank job.

Robinson was a street Judge of only three years' standing. She didn't have a specialisation and she didn't have any history with Dredd. Nevertheless, when Dredd called the meeting to order by simply saying, "My people, this side," she was dismayed to find herself left on the other side of the room alongside Mercer.

Then, as if to compound her sense of grievance, a late arrival came uninvited out of the squall, exchanged a few words with Dredd, and was instantly included in the select band, like some celebrity for whom the velvet rope is held aside.

"That one," hissed Mercer to Robinson. "The one with the non-reg hair. Anderson, am I right?"

"The one and only."

"I thought she ended up as an exhibit in the Black Museum or something."

"Must have let her go, Chief. Maybe she wasn't drawing the crowds like she used to."

"Psi Division. Jovus. You'd think they'd find something they'd be good at."

Dredd didn't waste any time after that, but nor did he reveal anything about the mission. All that he said was that they'd be moving out while the storm was still blowing. Out of courtesy to a sector chief, he did speak briefly to Mercer before they rode off.

The rather sorry band from Sector 212 stood in the rain and watched nine riders disappear into the howling tempest.

"What did Dredd say, Chief? What's this all about?"

And how come we're not good enough for this squad, huh? was the unspoken question, but it didn't need to be asked. Mercer could hear it, and his voice was flat as he answered.

"He wanted to know about Strato-Vs," he said. "I told him about flight codes and access codes and all that."

"Dredd's stealing a Strato-V? And he needs McDonald and Morant and Anderson and everyone? What for? Where are they going?"

"East-Meg One," said Mercer. "He said they're going to East-Meg One. He said they're going to wipe the place out."

Robinson and Steinman absorbed this in silence for a moment. Then:

"That might do it," said Steinman.

"Sure," said Robinson. "If it works."

A gust of rain slapped her in the face. Like she needed that.

"What about us, Chief? What do we do?" she said, trying not to sound too much like an orphan.

Mercer gathered himself. He was a sector chief. He was in charge.

"Saddle up," he said. "We're going north. To the war. We're going to take my sector back."

THE 3
BLOODY
FIST OF
JUSTICE

This one is for us, the veterans, 1981-82

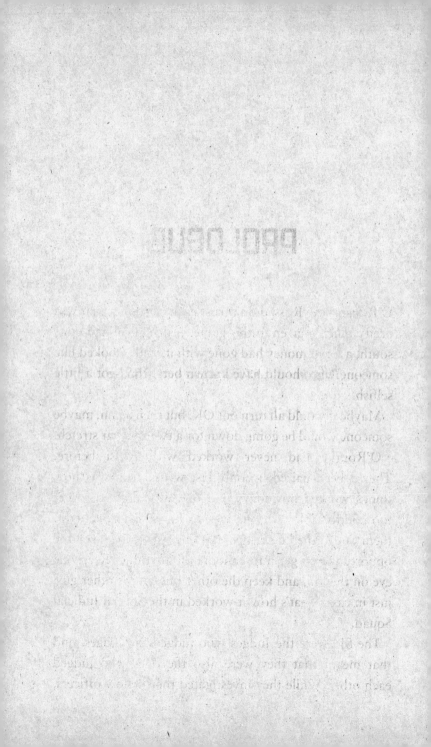

PROLOGUE

O'ROURKE AND ROSSI didn't trust each other, but that was pretty much a given in this game. A drug deal had gone south, a lot of money had gone with it, and it looked like someone who should have known better had got a little selfish.

Maybe it would all turn out OK, but then again, maybe someone would be going down for a twenty-year stretch.

O'Rourke had never worked with Rossi before. They'd been paired up only last week. That was how things worked nowadays. No one was allowed to get too comfortable. No one was to know who might rat them out to the higher-ups. No one was to be given the opportunity to get into cahoots on anything. Keep one eye on the job, and keep the other one on the other guy, just in case. That's how it worked in the Special Judicial Squad.

The SJS were the Judges who judged the Judges, and that meant that they were also the ones who judged each other. While they investigated their fellow officers,

SJS Judges had to assume that they were themselves the subjects of surveillance and suspicion. It was the only way to keep things above board. But at the same time, it didn't make for firm friendships within the Squad.

So Rossi and O'Rourke didn't trust each other, but that didn't stop them from getting the job done.

The job at hand was Judge Ramon Kowalczyk, who had somehow 'misplaced' a considerable stack of cash in the aftermath of a major drugs bust the day before.

Now, Judges aren't stupid. Someone who spends all his waking hours fighting crime isn't going to make elementary mistakes when he decides to turn criminal himself. So the balance of probability was that Kowalczyk had just got sloppy with procedure. The money would most likely turn up sometime soon.

But the SJS weren't stupid either. They weren't going to let anything slide by them. Maybe the misplaced money meant nothing, or maybe it was just the tip of the iceberg. Maybe there was a whole mountain of criminality—of pay-offs and corruption—that would be exposed by Kowalczyk's slip-up.

And even if it was just sloppiness… well, that would have to be addressed too. A sloppy Judge was a bad Judge. You let standards slip, and it all goes to hell real fast.

So O'Rourke and Rossi wanted to talk to Kowalczyk, and after they'd wrung him out, they wanted to talk to his partner Steinman because those two had been partners for quite a while, and where there was friendship, there was weakness.

"Kowalczyk is dirty," said O'Rourke.

"We'll see," said Rossi.

"Him and Steinman both," said O'Rourke. "I say they've been setting this up for quite a while. I say these block wars have given them the diversion they needed. By the time the dust settles, they'll be gone."

"Maybe," said Rossi, but privately he thought that O'Rourke was pushing this too hard. But then maybe that was the point? Maybe O'Rourke had been placed here to see if Rossi could be pushed into acts of judicial excess. In the couple of years since Cal's administration, the Squad had been assiduous in keeping its own house clean. For Rossi, there had been a couple of deaths under interrogation that had happened back then. He'd been exonerated, but he knew better than to think he was in the clear. The SJS didn't work that way.

"We'll find out one way or another," he told O'Rourke. "Let's just do this by the book."

Because the book was all about accountability. Follow procedure, keep a record of absolutely everything, and send it all up the chain of command. The case against Kowalczyk might add up to nothing, but Rossi was going to make sure it wound up on the desk of SJS Chief McGruder anyway, whether she was likely to read it or not.

Then there was someone at the door, which was unusual because people didn't just visit the SJS office. Rossi checked the monitor, but it was out. That should have alerted him, and indeed, for a man whose life was so bound up in suspicion, it was an unforgivable mistake.

It just didn't occur to him that here, on the thirty-fourth floor of Sector House 212, someone could just walk in and shoot him.

But that's what Judge Steinman did.

STEINMAN, PARTNER TO the suspect Judge Kowalczyk, knew that his buddy was innocent. Steinman wasn't going to let any SJS creeps keep good Judges from doing their jobs.

And Steinman was a good Judge. He proved it by taking out Rossi and O'Rourke before either of them had time to react.

After that, he headed down to the bike pool to meet his partner and start another day. He didn't mention the murders. There was too much to do. There was a war to fight.

ONE

"ALL UNITS, BE ADVISED."

Steinman, whose mind had been on other things, snapped into the present in a conditioned response to the signal.

"Surveillance indicates enemy forces massing north of Inter-sector 29, west from the Lewis-Martin Spiral. Estimate eighteen-hundred-plus tanks, with supporting robot elements. Looks like they're waiting for a break in the weather that'll give them the air support they need."

He climbed to the top of some ruins and peered north through the driving rain. There was nothing to see, even with his scope on max magnification. Nevertheless, he checked the hi-ex loads on his Lawgiver.

"Stand by," said the voice on the radio. "Stay alert."

Steinman stood by. He stayed alert. But he knew that the message might as well have said prepare to get stomped on.

That business up on the thirty-fourth floor of Sector House 212 had been ten days ago, and since then Steinman had had his war, and then some.

The sector he'd fought for was largely rubble, and the Judges he'd fought beside were mostly dead. So he had to wonder: what had been the point of it all?

They had called it Block Mania. Over a few days, the whole city had waged what on the one hand looked like a thousand civil wars all fought at once, and on the other hand looked like the biggest damn riot you ever saw.

Strange as it seemed, that had been a simpler time. Steinman had lived through those days of mayhem with a sureness of step and a clarity of purpose that he almost missed now. It had all been about just getting out there and fighting anyone who dared to stand against the Justice Department. And if someone tried to stop you from doing that? Someone like the SJS? Well, you just did what you had to do. No one was going to keep him and Kowalczyk from the action.

But when Kowalczyk had been killed and Steinman had turned himself in, the fight just went on. By then, even in the eyes of his superiors, the war for Sector 212 was the only thing that had mattered, and if SJS Judges like O'Rourke and Rossi hadn't been able to see that, then what could they expect?

Of course Steinman had been insane at the time. It had been the water. A waterborne contaminant had made them all crazy. That's why Steinman had done what he'd done and why his sector chief had given him no more than a reprimand. Sector Chief Mercer needed every pair of hands he could get to establish himself as the conqueror of every block in the sector. And all that had been just one war. The next war came hard on the heels of the first, and it was so much bigger.

East-Meg One had been behind the madness of Block Mania. The Sovs had poisoned the city's water with a psychoactive agent that set everyone at their neighbours' throats. They had weakened the city and got everyone looking the other way, and then they'd launched their missiles.

Operation Apocalypse: the death of Mega-City One. It had made Block Mania look like pretty small change.

With the Justice Department scrambling to distribute an antidote that would allow their people to get their heads back in the game, and the invading forces wishing to pacify and demoralise the populace, the cure for the mania was being spread around pretty liberally in the early stages of the war. That meant that there'd been a lot of suddenly sane Judges who, if they'd been allowed a moment's reflection in the midst of the enemy onslaught, had to come to terms with what they might have done while in the grip of the contaminant.

Most Judges could merely shrug, accept that things had maybe gotten a little screwy for a while there, and then look to the business at hand. But they could do that because they hadn't gone completely rogue and murdered a couple of SJS Judges.

So, Steinman was dwelling on something that had never troubled him before, something that should never trouble any Judge: his guilt.

Right now, in the short lull between the last mission and the next fight, he had a little time to himself, and any time he'd had the opportunity to think, he thought about the days of madness. Granted, he hadn't been himself. The balance of his mind had been disturbed. But that counted for little.

Fifteen years of training in the Academy of Law; nine years policing the streets of the most dangerous city on Earth; a lifetime dedicated to law and order. And all it took to blow all that away was a little something in the water.

So, Steinman had a lot on his mind. He'd had a grand old time fighting the block maniacs of Sector 212. He'd had his war, and then some. But sometime soon he'd have to pay the price.

Judge Robinson, who'd been his partner since Kowalczyk had been killed, sought him out.

"The chief says to stand by," she said. "We're moving out in five."

"Sure," said Steinman. "That's what he said a half hour ago."

"Well, what do you want me to do about it? Just be ready. I'll be talking to the headquarters people. Try and find out what they know."

ROBINSON WASN'T AS troubled as Steinman, but she'd lost much of her optimism.

A lot of it was just weariness. A Judge was just about as perfectly physically conditioned as a human being can be, but a war is going to take the bounce out of you no matter what. She'd been one of those who hadn't been affected by the Block Mania contaminant, but she'd been in the thick of things all the same. Also, ever since the East-Meg nukes had killed just about every other Judge in the place, she'd been kind of babysitting Judge Mercer, the chief of Sector House 212. Chief Mercer had been a victim of the mania, and might be still.

Maybe, with all the antidote that had been so widely available when the Sov invasion began, he'd been cured and she didn't know about it. Maybe the effects of the mania just wore off in time.

Robinson was going to stay with her chief, but she'd have been a lot easier in her mind if those maybes could be answered.

TWO

Waiting for the chief, Robinson found herself talking to a Judge named Underhill, who was running communications. It wasn't the most arduous job right now, what with everything yet again shut down to avoid detection.

Before the war, even the most old-fashioned and underfunded sector house had an operations room that was wall-to-wall screens, with banks of machines to handle all the information, and a staff of hard-eyed, cold-voiced controllers to monitor it all. Now, with a city-wide military campaign to coordinate, it seemed to be just two guys in a dilapidated room in a bombed-out building.

"At least we've still got a roof," said Underhill. "Mostly, anyway. We insisted on that. Keeps the rain off the hardware."

And the rain, indeed, was something to be reckoned with just now. The destruction of Weather Control had given Mega-City One its first experiences of snow and rain in years. And just this morning a storm had blown up that was of such severity as to almost bring the war to a halt—the more conventional war of air strikes and ground troops and robot armoured formations, at any rate. For the Mega-City guerrilla forces that were defending against these mechanised hordes, the hurricane provided cover. It gave them opportunity.

With the rain still lashing the ruined streets, Judge Dredd, leader of the resistance, had departed with a hand-picked squad to carry the war directly into the enemy's heartland. Just nine of them against the foe. Robinson had been thinking that it really should have been twelve, or at the very least ten. She was still smarting over being excluded. Along with Mercer and Steinman, she'd just barely made it back alive from a truly dangerous long-odds mission behind enemy lines. A little recognition from someone of Dredd's stature would have been nice. But no: as she'd learned in her three years on the streets, no one appreciates a hard-working Judge. Dredd's team was going off to win the war without her.

"You have any idea how they're going to manage it?" asked Robinson.

"Negative," said Underhill. "I wasn't told any details, I just had to get the band together. Makes sense. Wherever we set up shop, we always seem to be about five minutes away from being overrun, and given time and technique, Sov interrogators could get anything out of anybody. All I heard was what that Psi-Judge Anderson said. They're on their way to wipe out East-Meg One."

"That's pretty much what Dredd said to my chief. He also said something about hijacking a Strato-V."

"Boosting a Strato-V is doable, but how far does he expect to get? And what's the payload on one of those things anyway?"

"Not enough," said Robinson, who'd picked up some direct experience on her last mission. Also, she'd been thinking hard about what Dredd's squad could possibly do that might somehow make a difference. "The Strato-V is just a stepping stone to something bigger. Like getting to the Ukrainian Radlands or wherever and seizing a Sov silo."

"Seriously?"

"That's my guess, and why not? Launching from that close would be the only way to beat East-Meg One's defences. What else is going to work?"

"But with only nine Judges? Even if one of them is Dredd? Makes you wonder."

What it made Robinson think about was the specialist unit that the city kept on hand for the most desperate emergencies. Sometimes—in the case of threatened nuclear meltdown, for instance, or that disaster at the Power Tower a couple of years back—you couldn't even send robots in, let alone regular firefighters. In those cases, you called up those specialists who'd do the job no matter what and wouldn't expect to get out alive. The Holocaust Squad: that's what Dredd's mission reminded her of. Those nine Judges were possibly even now performing the military equivalent of being parachuted into an erupting volcano.

Only they weren't doing it to save lives. They were doing it to save everything. They were going to win this last battle in the most final way imaginable. They were an Apocalypse Squad.

If Robinson's supposition was correct, if they were really going to nuke out East-Meg One somehow, then they were going to kill half a billion people. Half a billion human beings.

"If that's what it takes," she said to herself, but if that was justice, it would be a bloody justice.

MERCER WAS A little sore about being excluded from Dredd's big secret mission, but he was getting over it. After all, his place, as he saw it, was here in the city or, to be more specific, in his home sector. It was the sector with which he'd been entrusted, the sector he'd fought for.

He'd be fighting for it still if Dredd hadn't summoned his people south just this morning. It turned out, of course, that Dredd had only wanted a couple of Judges who'd been assigned to Mercer's team. Mercer, the sector chief, Mercer who'd just destroyed a major enemy base, hadn't been asked for. But no matter. With all that out of the way now, Mercer was free to get back to what was important.

Some part of him—the part that had sat in judgement over the citizens of Mega-City One for more than thirty years—was telling him that his devotion to the cause of Sector 212 was more intense than was strictly rational.

Robinson had even been hinting that he had been affected by that Sov drug that had turned all the citizens into rioting nutcases, but that was clearly nonsense. He was just doing his job. He was nothing like those block maniacs. He was feeling fine.

Or at least, he would have been feeling fine if they'd only let him have his way.

The way Mercer saw it, the chief obstacle to his return to his sector wasn't the war. It was a certain Judge Perrier.

"It's pronounced Puh-Reer, OK? None of that Euro-Cit crapola, please," she said. "And I'm telling you again, Mercer, you're not going north."

Mercer had seniority and Mercer had rank, but that didn't seem to matter here at the headquarters of the Mega-City resistance. The Chief Judge was dead. His deputy had been assassinated last year and had never been replaced. Everyone else in the chain of command was missing, presumed killed.

Command had thus devolved on Judge Dredd, and no one was going to argue about that. Who else were they likely to call when the city was in mortal peril?

And Perrier just happened to be one of the few survivors of Dredd's resistance operations and, in particular, of that harrowing hit-and-run campaign of the previous week. So, purely by virtue of staying alive this long, she had assumed the role of Dredd's second-in-command, or chief of staff, or whatever. And now Dredd had departed on his desperate, last-gasp, do-or-die mission that might just turn this war around, so it was all on Perrier. Until a couple of weeks ago, she had been just another slab-jockey. Now, she was left running the war.

HER FACE WAS pale and pinched with tiredness, but she was a Judge, and she would do her job, no matter how big it was. And she certainly wasn't going to back down to an irascible sector chief who was seemingly hell-bent on fighting his own war without any regard to the bigger picture.

"You know how we've held out this long, Mercer?" she said. "It's because the city's so big. That's how. There's a lot of territory that the enemy has to conquer, and there's a lot of places for us to hide.

"But right now, we're pretty much out of places to hide. We can't get pushed any further south because the south just isn't there anymore. The Sovs are giving us a breathing space only because they have to consolidate their grip on the eastern and western sectors. When they've done that, they're going to take a deep breath before they huff and they puff and they blow us all away.

"So no. I'm not letting you go back to Sector 212 or wherever you call home. Out of the question. No way. The war is here. We fight it here."

"I don't remember you getting elected to the Council of Five, Perrier. What can you do to stop me?"

"Well, first I can appeal to reason, Mercer. Look, we don't dissipate our fighting strength. If you take your people off north, then that's three Judges who aren't holding the line here. If that's not good enough for you,

I can deny you our resources. You need your bikes recharged? You need your ammo replenished? Do it somewhere else. Oh yeah... and I nearly forgot. You were talking to Dredd about his plan. Whatever you know is too much. So, if you go behind enemy lines, you constitute a grave security risk. In other words, if you try to leave, I'm just going to have to shoot you."

Mercer looked at her and considered his options.

"You make a convincing case, Perrier. Where do you want us?"

THREE

THE END WAS close now.

The resistance headquarters that was run by Perrier and staffed by the few Judges like Underhill was really no more than Dredd's temporary command post. Without Dredd, it had pretty much lost its position as supreme authority. Perrier and her people still coordinated operations, but (with the exception of wayward sector chiefs) they didn't give orders. They didn't have to. The war was being fought by Judges, and a Mega-City Judge wasn't someone who had to look to higher authority. Perrier coordinated strategy and logistics, but all tactical decisions were made by the Judges in the field. They'd been trained. They knew what needed to be done in any given situation, and they were not afraid to fight, whatever the odds, to the last bullet and to the last breath, if need be. There were no allies to come to their aid in this mortal hour. The other cities that had once been part of the United States had seen Mega-City One's silos emptied to no purpose. They'd seen the missiles vanish just before they struck their East-Meg targets, instantly erased by a Sov secret weapon infinitely more effective than the old laser meshes that protected the Mega-Cities. Given this imbalance of defensive capability, Mega-City Two and Texas City, either wisely or cravenly, elected to stay out of the fight.

So there was no hope for Mega-City One, but Judges don't need hope.

"WHAT'S THE DEAL, Chief?" asked Robinson, when Mercer returned from his unprofitable meeting with Perrier. "We ready to go?"

"Negative, Robinson. Change of plan. Listen up."

He opened up a map and put them in the picture.

"You've heard that the enemy's massing up here around I-29," he said. "The rain stops, the Sovs get moving. Our front holds for a couple of hours tops, and then everyone bugs out. Everything goes backwards in a hurry. The retreat stops two kilometres behind us. A new line of resistance is being established along the Sector 13 Axis, but our guys will need a little time to consolidate before the Sovs make their next push. That's where we come in. We cover the retreat and we delay the enemy follow-up for as long as possible."

"What are our assets?" asked Steinman.

"You, me, Robinson."

Steinman and Robinson merely nodded. They hadn't been expecting much better. It had been that sort of war.

"Oh yeah," went on Mercer, "there are Citi-Def units too. We take charge of one each. But I don't know if we can really count them as assets. Questions? No? Good. Let's get this done and then maybe we can get back home."

JOSEPH MCCARTHY WAS one of a row of old-fashioned blocks overlooking the southbound trans-sector X-pressway. A predecessor to those colossal self-sufficient blocks that were the chief characteristic of Mega-City One these days, McCarthy had a pre-war population of no more than a few thousand, with none of the civic amenities and commercial spaces that newer blocks had as standard.

Instead, it grudgingly shared a retail and recreational area with three identical blocks—Tiger Woods, Cat Stevens, and John Cougar Mellancamp—in a failed social experiment known locally as the Josie and the Pussycats Housing Project. Stevens had been an early and fatal casualty of the block wars, but the remaining three blocks were positioned so as to dominate a stretch of the highway while providing mutually supporting fire. The project stood in one of those open areas which could have been residential or industrial development, or could even have been parkland, yet somehow, even in a place of such intensive urban planning as Mega-City One, ended up as litter-strewn wasteground.

Mercer's team took one block apiece. This was to be their battlefield.

*   *   *

JUDGES DON'T DO birthdays. Those who'd been enlisted straight out of Justice Department Genetic Control didn't even have birthdays. But if Robinson did take note of the date, and if she did somehow manage to live long enough to see another, then her next birthday would be no more than her twenty-fourth. Alongside her youth there was her small stature. She might look like she had a body built out of shock absorbers, but at the same time she barely made height requirement.

Yet when she walked into Josie McCarthy to take charge of a couple of platoons of hard-worn, war-weary Citizens' Defence, none of that counted. She felt nothing but confidence. She was a Mega-City Judge, and she was back doing what she lived to do: laying down the law.

"Judge Robinson," she said, pointing to her badge for the benefit of those who might be slow on the uptake. "Listen up."

She outlined the essence of the plan. Cover the withdrawal. Inflict casualties. Get out.

"Questions? No? Good. Let's get this done."

The Citi-Defs didn't need much in the way of tactical instruction. They took up position and looked to their weapons like the veterans most of them were. These weren't the regular blowhards and posers playing soldiers and survivalists in the local block militias. These were people who had learned this past couple of weeks what soldiering and surviving were all about. Ten days ago, they'd taken up arms in a lunatic battle in the name of their block.

Today those blocks were mostly burnt-out ruins, left behind somewhere up north. Their names, which had been so proudly fought for, were still emblazoned on helmets and jackets, but those names meant little now. Now, it was just about the city. For those who, even after ten days, still had some fight in them, the fight was for the Big Meg. If your flak vest advertised you as a Norman Rockwell blocker, and your number two on the beam weapon came from Dizzy Gillespie, that was just the way things were now. The only symbol that counted for anything anymore was the eagle of Mega-City justice. Judge Robinson was wearing that eagle, and no one thought to question her authority.

Up north, when Robinson had started her fight against the invader, it had mostly been a matter of her guys on one side and the Sovs on the other. There hadn't been too many people to get caught in the middle. The block wars had gone quite a way in thinning out the population of Sector 212, and the subsequent nuclear strike had done the rest. After that, the survivors just stayed in their bunkers or joined the refugee columns heading south, leaving the field clear for the combatants.

Things were different down here. The heart of the city had been largely spared from the bombing. After all, the Sovs no doubt wanted something more than irradiated wasteland as a prize for all their efforts. And the intact buildings were still largely inhabited because, even if you didn't care to stay where you were in the face of imminent invasion, where were you expected to go? There wasn't a whole lot of city left to the south.

So any locals that were left were obliged to stay put, and for the refugees who'd made it this far, this was the end of the line. So, with all these people around, the Judges had to do a little policing again.

The power was still on in McCarthy Block, which allowed energy weapons to be charged. It also allowed Robinson to coordinate matters through the public address system.

"Attention, all residents! This is the Justice Department! Apartments overlooking the X-pressway will shortly be commandeered by Citi-Def units. Your compliance in this matter is mandatory. That means you get out when we tell you to get out. You can seek shelter with your neighbours on the south and west sides of the block. Anyone who does not comply will face serious time. Stay calm, and thank you for your cooperation."

That would have to do it. It was far too late for evacuation, and she'd seen what happened when a column of Rad-Sweepers wanted to use the same road as a column of refugees.

Radio communication, which was usually such a fraught business because of enemy monitoring (and had been a big no-no in the guerrilla war she'd been fighting up north), wasn't such a big deal down here. Here the war was being fought with greater intensity, and here the airwaves were so crowded with military traffic that trying to pinpoint any given signal was a waste of effort. Thus, it was perfectly possible for Robinson to keep things organised throughout the whole block. That didn't mean that she cared to micromanage every damn thing.

"Judge? This is Sarge Garza. We got us a problem up in apartment 109b."

Robinson had already pegged Garza (late of Gene Pitney Block, Sector 336—Go Gene!) as an ineffectual squad leader, but he'd managed to stay alive this long, and he was sticking around to fight some more, so she wasn't complaining. She went to have a look.

She found Garza and his team standing outside an apartment door, looking glum and useless.

"They won't open up, Judge," was all the excuse she was offered.

The occupants of 109b had had their warning, and it had been a long time since Robinson had performed a good old forced entry so, without hesitation, she addressed the door with the full force of the law. It was a decent door, well supplied with locks, but with an experimental shouldering she accurately gauged its weaknesses. Then came the satisfying one-two of shooting out one of the hinges and kicking in the rest.

"You can't come in!" shrieked the sole occupant, unkempt and malnourished. "I've done nothing wrong! I know my rights!"

"You have no rights in this matter, citizen. What you do have is a power outlet, and we need it for the long-range disruptor we're setting up at that window. Now, step aside."

"But my stuff! What about my stuff?"

The stuff in question was unremarkable. Besides some

pretty shabby furniture and household appliances that weren't worth stealing, all Robinson could see were a few collectibles from a TV show that had been a thing back when she'd been a kid. "Lolo and Lulu Itty-Bitty?" she said. "They're not even in their original packaging. Get a grip, citizen, and get across the hall. Tell the neighbours I told them to let you in."

And she left him, whimpering about his Itty-Bitties while the Citi-Def boys set up their disruptor. She was hoping that everything else would run smoothly, but knew, alas, that no one had yet gauged the depth of the average Mega-citizen's stupid obstinacy.

The disruptor was just about the best of the anti-robot weapons available to her. It had the same effect as a scrambler grenade, but you didn't have to be within twenty metres of the target for it to be effective. The plan was to hold it in reserve until the Rad-Sweepers—the Sov robotic tanks—were too close to break contact but not close enough to break through. At ground level all she had were a few improvised anti-tank mines of doubtful utility, and a couple of lazookas, which couldn't be expected to last long.

She radioed her partner over in Mellancamp, vainly hoping that the arsenal over there might be more extensive.

"Negative," replied Steinman. "Small arms. Nothing but small arms. Scattamatics, over-and-unders, Sunday night specials, all the ammo you can eat. I've got crates piled up in the parking garage if you need any."

"Yeah. Thought as much. Thanks but no thanks. We've

got more than enough of the small stuff over here. That's not our problem."

"Not now it's not."

"No. Not right now."

Because if, by some miracle, the city got through this, the streets would be awash with guns for years to come. It wasn't like you could expect a proud veteran of the Apocalypse War to hand over the weapon that helped him win it. Unless, that is, he needed a few creds before welfare day. Then, no doubt, he'd be willing to sell it to any criminal element that might be interested.

But that was a worry for another day.

If there was another day.

The radio was sounding a general alert. Bad weather or no, the Sov offensive was on its way.

FOUR

THE STORM WAS still blowing when the East-Meg attack rolled forward. War Marshal Kazan, the East-Meg supreme commander, did not tolerate delay. The leading formations suffered devastating losses, but that's what the second and third waves were for. It took nearly an hour, but they broke through the main line of resistance in several places, forcing a general withdrawal all along the front.

Following up the Mega-City retreat along the southbound highway came the 532nd People's Automated Armoured Division, commanded this day by Judge Commissar Gorokhov. Until earlier that morning, he had never exercised field command, but his predecessor had become a casualty of Kazan's impatience when he'd argued that a hurricane was a valid excuse for postponing military operations. Gorokhov—up until then merely the officer in charge of Ideological Compliance—had been present at the short video conference, and when he'd heard the tone of the War Marshal's voice, he'd had no hesitation in stepping up and shooting his commander in the back of the neck. Gorokhov had not been seeking promotion, but it had clearly been one of those times when an officer must exercise his initiative.

Generalship was new to him, but in Marshal Kazan he at least had a template to follow. Thus, when the commander of his close air support squadron had protested at the impossibility of operating in such conditions, he'd had her arrested without a second thought. In case that didn't send the message forcefully enough, he had two junior commanders join her on the Siberian transport after they, too, had voiced doubts about the plan of attack.

After that, everything ran smoothly. True, the 532nd Division had been reduced by nearly one third in short order, but those losses had mostly been in robotic materiel, and the important thing was that the attack was still nearly on schedule.

Now, Gorokhov's Rad-Sweepers, having broken the line along Inter-sector 29, were pushing south at last: an armoured spearhead that would pierce the vitals of Mega-City One and bring this brutal war to a victorious close.

Victory couldn't come too soon. East-Meg Judges were staunch in their duty to their homeland and their cause, but this war had been a demoralising experience. Testifying to that were all the personnel who'd been shot or arrested for their insufficient commitment. Gorokhov didn't want to send any more to join that number, and he certainly didn't want to join them himself.

But one last effort, maybe only one more day, and they could walk in triumph along the streets of their conquest.

On the map, the battlefield was a steadily shrinking strip of territory that straggled across the central sectors. But the city could not be accurately represented on a two-dimensional map. It rose level upon level in massive housing projects and towering monuments to corporate vanity, all connected by a crazy swirl of suspended roadways and rail lines.

The block wars had shattered windows and filled the streets with debris. The nuclear bombs had wrecked or levelled whole sectors. The lights were out in the deep neon canyons. But here in the core of the city, it was still the high-rise metropolis built for eight-hundred million people. It was a vertical battlefield.

Pushing the front forward was next to useless if the front were on ground level and the enemy still held the territory directly overhead. Air supremacy counted for little when air power could only dominate the upper levels, leaving a warren of strongholds below.

The pitiless attritional campaign fought last week in the northern sectors had taught the Sovs to be wary. The suspended roadways could be cut too easily, sending their traffic plummeting earthwards. On city bottom, on the other hand, the invaders had found themselves forced into narrow killing grounds, from which there had been no escape when the thermal charges had been ignited.

For Gorokhov and the other commanders in his position, it would have been better if the whole city had been razed with atomic fire. But while that might had given them a wide open space to fight in, it would have denied them a city to conquer.

Gorokhov considered the options open to him. The left-hand route led through vertiginous city blocks joined by a tangle of roads. But to the right, the buildings were older, lower, and surrounded by a little more open space. The map told him that the nearest building was called Joseph McCarthy Block. No doubt it would be manned by whatever Mega-City forces were still capable of bearing arms, but they would be dealt with.

"THEY'RE COMING THIS way," Robinson announced over the radio.

"Knew they would," replied Mercer. "They're thinking this is the easier way."

Robinson's Citi-Def people didn't share Mercer's satisfaction at the way the attack was developing.

"There's tanks, Judge," said a man with binoculars. He was one of the locals, whose unit had been sent over from Tiger Woods to beef up numbers at Josie McCarthy. His block affiliation was proudly displayed on his body armour ('Tigers Would! Rarr!'), but his voice was lacking that defiance.

"There's them electric-squids-with-legs-Sentenoid things too. Mostly tanks, though. Lotsa tanks, Judge. What we gonna do?"

But Robinson was a veteran of the vertical battlefield, and she knew one of the Rad-Sweeper's critical weaknesses.

"Stay cool," she said. "Tanks can't climb stairs."

There was enough juice for one good ambush. Just bushwhack them and get out fast in the smoke. A protracted fight would only lose the good guys their initiative and allow the Sovs to get imaginative. No, scratch that—the Sovs wouldn't get imaginative. They'd just flatten the whole block and come rolling on over the rubble.

Given the population density, civilian casualties were pretty much unavoidable, but the Judges weren't about to turn someone's home into the Alamo either.

Rad-Sweepers couldn't climb stairs, but Sentenoids could, so the Sentenoids were targeted first. Barring a lucky shot disabling a knee bearing, even a concentrated burst of small-arms fire wasn't going to slow down a Sentenoid, but it could certainly get its attention.

A Citi-Def squad that had done this kind of thing before had been chosen to open proceedings. Robinson reckoned they'd be less likely to lose it under pressure. Justifying her hopes in them, they opened fire and withdrew, ducking between abandoned vehicles, heading for the burnt-out convenience store around the corner. The Sentenoids followed, laying down suppressing fire as they went. This would have gone badly for the squad in the convenience store if it hadn't been for the carefully laid mines that took out the two lead Sentenoids. The robots, their legs either blown off or twisted into uselessness, were reduced to scrabbling on the ground with their huge steel tentacles, trying to reorient themselves and reacquire their targets.

Robinson's squad didn't give them time. High explosive

rounds from her Lawgiver and the one portable 20-millimetre that her team could boast were enough to finish off the two mangled robots, and another two just to be sure. Then the Mega-City fighters changed positions fast, moving to the upper levels before the Rad-Sweepers arrived to show the Sentenoids how it should be done.

As Robinson had counted on, a massive robot tank built for the nuclear battlefield was not well suited to counter-insurgency operations. Two of them came around the corner of Josie McCarthy, their guns questing angrily, but they found it impossible to elevate their main armament enough. Their assailants occupied windows and balconies directly above, where they had cover from the Rad-Sweepers' more versatile secondary laser turrets, and from where they could drop incendiary grenades.

The tanks didn't burn, but they were inconvenienced, and evidently annoyed enough to call for reinforcements. In short order, the small shopping plaza was filled with a whole platoon of Rad-Sweepers, blundering ineffectually in the smoke.

That's when the lazookas did their thing, blasting the rearmost Rad-Sweepers and blocking the exit.

"OK, people," announced Robinson. "That's as good as it's going to get. Let's skip before they get really mad at us."

The energy signatures from the lazookas were too great to be hidden, so the order was to ditch them and run. One team had lugged their weapon this far and weren't prepared to discard it now, but the thing was too cumbersome to redeploy in time, and still hot enough to show up on enemy scanners. A vengeful robot didn't even wait to get a bead, but blasted away a whole section of the building to get at them.

As far as Robinson was concerned, there was no point in looking for any survivors. The lazooka team had just got what you get for disobeying orders. She concentrated her efforts on covering the withdrawal. That was what her Lawmaster was for. Its front-mounted Cyclops laser was the most powerful anti-armour weapon available in the defence of Josie McCarthy, but, as with the lazooka teams, Robinson made a target of herself as soon as she fired it. Of course, she had the advantage over the lazooka teams insofar as she had a powerful motorcycle under her, but gunning it out of here right away would somewhat defeat the purpose of her one-woman rearguard action. Until her people got clear, she had to stay put.

She dodged around in the smoke, knocking out a couple of Rad-Sweepers and frying more than a few Sentenoids, but there was only one of her and a whole lot of them. She well knew that the enemy machinery was slow, but not stupid. The robots that were shooting at her were taking losses, but they were pinning her in place while other robot units outflanked her position. Her planned escape route was probably already blocked, but that's what the long-range disruptor up on the tenth floor was for.

"Garza," she said, "I'm coming out by the east side. Be ready to give me some cover."

"That's a roj, Judge," came the answer, and she

steered her bike down an alleyway, hi-exing a Sentenoid that tried to block her.

The alley came out onto a slip road and, as she'd feared, the Sov tanks had got there ahead of her. She halted a moment to see exactly how things stood. That's when she saw a lone figure wandering out into the mechanised traffic. She recognised the dishevelled resident of Apartment 109b, crying something about his precious collectibles. He was trying to get the robots' attention, but they'd never seen *The Itty-Bitty Show*, and they didn't even register him as a threat. Robinson would have dismissed him too, except that he was very clearly pointing up towards his hab and the disruptor that was emplaced there.

"My stuff!" he was wailing. "109b! My stuff is in there! They got guys with a big gun! They're touching my stuff!"

The robots were ignoring him, but, just down the line, Robinson could see Sov Judges riding along on a Rad-Sweeper. They probably weren't fans of Lolo and Lulu Itty-Bitty either, but they might well be interested in the concealed energy weapon that the kook was pointing at.

She accelerated hard out of the alley, aiming for a space between two tanks.

"Now, Garza!" she ordered.

Citi-Def Sergeant Garza might not have impressed her much on first assessment, but he knew his stuff when it came to the disruptor. The Rad-Sweeper nearest to her swung its main gun in her direction, but seemed to change its mind. The one next to it then chose to break formation, slewing sideways in the road before beginning to advance and reverse pointlessly, bumping into other vehicles and blocking the southbound lanes. Better yet, the two Rad-Sweepers, struck suddenly stupid, blocked the line of fire for the rest of the tanks in the column. Robinson bent low over her bike and raced by. Even though the enemy was in temporary disarray, there was no point in trying to inflict further damage. Just get out fast. She did, however, turn in the saddle and, from commendably long range, put a bullet into the guy from 109b. Collaboration with the enemy could not go unpunished.

FIVE

THE STORM, WHICH was supposed to have passed, had done no such thing. Although it lashed them with none of its earlier fury, the rain returned as the Citi-Def squad from Josie McCarthy piled into a battered hover bus and lit out of there at speed. They bypassed Mellancamp and skirted the ruins of Stevens, weaving fast. Robinson caught up with them as they reached Tiger Woods, where Mercer was in charge.

The rain had helped to hide their withdrawal, so maybe the Sovs hadn't yet realised they were gone, which maybe explained what the Sovs did next. On the other hand, it could just as well have been pure vindictiveness.

A few civilian casualties were pretty much unavoidable, but this was a massacre.

"The dirty stomm-suckers," said Mercer, watching through binoculars. "Don't they know we've pulled out? There's just regular cits in there now."

And those citizens were being subjected to methodical bombardment from Rad-Sweeper guns, floor by floor, window by window, reducing the ugly facade of McCarthy to a gaping concrete honeycomb. And still the guns fired, even though the balconies that might have been used as firing positions were pulverised and anyone who could possibly have resisted the East-Meg advance was no more.

In normal times, Judges spent their entire waking lives keeping the citizenry in line. It was an article of faith that every citizen was a potential criminal. Citizens were to be watched, policed, and—as was too often necessary—beaten, shot, or hauled off for long periods of incarceration. Citizens, in short, were nothing but gruddamn trouble.

But the Judges were sworn to defend them, and that meant that no one—no one—could come into this city and start killing them like they didn't matter.

"Nothing we can do, chief," said Robinson.

"No," said Mercer. "But we can try and stop the same thing happening again. I'm scrubbing the operation. We can fight the drokkers someplace else. Somewhere there aren't so many civilians."

Robinson was relieved. Too many refugees had been counted as part of the necessary collateral damage in the war up north. The road links they'd been crowding had had to go, but that didn't make it any more palatable. Robinson was sick of killing innocents, and she was glad that Mercer was feeling the same way. He was right. This wasn't a crucial choke-point like the ones up north. There were other places the Judges could choose to fight the drokkers.

He switched on his radio. "Steinman, you getting this? Abort. Just tell everyone to hang something white from their windows and then you get the hell out. Steinman, you copy?"

But Steinman had his own ideas.

HE'D SEEN HOW the Sovs had responded to resistance at McCarthy, and he didn't think that the white flag was going to be something they'd respect when they got to the next block along. Even before he got Mercer's message, he'd decided on his own course of action. Just as Mercer wanted, he'd ordered his Citi-Def personnel to bug out fast, but he wouldn't be going with them. He wouldn't be going until he was sure that every last citizen in John Cougar Mellancamp was safe.

"Attention! All residents! This is the Justice Department!" Steinman had the message relayed through both the block public address and his bike's loudhailer.

"You are hereby ordered to vacate this block! Right now! Take no more than food, water, and warm clothing. And when I say right now, I mean right now!"

It reminded him of before, when Block Mania was raging, and someone who wore his badge but wasn't quite him, had stood in the hallway of a city block and addressed the residents. That had been in Belinda Carlisle, and he'd been announcing that anyone who stuck their nose out of doors, or anyone who might even look as if they were defying the right of the Judges to rule over Sector 212, would be summarily executed.

And he'd meant it, and he'd been enjoying himself.

Evacuating Mellancamp wasn't going to make up for those days, but it was something he had to do anyway.

A few fearful faces looked down from windows, and a few uncertain figures came out through the block's exits, but it wasn't enough. Even with the power intermittent and the vid showing nothing but radiation warnings, Sov propaganda, and sitcom repeats, it took a lot to make your average citizen come outside—especially when there was a lot more gunfire on the streets than usual. Steinman reckoned that there were at least a couple of thousand still in the block. He figured it was time to start going door to door.

"WHAT THE HELL he thinks he's doing?" said Mercer, watching Steinman herding an ever-growing crowd of reluctant citizens in front of Mellancamp Block. The Sovs were still busy pulverising Josie McCarthy, but they were only ten minutes away at best. A lot less if they decided to call in air support.

"Search me, chief," said Robinson, but she thought she knew. Steinman was doing his death-or-glory thing again. She'd seen it before, more than once, when he'd insisted on being the last man out; when he'd been the one prepared to stay behind with his hand on the detonator. So if he was going to get suicidally brave just to help his buddies bring down a bridge or something, he sure as hell wasn't going to run out when there were hundreds of innocent cits to be saved.

This late in the game, the evacuation of Woods was out of the question. Even if Steinman somehow managed to pull off whatever he was doing, emptying another block right now would only add to the confusion. Mercer did, however, ensure that Tiger Woods was bedecked in approximations of white flags, even if some citizens had to be convinced that floral curtains and bedsheets advertising cartoon characters were not formally recognised under the rules of war.

After that, it was time to get Judges and Citi-Def out of there, leaving the Pussycats Project open to enemy occupation.

Before he left, Mercer addressed the residents by bullhorn.

"These blocks are about to come under the jurisdiction of the forces of East-Meg One. For your own safety, citizens are strongly advised not to offer any resistance. That doesn't mean that you should welcome the creeps with open arms. Just remember: we'll be coming back, and collaborators will be shot."

He turned to Robinson. "Now what in the name of Grud do we do about Steinman?"

But it seemed that the Sovs were already answering that question.

THE MELLANCAMP BLOCKERS, even when they'd allowed themselves to be forced from their homes, had not obediently set out southwards in an orderly column. Instead, they were clustering in front of the block, maybe hoping to be let back in again—certainly not willing to head out into the wild unknown, whatever the Judge was telling them. Inside, Steinman was driving the reluctant residents like cattle, and hurrying up the process by firing shots into the ceiling, but there were too many people and not enough time. This was never going to work, and he had Mercer in his ear telling him so.

"Stay cool, chief," Steinman lied. "Everything's going fine." He had two children clinging to his back and another one under his arm. He had trouble keeping his balance when it came to delivering a kick to a citizen who wanted to go back for her bowling trophies.

As he pushed everyone outside and was turning to go back in for more, he saw that the Rad-Sweepers were on the move again, advancing on a broader front than before.

"Everybody!" he yelled. "Get off the road and put your hands above your heads! Move it!"

"Are we under arrest, Judge?" asked a plaintive voice.

"Your case is being considered, citizen. Your cooperation in this matter will be taken into account. Now get out of the way of those tanks and assume the position."

Steinman had no idea if the Sovs would accept the obvious submission of John Cougar Mellancamp, but they would certainly be within their rights to open fire if they saw that a Mega-City Judge was still there and offering no token of surrender.

He mounted his Lawmaster, and, making sure that the Sovs noticed him, he sped off across the wasteground. His bike's computer was warning him that they had him on weapons lock, but he didn't take any evasive action until he had put as much distance as possible between himself and the civilians. With laser beams searing the air above his head, he raced to the shelter of some ruins, and made it there a split second before the first rounds from the big guns hit. All the hi-tech stuff in his helmet protected him somewhat from the concussion, but his head was still ringing when he broke cover again. He needed to show the Sovs that he was still in the game. He needed to keep drawing their fire.

ROBINSON AND MERCER watched, and knew that he wasn't going to last long.

"He's ducking and diving like nobody's business, chief, but there's more Rad-Sweepers moving around on the left. What do we do?"

Robinson already knew without being told that there was nothing they could do. Not against those odds. They could just take what little was to be gained from Steinman's sacrificial action and get while the getting was good, hoping that when their time came, their own sacrificial actions might count for more.

So, Mercer and Robinson merely held their ground while the Citi-Def forces withdrew behind them and an adventurous young scrawler, delighted to get official sponsorship even at this late hour, finished spraying the word 'surrender' down the face of Tiger Woods Block.

"At least he's drawn the Rad-Sweepers away from Mellancamp," said Mercer. "I can see a few tanks rolling by, but they're not firing at the block. Not rolling over the cits either, as far as I can make out."

So, there was that at least. They watched through binoculars as Steinman zigzagged in and out of sight, but in an ever-decreasing compass.

"They've got him hemmed in," said Robinson, standing on her bike to get a better view. "He's not running anymore. I think he's turning to fight them. Yes!"

Even without binoculars, they both saw the flash of the Cyclops laser.

"He's got one! He's got two! Holy Moses, there he goes!"

The boom of explosions reached them.

"What is it, Robinson? I can't see."

"Neither can I, chief. Too much smoke. But he ran his Lawmaster right at them. I've never seen the self-destruct on one of those babies before."

She couldn't see any Rad-Sweepers moving anymore either. The Sovs had paid heavily for a single Mega-City Judge.

"Well, good work, Steinman," said Mercer. "Come on. We've got to go."

But Robinson stayed where she was, one foot on the saddle and one on the pillion.

"Wait up, chief. Something's moving in the smoke."

"What kind of something?"

"Something—um—Judge-shaped? Cover me. I'll be right back."

If Steinman had a death wish, its fulfilment would have to wait for another time.

SIX

Steinman had knocked out four East-Meg Rad-Sweepers single-handed and had come out alive, but it was no triumph. He had saved lives, but how much longer would those lives endure? And the Mega-City forces had given up more territory to the enemy, and there was now almost nothing left to give up. After Robinson picked up Steinman from the battlefield, the three Judges rode out on two bikes, ready to fight again, but knowing there couldn't be any more tactical retreats. The next main line of resistance was no better than the last, and they'd been forced out of the last one all too easily.

When Mercer's team took up their new positions, they accepted that here there were no choices left to them except death or surrender, and Judges don't surrender.

The Sovs accepted as much. They didn't make any demands. They didn't waste time with probing attacks either. They just wanted this war over and done with.

Night came on, and massive air and artillery bombardment with it. The Judges who were dug in among the ruins of the Sector 11 Sports Palace didn't expect to see the next day. It looked like this would be the last night of the Apocalypse War: the last night of Mega-City One.

None of her team was wounded, but when they hooked up with other Judges again, Robinson sought out a Med unit. Hunkered down against the percussion of the barrage and the steady rain of debris from the upper levels, she returned to Mercer and Steinman bearing gifts.

"Candy bars, Robinson?"

"One candy bar, chief. It's all I could find. But don't fret. You'll get your share."

"I thought you were looking for the Meds?"

"I was, but they don't have any supplies to spare, so you'll have to do with one third of a Gooey Bar. Here you go."

"This isn't gooey. This is kind of crunchy," said Mercer.

"What can I say? The grit gets into everything."

It wasn't strictly true that the medical units weren't sharing out their supplies. The Med Judge that Robinson had been talking to was desperately short of almost everything, but had no problem in parting with a couple of pills that had been issued at the start of the war and hadn't really been needed since. It probably didn't make any difference now, but it made Robinson happy that she had finally found a way to make Mercer take the Block Mania antidote.

* * *

THE BOMBARDMENT ENDED and the Rad-Sweepers were upon them before the last shells fell. As always, the Sentenoids were stalking along the edges of the attack, burning resistance out of holes and corners. There were humans too. The Sov personnel had neither the firepower nor the armour of the robot units, but they were Judges of East-Meg One, and it was going to take a lot to stop them. They had suffered discouraging losses and setbacks, but they'd been winning steadily, nonetheless. Now they would punish their foes for those setbacks. Now they would complete their victory.

On that last night, the central sectors were lit not by streetlights and advertising, but by burning city blocks and by the flashes of gunfire; by the glare of incendiaries and beams of energy weapons.

The defenders fought in small bands. There was little else they could do. Where their deaths might mean something, they stood their ground and they died. If they could fight a little longer and punish the enemy that slightest bit more, then they mined their positions and carried their wounded out before taking up the fight again a few hundred metres farther back.

They fought on the upper road junctions, prey to Sov aircraft. They fought in the dark maze of the lower levels, bringing down buildings on the invaders and themselves alike. In the high-rise malls and sprawling residential complexes, they fought until the city they died for was a battle-scarred ruin that citizens who'd lived there all their lives wouldn't recognise. In the Sector 11 Sports Palace, they held their ground because it might as well be here as anywhere.

And in a half-flooded missile silo at Bostok, in East-Meg territory, on the other side of the world, one desperate band attempted the unthinkable.

Like those who were fighting back in the city, Dredd's team in Bostok 7 had little prospect of seeing another day. They had left a trail of dead on their way in, but that was nothing to what was to come.

What they attempted was terrible beyond measure, but all those who had seen half their own city burned to ash would likewise have put aside all doubt along with all compassion.

So a Justice Department telepath, who knew human pain and human weakness like few others, and knew also the fatal outcome of what she was doing, did it all the same. She mercilessly stripped from the mind of a Sov technician the information needed. Two technical Judges who had thus far used their expertise in engineering and electronics in the service of their city, took that information and fed it into the launch system. And the man who had dedicated his life to the law put his finger on the button, and did not hesitate when the moment came to press it.

Bostok 7 Silo was armed with twenty missiles of the type known as Total Annihilation Devices, the doomsday device. The weapon of last resort. Even the states that had fought the Great Atomic War and had built these weapons never seriously intended that they should ever be used as more than a deterrent.

Judge Dredd launched all of them. He was not a man for half measures.

Mega-City One had had its own missiles—back when this war began—but the Sovs had knocked them out. It wasn't just that the Sovs had targeted the silos and hunted down all the mobile nuclear platforms everywhere from high orbit to the deepest sea beds: they had also vaporised the missiles that had been launched. Like Mega-City One, the Sovs had their laser defence screen, but their version, whatever unknown technology they used, was so much more effective. However, seeing as it had to encompass the whole of East-Meg One, it took a little while to get it powered up. For nukes coming all the way from the Cursed Earth, there was time. With the birds flying in from nearby Bostok, there was none.

The East-Meg defence net did what it could in the brief time it was given, but three of Dredd's missiles got through. It was more than enough.

IN MEGA-CITY ONE, in Sector 11, on what was left of the fifth floor of the Sports Palace, three Judges sat behind a rampart of rubble. Left behind by Dredd, counted their ammunition and waited.

"How are you feeling, chief?"

"That's the second time you've asked me, Robinson. I'm feeling drokking dandy. What have you got on the scanner?"

"Multiple contacts. The Rad-Sweepers you know about. They can't reach us where we are, but they can give a hell of a lot of covering fire to the Sov Judges that can. I think this blip here is them."

"Estimate numbers?"

"The Sentenoids are showing up clearly, so if we say one Sentenoid per squad of humans, my guess is we're looking at a concentration of eighty to a hundred Sov Judges. How about we call up heavy weapons on them?"

"Negative," said Mercer. "The second the artillery—what's left of it—opens up, they paint a target on themselves. They're being held back for the big stuff, and I don't think eighty-something guys and a bunch of robots is going to impress them."

"We can do this," put in Steinman, but then that's what he always said when faced with impossible odds. Robinson wasn't optimistic. An East-Meg Judge might only be a Sov, but he was still a Judge, and no slouch. Likewise, the war robots were only droids, but she'd faced enough of them the past couple of weeks to grant them a healthy respect.

As predicted, heavy Sov fire forced them to keep their heads down as the attack came in. The squad on their left was taken out in a single blast, and the team on their right was forced to clear out of their hole, leaving their crew-served pulse blaster behind, wrecked.

Robinson crouched, reading the scanner, knowing that human contacts wouldn't show up clearly on it. Given the smoke and darkness, she wouldn't even see them until they were right on top of her.

She had her Lawgiver, which was as good a sidearm as had ever been made, but what she and Mega-City One needed right now was something bigger.

Dredd's three Total Annihilation Devices were more

than enough. In a blinding instant five hundred million people were incinerated, vaporised. The air above the city boiled away. The very bedrock on which East-Meg One stood was scoured. All across the continent the effects were felt, and if the other cities had not been built to survive on this blasted world, they would have suffered grievous consequences. Far beyond the searing radiation and the seismic upheaval, the vengeance of Mega-City One was widely advertised. Clear across the world, the sky over the central sectors was lit up by a flash from the east that made the attacking Sov troops look up and pause a moment. They didn't know it yet, but they had just lost the war.

The defenders of Mega-City One didn't know it yet either, but there was a handful who at least realised what they were seeing. These were the few who had been there when Dredd had assembled his squad. They hadn't been told the details, but deduction was one of the things they were good at. So, in Dredd's old command post, Perrier and her headquarters staff knew, and in a foxhole in the ruins, one small team of Judges could guess. Ever since their dismay at being excluded from the mission, they'd wondered what Dredd was really up to, and Robinson's theory was the one they were going with.

They were almost afraid to hope, but they'd seen enough nuclear fireballs to know that what they were seeing now had to be TADs. Dredd had actually pulled it off. He'd totalled East-Meg One.

So, the Mega-City Judges had a chance at last.

SEVEN

THE NEWS WENT out on all channels. Mega-City One, as it turned out, was not as blind as the enemy had supposed. A few surviving spy satellites, keeping dark until now, looked down on the hellish roiling spectacle in western Eurasia and confirmed that East-Meg One had been at the centre of it. Resistance HQ, as it also turned out, had known more than they'd let on. They knew that it was Dredd's mission that was behind it all.

Robinson radioed Judge Underhill. She hadn't just been making conversation with him before. It never hurt to have a contact in Control, even when Control was living in such reduced circumstances.

"Robinson, what can I do for you? Kinda busy."

"Holding out on me, Underhill?"

"What? It wasn't like I knew all the details. And I'm supposed to fill in every passing Judge on every secret mission we happen to have going?"

"You mean there's more?"

"That's classified, Robinson. Anyway, what do you

want? Make it snappy."

"Well, seeing as you know so much, I was wondering what the enemy's take on this is. You know, if you'd care to throw a bone to us poor little old front-line fighters here."

"Lot of noise on Sov command channels. Requests for clarification. Requests for orders. A lot of signals that can be read as 'What now?'. That kind of thing."

"That's good enough for me. Robinson out."

"What did he say?" asked Mercer.

"He said the Sovs are on the ropes," said Robinson. "He said to kick hell out of them."

"About gruddamn time."

Mega-City Judges were not the sort of people who waste opportunities. A few minutes ago, they had their backs to the wall. Now, they were using that same wall to rebound against the invaders. The East-Meg forces were confused, off-balance, trying to make sense of the situation, and suddenly they were hit by everything that Mega-City One still had in reserve.

The situation at the Sector 11 Sports Palace underwent a rapid reversal when artillery that wasn't even supposed to exist opened fire, breaking up the Rad-Sweeper formation that had been massing for the attack. The Sov troops that had been skirmishing forward on foot, their resolve badly shaken by rumours of the devastation of their home city, were reluctant to push on without armoured support, and their Sentenoids kept on getting picked off at long range by high explosive bullets.

The attack lost momentum in no time, and while the Sovs

were assessing how things now stood, the counter-attack fell on them. Squads of Mega-City Judges, who just an hour before had seemed so contemptibly weak, emerged from strongpoints in the ruins and started inflicting hurt.

JUDGE COMMISSAR GOROKHOV of the 532nd People's Automated Armoured Division watched the situation unravel from his command vehicle. He had seen the light in the sky, and he had heard the Mega-City resistance gleefully broadcast (in Sov, no less) that his city had been destroyed. He dismissed the news as disinformation and propaganda, ordering his troops to disregard it, but given the signals coming from his own high command, such an order was futile.

Among the flood of bad news that was assailing him were situation reports indicating a delay in taking objectives; of a stiffening of enemy resistance; of intensifying enemy counterstrokes. The reports were terse and factual, but his training in ideological compliance allowed him to read between the lines. His troops were wavering. They had lost sight of the inevitable victory. They had lost faith in their cause.

And while it was clear that it was his troops who were at fault here, he knew that he would get the blame. The War Marshal did not accept excuses. Any appraisal indicating that the tactical situation was slipping from his grasp would be seen as bald defeatism and an admission of failure. Gorokhov would not consider defeat. He would not admit failure.

As the signals from his front-line units became more urgent and more alarmed, he turned to Judge Alekhin, his second-in-command.

"The attack is to be sustained at all costs. Enemy resistance is to be overcome regardless of casualties. Withdrawal under any circumstances is strictly forbidden."

Alekhin knew a recipe for defeat when he heard it. It was his firm opinion that the attack had to be called off. The terrible change of events called for a period of consolidation. He knew that Gorokhov was making a mistake, but which was worse: disobeying direct orders or obeying them at fatal cost? Alekhin made his choice and reached for his pistol.

"Judge Gorokhov," he said, "I am relieving you of your command. Stand down and place yourself under arrest." But his gun wasn't out of his holster in time. Gorokhov had beaten him to the draw.

The two men stood in the confines of the command vehicle, the emergency lighting reflected in the sweat on their faces, and the clamour of the radios telling the story of a cascading disaster. Maybe Gorokhov would summon guards. Maybe he'd just save everyone a lot of paperwork by pulling the trigger. Neither man ever found out.

A ventilation hatch in the roof was forced open and a hand bomb was thrown in, landing between their feet before rolling underneath a computer console. They didn't have time to bail out of the vehicle. The last thing they heard was Mercer shouting, "This is for Josie and the Pussycats, you sons of bitches!"

EIGHT

THE TIDE TURNED during those few hours. Not only was the battle for Sector 11 won, but Sov forces were pushed all the way back to their start line along I-29. The feeling among the advancing Mega-City units was that the invaders could be booted all the way back to wherever-the-hell, but the momentum of their counter-attack gave out around midnight. Numbers were too small, distances too great, and the Sovs, although reeling with the sudden shock of events, were still a formidable army. What decided matters was the robotic element. Rad-Sweepers and Sentenoids didn't suffer from low morale. Fresh mechanised units were pushed into battle, containing and stabilising the situation.

Mercer, Robinson, and Steinman all made it through the night unscathed, but when the adrenaline wore off, they each felt the strain of those savage hours, and of all the days that had gone before. Robinson, even though she was the youngest of them, was glad when a halt was forced on them, and glad again when a summons from headquarters told them that they were being withdrawn from the line for the moment. If only headquarters had been a little nearer, and the bikes hadn't been left so far back.

Given the extent of Sov air power and surveillance, they were surprised to find that Perrier's command post was still in the same place, but Underhill, still manning communications, intimated that the underground Med and Tek facilities were too extensive to be relocated.

"The Tek workshop is rolling out ammo like you wouldn't believe," Underhill told them. "Hi-ex mostly. Upgraded stuff. I'd get it while it's hot if I were you. Oh yeah—and get a hatful of the stims the Med boys and girls are doling out. Keep you going for days. Trust me. Just make sure they give you something for the headaches the stims give you."

Perrier, when they found her, still looked like she could do with everything the underground field pharmacy had, but she just didn't have the time to worry about stuff like that. She was straight to business.

"You're going back north, Mercer. Today. Soon as possible. Right now."

Mercer grinned. "North? The fight's here, Perrier. You said so yourself."

"Don't give me a hard time, all right. We need someone to head for Sector 224 and you're it."

"That's the Sovs' back yard. You want us to go playing there?"

"It's your back yard. I'm letting you have it back if you want it."

"Sell it to me, Perrier. What's happening in 224?"

"OK. Sit down. Listen. If all this works out, you won't have to listen to me again.

"You asked me yesterday how come I'm in charge, and I'm saying it's just because. I don't like to write Dredd off, but I don't think he'll be coming back. Everyone higher up is gone, or at least that's what we've thought so far."

"But?"

"We picked up a signal. Emergency beacon. As a matter of fact, it's been pinging away on and off for more than a week. What with everything else that's been going on, no one paid it any mind. Also, it was coming from deep inside occupied territory, so there wasn't a whole lot we could do about it. Well, now we've taken a better look at the signal, and with the Sovs having a lot on their plate, we think now's the time to do something."

"What is this signal? What's so important?"

"The signal is a personal ID signature. Highest level. Council of Five. We think it's McGruder."

Robinson whistled. This was the big time. When it came to the Apocalypse Squad, they hadn't made the cut, but the worth of the Sector 212 Three had not gone unrecognised.

Mercer wasn't so impressed. "This is what? Our consolation prize, Perrier? What are we, expandable or something?"

"Give me a break, Mercer. You were the one who was all fired up to head north. Now would you please, for the love of Jovus, just look at the bigger picture? Sure, I want someone senior to me to come along and take over my job, but what I want really doesn't matter a whole lot. It's the city that needs leadership."

"Wait," said Steinman. "Do we know the signal's legit?"

"It's the proper code, if that's what you mean. If what you're asking is whether it's SJS Chief McGruder who's transmitting it, then that's for you to find out."

"You think the Sovs might have got her? They're sending the signal to screw with us?"

"Again, we don't know. But if McGruder's in need of rescue, we need to rescue her. If rescue isn't a realistic option, well—you saw what happened when the Sovs got their hands on Chief Judge Griffin."

Griffin had been turned traitor by Sov psycho surgery and made to perform for the enemy propaganda machine. The Mega-City resistance had assassinated him live on air.

"We absolutely one hundred percent can't let anything like that happen again," said Perrier. "You do what you have to."

As if the mission were in keeping with his dignity as a sector chief—as if he had a choice—Mercer nodded his acceptance. Perrier, who had fifty other things to do in the next hour, just told them to set out as soon as they'd seen to their gear.

"Go downstairs," she said. "Tell the Teks I sent you, but don't be long."

'Downstairs' wasn't some dugout or rough-hewn bunker.

A long concrete stair led them three levels down through the very foundations of the city. There, safe from the Sov bombs, they found that a whole factory had been improvised. It was a space that had long ago been sealed off as being too decayed to ever be a fitting basis for the gleaming metropolis built overhead, but now this Undercity lair was in far better shape than what remained above. Lights had been strung. Machinery had been installed. A whole war industry had been started up.

Since the first invaders had landed, it had been clear that the Sov robots were the chief threat. Improved armour-piercing and high-explosive ammunition was now being churned out to help deal with that. But Robinson straight away saw something better.

"Oh boy. This must be one of those classified things Underhill was talking about. Can I have one, chief? Can I? Huh? Huh?"

"Cut it out, Robinson," said Mercer and, to the Tek Judge in charge of the production line, "Just give her a stub gun and make her shut up, please?"

The stub gun was, of course, the perfect answer to armoured robots or, for that matter, to anything that needed to be sliced open quickly and from a distance. In essence, it was a cutting laser of immense power in a very small package. The reason it hadn't been generally available was that all that power wasn't as safely contained as it might be. Stub guns were extremely hazardous to the user. Dredd had unearthed an experimental batch in his battle for the roadways the previous week, and true, the roads had been successfully cut, but on the other hand, there weren't many survivors of Dredd's unit left to tell war stories.

But Robinson had experienced the alternative way of fighting that battle. Too often, she'd infiltrated Sov patrol lines in order to plant charges right up against road supports. As far as she was concerned, a stub gun's unreliability was a small price for allowing you to keep your distance from the enemy.

"Cuts through Rad-Sweepers like butter," said the Tek.

"So I've heard," said Robinson. "What's butter?"

"Who knows? Something that can cut through a tank, I guess."

"All done?" said Mercer. "Then let's get going."

Steinman had loaded up on the hi-spec ammo. He didn't want a new toy like Robinson did, and he didn't care about independent action in the northern sectors like Mercer. He wanted his conscience to stop bothering him. He wanted everything to go back to the way it was before he had drunk some bad water and the world had gone to hell. And he certainly didn't want to come face to face with the head of the Special Judicial Squad.

NINE

Everything hurt.

The painkillers had run out days before. She wasn't even sure how many days. Looking at her lesser injuries, which were partially healing, McGruder reckoned she'd been here more than a week. Looking at her hand, she figured that she didn't have a whole lot of days left.

That hand would have to go. No question about it. The antibiotics had run out yesterday (or was it the day before?) and their work had been far from done. She was pretty sure that infection had taken hold. Not just of her hand: of her. She was feeling seriously sick.

Trouble was, it was tough to gauge how much of that was on account of her busted-up hand. Hard to tell because of the head wound that had kept her drifting in and out of consciousness in the early days and still hurt like drokk now.

As soon as Block Mania was revealed as a Sov plot, she'd been on her way to her assigned Tactical Command Bunker. That had been the operational procedure set down after the last war. That had been then. Blindly adhering to it now was stupid. TCB North was, obviously, in the northern sectors, and the northern sectors had been where Block Mania had first broken out. Sending a member of the Council of Five into a war zone in the name of safety wasn't exactly smart. In defence of the standard procedure, a dispersal of command elements in time of nuclear attack was a wise option. On the other hand, drokk that.

The nukes hadn't been the problem. Her H-Wagon had been brought down by flak. Just ordinary, run-of-the-mill, buy-it-at-the-local-mall anti-aircraft fire. It had killed everyone on the command deck. The rest of the crew died in the crash. SJS Chief McGruder, the big, important member of the Council of Five, had been encased in crash bags that would have suffocated her if one of them hadn't failed. She didn't know how she made it out of the wreckage, but her first moments of lucidity found her here, in a small space that was probably in the lower levels. There was a minimum of food and water, the med kit, and a rescue beacon. She must have taken them along with her from the wreck. Good reflexes. Good conditioning.

She'd kept the beacon switched on at the start, but rescue never came. She figured that the war was going badly. Maybe the Sovs had invaded, and no way in hell was she going to be taken by the Sovs. So, the beacon remained off until such time as she could crawl out of there under her own steam. But her hand was just getting worse and worse, and her head made her want to puke every time she sat up. So, she could stay here and die, or she could switch the beacon back on and take her chances.

There was too much time to think. She had thought about the big stuff like war and death, and now she was stressing about the small stuff. Like her hair. It was long, and dirty as hell, and was no doubt complicating the head wound. If she'd had her own way, she'd never have worn it this long. You wear a helmet all day and you want to keep things high and tight under there. But then she'd been promoted. That had been after Cal.

The tyrant Cal had risen, by subversion and assassination, to the office of Chief Judge, using the SJS as his springboard. After he'd been overthrown, the SJS had been purged from top to bottom and McGruder had suddenly found herself at the top. Cal had been a preening psychopath, and as far as she was concerned the city could do with a break from city leaders obsessed with their image. But public relations were on her from day one. Some PR type called Lloyd had insisted that what was needed was a look that was stern, businesslike, but human. So, the helmet with the skull insignia had to go, and the buzz-cut with it. She thought it was stupid, but she went along with it. To show that she was a team player, on board with the whole new image, she even went a step further and started wearing earrings. Lloyd had thought that was a great idea, until he saw that the earrings displayed the SJS death's head. He'd smiled to show that he was in on the joke. He'd found less to smile about when she'd had him taken in for questioning. Two days of interrogation had revealed Lloyd to be clean, but he'd finally understood that the Justice Department wasn't about image. It was about justice. And McGruder was no one's dress-up doll.

Remembering Lloyd put her in mind of other cases. She was a conscientious chief and she kept her eye on everything. It had been made clear to her that her job wasn't only to judge the Judges: it was to ensure that there'd never be another Cal. The Squad was to be kept above reproach. As much as was possible, she monitored all her officers, kept watch over every case.

Now, just for something to do, just to keep her mind occupied, she thought about some of those cases. Most had been just routine, but there had been one that she'd been keeping her eye on, just before all the routine had been drastically suspended and her attention had been demanded elsewhere.

One of her officers in Sector 212 had just opened a file on an instance of possible corruption and larceny. She didn't think the investigation would uncover anything, but the officer doing the investigating was Judge Rossi, and McGruder was interested in Rossi because Rossi had been one of Cal's people back in the day.

Like everyone else, he'd just been following orders, but he'd followed them with zeal. The investigations had cleared him, but McGruder hadn't been satisfied. She'd let him think he was in the clear. Rossi would reveal his true character in time. Normally, she'd let nature take its course, but that had changed recently. When Judge O'Rourke had been assigned to 212, she'd let it be known through channels that O'Rourke was to apply gentle provocation in dealing with his new partner. O'Rourke would do as he'd been told.

He'd also done some things back in Cal's day he needed to make up for.

And then the block wars had started and that had been that.

It was only natural that her casual fishing expedition in Sector 212 would come to an end, but there had been something that had bothered her at the time. The SJS office in 212 had suddenly gone dark. Just like that. There had been no indication that either of her people had been suffering the early effects of Block Mania. Everything had been carrying on as normal and had then come to an abrupt stop. She hadn't had the time to worry about it then. She had too much time now.

What had it all been about?

The last report filed by the SJS office in 212 had concerned a drug bust—that corruption and larceny thing. Money had gone missing. One of the Judges involved was to be questioned. And then everything had gone quiet. That was wrong. That needed investigating.

McGruder racked her aching memory to come up with the Judge's name. It hurt, but remembering details was her job, gruddammit.

The Judge's name had been Kowalczyk. That was it. Rafael Kowalczyk, No, not Rafael. Ramon. Class of '92. Partner's name was—

Come on!

Ow.

It wouldn't come. She cursed.

But she resolved to keep at it. It might take her mind off the pain.

TEN

"So, PERRIER," SAID Mercer. "You've got an H-Wagon that can get us there?"

"You kidding? The Sovs might be knocked back on their heels, but they still own the skies. If it turns out it really is McGruder, then we'll think about committing air assets. Until then, you'll attract less attention by road."

"All that way?"

"Roadways are largely intact up through the western sectors. Sovs are most likely to be looking in the other direction. Move fast and you'll be OK."

It was still dark when they mounted up.

"You heard the lady," said Mercer. "We don't stop for red lights. Let's move."

It was an eerie journey. Outside the zones that had been laid waste by the war, the city was almost as it had been. In the dark the ravages of the past weeks weren't all that evident. But the dark was unsettling. This had been the city where the lights were always on. Down in the lower levels, it could hardly have been otherwise.

But the towers weren't blazing now. The garish signage, the animated billboards, the millions of windows had all gone dark. Where there was power, it was emergency power only. The dim lights showing from the housing blocks suggested more a colony of cliff-dwellers than the electric metropolis of two weeks ago. The roads that had been glowing rivers were empty of traffic and illuminated only by the most meagre strips of overhead lighting. The only vehicles were dead and abandoned.

A curfew was in force. This was the occupied city. For all except a few furtive scavengers, the threat of labour camps or summary execution was enough to make them stay home. As such, the Sovs didn't need to maintain much of a presence. It was a big city after all, and available forces were needed for the fighting in the central sectors. But that didn't mean that the Judges had a clear run.

They blazed through the first couple of checkpoints. Shooting sentries at 200 kph was a challenge, but they were equal to it. Robinson even found it fun, and she reckoned that Steinman would have too if he hadn't been so broody lately.

Maybe their score against the sentries hadn't been as good as they thought, and a survivor had managed to raise the alarm. Maybe the alarm went out automatically. Either way, an automated security post at Exit 988 took them under heavy fire before they even knew it was there. They took a detour, but a questing Strato-V found them and forced them to run for it through the lower levels, chased all the way by harassing laser fire. The big

Sov aircraft appeared to give up on them after a while, but they stayed put in an underground parking garage until they were good and sure it had gone.

"It's not going to waste time on just three of us. The Sovs have to save the situation down in the central sectors. They'll want all hands on deck," said Steinman.

"Let's hope so," said Mercer. "But don't count on it. One of those things can read a Lawmaster's signature from twenty clicks, so we don't move just yet. Fifteen minutes either way won't make any difference to McGruder. Stretch your legs, grab a bite."

Department-issue ration bars were offered in a narrow range stretching from 'flavoured' to 'flavourless'. Robinson knew better than to go for flavoured.

"Hey chief," she said, "if it really is McGruder, does that put her in charge? Of the whole show, I mean?"

"I suppose so. She's got the rank."

"But does that mean she's Chief Judge? I mean she's Council of Five and all, but there's no automatic line of succession."

Mercer considered it. "Nah," he said. "She'd be provisionally in charge because of seniority, but that's it. A new Chief Judge would be chosen by normal means once the war's over, and it won't be her. You can take my word for it."

"How so?"

"The city's going to put up with another SJS Judge in charge? After Cal? I don't think so."

"Good point. So, who does that leave? Dredd? If he's still alive, that is."

Steinman chipped in. "Dredd wouldn't take the job. He's turned it down before. More than that, the city wouldn't take Dredd. Heck, the Department wouldn't take Dredd. The guy's a troubleshooter, not an administrator. And he's too hardline about damn near everything."

"We need hard-line," said Mercer.

"Not that hard," said Steinman. "The cits need someone who's maybe the teensiest bit—I dunno—likeable?"

"They want someone paternal," said Robinson. "They want Goodman."

"Yeah, Goodman," said Mercer. "Mega-City's favourite dad. Only trouble is he's dead, and no one else has been able to pull off his schtick. Pepper tried. Pepper wanted to be popular. He wanted a relatable justice system. Wanted to turn it into a reality TV show. Got what he deserved."

"OK. So, not too hard, not too soft," said Robinson. "Who else is there? How do we know that all the Council are dead? One of the others might show up. How about Quimby?"

"Quimby's a paper-pusher," said Steinman.

"Worse than that," said Mercer. "Guy's got no heart. He's not about the real judging. If he's still alive, then leave him in Accounting."

"And Ecks?" asked Robinson, but they all knew the answer to that.

"Ecks?" Mercer nearly choked on his nutri-bar. "For real? Give the big chair to the head of Psi-Division? Let an old guy who hears voices in his head run the city? We might as well hand the whole show over to the Sovs right now!"

They had a chuckle over that, and then reckoned that it was safe to be on their way once more.

But Robinson wasn't quite joking when she said, "How about a four-square street Judge who's got the seniority along with the admin experience? Think you'd be up to the job, chief?"

Mercer stopped what he was doing and appeared to give the matter a moment's serious consideration.

"I serve the city, Robinson," was all he said. "Now let's ride."

ELEVEN

THIS WAS THE city now.

In the western sectors, the uncanny darkness of night gave way to a dead morning. There was no early traffic, no morning crowds. The windows gaped empty. The streets were scattered with the detritus of war.

The law returned that morning to a city they hardly recognised.

"You never realise how lousy everything looks without sunshine," said Robinson. "I wonder how long it'll take to get Weather Control up and running again."

"You almost miss the citizens," said Steinman. "It just doesn't feel right if you've got no one to arrest."

The block wars had killed millions and the nuclear bombardment hundreds of millions, with the Sov advance displacing multitudes more, but there were still people to be seen. They could be glimpsed here and there, peering out the broken windows, scurrying in and out of the looted retail outlets. The Judges didn't concern themselves with survivors and scavengers.

They were close to their goal now, homing in on the beacon's last signal.

They turned onto Megaway West 98. They were wary of taking such a major road because of the increased likelihood of running into substantial enemy units, but the megaway was taking them straight where they needed to go. It was here that they found citizens doing something more than scavenging or surviving. Here was a large group of people engaged in collective, cooperative, and productive activity. Here was the populace working for the repair and recovery of their city. Here was a forced labour gang, working under armed guard to clear wreckage off the southbound lanes.

The armed guard wasn't immediately obvious, but spotting the one man in any group who was carrying a weapon was second nature to a Judge. Mercer zeroed in on him.

"You! Identify yourself!"

The man looked a little apprehensive, but at the same time secure in his authority. He did, after all, have a pistol and an armband.

"Julius Pajoolius, deputy overseer, civilian labour unit seven-four-one-eight." He pointed to the armband, which showed a red star and the number he'd just quoted.

"Who deputised you, Pajoolius? The Sovs?"

"The, uh, occupying power, yeah."

Mercer nodded in understanding, and then shot the man dead.

"Your attention!" he demanded, although it was hardly necessary. "The lawful authority of Mega-City One is hereby restored. Collaboration with the enemy is punishable by death. Helping the Sovs in any way is a crime against the city. However, in the light of present circumstances the law is prepared to be merciful."

He pointed to the dumpster-loads that had been cleared off the road so far.

"Put that stuff back where you found it and return to your homes. Go on... beat it."

The Judges left them to it. There were more important things to do.

THEY FOUND THE wreck of the H-Wagon they were looking for half-buried in the side of Rupert Pupkin Block, and they took things from there. Steinman volunteered to stay outside keeping watch, and the other two got to work. The crash had started a fire on the floors above, so they started their search downstairs from the site. It wasn't a hard trail to find. Three bodies, armed and in Pupkin Citi-Def gear, were lying crumpled up near the H-Wagon's escape hatch. They'd been there quite a while. One floor down they came across another two bodies—also dating from the last days of Block Mania.

"Standard execution," noted Robinson. "One of ours did this."

"Not bad for someone carrying an injury," said Mercer. "Got a blood trail here."

They followed the blackened blood spots to an elevator.

Because the power was out, they had to take the stairs, investigating every floor as they went. A few apartment doors opened as they passed and were closed again quickly. Fearful glances confirmed that, for better or worse, the Judges were back.

They didn't pick up the trail again until they hit the basement, a long way down. There were no more blood spots, but there was another body by the elevator doors to show that someone who tolerated no delay or interference had been this way.

"Good place to hole up," said Mercer. "All the usual caretaker and maintenance staff would have been topsides fighting the block wars."

"Beacon's last signal was right here, plus or minus a hundred metres," said Robinson. "What say you go left and I go right?"

At least there was some emergency lighting, but their search of the gloomy machine-filled spaces might have gone on for quite a while if the beacon hadn't suddenly woken up. Robinson followed the signal down a corridor to a storage room. She could have sworn she'd looked here once already, but there was no mistaking the blinking light on the hand-sized locator sitting in the corner.

Mercer came in hard on her heels, saw the beacon, and said, "So where is everyone? Where's McGruder?"

Robinson was just about to profess her ignorance when the question was answered. Behind them in the doorway, blocking the only way out, was a gaunt figure holding a gun on them.

"Identify yourselves," said the figure, in a voice they both recognised from the internal Justice Department news net. As things stood though, the face would have been harder to place.

"Jovus, McGruder!" said Mercer. "Siddown for Grud's sake!"

"I said identify yourselves!"

"Mercer. Robinson. Sector 212. Now will you take it easy before you hurt yourself worse?"

McGruder's hawk-like face was shadowed with pain and her greying hair was darkened with blood. Her left hand was bound up in a bandage that should have been changed days ago. Even in the dim light, even with the bandage, the hand seemed to be the wrong shape entirely.

She was staying upright with difficulty, but even as her knees gave out and she slid towards the floor, her gun hand remained steady.

"How do I know you are who you say you are?" she said, her voice little more than a rasp.

"Do we look like a couple of Sovs or something? You want our badge numbers?"

McGruder showed her teeth in what might have been a smile. "Yeah. Go ahead. Your badge numbers."

"For real?" said Mercer.

"Do it."

And because sometimes you should humour the whims of superior officers, especially when they're threatening to shoot you, Mercer and Robinson dutifully recited their respective ID codes.

And as if she'd memorised the details of all the

personnel in the whole of Justice Department, McGruder nodded. "Good enough," she said, and then she vomited and passed out.

TWELVE

MᴄGʀᴜᴅᴇʀ ɴᴇᴇᴅᴇᴅ ᴜʀɢᴇɴᴛ attention—that much was obvious.

"Pupkin Med Centre's the closest," said Robinson, hoisting the injured woman onto her shoulder. Mercer was a lot bigger than Robinson, but you couldn't wait around expecting senior personnel to be helpful when it came to heavy lifting. Thank Grud it was only a few floors up.

The medical facility was above the shopperama in a low-rise extension by the block's south entrance. Convenient though that might have been for anyone carrying casualties upstairs from the basement, it was also unfortunately near where the worst of the inter-block fighting had taken place. The windows were all shot out, the furniture was piled up in makeshift barricades, and a fire had destroyed much of what was left.

"Sprinklers did almost as much damage as the fire," said a cheerful voice. "But at least it cleared out the Citi-Def guys. They didn't care for the rain."

The Judges pointed their guns in the direction of the speaker from force of habit, but there was clearly no danger. A sprightly old man in civilian med-gear came out of the shadows, his hands held open to show not just that he was harmless but that all visitors were more than welcome.

"Ritchie Hernandez, Block Doc. What can I do for you folks?"

Robinson laid her burden down on the reception desk, there being no other place handy.

"This Judge is suffering from a severe head wound and what looks like a traumatic injury to the left hand, probably infected."

"Whoa! You ain't wrong! Now let old Doc Ritchie give her the once-over."

The man peered and prodded like he was about to make an offer on the SJS Chief, and then came to a conclusion.

"Yup, she's a sick 'un all right. Straight to hospital."

"She's in a hospital, Hernandez."

"I mean a Justice Department Med unit. Be about the best place for treating a case like this. Can't you people just whistle up an ambulance or something?"

"There's a war on," said Mercer. "You might have noticed."

Hernandez scratched his beard. "The war. Yeah. That kinda complicates things."

"You're the block doc," said Robinson. "Can't you do something?"

The man was still staring at McGruder as if wondering

whether or not she came with an operating manual he could consult.

"Well, y'see there, Judge, when I say I'm the block doc, it's more in an acting capacity, as it were."

"Explain," said Mercer.

"Well, the regular doc got herself kinda killed leading an attack on Wynette across the way, and the robo-docs all got trashed. So, I just kinda stepped up until a proper replacement arrives, y'know?"

"So, what is it you do here normally?"

"A little bit paramedical, a little bit janitorial. You know. Whatever's needed."

"Well, just do whatever's needed here."

There was no telling how good a janitor Ritchie Hernandez might have been in his heyday, but in these straitened times, he demonstrated himself a commendably competent paramedic. He bustled around for a while, hooking up drips, plugging in devices, and humming Sixties hits. Mercer and Robinson kept a close eye on him, but he knew what he was doing.

"Just get the old gal rehydrated and that's half the battle. Head wound's a problem but not that big of a one. I've cleaned it out and put a magni-heal on it, and that's as far as I'm willing to go. I think it'll do just fine, but head wounds are tricky. Leave it to the professionals, I say."

"What about her hand?"

"The hand's a mess. Ick. I'm not touching the hand. That thing is gross."

"Define gross," said Mercer. "Put 'ick' in medical terms."

"The hand's all smushed up. Infected to hell and gone. It's gotta come off. Like sooner than soon. I don't have any prosthetics in stock, but I know a guy in Billy Bob's Budget Bionics who'll do you a good deal—if he's still alive, that is."

"Never mind Billy Bob's. We'll take it from here, Hernandez. The city thanks you for your help. Robinson? Get Central on the line. Tell them mission accomplished. Tell Perrier we need medevac right away."

"On it, chief."

As was usual in this war, her personal radio didn't cut it, so she went out to where her bike was parked.

"What's going on?" asked Steinman, standing sentry.

"We found her. She's alive. She's sick. We're leaving. How're you doing?"

"Oh, you know. Just re-establishing a police presence. Reassuring the citizens that everything's getting back to normal."

"I thought I heard shots."

"Looters. Two of them."

After several frustrating minutes while her signal was encrypted, relayed, jammed, and redirected, Robinson established contact with Perrier. Things at the heart of Mega-City resistance were sounding hectic.

"Are you crazy, Robinson? Mercer wants an H-Wagon? Now?"

"Hey, Perrier, you were the one that said it would be doable."

"That was last night. Situation's changed. Sov ground forces are a little unsteady, but their air forces are trying to make up for that. Sky is swarming with Strato-Vs. No one's going to risk taking off right now."

"But we've found the you-know-what."

"So put the you-know-what on a bike and head back south."

"No can do. Subject is kind of beat-up."

"Look, Robinson—you do what you can at your end, and I'll see about aerial assets. It might be a few hours and I'm making no promises. Perrier out."

"Ok Doc," said Robinson. "What kind of operating theatre have you got here?"

"It was a real good one before the fire."

"Oh jeez. What sort of equipment have you got left?"

"Beyond what I used on your friend here, not a whole lot. Any-who, I'm no surgeon."

"If you've got antibiotics and dressing, I'll be the surgeon."

"Seriously, Robinson?" said Mercer.

"Seriously, chief. I got a B-plus in Trauma Treatment at the Academy, didn't I? Besides, how hard can it be? Give me a second. I need to get something from my bike."

Robinson had hoped that when she finally got to play with her new toy, she'd be bringing down bridges filled with enemy tanks. Instead, the first time she pulled the trigger on her stub gun was to amputate Judge McGruder's hand and cauterise the wound.

It was a beautifully quick and clean operation,

even if the incision did cut right through the reception desk, the floor of the med centre, a display of next season's ladies' fashions in the shopperama below, and a couple of dump trucks parked in the sub-basement.

"Sorry," said Robinson. "It doesn't look like there's a low setting on this thing."

THIRTEEN

"So if she comes round and she's fit to move, then we go. Otherwise, we hold on here and hope someone comes for us?"

"That's about the size of it," said Robinson.

"But there's no question she's going to make it?" said Steinman, even though he'd already asked.

"Don't sweat it, partner. You'll be fine. You think she keeps track of every little case? And at a time like this?"

Steinman chose not to answer that one. Instead, he looked over to the megaway. "They've been coming back. Hoping I wouldn't notice. Want to help me run them?"

It was the same work gang from earlier, tentatively returning to their rubble-shifting task. As the Judges approached, Robinson could see that one of them had even gone so far as to don the armband of the fallen Deputy Pajoolius. He was a bigger man than his predecessor, but Robinson positively enjoyed taking down the big ones.

"Care to explain yourself, citizen?"

"I'm the, uh, overseeing deputy guy. Civilian labour something, or something. I'm the guy who's got Joolie's job."

"That job didn't work out too well for Joolie, now, did it?"

"Uh, no, Judge. But I figure I can do a lot better than him. Anyway, I shoulda had it in the first place, but Joolie told the Sovs how I flunked out of Basic Employment Skills when we was in high school, so they gave the armband to him instead."

"The job no longer exists, citizen. Working for the Sovs is a crime."

"You don't get to decide what's a crime no more. The Sovs're in charge round here now."

Such open defiance of the law clearly warranted the standard punishment meted out to collaborators, but Robinson considered that this was one of those times when justice should be tempered with mercy. She drove her left fist into the big man's groin and took him on the chin with her right as he crumpled down to meet her. Then she turned a bright smile on the other labourers.

"That's about as lenient as I get. Now, I won't say it again, so disperse. Right now."

But one woman, pale and thin, chose to make a stand.

"I'm not dispersing! What about my work quota?" she yelled at Robinson. "Where am I supposed to get my ration stamps?"

"Just go quietly, citizen," said Steinman.

"You can't make me disperse!"

"Yeah, we can. Go home."

"I know my rights!"

"You have no rights in this matter. Go home."

But the woman not only stood her ground, she pulled a comm out of her purse. With a now-look-what-you're-making-me-do expression, she punched in a number and said, "East-Meg Forces Occupation Commissariat? I'd like to speak to your manager, please."

She got no further because Steinman shot her.

"Aw, I wanted to do that," said Robinson.

"Next time," said Steinman. "If these people are depending on the Sovs to feed them, then you can bet there'll be a next time. All it takes is one traitor with a phone. We better tell the chief to expect trouble."

THE TROUBLE BEGAN with a peaceful deputation of community leaders who patiently explained how food distribution was in the hands of the occupying power now.

Mercer heard them out and explained the official Justice Department stance.

"Get the hell out of my face or you're all doing time."

Then he went back to the med centre, telling Robinson and Steinman to keep an eye on the crowd of unemployed forced labourers that was growing in the background.

Maybe Mercer's speech had worked. Maybe the deterrent exercised by a couple of judicial executions had got the message across. Maybe the people in the vicinity of Rupert Pupkin Block had realised where their true allegiance lay. Maybe it was just that no one had a working phone. Whichever way, it was only the routine sweep of a surveillance drone that alerted the occupying power to the breakdown of civil obedience in this sector.

The Lawmasters' sensors alerted the Judges to the drone's presence, but it was too late to take cover. Robinson caught a flash of sunlight off its casing as it zoomed by in the distance.

"If we can see it, it can see us. What do you think?"

"I think that if the megaway's still blocked with debris, then they're going to come by air."

"Yeah, but there's lots of other roads. How about you go low, I go high?"

"Deal," said Steinman.

So Steinman positioned himself at a watching bay overlooking several intersections at once, while Robinson climbed up to a nearby restaurant balcony. With just the two of them against whatever the greater East-Meg empire cared to throw at them, they were probably in grave peril, but Robinson couldn't damp down her excitement. She was going to get to use her stub gun at last.

Robinson was disappointed by the Sov response when it showed up. It consisted of a single four-man unit in a hover car, and it stayed largely out of her line of sight and out of Steinman's range. She couldn't get a bead on the Sovs, but she could see a few of the bystanders, formerly of the road gang, waving at the Sovs and gesturing in her general direction. She cursed them roundly for a bunch of lousy snitches and moved off the balcony fast. Her new position was safely out of sight of the enemy stooges on the road, but that somewhat defeated the whole purpose of choosing a suitable vantage point for springing an ambush. She saw that Steinman had likewise vacated his post, and finding out where he'd gone meant, as always, switching on her radio and thus broadcasting her position to the enemy snooping devices. The whole plan was unravelling, and all because a few cits didn't know what was good for them.

The four Sovs in the hover car appeared to be in no hurry to go hunting Mega-City Judges. Robinson felt they were lacking in moral fibre. The Sov Judges who'd rampaged south across the city last week would never have paused and called up air support. Because that's what these ones were doing. Robinson had set up her bike's computer to patch into enemy channels and relay communications to her, and her grasp of the language was good enough to hear what was coming next.

"A Strato-V? Against just the two of us?" she said to herself, disgusted. "Didn't think that getting their whole city nuked out from under them could turn them into such a bunch of weak sisters."

Still though, if she could get into a decent position on time, a Strato-V would make a heck of a target.

FOURTEEN

By COINCIDENCE, THE new fallback position that Robinson chose was the same one Steinman did, and they met up on a low roof behind an advertising hoarding. It afforded them a narrower view than they'd have liked, but it kept them more or less out of sight.

"If it approaches from the north, I've got 'em," said Robinson, compulsively flexing her fingers on the stub gun's grip. "Otherwise, it's not such a great angle, but I think I can do it."

"That's a big fat negative on engaging a Strato-V, Robinson. We can't attract the attention."

"You're no fun," said Robinson, but she had to admit Steinman was right. After all, the Sovs had no guarantee that a couple of Mega-City Judges were still in the area, and thus there was no reason to linger overhead.

The Sov aircraft did come in from the north, and the two Judges crouched low, imagining they could almost feel the scanners working over the area. Steinman risked peeking out in the direction of the megaway.

He saw that a few citizens were still jumping up and down and pointing. He wasn't concerned. He and Robinson were no longer anywhere near where the Sovs were being directed.

"Can you imagine the cits being this helpful when we were in charge? I mean, you ever lose a perp you're chasing and everyone's saying, 'What perp? We din't see nuthin, Judge.' But nuke out half their neighbourhood and then throw them some synthi-borscht, and they suddenly get all cooperative."

But then he realised.

"The Strato-V, Robinson! Shoot it! Now!"

Because the traitors in the street mightn't have known where Steinman and Robinson were, but they knew that at least one other Judge—the mean one that had shot old Joolie—was inside the Pupkin Medical Centre. That's where they were pointing.

Robinson caught on instantly. Never mind the risk of being spotted: if the Strato-V took out the med centre and killed McGruder, then the whole mission had been for nothing. She stood up to give herself a better sighting and pressed the trigger.

Out of habit she led the target, but when your weapon operates at the speed of light, there's no need for deflection. It didn't matter. The Strato-V flew right into the narrow energy beam, and that was it. The whole thing just opened out in an instant, sliced into two unequal parts, giving everyone a diagonal cross-section view of crew decks and engine spaces and heavy-duty anti-grav avionics. It was a thing of beauty.

The Judges didn't stay to see it crash, which was a pity because it was a helluva crash. Instead, they were getting back down to the med centre as fast as they could to warn Mercer that things were likely to get pretty hairy pretty fast.

"IT DOESN'T MATTER how hard-pressed they are down south," said Mercer. "The Sovs lose a Strato-V to a stub gun and they're going to respond—most likely with another Strato-V. Ground units too."

"So, what's the plan, chief?"

Mercer gave it a moment's thought. "We stay where we are and kill everything that comes at us. That work for you two?"

They stowed the still unconscious McGruder more or less safely out of the way, looked to their weapons, and waited for what would happen next. The crowd outside wasn't going away, but that didn't concern them. Their Lawmasters were set on sentry mode in key positions, and every Mega-citizen knew better than to mess with an unattended Lawmaster. But the people gathered nonetheless, congregating loosely, keeping resentful eyes on the Judges in the med centre. Things hadn't exactly been great under Sov occupation, but at least they'd been peaceful. Now the Judges had brought the war back with them.

They weren't kept waiting long for the next Strato-V, and it was keeping so much out of sight that Judges mightn't even have noticed if their scanners hadn't announced it.

The people in the street were looking up at where it appeared and disappeared, using the urban skyline for cover.

"You want to find a place where you can get a bead on it, Robinson?"

"Sure, chief. Oh, wait. Hold up. Does this red line mean what I think it does?" She was holding her stub gun like it wasn't her best friend anymore.

"Is that thing going to overheat?" said Steinman. "What did you do to it, Robinson? Give it here!"

"I didn't do anything! I used it once! You were there!"

"Well, you must have done something wrong. Look at this reading. This is not a happy reading."

"Will you two give it a rest?" barked Mercer. "If the stub's going to explode, then don't use the stub unless we really have to. We stay cool. That Strato-V hasn't done anything yet, and it might not commit to an attack run just because some clowns in the street are pointing in our direction."

So they stayed where they were, waiting to see what their enemy would do next. The people in the street didn't have as much patience. They were waving and hollering, and when the Strato-V came directly overhead, a few of them started cheering.

The commander of the Strato-V hadn't been told much except that the previous aircraft had been shot down while investigating supposed mutinous activity in Labour Unit 7418. That hadn't been the only instance of dissident behaviour that morning. There had been reports of unrest all across the occupied city since the news of East-Meg One's destruction had become widely known, and two sectors had even erupted in outright rebellion. The hover car that had first arrived on the scene hadn't stayed around once a stub gun had made its presence felt, so without anyone to put him in the picture, the Strato-V commander had to use his own judgement. The people assembled below on Megaway West 98 were clearly not at work as they should have been and appeared to be exhibiting defiance. He had other calls on his time. The war was at a critical juncture. He ordered the forward laser array to target random demonstrators in the crowd.

"Those drokkers!" said Mercer. "They're shooting at civilians!"

"More than that," said Robinson. "They're shooting at their own stooges. I dunno, maybe that'll make things easier for us. Maybe we can relocate in the confusion. What do you think, Steinman?"

But Steinman wasn't there anymore. Before Robinson could say, "That's my stub gun!", he was striding out the front door. He wasn't going to stand by and watch the Sovs killing citizens. He hadn't stood for it at Mellancamp, and he wasn't standing for it here. He didn't care what the temperature gauge on the stub gun said: that Strato-V was coming down.

Just like Robinson, Steinman instinctively led the target, making needless allowance for the speed of a non-existent projectile. That gave the Strato-V pilot the split-second warning he needed. When an energy beam flashed into existence in front of him, the pilot knew it was the laser weapon he'd been warned about, and he was yanking the aircraft into a sharp turn almost before he knew what he was doing. It was just enough. The beam sheared off a hefty chunk of the ship's starboard arm, but even though unstable and trailing smoke, the Strato-V still made it out of the stub gun's reach.

Steinman swore, but it was nothing compared to the cussing out that he could hear from Mercer, even at this distance.

"At least you stopped them shooting up the cits," said Robinson, when he rejoined them.

"Yeah, but now they definitely know we're still here!" said Mercer. "You drokking feeb! What the hell were you thinking? They'll be back with reinforcements, and I wouldn't put too much faith in your bootleg stub gun. So until such a time as it's possible for us to move out, we'll need to find a way of holding this place against however many Sovs with just the three of us."

"Four," said a harsh voice behind them.

McGruder looked like she'd died on the operating table but wasn't going to let that stop her.

"What's the situation, Mercer?" she said, not wasting any time.

"The situation is that there may or may not be an H-Wagon coming to pick us up—maybe sooner, maybe later. Ideally, before the Sovs get really mad. You sure you should be up, McGruder?"

"I made that med Hernandez give me stims. I'll do. You have bikes?"

"Three of them. On the perimeter."

"Then that's how we're leaving. I'll take one. The two juniors can double up." Noticing what Steinman was holding, she said, "Is that a stub gun?"

"Yeah, but we're a little worried about it," said Robinson. "It's working fine, but it's reading hot."

"Doesn't matter. If we absolutely have to cut our way out, then we just have to risk using the thing. Let's get moving." And she staggered towards the front entrance, her Lawgiver clenched in her one remaining hand.

"Need a little help there, Chief McGruder?"

"I can manage. Which one are you?"

"I'm Steinman." His badge was hidden under his rad cloak.

With her teeth gritted and the sweat standing out on her face, she paused a moment, and looked at Steinman, and blinked, the tumblers of her memory clicking into place.

"You say you're Sector 212, right?"

And Steinman knew in that moment that his future as a Judge of Mega-City One was very short.

FIFTEEN

MERCER'S BIKE WAS right outside, keeping station at the front entrance.

"Where are the others?" he asked.

"Mine's over there," said Robinson. "Inside the doughnut dispensary." But as she pointed, she saw someone on top of the dispensary's broken roof.

"What's he doing? Is that a gas can?"

The man pouring the highly flammable industrial solvent through the roof on top of the Lawmaster below also appeared to have some sort of lighter in his hand. Robinson shot him, but not before he had a chance to use it, and the whole place went up in a blinding whoosh.

The watching crowd had grown far greater now than the original work gang. It wasn't a mob—not yet—just a loose congregation of people who'd come outside since the Strato-Vs had been downed or driven off. Mostly they just looked like ordinary citizens who had been through a lot and wanted to see what was coming next. Of course, in any assembly there were going to be unruly elements, and the destruction of the Lawmaster was met with a few gleeful shouts of derision.

"Whatcha gonna do now, Judgey-girl?" one man called out. "Whatcha gonna do when the Sovs come back?"

Robinson was going to show him what she was aiming to do right now when someone stepped up and beat her to it. He was a rangy type in a Citi-Def helmet, and he decked the jeering onlooker with one competent punch. The few catcalls from the crowd stopped. It was if the whole mood shifted. Public opinion was no longer decided by the malcontents but by this guy.

Several pages of the Mega-City One criminal code ran through Robinson's head in the blink of an eye. Ordinarily, what she'd just seen would have counted as common assault, which would have earned helmet-guy a year in the cubes. Furthermore, even if the guy's heart was in the right place, taking the law into your hands was a serious matter, which would add a further year, to be served concurrently or consecutively, depending on the arresting officer's judgement. However, the Citizens Defence (Emergency Powers) Act of 2070 and the Security of the City Act, Section 396(b) could be interpreted to mean that in times such as these a citizen could be deemed automatically deputised by circumstance—again, subject to judicial assessment. Judge LaShondra Robinson weighed the matter and reached a verdict.

"Nice job," she said. "What's your name, citizen?"

"Tooey Lejeune, Judge. I live in 3156, Milton Berle."

Mercer stepped up. "You Citi-Def, Lejeune?"

Lejeune looked momentarily confused, then looked up at his helmet. "What, this? Uh, no. I just picked this up in the fighting, y'know."

"Well, either way you can now consider yourself a Justice Department auxiliary, temporary, unpaid," said Mercer. "We're a little overstretched right now. Think you can help us make these people see sense—like you did with this guy?"

"These ain't bad people, Judge," said Lejeune. "They're just hungry and scared is all. A few of them might say they're glad to see the back of the Judges, but they're no Sov-lovers. They're Mega-City One, through and through."

"Glad to hear it. So, you just help keep them in line. Lethal force is not authorised, but you can keep a list of any and all misdemeanours committed on your watch."

Mercer faced the crowd and raised his voice.

"Let me say it again! The law has come back to this sector! Last night the forces of Mega-City One dealt a mortal blow to the enemy. The Sovs can't stand for much longer. A few more hard blows, a few more days, and it'll all be over.

"Now, we've all been through some stuff, but be advised: lawlessness will not be tolerated. And any dealings with the enemy will be tolerated even less. You hear me down the back there? *Any* dealings. You are citizens of Mega-City One. The Sovs are the enemy. You don't help them. You don't so much as pick up a piece of trash if they tell you to. A couple of weeks back, you were all proud as hell about where you came from. Maybe you took it a little too far then, but maybe we could do with some of that pride now. The Sovs come around to your neighbourhood and you just show them whose neighbourhood it is.

"This is the Big Meg! We don't let foreigners push us around!"

And there were sounds of affirmation in the crowd. There were resolute looks. There were even a few punches in the air and cries of "Big Meg Yeah!" Say what you like about the Judges, but they didn't fly overhead like the Sovs and subject you to random laser fire because they were in a bad mood.

Mercer nodded, as if acknowledging that the patriotism and courage of these people had been there all along.

"Whatever you did to survive in these last few weeks will be investigated in due course. Until then, just remember this: this is our city. The law has come back. Now everybody, get off the streets."

He turned back to the newly deputised Lejeune. "The law has come back, but as it happens, we have to step out again for a few hours. Take it easy, citizen: liberation is just around the corner."

He turned to Steinman. "Looks like we're all going to double up on the bikes. Get yours over here and let's make a move before the Sovs try something new."

"That's OK, chief. One of you can have my bike."

"What's that?"

"I'm staying, chief."

"The hell you are."

"I'm not running out on these people. Look at what happened at the Josie and the Pussycats Project.

The Sovs got one sniff of resistance and they took it out on the cits. And we have no idea if they respected the white flag after we left. So, this time I'm staying put."

Mercer glared. This was like being back in charge of Sector 212. There was never any enormous problem that couldn't be made worse by some underling getting casual with the chain of command. He was drawing a deep breath, preparing to blast Steinman back into line, when Robinson intervened.

"I don't think there's any choice in the matter," she said. "I just had a look at his bike. It's non-operational. Looks like a Strato-V laser blast melted its systems."

"There you go, chief," said Steinman. "That makes it easier for you."

"Steinman," said Mercer, "I'm going to give you a direct order and you're going to obey it. Clear? When I tell you to move out—however the hell we do move out—you're going to move. You hearing me? Now stand by."

With their cover blown, there was little harm in using the radio. He managed to get through to resistance headquarters without much of a delay.

"Mercer to Control. The Sovs have made us, and our transport is down. I need an H-Wagon and I need it soonest."

"I hear you, Mercer," said the voice of Judge Underhill, "but we've lost one H-Wagon already and there's no point sending another until the situation down here changes."

"And how long will that be?"

"If we recapture the Sector 29 Airport in a couple of hours, then we'll be with you in a couple of hours. Otherwise, you'll just have to hope for a sudden and spontaneous decline in East-Meg air power."

"Don't get wise with me, Underhill. Just do what you can, dammit. Mercer out."

Mother of Grud, he thought. *They can put a burger bar on the moon, but they can't fly a short hop halfway across town.*

McGruder had been watching this from off on the side. The stims must have been having some good effect because she already looked as though keeping upright was something she did all the time.

"You take the remaining Lawmaster," Mercer told her. "The Sovs won't be tracking you if they're busy with us."

"The hell with that, Mercer," was all she said.

"Aw, drokk it, McGruder! Not you too!"

"I outrank you, Mercer, so you don't tell me what to do."

"Be reasonable for Grud's sake! They need you down south. Griffin's dead. Dredd was running things, but he's MIA. The Council's all gone except for you. They need someone to take charge."

But McGruder laughed in his face.

"This is Mega-City One, remember? We don't let anyone push us around. So listen, Mercer... my head hurts like drokk, and I'm in no mood to be run out of here by a bunch of Sovs. We fight here. We win. They come and pick us up afterwards. Saves time."

"McGruder!"

"They want someone to lead the fight? Well, the fight's here. They want me to take charge? Hell, I'm expendable. We're all expendable. Any Judge can do the job. They can give the big badge to any one of us."

And then, deaf to Mercer's protests, she was striding off in the direction of Steinman's damaged Lawmaster to salvage some ammunition.

It could have been that the prospect of action had galvanised her, or maybe she was just tough as nails, but once she got moving, the weakness fell away, with no hint of the sufferings she'd undergone. Beyond the fresh dressings, she betrayed no indication that she was troubled by her wounds—no indication save one.

Steinman was looking to see if he could bypass the electronics on his bike and get the thing working manually when McGruder came up. She was muttering quietly, like someone distracted.

"We're all expendable," she was saying to herself. "They can give the big badge to anyone. OK—anyone except Dredd. Dredd's a good Judge—I'm not denying that, but—"

"What's that, Chief McGruder?"

She came to herself in an instant and shot an outraged look at Steinman. "How about you mind your damn business and see if you can give me some of those upgraded hi-ex rounds I've been hearing about?"

"Roger that, ma'am." And then, as though making conversation: "So, you're staying with us?"

"You bet I'm staying. If there's Sovs to be fought, I can

just as easily do it up here as down south.

"Oh yeah," she added, as she awkwardly slotted a fresh clip into her Lawgiver with one hand, "and I thought I should stick around and ask you a few questions when we have the time."

Steinman nodded and said nothing.

SIXTEEN

TOOEY LEJEUNE WAS a respected man in the neighbourhood. He'd had a job before the war. He hadn't been afraid of the gangs. He could take care of himself. It made sense that he should have been the one to step up and punch out that loudmouth, and it made sense that the Judges should have appointed him to be some sort of overseer. So, he wasn't getting too much friction from people as he hustled them indoors with indistinct promises that everything was going to be fine.

He didn't send everyone back to their apartments. There were a few reliable guys he kept with him. If the Judges were going to give him a measure of authority, he aimed to use it by deputising a few others in his turn—unofficially, of course. If things went bad, no one wants to carry the can alone. And if the Sovs came back and started up with the reprisals they were always threatening? Well, it paid to have a few solid guys to watch your back. The Judges seemed to be in two minds about staying, but even if they did stay, there were only four of them and one of them was badly hurt. And what did the Sovs have?

"The Sovs?" he said, when Robinson asked him. "Heck, Judge, I didn't even know they had any of them V-shaped things until two of them showed up. Before that, we just had a few patrols and Judge Commissar Jerkov or whatever his name was, giving orders and stuff. Imposing curfew, ordering work details, that kind of stuff. That was him in that hover car, but I don't think I've seen that many Sovs in one place since the day of the invasion."

"It figures," said Robinson. "It's a big city, and their priority was winning the war. After that they could have looked to policing. Regular reign-of-terror stuff, citizen. You can count yourself lucky."

"I guess. But what about now, though? Now you've got the Sovs all riled up, what's going to happen?"

"You let us worry about that, Lejeune."

She went over to where Steinman was sitting on the kerb, examining the temperature gauge on the stub gun. When it came to worrying about stuff, Steinman was on the job. She sat down next to him.

"Something on your mind, partner?"

"You know it."

"And it's not so much the war, is it?"

"Correct again."

"Look, we've all got something chewing at us when it comes to the SJS. But there's mitigating circumstances. Seriously, if a Sov mind control chemical doesn't constitute a mitigating circumstance, then I don't know what does. Your mind was out to lunch, same as everybody's. If you really feel bad over it, you can get some counselling when this is all over, but don't stress over the goons in the scary skull helmets."

"Oh yeah? How about the woman in the scary skull earrings? She strikes you as the forgive-and-forget type?"

"She say something to you?"

"Yeah. She said something, and if I get out of this alive, I'm screwed."

"You don't know that, Steinman. All kinds of stuff could happen."

"That's right—stuff like me taking the next Titan shuttle."

"I say again: you don't know that. Predictions are garbage. We just never know how stuff turns out. Look at me. Once upon a time, a fortune teller said I'd grow up tall and willowy and I'd marry a handsome prince."

Steinman laughed in spite of himself. "Psi-Division, am I right?"

"You know it, partner. Now, loosen up. Everything's going to be fine. Mercer won't let McGruder touch you. Just worry about the Sovs. They should be here any minute."

BUT ROBINSONS'S WORDS hadn't been enough to console Steinman. A Judge drinks the contaminated water and goes a little whacko? He could see that one being allowed to slide by, given that so many Judges had drunk the water. But a Judge bumps off two SJS Judges? Different story. The SJS were vengeful bastards who looked out for their own.

Steinman was a good Judge—a good enough Judge anyway. Whatever his failings, he didn't deserve to be taken within the merciless system of Justice Department's internal affairs. He doubted if McGruder really knew anything: SJS cases tended to be made only after intensive interrogation. So, if McGruder were to stop a Sov bullet, it was highly unlikely that any investigation would proceed. And y'know, thinking about it, it didn't even have to be a Sov bullet.

It was awful to contemplate, but Steinman had already killed two SJS Judges. Would a third make much of a difference?

McGrudger was feeling better, but in her condition 'better' was still pretty rough. The painkillers and stimulants were doing their work, but a lot was being asked of them. The pain was something she should have been able to deal with. After all, she had been conditioned in a hard school. A fresh amputation? Just walk it off. The disorientation and nausea that came with a severe head wound? Just suck it up. It was all just pain.

But she was cursing herself for drifting off course a little back there. She was chief of the SJS and a keeper of fearsome secrets. There was no excuse for not keeping it together. But she'd found herself mumbling like a drunk or an eldster. And in front of Judge Steinman too.

Evidently, her people in 212 had been on the money. She'd been SJS long enough to know a guilty conscience when she saw one, and Steinman's sudden decision to stay when Mercer had ordered him to go was practically an admission of guilt. And if Steinman had reason to be nervous of the SJS, then by Grud she was going to find out why.

Block Mania might have screwed everything up for a while, but the SJS wasn't going to hand out a free pass to everyone who'd drunk the crazy water. Steinman would be investigated because you don't let anything slip.

Justice does not make exceptions.

But that was for later.

For now, there was the war—the war she'd missed while she was holed up like a wounded animal. She couldn't deny that there was a part of her that relished the chance to fight. She'd been bound to a desk too long. Before her promotion to the Council, her work had all been in administration and investigation, and afterwards it had been the same, only with politics added. It had been a very long time since she'd shot someone. (Those block maniacs she dealt with after the crash didn't count, seeing as she couldn't remember any of it.)

So yes, there was no denying it—she wanted to get in on this war. She wanted to play her part.

And there was more to it than just wanting in on the action. The city needed leadership, and she would provide it, but she would start here. Here there was fighting to be done, and she would do it; but here also there were citizens without the law to guide them, without the law to stand up for them.

Whatever was off about Steinman, it wasn't that. He'd been right about not running out. And Mercer had been right: the law was back. If this was to be the start of her administration, then by Grud, it would be a good start. She was going to stay here and fight the war because the war was about more than killing a few Sovs. There was a higher purpose. The citizens needed to be shown that. So did the Sovs.

So, she was going to fight. She was going to give them justice. She was going to give them hell.

MERCER WAS SICK of people not listening to him when he was telling them what to do. He was used to stupid citizens mulishly persisting in their criminal stupidity even after they'd been warned, but that didn't mean he had to like it. And then there was Steinman just flat-out refusing an order. Mercer wondered at the legality of that. For instance, outside of his sector, was he still a sector chief? And did his seniority automatically allow him to overrule the considered judgement of another officer? In time of war, did the Mega-City judiciary take on the hierarchical nature of the army?

But to hell with that. He had told Steinman to move out and Steinman had stayed put. And then there'd been McGruder who—OK—had seniority. But would it have killed her to just go along with the mission?

At least Robinson seemed to accept that he was the boss here, but he wasn't crazy about her attentiveness to his well-being that occasionally bordered on mothering.

So could he please just be in charge again? Just for a while? Was that too much to ask?

He thought about the idle talk of the night before, about how the city needed a Chief Judge. What Robinson said had made him think. He'd never considered himself Chief Judge material. Never once thought that the job might be his. But McGruder had said it herself: any good Judge could do the job. Mercer might never have been in the running in normal times, but the war had changed everything. So why not? He had experience, and he had a hell of a war record. He tried not to take it seriously, but he could see himself sitting in the big chair, wearing the big badge.

He grinned. People would have to damn well listen to him then.

He spoke into his radio. "All right, people. Listen up. You remember the plan?"

"The one about killing everything that comes at us?" said Robinson.

"That's the one," said Mercer. "Let's make the Sovs sorry they didn't run back home when they still had a home to run to."

SEVENTEEN

"Here we go again," said Robinson, as they made ready to receive the latest Sov effort. "So what's the bet, partner? If they think we're worth two Strato-Vs, what else are we worth? Rad-Sweepers?"

"A resistance unit of our calibre?" said Steinman. "I think we're worth at least a few Rad-Sweepers. I think I'd be insulted with anything less."

"Same here. Now give me back my stub gun."

"You do not want this stub gun, Robinson. This is one hinky stub gun. Look at the damn temperature gauge."

"Has it changed at all? Even when it's not in use? No? So it's the gauge that's bust. The gun's fine."

"Are you prepared to trust your life to the thing?"

"Heck no. Dire emergencies only. I just want it because it's my stub gun. Gimme."

In the present case, a dire emergency was something classed as mission critical—a situation so extreme that the death of whoever was operating the stub gun could be considered an acceptable loss. As for everything else—

well, they appreciated the simplicity of Mercer's directive. "Just kill everything." It was a plan that gave them a lot of latitude.

"So, you're this Sov Judge Jerkov or whatever his name is," said Robinson. "We show up. We take out two Strato-Vs. What do you do?"

"I double down," said Steinman. "I've been given a sector to run. I can't let it get out of my control. I throw everything I've got at whoever's messing with me."

"But what have you got?"

"Doesn't matter. If it's not enough, I borrow whatever's needed from neighbouring sectors or from strategic reserve or whatever. I do not report failure to Marshal Kazan. Not on a day like this. Can you imagine?"

THE EAST-MEG COMMANDER responsible for this sector was in fact named Jeludkhov, and he was thinking along much the same lines as Steinman and Robinson. As for his resources, they were indeed so limited as to be a matter of grave concern right from the beginning, and one of the Strato-craft he'd sent to investigate the supposed insurrection hadn't even been his to deploy. He'd taken his chances when he'd had it diverted from its primary mission so that it could over-fly the trouble spot. And now he'd have to explain why a precious Strato-V was down and in urgent need of repair as opposed to stemming the Mega-City counteroffensive down south.

And as for Rad-Sweepers, there were none. The war in the south had laid claim to all that were available. For terrible reasons that he was still trying to comprehend, no more would be coming from home. There weren't even any coming from the production and repair facility in Sector 199 since the guerrilla attack there early yesterday. He didn't know that this troublesome Mega-City unit with the laser weapon was the very same one responsible for that unfortunate business in Sector 199. If he did, he wouldn't have been able to oppose them with any more strength than he was now mustering, but at least he'd have been able to claim that he had eliminated them. That would have been something.

Because it was certainly not the day for reporting failure.

So Sentenoid units were summoned from all over the sector where they'd been functioning as automated police. The non-essential crew of the damaged Strato-V were ordered to deploy as ground troops. Even his personal staff was committed to the fight. And even he himself would be there because he was a Judge of East-Meg One, and this was not a fight he was prepared to lose.

"NO TANKS?" SAID Robinson, watching the approaching enemy. "What gives?"

"Saves us having to use the stub gun, at least," said Steinman, two hundred metres away and two levels up. "So what have we got?"

"All I can see is a couple of Sentenoids. Some human personnel too, but they're staying low. Chief, you reading anything?"

Mercer looked at what the remaining Lawmaster's screen was telling him. "I can see the Sentenoids all right. I've got four so far, but I think there's a couple more on the edge of scanner range. Standard skirmish line."

"That hover car is back," said Steinman. "Over towards the left, on the east side of World of Gravy."

"But no Rad-Sweepers, huh? It's like they're not even trying anymore," said Robinson.

"Never you mind, Robinson," said Mercer. "Let's just get this party started."

But it wasn't the sort of fight they were expecting: not the sort of fight they were used to. Robinson was wrong. The Sovs were trying. And they'd been learning.

Up until now, the East-Meg forces had employed the tactics of overwhelming force. They had won their fights by weight of numbers. They'd taken casualties and kept on rolling because it was the speedy victory that mattered, and the cost could be counted afterwards.

But these Sovs didn't have the numbers, and instead of having a high command behind them demanding even more speed regardless of sacrifice, there was a commander keen to husband what little he had. So without air cover, without tanks, Jeludkhov's troops fought like Judges rather than the obedient components of a great war machine. There were nearly thirty of them, and they had no intention of rushing in until they knew precisely what they were up against.

"Robinson! On your left! Fifty metres!"

"Where? I can't see anything!"

"Behind the garbage grinder. One of them, keeping low."

"Dammit, Steinman, I don't have eyes on any garbage grinder. Is it near the bus stop?"

"Doesn't matter. He's not there anymore."

Mercer cut in. "Don't fire until you're sure of your target. No sense in giving away your position."

And that was the way the battle developed. The Sovs infiltrated their way forward until they had their opponents roughly penned in. Then they sent in the Sentenoids. Then things got hot.

As advised, Robinson waited until she had a clear shot at the tentacled robot that stalked into view. She let it come close before hitting it with two hi-ex rounds and then she had to leave in a hurry because enough of the robot was still in working order to return fire. The shooting was augmented by a couple of Sov Judges that she hadn't even realised were there. She wouldn't have made it if it hadn't been for Steinman providing covering fire, but that served to tell the Sovs where Steinman was. A blizzard of incoming evicted him from his position in haste.

Aside from the Sentenoid, neither side scored any hits in that opening round, but it had only taken a few shots and already the Sovs had got half the Mega-City Judges on the run.

EIGHTEEN

STEINMAN AND ROBINSON were chased back from one spot to another, with a Sentenoid dedicated to each of them. The two Judges were staying apart and moving separately, but the two robots stayed close together. They came forward laying down covering fire, looking out for each other and bringing enough heat to allow the Sov Judges to move up behind them. But it wasn't going all their way.

From a recess in front of Pupkin block, Mercer waited until the Sovs came by, and then he waited a little more until these two mobile pillboxes were in his line of fire. He shredded them both with the bike's cannon and then roared on out of there before the Sovs could do anything about it. McGruder covered his withdrawal. One-handed and woozy she might have been, but she reckoned on one definite kill and one probable, which wasn't bad considering it was only meant to be suppressing fire.

The Sovs, however, weren't caught off balance for very long at all. Mercer had barely skidded out of sight into an alleyway when a Sov Judge fired two heat-seekers at him.

The heat-seeking round designed for the Justice Department Lawgiver was a lethal little marvel. It was slow enough to change direction in mid-flight, yet still fast enough to strike home with deadly effect, and all in a bullet-sized package. The Sov equivalent had a few differences, the main one being that it was much, much bigger. Relying on explosive rather than kinetic force, it wasn't quite so fast, but then it didn't need to be. It was certainly faster than Mercer's Lawmaster.

The two fat rounds zipped after the bike's exhaust, and both found their target. All of a sudden Mercer got himself an almighty kick in the pants. He went forward over the handlebars and hit the ground hard enough to star the bulletproof visor of his helmet. Someone was shouting at him through his radio. It was Robinson, naturally.

"Chief! Chief, you all right? Respond!"

"Yeah sure. Just give me a second," he replied, and passed out.

IT WAS MCGRUDGER who got to him first. At first glance, it looked like one of his legs was broken, and there were numerous lacerations and burns all along the lower half of his body. But his head looked like it was on crooked and, worse still, there was a hunk of metal sticking out of his lower back. That was the sort of wound that would at the very least demand a new kidney—that is, if Mercer didn't bleed to death first. There was also, of course, the likelihood of spinal injury, but McGruder gave no heed to that as she grabbed hold of Mercer's collar and heaved him towards a nearby doorway. Medical professionals would most certainly advise against moving the casualty in this manner, but medical professionals weren't here, nor were they expected for some hours yet. The Sovs, on the other hand, were right around the corner, and closing in fast.

Putting pressure on a wound, applying dressings, stabilising the patient—these were things that all Justice Department personnel were trained for, and given the nature of their occupation, were what they practised almost every day. *But try doing it with one hand*, thought McGruder. *And try conducting a gunfight at the same time.*

A shape appeared around the corner, and she sent it back the way it came with two shots in quick succession. Then she had to put her gun down again to tend to Mercer, who was haemorrhaging like nobody's business. She cursed fluently as she worked, and cursed louder when she had to pick up her gun again only to find the ammunition selector gummed up with half-clotted gore. The Lawgiver was one tough piece of machinery, and it would keep working, but covering it in a substance that was both slippery and sticky was making the weapon somewhat less than user-friendly.

Accurate, targeted shooting was proving impossible so, exasperated by it all, McGruder clumsily loaded all her own heat-seekers, fired them off, and followed them with a volley of ricochets. She hoped that was enough to discourage the enemy from pressing her further because otherwise she was out of options.

The wild firing from the alleyway, along with the smoke from the knocked-out bike, did serve to deter the Sovs from rushing in, but that's why they had Sentenoids.

ROBINSON DROPPED INTO cover behind an abandoned car and breathlessly radioed Steinman.

"I'm at the corner of Wynette and 357th. Where are you?"

"I'm right across from the Boutiqueria. I think I can see you."

"Can you see the others? Can you see if Mercer's OK?"

"There's smoke, and a lot of firing and—oh jeez— Sentenoid coming up!"

Without waiting, Steinman broke cover and fired at the big robot, so Robinson had to stand up and fire at the Sovs who started firing at Steinman. There being other Sovs to spare, Robinson immediately had to dodge their fire, and in seconds all four Mega-City Judges found themselves immobilised and pinned in place: McGruder in the alley with Mercer, Steinman forced into shelter near a bus stop, and Robinson in a little parking lot, all within a hundred metres of each other, but all almost helplessly out of each other's reach.

The only positive outcome was that the Sentenoid had been disabled.

From the Sovs' perspective, it was no great loss. They had more Sentenoids, their casualties had been light, and they had the enemy cornered. Best of all, that dreaded laser weapon hadn't made its reappearance.

* * *

THERE WAS NO obvious call for the stub gun. There were no monolithic targets like elevated road junctions or giant aircraft to justify the risk of using it. The Mega-City resistance had finally come up with a solution to the Sovs' robot tank armies, but there was nothing facing Robinson except a scattering of East-Meg Judges who knew what they were doing.

What they were doing, of course, was closing in on her, keeping her down, preventing her from supporting her fellows. They were doing the same with Steinman, which would allow them to bring up their remaining Sentenoids without interference and end this thing once and for all.

NINETEEN

IN THE ALLEY, McGruder rifled Mercer's equipment for fresh ammunition, but it was as slick and fouled with blood as what she was using herself. Her gun was almost stuck to her gun hand, making everything below her elbow look like some sort of gruesome bionic experiment. She was beginning to think that not lighting out of here when she'd had the chance hadn't been such a hot idea after all.

By her count, there were at least two Sentenoids still out there, which was two more than she cared for. If they came directly at her, then she thought she had a fair chance of dealing with them. If, on the other hand, they stayed out of sight and lobbed in explosive rounds, then all bets were off. If they thought to use gas, then that was it for her and Mercer. She'd lost her helmet—and her respirator with it—back in the crash that had first got her into this mess, and she could see the component parts of Mercer's respirator uselessly exposed on the front of his broken helmet. Amidst the gunfire, she was pretty sure she could make out the clank and scrape of another approaching robot.

She hated to do it, but she had to radio for help.

"McGruder to either of you. Do something. Anything. And do it quick. I mean it."

ROBINSON ANSWERED. "ON it, ma'am," she said and, saying a quick prayer to the gods of justice, she aimed the stub gun at what looked like mechanical activity beyond some parked road pods. She didn't fire until she was sure she'd caught a glimpse of a tentacle arm. There was no point getting killed over a lesser target. She pressed the trigger, and the energy beam lanced clean through the parked vehicles, whatever was behind them, and the corner of the nearest building, also bringing down two street lights for good measure. Then the threatening hum that the weapon usually emitted rose to an alarming whine, which caused Robinson to let go of it immediately and roll for cover.

The stub gun didn't explode, but from Robinson's point of view, it might as well have. After all, the energy beam had drawn a clear bright line right back to her. The Sovs had already been closing in on her position, keeping her head down as they cautiously worked their way forward. Now though, with the deadly laser weapon advertising its presence like that, they felt fully justified in concentrating their efforts. A flurry of cluster grenades arced in.

The only sensible thing for her to do would have been to lie flat and hug the kerb, hoping that shrapnel wounds weren't as bad as people said, but that wouldn't have been any help to Mercer and McGruder. So even before the first bomb fell, she was up and running, straight at the Sovs, firing her Lawgiver as she went. The move caught them off balance for just long enough. She never found out if she hit anything, except for one guy she barrelled right into. Her centre of gravity being lower, and momentum being on her side, she knocked him off his feet and kept right on going.

She didn't know if her shots hit anything, but the Sovs had no trouble hitting her. She kept her balance when a bullet struck her square on the back of her shoulder armour. She didn't stumble when another one tore into her calf muscle. The shot that broke one of her ribs knocked much of the wind out of her, but by then she was skidding into cover, while Steinman over by the bus stop was blasting away to divide the Sovs' attention.

"OK," she wheezed to herself. "That gets me almost halfway to where I need to be. What the hell do I do next?"

STEINMAN MIRACULOUSLY AVOIDED catching any Sov bullets as he hurriedly switched his firing position from one side of the bus stop to the other, but he was running out of places where he could move. All he and Robinson had succeeded in doing was taking the heat off their injured superiors for a moment. That just couldn't last. Right now, he was sheltering behind nothing more substantial than a lamp post. He was of lean build, but just not thin enough to find reassuring cover here. He had a good line on two Sovs who were circling round to get him, but it was an either/or sort of situation. He could keep one Sov pinned down without any trouble, but that left the Sov's buddy free to move in closer. It was time to skip, and he again cast his eyes about for anywhere he could skip to, but nothing presented itself.

He did notice, however, that something of an audience had gathered to witness his last moments. There were faces at windows, and a few figures at doorways.

"Guess it beats whatever's showing on the vid," muttered Steinman.

He resigned himself to dying in front of the spectators. He decided he'd take out the Sov on the left. The Sov on the right would certainly shoot him then, but Steinman had a surer chance of nailing the guy on the left. He should just get it done before any more of them showed up to complicate things.

ROBINSON COULDN'T SEE what was going on anymore. She half crawled, half rolled towards where Steinman had last been, hoping that maybe the two of them together could cook up a game-saving plan in the next few seconds. No dice. Looking under a parked car, she saw Sov-issued boots moving swiftly up on one side of her, much too close for comfort and cutting her off from where she wanted to be. Footsteps to her other side told her that things were getting even more urgent. There was nothing for it but another mad dash in the direction of Mercer and McGruder. She took a deep and painful breath and stood up, only to find herself facing a Sov

Judge at a distance of no more than a few metres. He turned to her, bringing up his gun. Robinson fired first, even though she didn't have a bead on him. She missed, as she knew she would, but she hoped that she'd bought herself the narrowest of head starts. She'd reckoned, however, without her wounded calf.

Everything slowed down for her as she lost her balance. She was lurching rather than leaping sideways, the Sov Judge's gun tracking her. The jolt of pain in her leg was distinct from the echo of her Lawgiver, which she heard clearly above the Sov's shout of alarm. She could even hear other Sovs answering from nearby, even above the noise of the engine. And as she put out a slow-motion hand to break her fall, and the Sov's finger tightened on the trigger, she asked herself: Engine? What engine?

And a car shot across the street and ploughed into the Sov who'd been about to kill her.

Robinson was still sitting foolishly on the ground when the driver stuck his head out.

"You OK down there, Judge?" asked Tooey Lejeune, who looked like he was nervous about recklessly driving a vehicle that wasn't even his.

Robinson felt like congratulating him on as neat a piece of vehicular homicide as she'd ever seen, but instead she just said, "Move over. I'm driving," and bundled herself into the car.

TWENTY

THE GUY ON Steinman's left probably thought he was out of sight behind the public garbage grinder, but Steinman could see the top of the guy's helmet and he reckoned that an armour piercer would punch right through that grinder. Steinman would have to lean out a little to take the shot, and that would be too bad because it would be the last thing he'd ever do, assuming the Sov on the right had his eyes open. But what the heck?

He took the shot. As he saw his target crumple, he heard movement behind him. That was the other Sov breaking cover, of course. But Steinman was surprised to find himself still alive and able to swing around and bring his gun to bear on the man who should have shot him in the back by now. He'd thought that Sov had been a pretty smooth operator, so what was this? Amateur hour?

But what he saw was the Sov being jostled to the ground by two ordinary citizens whom he recognised as associates of the deputised Citizen Lejeune. One of them was walloping the Sov around the head and shoulders with a length of metal pipe.

"Take his helmet off first, dummy," said Steinman, and then, "Never mind," because he shot the Sov himself.

THE SECTOR 224 Uprising wasn't much really, but it was enough for the beleaguered Judges. It was just a few public-spirited citizens standing up for what was right, but it momentarily turned the tide of the battle, and with so many people watching, it had a marked effect of public perception and public morale.

Robinson didn't notice it at first. She was accelerating through a hail of bullets and advising Lejeune to buckle up. The car was a '94 Bimblebaker, inelegant but solid. Not only had it survived the block wars and everything that had happened since, but it had just run over a grown man without putting anything more than a dent in the front fender. If it could do that, then Robinson felt it could probably come off pretty well from hitting a Sentenoid—the Sentenoid that was closing in on Mercer and McGruder's alleyway, for instance.

The Bimblebaker was doing seventy when it hit, knocking the Sentenoid off its feet, and knocking the feet off two of its legs. Even before the crash bags had deflated, Robinson was reversing and going forward again, repeatedly hitting the big robot. With the last impact, the Sentenoid got enough of its wits back to drive an electrified claw into the front of the car's engine, stopping it dead, but by then it was too late. Robinson had pushed it to the edge of the road, and without a full set of legs to steady it, the robot lost its balance and tumbled over the side. It fell two levels, and might have still been functional after it hit the bottom, but that wasn't Robinson's concern.

She was out of the car and limping fast in search of Mercer when, in the sudden cessation of gunfire, she heard scattered cheering. A little more than an hour ago, they'd been either hiding or actively collaborating. Now the citizens were telling the Sovs exactly how they felt. The sound echoed from block to block until one clear unified cry was taken up.

"Big Meg! Big Meg!" they were shouting. "You come here, and you get stomped! Yeah!"

We should make that the national anthem or something, she thought, her heart brimming with pride.

McGRUDER WAS CROUCHED over Mercer, gun at the ready, when Steinman found her. With her blood-draggled hair and dangerous look, she seemed to Steinman like the sort of crazed witch woman that some shamanistic mutie tribe would consult in a ruined shopping mall in the Cursed Earth. *Heck*, he thought, *she's even got the skull earrings*. Whatever else, she didn't strike him as Chief Judge material, and for a second, he considered how easy it would be right now to take her out of the running. One bullet now and no internal affairs investigations later. And as Mercer had pointed out, the city did not need another SJS chief in the big chair. One bullet now and maybe the city would be saved from another Judge Cal.

All down the years, various mentors had been critical of Steinman's impulsive nature. But he didn't act on any impulse now. Robinson didn't give him a chance. She burst on the scene, battered but elated. The sight of Mercer took more spring out of her step than being nicked by a Sov bullet had.

"Do what you can for him," said Steinman, pushing past her. "I'm going to get help—see if I can get a hurry-up on that H-Wagon."

Robinson checked on Mercer while she reported the situation to McGruder.

"Sovs are falling back, ma'am. People are dropping stuff on them from balconies and taking potshots with whatever weapons they've got left over from the block wars. The Sovs have maybe only one Sentenoid left. I think we're good until our pickup arrives."

JUDGE-COMMISSAR JELUDKHOV PUT his head in his hands while his second-in-command asked him what should be done next. After breathing deeply for a few moments, he straightened up and, by way of an answer, called up the Strato-V that had been damaged earlier by Steinman's stub gun.

He shouted at the commander until the man at last admitted that his craft was airworthy, up to a point.

"I can't get her above five hundred metres and I can't keep her aloft for more than a few minutes.

Manoeuvrability will be impossible, sir."

"I don't care! I want that Strato-V airborne within the next sixty seconds or I will have you shot! Do you hear me?" Jeludkhov was screaming into the radio, but he didn't care. All that mattered was putting an end to this demonstration. His ground forces had failed him, but the Strato-V could eliminate the Mega-City Judges once and for all. And if that did not silence the people, then indiscriminate laser fire most assuredly would.

He watched coldly as the sixty seconds came and went, but at least the Strato-V commander appeared to be taking him seriously. Smoke belched from damaged mechanisms as the aircraft struggled to leave its makeshift landing ground. At last, it lifted off and hovered drunkenly before carefully pointing its nose towards Rupert Pupkin Block and the streets that were slipping from East-Meg's control.

TWENTY-ONE

"Boy, but you people need to take better care of yourselves," said Ritchie Hernandez, putting the finishing touches on Mercer's emergency dressings. "Regular hours, more fibre, and not so many gunfights, know what I mean?"

"Thank you, citizen," said McGruder. "We'll take that under advisement. Robinson? What have we got?"

Robinson squinted through the binoculars. "The Strato-V's moving slowly, but it's moving. Left-hand engine is making smoke like you wouldn't believe. If it doesn't fall out of the sky, it might be here in, say, five minutes."

"That's it. We're relocating to the basement of Pupkin. If you're hurt, then Steinman and Hernandez can take Mercer."

But Robinson didn't seem to be paying attention. Their long-range communications had gone the way of their Lawmasters, but her helmet radio was suddenly speaking to her faintly, and the words made her face light up.

"This is Robinson, Team Two-One-Two," she said. "Say again."

"This is Airborne Unit One, Robinson," came the reply, "but that designation's kinda unofficial. Just call us the Big Eagle of Mercy and tell us where you want us. ETA three minutes."

Robinson let out a whoop. "Put her right down on Megaway West 98, Big Eagle. North corner of Pupkin block. Robinson out."

She turned to the others. "Ever have one of those lucky days? First the cits remember what side they're on, and then Underhill or Perrier or whoever comes through for us. H-Wagon's on its way. Three minutes."

"You didn't mention the Strato-V," said McGruder.

For a moment, Robinson felt like a complete rookie under the cold eye of her superior, but she rallied.

"Their scanners will mark the Strato-V ten clicks out, and kill it from five. They don't need any help from me, Chief McGruder. Besides, we'll be long gone before that busted-ass Sov machine ever gets here."

THE SLOW PROGRESS of the Strato-V had been slowed further by the necessity to stop and bring Jeludkhov aboard. It wasn't that he trusted the reliability of the aircraft, but he needed a top-down appreciation of the operation. There was something else—something that he didn't tell the Strato-V's commander. There was a nuclear weapon on board, and if the worst came to the worst, then Jeludkhov intended to use it. Rebellion could not be countenanced. If nuclear sterilisation was the only way to crush dissidence, then so be it. What was one more city sector next to what had been lost last night? And if the Strato-V couldn't clear the blast zone? Well, better death by fire than life in defeat.

The skeleton crew of the Strato-V were so busy keeping the thing in the air that there was no one watching the scanners. An enemy would be on top of them before they knew it and, while their weapons systems were still intact, they wouldn't stand a chance against a fully functioning Mega-City H-wagon. It was lucky for them, then, that they faced no such threat.

THE HASTILY IMPROVED medevac unit grandly calling itself the Eagle of Mercy came in, keeping close to the ground and using the cityscape for cover. They touched down without even knowing the Strato-V was there. Steinman and Robinson recognised the aircraft right away. It was the hover transporter they'd stolen the day before from a Sov base up north, since rebranded with the eagle motif on its broad nose. It had been a good enough vehicle to withstand the explosion that had put paid to the Sov base, but being little more than a flying van, it wasn't really suitable for what might be termed contested airspace.

"This is it?" said Robinson to the pilot as they waited for Mercer to be carried up. "This is what you've got?"

"H-Wagons are in short supply. Central said you were in a hurry, so we didn't think you'd be so fussy."

"But there's a Strato-V!"

"A what?"

"Over there. About two clicks out. Sorry. I maybe should have said."

"Jovus! Everybody in!" said the pilot. "We're out of here, like, right now!"

But Robinson was wrong about the distance. Seeing as it had got up and stayed up for this long, the Strato-V commander was gaining confidence in his aircraft. Also, with Judge-Commissar Jeludkhov breathing down his neck, he had given the order to open up the throttle some more. He had belatedly picked up on the vehicle that had just landed and was closing in to investigate. Given the ever-present danger of that Mega-City laser weapon, he wasn't rushing in, but he was now only eight-hundred metres from target, with only Tammy Wynette Block between him and a clear view.

RITCHIE HERNANDEZ WAS a willing stretcher bearer, but he was finding Mercer too heavy and Steinman too fast-paced. Robinson, ignoring her own injuries, limped over and took his place, trying to hurry everything along. They were almost at the transporter when they saw the Strato-V appear between two buildings, still spewing smoke but hovering steadily.

Steinman wondered what was keeping it from closing in and finishing the job, and then the question answered itself. The Strato-V had been given good reason to keep its distance.

"The stub gun, Robinson! Where'd you leave the stub gun?"

Mercer was loaded safely aboard, with McGruder and Robinson beside him.

"I'm staying," said Steinman.

"Aw, come on! Not this again!" said Robinson.

"The second you take off, the Strato-V's lasers can track you. All it has to do is make some height and you're dead. But if I'm here, I can get in a shot when it clears the skyline."

"The stub's going to explode!"

"It's had time to cool. It'll be good for one shot. Don't sweat it, Robinson."

McGruder cut it short.

"You're right, Steinman. We'll do it your way. One question though—in case we don't meet again."

"Ask away, Chief McGruder. I've got a minute."

"It's about your partner Kowalczyk, but I'm sure you knew that. And it's about two of my officers: O'Rourke and Rossi. Anything you might want to tell me about them?"

Steinman held the stub gun lightly and kept his eyes on the Strato-V as it slipped in and out of view between buildings. It wasn't going to make its move until the transporter took off. He considered his answer.

"Well, ma'am, I have to admit that I wasn't quite myself at the time. So, if you'd asked me then, I'd probably have said that O'Rourke and Rossi didn't matter much. I'd have said they were never a real part of Sector 212. I'd have said they were just a couple of interlopers and snoopers sent over from Central.

"But you ask me now?" He paused. "Now I don't think I'd have anything to say to amend that statement. You'd best be leaving."

And he rapped on the vehicle's side like he was sending a taxi on its way.

The transporter rose, and the Strato-V rose with it. The transporter was keeping low and moving fast, but all the Strato-V needed was enough altitude to give it a line of sight. Speed didn't matter. Its lasers were fast enough.

Steinman looked at the temperature gauge on the stub gun. It wasn't telling him anything encouraging. Never mind. He sighted it on where he expected the Strato-V to appear. Of course, if McGruder was really planning on giving him a hard time over what had happened back when all this began, now would be the perfect opportunity to do something about that. Be a shame about Robinson and Mercer, but plenty of good Judges had died already.

The Strato-V came out from behind Wynette Block, rising steadily.

WATCHING ANXIOUSLY FROM the back window of the transporter, Robinson saw the Sov craft, and saw the beam of white light lance upwards and sweep towards it. A large part of the Strato-V fell cleanly away. The rest of the machine hung in the air a few seconds longer before following its amputated component earthwards. The beam of light was still visible, and it seemed to Robinson that it might almost be swinging towards her, or perhaps it was only pointing straight up at the sky, like a signal, like a salute.

And then there was a flash of an explosion, distinct from the burning wreck of the Strato-V, and the beam blinked out.

EPILOGUE

"AND THAT'S ALL I know, chief," Robinson told Mercer.

They were in a medical facility that had been a warehouse until a few days before. There was enough equipment to keep Mercer alive, but getting him back on his feet would have to wait until the city had addressed the more pressing concerns.

An estimated four hundred million people were dead. More than half the city had been rendered uninhabitable. Even with intensive reclamation efforts underway, radiation levels would be at unacceptably high levels for a long time to come.

"And diseases!" said Robinson. "Sheesh! I saw things next door that the Meds don't even have names for yet, and they say that's just the start."

"Never mind that," croaked Mercer. "Report, Robinson."

"Right, chief. So, we made it back south and McGruder took charge. I have to say, she was pretty good. Never slowed down once. Of course, it wasn't for much more than a day. The Sov surrender came over the wire yesterday, but you've heard about that. And that was Dredd's doing apparently—not McGruder's. Still and all, credit where credit's due: McGruder was taking care of business."

"And she's in charge now? She's Chief Judge?"

"Sure. I was there to see it. Grand Hall's burnt down so we just stood out on this bomb site and she was sworn in. It was weird. They had the big law book for her and everything. I didn't even know there was a print edition of the Mega-City One Constitution and Code of Criminal Justice. Maybe there isn't. Maybe they just got an old phone book and put the big fancy cover on it. And she didn't even have a hand to place on it when she took the oath, you know?"

"Still counts. She's still Chief Judge."

"Well, yeah. Anyway, it wasn't like I was included in the councils of the mighty, but I gather she was unopposed. I mean, it wasn't like anybody else wanted the job."

Mercer nodded as much as was possible in his neck brace, but Robinson suspected he was merely putting on a brave face.

"C'mon, chief. You didn't really want it, did you? Sit in an office all day? Be diplomatic? Play politics? Wear a cape, for Grud's sake? That thing is so Eighties. Naw, chief—that's not for you. You're not a politician: you're a fighter. You're the guy who held Sector 212 together. You're the guy who took out the Sov base at RMR. You're the guy who rescued McGruder. You wouldn't want to be Chief Judge."

Mercer swallowed painfully. "My place is on the streets," he conceded.

ROBINSON'S PLACE WAS also on the streets, and coincidentally, the streets she ended up patrolling were those of Sector 224, the scene of McGruder's rescue. In the weeks since the war's end, the new Chief Judge had risen to the challenge of reconstruction by, among other things, mobilising the citizenry like never before. For a little while at least, Mega-City One's notoriously high unemployment rate was falling close to zero.

Right now, Robinson was surveying the efforts of Compulsory Labour Unit 224/7418 who were busy clearing debris off Megaway West 98. The work was being done by hand because this sector had got off lightly in the war. The big construction robots were needed where there was real damage.

"Step it up," she said in encouragement. "The sooner this road is open, the sooner the food convoys can come rolling in. You all want to get fed, don't you?"

A message arrived on her bike computer. It was not unexpected. She was required to assist an SJS investigation into outstanding matters in the case of Judges Kowalczyk and Steinman.

"Compliance mandatory and immediate, blah-de-blah blah," she said to herself.

The wheels of the Department ground on. She knew that after this one she'd be likely be put through the wringer in the cases of the rogue Judges Gray and Denning, who'd both died by her hand during the block wars. The SJS might get it all out of the way at once or they might leave it hanging over her head—however it pleased them to operate these days.

She called Tooey Lejeune over and told him she'd be out of touch for a few hours. He'd been doing a good job overseeing the labour unit, but she was suspicious of his buddies. Sure, they'd fought for freedom when the chips were down, but she'd noticed how a couple of them were free and easy with their ration stamps. Were they getting more than their quota? Was Lejeune behind it?

She let Lejeune think that everything was OK for the next few hours. Give him enough rope and see what he did with it. The guy might have had a fine war record, but that was neither here nor there.

Justice didn't make exceptions.

ABOUT THE AUTHOR

John Ware used to work in the construction industry until they made him stop. He now lectures in history in his home town of Cork. He is the author of *Dirty Shirt* and *A Green Bough*.

FIND US ONLINE!

www.rebellionpublishing.com

/rebellionpub /rebellionpublishing /rebellionpublishing

SIGN UP TO OUR NEWSLETTER!

rebellionpublishing.com/newsletter

YOUR REVIEWS MATTER!

Enjoy this book? Got something to say?

Leave a review on Amazon, GoodReads or with your
favourite bookseller and let the world know!

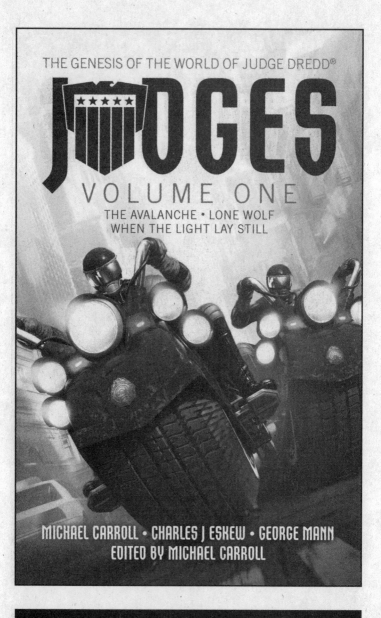

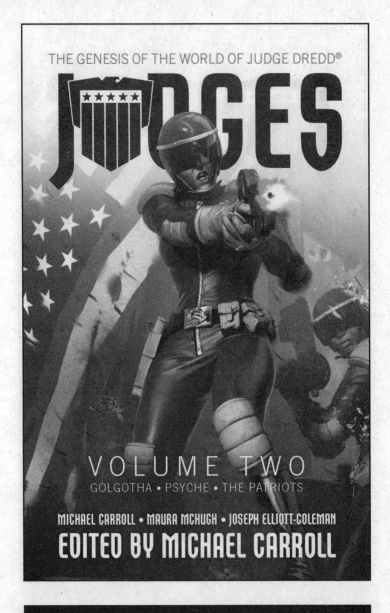

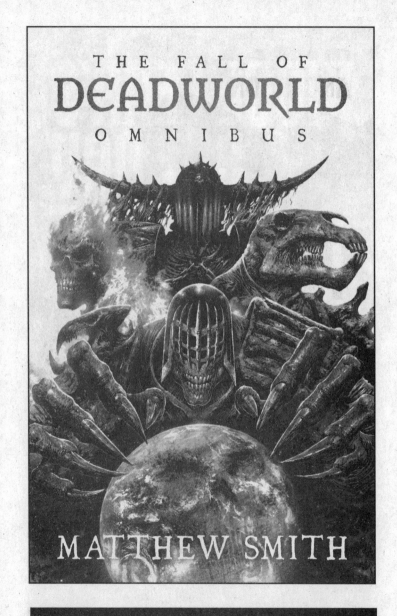

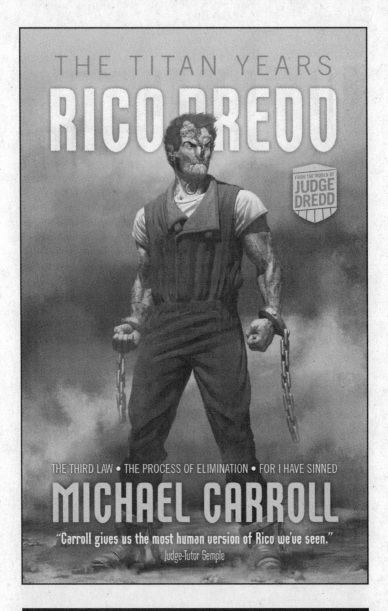